NECESSARY

MEASURES

J. M. Barlog

BAK
BOOKS

WHEATON, ILLINOIS

LC treff meeting set Tango-12. Jaffe
arrives the seventh.

                                    Brax

Too-goddamned-hot Nigeria. A silvery moonlight
washed over an indigo Range Rover racing with
pegged speedometer across a lifeless stretch of
tarred two-lane highway. Carved out of a barren landscape, the trunk provided the only overland connection between Kaduna in central Nigeria and Kano in
the northern territory. Scattered about like discarded
rubbish, shards of mangled guardrail and the rusted
carcasses of earlier, less fortunate, travelers littered
an otherwise desolate causeway. Courage set the
speed limit. To even attempt this crossing invited
mayhem. The *Pu'dalla*, pirates of the highway, owned
this stretch of useless sand, preying unchecked upon
those foolish souls who ventured over this route.
Robbery and murder prevailed here like the giant ter-
mite mounds standing sentry along the way.
      Only the desperate or the determined traversed
Nigeria's nocturnal middle zone during the searing
tail of the hot dry season. A time when *sirocco* could
drain every ounce of vitality from even the stoutest.
      Ahead, a single red flicker danced across the gray
shrouded curtain. A clattering, soot-spewing and
overloaded bus of day laborers bound for the meager
returns of work in Kano arose as a slight annoyance
to the Rover's steady hum. *The desperate.*

Brax eased off, reining the vehicle to a hundred. He engaged the idle moment to recalculate, for the fifth time, their arrival into the old section of Kano. Every detail had been meticulously plotted to time their arrival coincident with the dawn. Darkness cloaked their passage, fostered a tenuous security.

For a long moment, Brax gazed into the night. Would Kano hold what they so desperately sought? Hellish flashes of the World Trade Center—her belly smoke-infested and heaved into chaos—played across his mind. They had erred. Now they must put right their mistake.

Brax's face, shadowed behind a four day growth, could commandeer a Christian woman's heart one moment, vanish into a crowd the next. He appeared ordinary in most ways, even passive and academic, though his profession was neither.

Ahead, the road snaked northward like a sleeping black viper against snowy sand, to where the first glimmering peaks of Kano buoyed over the rise.

In thirty-seven minutes they would know.

A sleeping Jaffe shifted in the reclined passenger seat, his swarthy chiseled face hidden beneath a straw hat that allowed only a sliver of his piceous, jaw-line beard to slip through. Both dressed congruent with the region, clad in khaki gone stale from the arduous nine-hour zigzag journey. A necessary precaution for this place.

Kano's bevy of mosque domes glinted like miniature golden treasures in the distance, etched by the nascent beams of morning. Beyond the city proper, a serried array of clay houses crammed Kano's old section, their corrugated metal roofs arranged like scales, shimmering mirror-like against the soon-to-be-scorching sun.

The Rover skirted the clogs of human congestion that rose and abated with the daylight. In its stead, Brax chose the less-traveled, rutted roadways bypassing the indifferent knots of foot traffic in the awakening city streets. Only the privileged owned autos, and it seemed right and proper that they should become victims to the masses, who hindered their passage as if it were their intent to punish drivers for their wealth.

"Time to prepare," Brax said. He turned a hawkish eye toward the squalid Nigerians crowding their vehicle, patting the hood insistently with open palm, while extending the other in hopes of gaining a single dinar. Brax grew uneasy navigating through crowds; they put the two at risk. He, by nature, kept his distance from people whenever prudent.

"I thought I detected the stench of an African city," Jaffe said from beneath his hat. The virulent fetor of open sewage saturated the air like humidity.

Jaffe awakened to a foul disposition. Maybe that was his way of dealing with the stress that crept into these exchanges. *Too many variables.*

He tapped his hat back, and without expression, leaned forward in a stretch. Opaque eyes worked the panorama with a soldier's ardor. He studied their wake in the side mirror for a time before unlocking the glove compartment. Using his index finger to pry, he dislodged the secret panel inside. One by one he extracted their arsenal, careful to keep the tools of their profession out of view of the street beggars.

"The signal?" Brax queried. His eyes worked the mirrors like a bad habit. No one but the street beggars took an interest in the Rover crawling the narrow roads, and they quickly faded away once they realized no money would be forthcoming.

"Red vase, single white flower and blue curtains drawn," Jaffe said. "Red, white and blue, get it."

Jaffe's cool exterior seemed all but impenetrable. If what lay ahead intimidated him, he concealed it from Brax. Jaffe exposed little outside his tough professional armor. Armor now tarnished by those he once believed in.

Surrounded by old Kano, mounded streets of packed sand separated rows of cube houses. Modest means for a modest people. A people rich in resources yet poor in their efficacy to convert them to wealth.

Jaffe scanned with fired intensity. Unlike Brax, who now withheld expression, Jaffe's smile took on an almost sinister glint. Those lifeless unblinking eyes immediately fueled suspicion. But Jaffe was a master at his craft. Those unfortunate enough to witness his work came away convinced this one had no soul.

"Turn right here; then three streets. Then left," he instructed, forcing a yawn to wipe away sleep. Or was it to mask a fear swimming beneath the surface?

Too many variables.

Brax slowed, anticipating his turn.

"Should've used a dead-letter drop," Brax said, his roving steely-gray eyes working the flanks like a mercenary breaching a hot zone. Eyes trained to miss nothing.

"We've been through this fucking shit a dozen times, college boy. Christ, you worry more than a Russian grandmother. Left at the next intersection," Jaffe said with a kind of unsettling flippancy. The kind Brax had come to resent. The kind that set Brax on edge.

They were players in a deadly game. The stakes were lives. Six lost in the World Trade Center, another fourteen in three London bombings in a little over a year. The ante kept going up. They had yet to win a hand.

Brax glanced at his watch. They would arrive at the precise time. He made the left turn and slowed while Jaffe inventoried their tool chest.

"Who prepped the safe house?" Brax asked. A question asked at least a dozen times in the preceding six hours. He asked it again anyway.

"We're clean going in. Get off my fucking back."

Jaffe checked his Glock 22 as if it were a toy. The *click* of the twenty-two round clip sliding home brought a boyish smile. He locked in the silencer and traced his finger along its length. Then he palmed a Soviet Makarov PM with special Tokarev rounds, designed to eliminate any need for a second shot. Giant Slayers. He brushed his thumb over the safety, turning the gun over in his hand, all the while maintaining the weapon below the window. He relished the weight and feel.

"I'll make it look like a Soviet clean-up."

Nothing could go awry...they hoped.

"In and out. Five minutes, not one second more," Brax delivered with the cadence of a General's order.

"I know my job, college boy. I've got five years on you in the field. Every one of my terminations were clean. I know exactly what the fuck I'm doing."

Brax shed the stab.

Jaffe had super-glued a chip to his shoulder. Finding himself suddenly forty-four, friendless and subordinate to a man ten years his junior, maybe he felt he deserved that chip. Nothing personal. He had sacrificed everything to climb the Company ladder, and one screw-up pummeled him back down to the bottom rung. They're all fuckers.

But as Wolf Pack leader, Brax had to sweat every detail, anticipate every contingency; he accepted nothing at face value. *Nothing.* Mandigo was Jaffe's man, Jaffe's show. Something tugged at Brax's brain; something kept his stomach on the verge of upheaval. Something about this meeting seemed out of place, but Brax couldn't get a handle on what.

"I don't like it. He's skittish. Can we coddle Mandigo through this?" Brax said changing the subject.

"He's a fuckin' lowlander. I had to promise America if he delivered. Only a face-to-face would appease the little fuck. Slow down, it's coming up on the right."

The Rover rolled through an intersection to the spray of gravel against the side panel. They crawled past the safe house. Neither looked directly at the window.

"It's show time. Our little fuck's inside."

The Rover continued, made a turn at the next intersection three houses beyond, then stopped discreetly out of sight.

"I worked the Liberian coup. I can handle Africans. I'm comfortable with this, are you?" Jaffe prodded.

Something gnawed at Brax's sense of equilibrium. He could abort *any* operation at any moment without justification. Instead, he nodded, despite something shredding his confidence. Something sinister taunted him from the outskirts of recognition. A deep breath cast doubt aside. They had to risk it. They needed what Mandigo had come to deliver. Brax mashed a micro-receiver into his right ear. He then felt for the comfort of his own Glock 22 under his shirt.

They were so close.

"Mike check," Brax said.

Jaffe's stare turned ominous.

"It's by the book. I'm the handler, we're in a neutral zone. I get what we came for and then release Mandigo of further obligation. Relax," Jaffe said with a laugh that would send chills up a spine.

The Company put that bitter taste in the back of Jaffe's throat. They fucked him good putting Brax in charge of something as important as Wolf Pack. He served his time in the trenches. The roles should have been reversed.

Brax's restless gaze swept the street. No room for trust in a profession intolerant of human frailties.

"Time to go. Let the wiser rule on this one, will ya," Jaffe said. He stepped out, shifted his concealed weight and turned back to face the car.

"Abort signal?" Brax asked.

"It is my mistake, I must have the wrong house."

Jaffe's face went slack. In a glance, he took in the street behind the vehicle. The moment had arrived. He switched to his business face, smileless and devoid of compassion.

"We fix other people's fuck-ups. If those Fools, Boneheads, and Idiots had been doing their job, the WTC would have been prevented. When this thing's over, I'm retiring. Fuck them all. Think I'll set up a bird sanctuary," Jaffe said, testing the button microphone as his eyes worked the street ahead of him. His face lost all luster; for the first time since beginning their journey Jaffe's usual unshakable facade dulled.

Brax shot a thumbs up, read the uncertainty in Jaffe's eyes. At that moment, something inside Brax ordered an abort. *Too many variables.* Too little preparation time. However, no words left his throat.

Jaffe ambled off as if this were to be a morning stroll, carrying at his side a black attaché extracted from the Rover's back seat. Seconds later he disappeared around the corner.

"Did you know there's less than two hundred bald eagles left in North America. Nobody else gives a fuck about the country. After I retire, all I have to worry about is...birds...shit...ting..."

A sudden dead silence.

Brax's heart surged. He clutched the door handle.

"...rather have bird shit on my head than people shit," finally marched into Brax's ear piece.

Brax siphoned off some tension. Communications went to one way. Brax had to allow Jaffe to make the calls from now on. He settled back, checking his watch. Five minutes...not one second more.

Jaffe knocked twice. A door opened with a rusted screech.

"I'm looking for Mr. Abu-jah'wanni," Brax heard Jaffe say.

The door closed; Jaffe was on his own.

"Mandigo," Jaffe blurted in a hurried burst, "meet one week from tomorrow in southern Sokoto at five-seven-seven."

Having quickly dispensed with the formality of assigning an alternate meeting should this one abort before an exchange could be consummated, Jaffe plowed into the business for which the meeting had been arranged.

Brax allowed himself the luxury of a faint smile. But those restless eyes continued their sweep of the locale. His foot never left the accelerator. He recited their escape route in his head while the engine idled ready.

They could draw one step closer to Leviathan. They could fit another piece into a diabolic puzzle.

Brax listened.

Footsteps. Nervous shuffling.

"I do good, Jaffe?" a Mediterranean voice said with an edge of anticipation. He pronounced the name as if it were French, changing the e sound to an a.

"I need a minute," Jaffe said over the continued shuffle of feet.

Then dead silence hung between them for an unending moment. No movement, no breathing. The mike must have cut out again.

Brax adjusted his ear piece, praying the microphone would return. It did a moment later.

More shuffling. Mandigo must be pacing.

"We go. You get what you ask."

Tension tightened Mandigo's vocal cords, forcing his voice to rise an octave.

"First I must authenticate the list," replied Jaffe.

"It is good. Show me my passport. Damn it you. They are suspicious. I am watched, excluded from high level meetings."

Jaffe's breathing filled the silence. More foot-steps.

"This isn't it," Jaffe said finally with deep disappointment smothering each word.

Brax felt his heart sink into oblivion. All their painstaking planning had turned to vapor. The ensuing silence drew Brax to the edge of his seat. He gripped the steering wheel until his knuckles paled.

Something didn't ring true.

"Get out of there," Brax whispered, rubbernecking the surroundings. Jaffe knew the drill. If the information turned out to be bad, evacuate without delay.

Something was out of whack. Mandigo had been fully briefed. He knew what to look for and how to authenticate the list himself.

"It *is* good. From minister's safe. Show me my passport!"

Mandigo's voice rose another octave in anger.

"Listen, we know you fuckin' Libyans issued thirty-seven passports to terrorists to get them safely into Nicaragua. This list is incomplete."

"No! Fuck you. You take me out." Mandigo was screaming.

Brax pulled his Glock—clicked the safety off.

"Mandigo, listen. Here's another fifty thousand dinars. You must return. Find the correct list."

"No! No money. Passport to U.S. I memorized your watch list. Look! The name...Loni..."

Silence. Dead sickening silence.

"Damn! Jaffe get out of there," Brax uttered barely above a whisper.

A second later the microphone returned the conversation.

"You lie, you bastard! You're going to kill me," Mandigo screamed.

"Mandi...goddamnit, I've been set up!" Jaffe ejected in a voice strapped in sheer panic.

Brax kicked open the Rover's door and flew from the vehicle just as the explosion's driving force battered him back against the spare tire affixed to the vehicle's rear. The percussion pummeled him to the road like a rag doll. Then a sweeping orange fireball swarmed over the neighboring houses.

For an unending moment, Brax lay stunned and immobile. Scorching heat sucked the oxygen from his lungs, forcing him to gasp to stay alive. His throat turned into an inferno; his eyes felt like they had been socked back into his head.

A few locals rushed from their homes to witness the aftermath. When a white-bearded elderly Nigerian reached down to aid Brax, Brax fought his grip and blindly pushed his way back to the Rover. Through a blur, he fumbled at the door, dragged himself into the seat and tromped the gas pedal to the floor.

Nothing could help Jaffe now.

The Rover roared to the red line as it took over the center of the road and disappeared behind a cascading cloud of sand dust. Brax rammed into second, swerving away from the scene onto the first side road he encountered.

To keep focused, Brax recited the emergency escape steps—the plan set up to get *them* out of Nigeria alive if anything went wrong.

In his wake rose the first faint whir of klaxons.

2

Meeting compromised. Coming home.

Brax

By mid-morning, an unorganized gathering of Right-To-Lifers cluttered Pennsylvania Avenue outside the White House fence. The crowd appeared loquacious but at the same time incapable of melding their forces into a unified whole, despite attempts from some members to initiate an affirmative course of action. Most cast their eyes askance when the moment came for a leader to emerge and bring order to this chaos. The D.C. police chose wisely to allow the protesters their space, positioning themselves clear of the gathering, yet maintaining a presence that included a helicopter overhead in the event the protest did take form and escalate.

Brax emerged phantom-like from the clustered core of the crowd, his face a shadow beneath a Yankees baseball cap pulled low over his forehead. He stuffed his hands into the pockets of a well worn black leather jacket, making the newspaper he tucked under one arm more pronounced. Spring had been unkind to the nation's Capital. Shrouded snow clouds threatened in the western sky. Brax regretted selecting a coat ill-suited for the weather. He longed to be in a different place, a temperate place some distance from here. But the fired heat of Kano still burned inside his soul.

Brax drifted off like a man who had become disillusioned in the cause. He strolled into Lafayette Square against an accosting north wind that tousled his collar-length chestnut hair. Seemingly at random, he took a bench facing a warming late-morning sun.

For a moment Brax stared vacantly, though in fact his eyes reconnoitered his surroundings. No distant faces took an interest in his presence. No bodies shifted strategically to maintain a vantage point from which to observe. Opening the newspaper signaled the meeting to proceed. If he rose instead, the meeting would abort and another attempt could come twenty-four hours from now in an alternate location.

Once at ease with his surroundings, Brax pulled his Post. He stopped midway when skinheads dressed like twins in green fatigue jackets and scruffy combat boots, traipsed toward him from behind. Brax considered aborting. He dropped the paper as a way to disguise his examination of the situation. Uncovering no markings that could identify the two as point men for a surveillance, he retrieved his newspaper.

Brax opened to the middle section, where he skimmed. His heart settled. An editorial blasted the House Appropriations Committee's stormy debate over the president's latest proposal for deficit reduction. All just rhetoric. The president blamed Congress. Congress blamed the president. Sibling rivalry destined to end with inaction. Nothing ever got resolved in Washington. But something else in the article snared Brax's attention. A growing number of Senate committees urged tightening the presidential purse strings, namely operations within the CIA that the president had direct control over. A growing majority in the Senate accused the CIA of being nothing more than a useless drain on tax dollars. The cold war was over. Spies were a romance of the sixties. Brax considered Wolf Pack. Foolish arrogant power mongers stood ready to trade dollars for lives. The mood among Washington insiders took a dramatic shift after the Soviet break up, and more and more senators questioned the need for any intelligence gathering agency. The WTC should stand in testament to a virile threat that had yet to be extinguished.

Minutes after the skinheads disappeared, Theodore Whittier Calfield, Deputy Director of Operations, a man approaching seventy but with the gait and wit of a *thirtysomething*, and whose black furrowed brows rimmed his eyes like trimmed bushes, took a seat on the adjoining bench. Brax and Calfield sat back to back at opposite ends, and each found something to keep their eyes from meeting.

Calfield fumbled through his pocket with an arresting preoccupation, like someone searching for a nitro-glycerin pill to stave off cardiac arrest. His dull green probing eyes never once crossed Brax's path.

"I've had some time now to digest the report," Housemother said with a voice raspy from years of tobacco. He unwrapped a cough drop he withdrew from his pocket and slipped it into his mouth. His violent coughs rippled through his considerable girth.

"Did it get cleaned up?" Brax asked from behind his paper.

Housemother shifted his gaze in a new direction, at the same time tightening his knee-length tweed coat around his barrel waist. Nothing, it seemed lately, could stave off the chill in the air. Maybe it was time he retired to the warmer climate out west?

"Nothing to clean. It was all over by the time our crew arrived. Incoming intelligence indicates the Nigerians are clueless. What the devil went wrong out there?"

Calfield allowed his characteristic patient, paternal tone to rise above his words, despite having lost a vital member of his top secret team.

Brax flipped a page, wishing for some simple, logical explanation. *'Too many variables,'* flooded his brain. The action of folding the paper back on itself

hid the pang in his chest. He and Jaffe had their dif-
ferences. But they were fighting the same battle. They
had both escaped Leviathan's wrath in the past. Brax
needed a moment to put it in order, even though he
spent six hours on a Concorde working it through in
his mind. Too many deaths, he thought. He took failure—every failure—personal. There had to have been
something they missed.

"It was strictly routine. Our mole had pulled a list
of Libyan passports issued directly from the Interior
Minister's office. We were picking it up."

"Why face to face? Andrew knew better."

An edge of embroiled anger slipped out with
Housemother's words. Anger borne out of concern
for the mission rather than a fallen soldier. The players knew the risks. They were intimately aware of
their hard target and his penchant for killing.

"Had to be personal. Jaffe promised to yank
him."

"I softened it for Valentine. He's gravely concerned. Can't let this out. Heat's being turned up
right now. Senate Intelligence Committee is poking
around for information about on-going operations.
I've made Andrew out a hero for now. We come away
with anything?"

"Nothing. All Andrew could convey was that Mandigo's list was incomplete. Could have been a
dummy, if his superiors realized he had turned on
them. Then his man went ballistic."

"Literally."

For a moment neither spoke. Brax turned the
page; Housemother fished through his pocket for
another cough drop. Coming up empty, he set a withered pale hand with fingers yellowed by nicotine on
the back of the bench.

"Andrew have anyone?" Brax asked.

"Wife."

The words ignited a salvo inside Brax. He shuffled the newspaper to hide it. He had always figured

Andrew for a loner. No ties, no tears. Being alone didn't make the job easier. It just made dying easier.

"Nothing that intimate. Marriage ended long ago. Just never went through the formality of divorce. Seemed the little woman would rather turn tricks than care for hubby. He named the Madison Aviary Preservation Society in Wisconsin his beneficiary."

"Parents?"

"An aunt in Bangor. If she's still alive when this is over, we'll tell her and the wife. Right now security's paramount. Andrew had enemies in a score of governments. Can't let out that he's out of commission."

Another silence settled in. Not for lack of words. Rather for a moment of respect for Andrew.

Housemother stifled a hacking cough and wrapped the lapel of his coat around his fleshy neck. For the first time since taking the seat, he connected with Brax. They had a decade's history together. Eight top secret Black Ops missions between them. They knew how each other thought most of the time. And they came to trust each other's instincts.

"Mean business," Housemother muttered more to himself. "Any chance they made Andrew?"

"Squire's digging. Andrew never acknowledged any watch list names. Do we abort?"

"Your call."

Silence answered.

"Good. Let's nail that bastard's coffin shut. I'll get moving on a replacement. Won't be easy, Andrew had a sense about the target. You and the team be careful. Let's run down all ravens in flight. See if the Russians are running interference for Leviathan."

"We were clear going in. I would have aborted otherwise."

Brax flipped to the back page. He stared at the print, seeing nothing.

"I know you would have. No need to explain."

"Opening day's next week. Andrew was a Cubs fan."

Housemother's laugh turned into a cough.

"I owe Valentine an immediate risk assessment. A leak now might ruffle some political feathers."

Housemother rose, steadying momentarily on the bench before strolling off. Brax remained, thumbing through Sports before tossing the paper and marching off across the soggy field with hands stuffed into his pockets. He had another plane to catch.

🔫

The six hour flight to San Jose provided Brax time to reflect upon the events of Kano. At times he tried, albeit unsuccessfully, to put the whole mess out of his mind and sleep. Hazards of the job, he kept instructing himself. Shake it off; go on. It came with the paycheck. Though he never once flinched, a dozen times in his mind's eye he relived that tumultuous raging explosion and the deafening percussion that ensued. Each time, the fireball roared closer and closer. Brax had to run to keep from being engulfed. He could feel his heart hammering two hundred beats a minute—convincing him he was still alive. One of his team was not.

Emerging into the terminal from the gangway, Brax fell into his role of Kevin Chambers as easily as if it had been some magical transformation. He had passed through the metamorphosis so many times in the last three years that it became a Pavlovian response. No conscious thought required. Years of focused effort made his deception so complete, so infallible, that regardless of circumstance, his responses rang natural and spontaneous. Kevin Chambers sold super-sophisticated mini-computers in 22 countries around the world. Kevin Chambers could talk *mega*ram, gigabytes and virtual reality as if it were his second language.

Exiting the airport loaded with suitcase and product cases, Kevin Chambers spoke to no one, paid three weeks of parking, and roared out of the lot shifting his black Beemer ferociously up to third gear.

Picking up Route 17 east of the airport, the drive through the dappled beauty of the Santa Cruz mountains seemed more a blur than a passage. He maneuvered easily around chugging, churning trucks without thought. The scene transported him back to Kano and the bus of migrant laborers. He shut down his mind before facing the explosion anew.

Beyond the crest of these tranquil forested mountains lie Oz. A place where Kevin Chambers was safe. A sense of renewed vigor flooded in when specks of the Pacific Ocean gleamed through the gaps in the lush greenery.

Home.

The Kevin Chambers secret he kept from everyone, including the Company. Only he knew this side of Brax. Kevin remained sheltered and free, and he enjoyed a modicum of normalcy, despite a plaguing inner voice warning with the insistence of a spoiled child that normal could never exist in his world. That same dark cynic nagged that even Kevin Chambers might someday turn against him.

The plangent rush and rhythmic pounding of white caps applauded his arrival as he pulled into the garage of his split-level perched a scant four feet in from a thirty-foot rock cliff just south of the sleepy, out-of-the-way coastal town of Aptos. Here, Kevin Chambers became just another successful *techie*, in a guarded elitist colony of mega-rich techies, who amassed fortunes 'over the hill' in Silicon Valley, feeding off the hunger for computer technology.

Once inside the guarded walls of his fortress, Kevin paused before the glass wall facing the rushing waves while saffron light streamed over him. Elevated from the shore, he lost the sight of the waves rolling up the sand, but the awesome forces crashing below vibrated his window panes. Like a heart beat, the ocean rose and fell without arrhythmia.

This isolated world he meticulously constructed beyond the rest of the world was to be a sane, pristine refuge segregated from the black streets of his profession. This world established a haven from the nightmares that haunt the men who have witnessed and even instigated the things he had seen.

Kevin dropped his bags, collected up the pile of mail stacked on the foyer table and drifted into his den, which also looked out upon the dappled cerulean water. Only the kitchen and guest bedrooms in this house lacked the ocean's constant companionship.

He settled into a well worn, high-backed leather chair behind a rich, uncluttered mahogany desk. His mind sought to return to Nigeria. Instead, Kevin grabbed a remote, leveled it at a small television set on the wall of shelves to his left and fired. While he opened the first few pieces of mail, he listened.

After's a moment's pause, the word 'PLAY' flashed across the dark screen. Then sirens and chaos crowded out the serenity.

"*Shortly before one o'clock an explosion rocked the World Trade Center. The blast is believed to have originated in the basement garage, sending churning black smoke through the lower floors of the building.*"

The female reporter's plaintive, detached voice fell victim to the cries of the terrified. People scurried to escape the building's smoke-infested bowels.

A persistent snow danced up the scene, the result of areas on the tape where the signal had been worn away by the thousands of passes made across the magnetic VCR heads. Brax had replayed this tape inside his head an additional thousand times. He could recite every word spoken, duplicating the inflection until it became impossible to tell his voice from the voices on the tape.

"*It will be hours before the total number of dead and injured can be tallied. My God, who could have perpetrated such an act.*"

Nigeria demanded him.

Had Andrew overlooked subtle signs of compromise? Shouldn't Andrew's sixth sense have picked up Mandigo's volatility and penchant for self-destruction?

Should he have aborted? The past becomes granite in a fleeting moment, forever unchangeable. Contemplating it was a fool's folly. Only the future can be altered, by heeding the lessons of the past. At least that's the substance of what history professors tout while nestled in the sterile confines of their classrooms, where their greatest adversary becomes some snot-nosed kid angered over a grade less than an A.

"I's never been so scared in my life. The smoke was choking me. Alls I could think about was dying alone. I didn't want to die without having the chance to share my life with someone."

Brax stared vacantly out the window. Anger poppled like a pot on the boil. He had lost a crucial team member. It was difficult to think of Andrew as anything more. Too many clashes had prevented friendship from seeping in. All too often it was Andrew's way or the highway. It had gotten him killed.

Unconsciously, Kevin switched off the television only to remove a black and silver marble from his pocket. He began working it in his hand the way an man of meager means fondles loose change. It carried the same significance. The marble was more than a charm; he had carried it since age fifteen—when he discovered its potent value.

A multimedia computer, a unremarkable desk telephone and an answering machine populated half the desk's surface. He kept the other half clear. No papers, no folders. All items professional in nature were encrypted and stored electronically. Only he held the key. Only he had access to the secrets. Taking himself out of that wandering moment, Kevin unlocked a side drawer, removed a cellular phone and dialed a number inside Systech Software Solutions over the hill in San Jose. Dummied telephone records listed a Dr. Manuel Cortizina, a very real doctor in a very real Watsonville clinic, as the telephone's owner. Another layer of deception to further isolate him from the world beyond his fortress.

Kevin listened to three beeps; Squire had left no new messages. For the moment, Kevin could tuck Brax and everything to do with Wolf Pack into the darkest recesses of his mind. He could allow himself some time, time for Kevin Chambers to emerge and find balance in his life.

But Andrew's death plagued him, sparking new thoughts. Dying alone seemed unforgivable—living alone now unbearable. A vital part of Kevin's life remained unfulfilled. He had promised himself when he was twenty that he would marry by thirty and fill his house with children by thirty-three. Now thirty-five, he had neither. He snapped out of the chair, intent on remedying that.

He made two phone calls from the phone on his desk, tossed the mail into a tray as if it were all useless junk and dashed up the stairs, where he changed into running shorts and a tank top. No sooner had he dressed when he heard a Carmen Ghia's tinny whir rolling into the drive. With the swiftness of flight, Kevin dashed down the stairs in time to pull open the front door just as Suzanne strode up the walk shifting grocery bags and cursing her errant house key.

"Kevin!" she chimed as the door swung open for her. Grocery bags dropped with complete disregard for the eggs on top as she rushed into his waiting arms.

Their kiss came more out of urgency than welcome, and for a long moment neither spoiled the embrace with a breathe.

Suzanne melded her boiling soft form into Kevin's arms. She smelled of some exotic fragrance. Then Kevin noticed orchards that had spilled from a grocery bag and tainted with egg yoke.

Finally Suzanne withdrew.

"God, I've missed you," he said, gazing upon the sparkling blue of her eyes as if they were a treasure that he himself had unearthed.

"I thought you..."

Kevin's lips silenced her. His fingers worked beneath her willowy, honey-colored hair to caress the nape of her neck. The touch sent shivers up Suzanne's spine.

"I thought you were going to be gone a month?"

"The deal went better than I had hoped. I closed it two days ago."

Inside, a trail of discarded clothes led up the spiral staircase to the master bedroom anchored at the very edge of the rock cliff, and from which the vibrant sea air swept in while Kevin and Suzanne made love with unbridled passion. The fires of their excitement died slowly in a lasting embrace, while Michael Bolton love songs drifted out the stereo on the wall unit, just loud enough to be heard, but not so boisterous as to interfere with the lapping ocean below. Their heralds of pleasure became lost amongst the rushing waves and the sweet music. Afterward, exhausted from the intensity with which they made love, they collapsed in each others' arms. Neither sought to sever the bond holding them until hours later when hunger settled in.

They showered together as the sun sank into the glistening watery horizon, then wound their way up Highway 1 into the city for dinner at Skonidia's on the wharf.

Skonidia's offered that special ambiance Kevin sought for this night: Subdued romantic lighting, exquisite furnishings, and the kind of care and attention to detail that made a patron feel special. In fact it was the only restaurant on the bay Kevin frequented, and Orienda the owner, knew him well. When the silver-haired woman picked him out at the crowded entrance, her face alighted, she cleared a path with the wave of her fleshy arm, and upon reaching the couple, hugged Kevin the way a spinster aunt hugs her favorite nephew after half a lifetime apart. Her peck on his cheek left a ruby smear, which she removed with her finger before releasing him.

"I have missed you, Kevin. How many months has it been since your last visit to Skonidia's?" Orienda said in an English tongue waited heavy by an accent from an Eastern European region.

"Far too long, Orienda. You are looking more beautiful than the last time I dined here."

"You tease an old woman."

Orienda smiled and waved her finger as if to dismiss his compliment as perfunctory.

"What's that all about?" Suzanne asked as they wormed their way through waiting faces turned bitter by the treatment the two received.

Orienda removed a RESERVED sign from a prime choice table, setting them with a view of the Golden Gate bridge, and before leaving, she ordered a bottle of Chateau Carbonnieux '86 for their table.

Sitting in a darkened alcove in a prolonged silence, Suzanne sensed a different Kevin emerging from the very moment they left their bed. He held back, seemed uncertain. She saw it in his eyes and felt it in his silence. They shared their meal this night in an uncharacteristic somber atmosphere.

Midnight crept in by the time they left Skonidia's. Waves clapping the deserted wharf beckoned. At this time of night, no street urchins cluttered the streets and an eerie air clung to the wharf.

Kevin, always the observer, appraised the scene in a glance, then took Suzanne under his arm as he motioned her toward the water.

Even the envelope of his warmth failed to dissipate the lingering chill Suzanne felt since dinner. No funny witticisms nor salesman's raunchy humor. No stories, no anecdotes. Concern shuddered through her. Something was stealing her lover's attention.

"You think this is a good idea? Walking around here at night is dangerous."

"It's fine," Kevin said, kissing her cheek. Her heady scent wormed its way into his head. She wore the perfume he had brought her from Paris three months earlier. Sweat came up on his palms; he wondered if Suzanne could sense his anxiety.

What was he doing, anyway?

Across the choppy bay, Alcatraz's faint desolation cut into the indigo skyline. Beyond, a fog horn bellowed through a gray spreading mist that swallowed up most of the Golden Gate on its way inland. In an hour the wharf would also fall victim to the shroud.

Kevin walked in silence, tucking Suzanne close, savoring her warmth against his. They stopped at a fence where below the water lapped against the piles of the wharf. Overhead, a single gull clung to the air currents as if expecting something from the two lovers. For a time they stared at nothing and listened to the gentle rhythm. The universe elicits a rhythm all its own. A rhythm men must learn to live within.

"How long...before you leave again?"

"Don't know. A French deal's shaky. I may have to appease them. They can be so demanding."

"A week? Two?"

"Suzanne, we've meant alot. I mean, I'm not always great at saying... I wish I knew how..."

A fist clamped around Suzanne's heart. Her mind blocked out the rest of his sentence. *Oh God, it's the old heave-ho!* Something sucked her stomach right out of her. For three years they had been consummate lovers. Passion's fire never once so much as flickered in this past year of sharing their lives. This had all been a dream. The gorgeous house on the ocean, making love for hours when he returned from a trip, secretly planning all the little details of a life with him. He was about to burst her whole bubble.

She wanted to take his hand but refrained, fearful his response might telegraph intent. What if he pulled away? He avoided her eyes.

"I..." he wavered.

Something inside yelled for Suzanne to turn away. Maybe it was the unctuous way Kevin's eyes now slid off hers, avoiding any sustained contact.

Speak damnit, she thought, braced for the worst. He had found someone new. He got lonely on the road so much. *Goddamn him.* He found someone more beautiful, more loving.

"I need you to know...I really care for you."

Oh Christ, here it comes...

Suzanne swallowed. She reminded him constantly of how much she loved him. A thousand times isn't enough? That's it, goddamn him, goddamn hi...

"Suzanne...uh...Suzanne Elizabeth Masters, will...you...marry me?" He uttered the words as if it required tremendous effort to eject them. Words so heavy and unwieldy that he barely mustered the control to get them out.

"What?"

Suzanne rushed into his arms with such force that they clanked into the fence.

But without answering, without so much as a kiss of reassurance, Suzanne released him with an arresting jolt and retreated. Her eyes shifted from excitement to something else.

Something that stopped Kevin's heart. Had he misread her feelings for him? He thought she loved him enough to spend the rest of her life with him. Had he erred in asking for that now?

"I love you, Kevin Chambers. I've loved you since the first time you kissed me, the first time you took my hand in yours. But even after three years, I don't really know you. There's a side I'm not been privy to."

Kevin wrapped his arms around her. He brought her supple body against his. He wanted to kiss her, yet he resisted. She had still to answer.

"Will I marry you? My life would be incomplete without you. I'll be the candle that burns in your window and the hand that reaches out to you in the night. I will love you—and be your wife—for as long as you love me."

Their kiss lasted but a moment.

By day, Suzanne doled out reading, writing and arithmetic to fourth graders at Rio del Mar School, a marginally adequate institution set a hilly mile from the house they shared. But by night, under the moonlit sky, she became an insatiable pleasure seeker. A lover whose uninhibited energy rivaled her students.

Later, as they lay as one in their bed, Suzanne slept motionless and soundless. Kevin watched her. Even in sleep she was more beautiful than anything he could conjure up in his imagination. The satin sheet molded to her petite frame that needed to be soaking wet to hit triple digits on a scale. But now doubts crept in where assurance once reigned.

Had he acted on a foolish impulse? He could endure an empty existence no longer. Life was slipping away from him. Was he insane to hope for a normal life? That was exactly what he was doing. Long ago he sold his conscience for an ideal; now he was no longer certain he could ever really buy back his soul, even if he wished.

🔫

Kevin awoke to shallow darkness. He lived with sentinel sleep habits—asleep yet alert, capable of a lethal response in an instant. Motionless, he took in the world around him: Suzanne's soft breathing, the gentle rhythm beyond his window, her lingering scent that had been transferred to his pillow.

He expended his first waking minute confirming his location and identity. To prevent incriminating errors from surfacing, he routinely re-enforced the role he played. Forgetting his current identity any given moment could become costly.

Discerning only Suzanne's sleek curves, he fought down the urge to touch her, to stroke her hair, to slip his fingers between hers. She was at peace and too beautiful to disturb. Too safe in his bed sharing her life with him. A life cluttered with secrets, secrets he might never be able to reveal to her.

Kevin crawled soundlessly from the bed and pulled on a black sweatsuit. His was a profession of undetectable passage, seeing with fingers in complete darkness, traversing chasms in utter silence. During a moment's pause at the door, Kevin questioned the sanity of his decision. Could she live in his world?

Padding down a path of rotted timbers implanted as steps to the shore, Kevin once again felt the sting of loneliness. At his back, the first weak glow of dawn appeared over the housetops and the cool morning air slapped him awake.

He inhaled the rich majesty of the ocean's roar. Constant, unrelenting, powerful. He drew strength from the awesome powers surrounding him, as he had been taught in his youth. *If we could harness the forces that bind us to this place, we can arise with the power of a hundred against our enemies*, his master had said so many years ago.

Foaming waves erased his first driving footprint left in the wet sand. Then the next and the next as Kevin kicked into his run. A mile down the beach he launched into a fierce rage, reliving those deadly moments in Kano, racing to escape the raging fireball barreling down upon him. He pounded harder to escape the rolling blast. He relived the swarming inferno that seized him back in Nigeria. Moving in and out of the waves, his tracks vanished as quickly as they appeared, leaving only circling gulls to mark his trail.

Andrew had been flippant, careless. Goddamn him to let himself be killed.

The moment the fireball consumed his mind's eye, Kevin kicked into full pelt. His scream fell lost amongst the cries of the hungry sea birds.

A fire burning up his lungs forced him to cease. The fireball had vanished; the memories of Kano never would. Kevin checked his pulse at his neck and settled into a voracious walk.

Block the incident from the mind. Its very presence destroyed concentration and confidence. Two things Kevin needed intact.

The walk ended at a secluded crevasse in the rock-ribbed cliff lining the beach a mile from his house. Twenty paces into the shaded hollow, the outside world fell silently away. Kevin entered yet another world.

Bushido. The world of the warrior.

A pair of fallen, rotted trees awaited him.

In this world, Brax ascended to supreme master. He stopped and focused. His eyes became ice—his face stone. He assumed a deadly stance before a chest-high stump and closed his eyes. *See the enemy, destroy your enemy first inside your mind.* One after another, he mentally reviewed the deadly kills of *wing chun.* Another weapon he had mastered by age twenty. A weapon few could deliver with the kind of force and accuracy to make them lethal.

In a controlled flurry of flying feet and fists, he attacked the tree trunk until his hands and feet ached. As soundless as a shadow, as lethal as a cobra, he struck with the same fluid ease as the great ocean, yet he delivered each blow with a surgical precision. He lived every day with the knowledge that he would likely only get one shot at Leviathan. If his first strike went astray, he would have no second chance.

Bushido—giving without asking in return. Even to the ultimate sacrifice.

He understood his nemesis more intimately than the woman he had just asked to marry him. He had cataloged every nuance of Leviathan's diabolic mind.

Not a day passed without him thinking about Leviathan. Even with an arsenal of high-tech weapons, it would come down to tenacity and cunning that would ultimately defeat their enemy. Leviathan was responsible for Andrew's death. Brax knew that as deeply as he understood why he must risk everything to stop that monster. He could never rest until he had achieved his objective.

3

BX phone home.

                                    Squire

Stainless steel elevator doors parted with a soft sucking whir, allowing Brax access to a windowless third floor wing of the Central Intelligence Agency headquarters. He swiped his access card across the security reader to gain entry through an oaken unmarked door at the far end of the corridor.

"Morning, Mr. Nash," a polite, chesty-voiced secretary said, which made her sound gruff despite her pleasant smile. "Mr. Ford's expecting you."

"How's his mood today, Angel?" Nash asked with a wink.

"Glad it's not me."

Angel buzzed him through the inner door to the station chief's private office.

"Philip, how was the flight?" Dixon Ford asked without lifting his eyes from his reading. With a timorous face and the frame of a junior accountant, Dixon's agency talents extended only as far as organization and resource management—of the human kind. That kept him always within reach of his desk, though he began his unremarkable fourteen-year career romanticizing of fieldwork and tradecraft. Now he resigned himself to the security and routine that his internal assignment afforded him. Four children and a wife became far more important than the fantasies he nurtured from his college days. Over the course of the last decade at his desk, he convinced himself of the crucial role behind-the-lines support played, well maybe not as crucial to success as front line involvement.

Dixon's unimposing green eyes rose lazily off the page to meet Nash's. There seemed no way his appearance could ever intimidate.

"Pleasant."

"Sorry about Andrew. Good man. Heard he hid his condition even from our doctors. Should have been pulled in house years ago. Nothing demeaning about administrative work."

Nash said nothing. A hastily arranged cover story provided those who without a need to know with a cause of death as fatal heart attack. Dixon, as well as everyone else privy to the story, harbored suspicions of their own.

Dixon closed the file, whereupon he shifted his attention to a single unmarked file that had been relegated to the corner of his tidy desk.

"This room only," he said, handing Nash the file before settling back into his chair.

"What's this?" Nash asked perplexed, without opening the file. "What about the others?"

"Others? I was given to understand you knew. Decision's been made. Out of our hands."

Dixon shrugged as if to relieve himself of any responsibility and vacated his office.

"I'll return after you've had time to review the file. Strictly perfunctory though," he added at the door. He left with no trace of a smile on his face.

Nash wasted little time delving into the numbered file. No name, no identifying marks. But the file did elicit sufficient supporting documentation to warrant a Congressional Medal of Honor. Sensitive surveillance in Bulgaria just before the fall at grave personal risk. A stack of outstanding performance appraisals. High level counterterrorist work in Germany and Ireland. A letter of commendation and praise from an Irish station chief was attached to another stellar performance appraisal.

Only the absolute best received consideration for Wolf Pack. Integrity and commitment had to be untouchable. But this one, it would seem, had somehow bypassed the normal chain of consideration. Housemother had removed Nash from the selection process. That set Nash's mind to wondering. Who could be *that* good to move to the front of the line? And if he were that good, why haven't Nash been informed of him earlier? Nash had worked with a few in past years that he believed worthy of this assignment. Now his input was being shut down.

Still, he churned uneasily over having to accept this replacement sight unseen. Paper's a fool's way to judge efficacy. Performance determines efficacy in this line of work. Can this 791 perform? Was the question. Housemother must have something to warrant the decision.

Nash forced intuition to the forefront. He began picking and probing between the lines, diligent to uncover the chink in this knight's armor. Everyone had one. Yet this one's seemed to be well concealed in flowered Company rhetoric. That which seems too good to be true, usually isn't true.

Exactly fifteen minutes after departing, Dixon returned. He slid into his chair with no hint of a pleasure on his face. For a moment, he studied Nash's eyes, which as usual revealed nothing.

"I suppose if you're dead set against number..."

"791."

"I could go to bat for you. But I can't imagine what more you could want. Sound school, Bulgaria, martial arts...*bushido,* like yourself. I think that hokey crap is overrated. Give me a big gun any day. Did you read the '92 report. Top notch stuff in Belfast."

Nash stared at the paper.

"Clairvoyance. Able to leap tall buildings. Stop a bullet with his teeth."

"That's not in there? Let me check with personnel," Dixon said, then paused to reflect. "Besides, the way I hear it, you'd be rubbing some very important people the wrong way if you oppose this."

Nash closed the file. He opened it a few seconds later. There had to be something. Why was this one being pushed on him?

"No scars."

"And that's bad?"

"Either never been in a fight, or..."

"Damn good?" Dixon injected.

"Damn lucky."

Dixon leaned forward, resting the full weight of his frame on his elbows as if he were about to share something only he knew. Nash watched Dixon's eyes alight. He had something that made him feel important.

"Word is...that file came from God," he said as if he were sharing an Agency secret reserved for the inner circle. Something one at his level never gained access to.

Dixon pushed himself back in his chair in a boastful way. A slight smile turned the corners of his lips.

"Then I guess it's time I meet 791," Nash said, sliding the file back onto the desk. Something, however, triggered a cautionary flag inside his head.

"How's ten minutes. I'll have the south cafeteria cleared, then you two can get acquainted over a nice quiet lunch."

Nash remained silent. His mind scrambled to set up a quick scenario analysis.

"Is D9 available?"

"Right now? You mean right now, this minute?"

Nash nodded, releasing only the faintest glimmer of a smile.

Dixon shot forward in his chair and snatched up the phone. A wicked smile crossed his face while he dialed.

"A little one on one in order? Nash you are one sly devil," he said.

Dixon had half expected that Nash might find some way to challenge the decision. And he had chosen the best way he knew to test this one's abilities. Nash, it seemed, required more convincing before accepting God's word. And D9 was Nash's territory.

"All clear. You get thirty minutes. Proctor's setting the place up now. I'm glad *I'm* not the one under consideration."

"If 791 makes it through, I'll need a briefing tank for an hour, then you can clear the cafeteria."

"You got it."

While Dixon handled the arrangements, Nash retreated to the outer office, where he used Angel's phone to contact Squire and invite him to lunch. He disliked eating alone when it could be avoided, and the cafeteria would already be cleared anyway.

Nash tightened Velcro wrist straps as he stood at the entrance to the D9 stealth facility. Clad in a black jumpsuit and rubber-soled shoes, he pulled the knit hood over his face and fitted the black gloves onto his hands. The exercise was simple: one man must oppose one aggressor in a labyrinth of corridors and rooms. No weapons except what could be gained in the exercise. Only cunning, wit and martial arts. Five-watt red lights spaced at thirty meter intervals throughout the course threw off just enough luminescence to overcome complete darkness.

A red-lighted entry sign above Nash's door flashed. Agent 791 had entered at the other end. The contest had begun.

Nash penetrated the maze soundlessly. Arranged much like a series of movie sets, connecting rooms had been populated with a variety of motifs. A fully furnished living room opened up to a warehouse filled with crates that might lead to a garbage-infested dilapidated building. Walls were easily added or removed to alter the course and change the settings. Each time through presented new challenges to overcome. Nash listened, heard nothing.

Students received a complete briefing as to expectations before entering, and they were informed they were on a clock from the moment they passed through the door. Nash expected 791 would attempt the path of least resistance, and therefore try for the lowest time score.

Two minutes and three rooms into the exercise, Nash's opponent still evaded detection. Few could advance through unfamiliar territory so efficiently. He stopped inside the warehouse and became swallowed up by a blackened corner. No doors to creak, no footsteps to betray movement. Only faint shadows to forewarn of an approach.

The faint outline of a skulking shadow crossed the far wall. Nash readied himself to strike. This would be easier than he thought. As the form emerged, he launched himself to deliver a flying round-house kick. His war scream worked to disorient. They did neither.

A quick thrusting arm neutralized his attack. Nash buckled when a fist slammed upward and inward at the base of his rib cage, a very careful strike meant to wind him and minimize any potential counter strike. When Nash straightened, the figure skirted swiftly and silently into the next room.

Rather than pursue directly, Nash fled the warehouse, slipping into a corridor off the living room. He waited. His adversary had to pass this way to reach the exit. His location gave him the advantage from which to strike.

The sucking sound of quick inhalation blared inside his head. He spun just in time to fend off a double-fisted attack from his flank. 791 had doubled back to follow him instead of going for the exit.

Nash delivered a sweeping kick, hoping to drop his adversary to the floor and end the exercise. However, his opponent curled, somersaulted over the leg, bounced off the side wall and landed a flying elbow to Nash's jaw. The taste of warm blood leaked into Nash's throat. The strike had been measured well and delivered with less than full force, but still sufficient to draw blood.

While Nash used a kip to return to his feet, his opponent disappeared down a side corridor in a race to reach the exit.

But victory would not come this easily for 791. Nash had one shot left. He slipped through a blackened room resembling a crowded office and took a position near the last corridor before the exit door. He leapt from a dead stop to punch out the light affording his opponent the benefit of sight. Now in total darkness, he waited. His bruised rib throbbed. The blood still trickled from the cut inside his lip. Nash could still win, though winning became secondary. For the most part, this exercise was over. This one had proven himself. He had earned his spot on Wolf Pack.

Nash listened. Nothing. Stalemate, he thought.

He learned young that patience as a weapon could be far more potent in victory than force. It would seem that 791 also understood that lesson.

When Nash advanced to the end of the corridor, a flying foot came down from above to clip him in the chest, though his opponent could never have known his precise location without night vision goggles.

The black jumpsuit sallied forth with flying fists, intending to force Nash into retreat just long enough to make a dash for the exit. Escaping the maze was the objective, not destroying the aggressor.

But in that moment, Nash analyzed the strategy and went for the legs. He missed, had to throw up a forearm to deflect a fist, then took hold of 791's hood to bring him down. His hand came away with the hood and a handful of hair—long hair. That sudden incongruence shattered Nash's concentration. He allowed his opponent to turn his arm outward and throw him over his shoulder to the floor.

A forearm pinned Nash's throat to the tile.

Nash raised his arms in surrender immediately. The proctor, monitoring the exercise from an overhead control booth, switched on the overhead lights. Nash lay staring up into the hard blue, very feminine, eyes of the newest member of his team.

"I pass?" she asked, The glint in her slight smile being borne out of dominance over the one sent to evaluate her. Those eyes never strayed from Nash's. And she made no effort to release him.

In that taut moment, 791 wondered if a man would have been tested.

Nash offered no resistance

Slowly, 791 removed her lock on his throat. Nash released his grip on her arm. Standing over him, she offered her hand. Nash accepted it.

"You're Philip Nash," she said when they had both returned to their feet beneath the last light before the exit. An escaping admiration weighted her words. She had bloodied the lip of the one Company man she most admired. She stood face to face with a legend she had only heard about in whispers.

"791?" Nash was hoping there had been a mistake.

The briefing room door was self-locking. Only a key could get you in from the outside. Nash sat across from 791 in the eight-by-ten reading room, waiting for Dixon to bring in the sealed files on Leviathan and Operation Wolf Pack. Waiting and wondering. For a long moment neither spoke.

"Virginia...Soo-Ling Watkins," she said finally, when Nash remained comfortably silent. The one vital statistic absent from her file. "I hate being thought of as a number."

Ford entered, guarding the files as if they were written with gilded ink. He set them on the table and turned away as if upset that he had been excluded from their contents.

"When you're finished, seal, sign and ring my secretary. She'll see that the file accounting is in order," Dixon said at the door. He couldn't resist offering a thumbs up to Virginia before leaving. *Great job*, he mouthed. No one equaled Nash in the stealth facility. No one.

Virginia could have easily been mistaken for an Asian movie star or a model. She was that beautiful. Those glistening blue Amerasian eyes cast off a purely captivating quality. The most alluring aspect of her appearance though, was the one thing that marked her a freak in the land of her birth. Having spoken, Watkins seemed content now to wait for Nash's response. She knew better than to ask questions. She would receive what she needed to know, and *only* what she needed to know, even though she had already pieced together much from the exercise and Nash's presence.

"You did well. Very well. You have any idea why you're here?"

"None." The correct answer to his question. She had suspicions but believed it better to keep them buried at this point.

Nash slit the file's seal. Without examining the contents, he slid the file across the table—a file much too thin for a monster the Company codenamed Leviathan.

'EYES ONLY' had been stamped boldly in red on every page.

Virginia read, stopping long enough to study the face in a blown up, grainy photograph that topped the stack of sketchy incidence reports and assessments. The reports offered enough information to purport that Ranzami could be Satan incarnate. This man was ruthless, cunning and elusive. Invariably, those who ventured too close ended up dead.

"I'm getting Wolf Pack?" Virginia let slip, her voice betraying her excitement.

"What do you know about us?"

"Only that you exist."

"And you're aware of Ranzami Abu Mabbas?"

"I'd have to be dead not to. You don't need a Cray One computer to figure out something big's going on."

"Where did you study?"

"Bushido?"

Nash nodded.

"My father."

"Who is?"

"Was Captain Nathan Watkins, Special Forces. I was a Company baby. He loved my mother enough to get me out before the fall. She never made it. The Company helped him. I was eight. I earned my black belt by high school. After my father died, I completed my training in three years under a Koji master in Korea."

A Korean influence in her training spawned an uneasiness in Brax. None proved more vicious than the Koreans when it came to silent killing. Korean terrorist training camps were vying for popularity and funding, turning out master assassins to propagate urban guerilla warfare.

"Why intelligence?"

"Father said I owe my freedom to the Company. My way of repaying the debt."

"How much do you know about Leviathan?"

"Almost nothing. I had a rodent in Belfast who claimed one man was organizing terrorists across political lines. Some kind of mastermind for international terrorism. Maybe Ranzami was the one he meant."

"We know he engineered the World Trade Center bombing and a half dozen London explosions. We've attributed twenty-two dead to him for sure. We also believe he orchestrated the kidnap/murder of Thierry le Carta, the French diplomat in Singapore."

"I read the briefs. He took out five innocents to get to his target."

"About six months ago, we intercepted some intelligence indicating Leviathan had used the WTC to convince extremist financiers of his ability to penetrate deep inside the U.S."

"So he's after something bigger?"

"Maybe our throat. What you heard in Belfast was true. Ranzami's bringing together a global terrorist network. And we believe he's made the U.S. his prime target."

Virginia closed the file, slid it back across the table with a hesitation. A moment of silence lingered.

"And Wolf Pack's mission?"

"Eliminate the threat."

This was unlike anything she had worked on before. Counterterrorism was the deadliest of all the games. Terrorists are too willing to die for their causes, too willing to kill to achieve an objective.

"Our hard target is Leviathan's plan. Uncover it, neutralize it, and make sure he no longer poses a threat to western governments."

"How many?"

"I get to keep asking the questions. You got a codename?"

"Snow White."

Nash thought for a moment.

"Now it's Cali. I'm Brax. The names are secure—I expect you'll keep them that way. You'll meet the team before we go into the trenches."

"Then I'm in?"

"Unless you decline."

Cali let a smile slip.

"What are our operating parameters?"

"Necessary measures."

Cali reacted not to the words, but to their implication. *Giving without asking in return. Doing what must be done without prejudice.* Her heart raced.

"Seven know. Our directives come from the highest authority."

"This isn't just a covert?" she said, raising a brow. A knot twisted up her stomach. The words 'necessary measures' churned inside her head.

"Your record's exemplary. Better than exemplary. You came down from the top."

"But?" Cali asked. There was something in Brax's delivery that warranted her response.

"You don't blend well. Your face can be made in a crowd. Amerasian features are easily marked."

"So you're dumping me for the way I look?"

"No. But it increases our risk. And maybe this isn't for you. If you'd rather pass…"

"You crazy? I busted my ass for eight years hoping for this."

Nash rose, reached across the table and took her hand. It was warm, steady and dry. This one had steel cables for nerves. Most would be quaking at the thought of going up against a demon like Ranzami.

Cali accepted his hand; her forearm muscles locked tight and ready. Still too soon to trust. Their eyes never strayed from each other. Cali didn't know how to read them. Was Nash pleased?

"Why you?" Nash asked, "Why were you singled out?"

"Before my father died, he worked the halls on Capitol Hill from a wheel chair. His persistence got people to listen."

"How'd he die?"

"Doctors said Cancer; he said Agent Orange. He lasted long enough to get the politicians to at least consider what he had to say. I believe he made a difference."

"I'll arrange preliminary contacts. Put your affairs in order and make no personal plans for a while."

Nash collected up the files and returned them to their envelopes. Then he sealed and signed them.

"How long is a while?"

"I'll let you know. To be honest, I don't know if someone important really likes you, or hates you."

Nash started for the door. Cali's words stopped him, bringing him back to face her.

"Nash, you as good as they say?" Virginia blurted as if the words erupted on impulse. She tried without success to bury a concern racing about inside her mind. Maybe the full weight of what she had agreed to had begun to take root.

Had her confidence faltered? Those sparkling eyes revealed nothing. Was this her way of exposing that she now harbored second thoughts about her decision? Nash wondered.

"Better."

Nash opened the door.

"Let's get lunch," he said.

Cali remained at the table.

"One more thing. Why me? Why am I on the team?"

"A replacement," was all Nash offered.

Brax and Cali entered a deserted south cafeteria, where they selected their fare from unmanned serving trays, then settled at the first table. The depth of the vacant room lent an eerie undertone. It also served to punctuate the significance of the two.

"You guys really are invisible," Cali commented, taking in the arranged extremes. No wonder Wolf Pack never grew to more than a whisper on the wind. Something this secret could only come down from executive order.

"*We're* invisible, and never forget that."

A few moments after they began eating, the cafeteria doors opened with a squeal. A lanky, thirtyish black man with studious face behind wire-rimmed glasses strolled in as if he belonged there. Without looking up, he collected his tray and silverware, filled his plate to overflowing, which seemed odd for one with such a lean frame, and turned with a stilted smile to join them. But the smoldering in those dark eyes escaped Brax's notice, since Brax sat with his back to Squire's approach.

As Squire came around to take a seat facing Brax, Brax read the disappointment across Squire's face. Even the way Squire slid his tray onto the table and dropped his weight into the chair beside Cali telegraphed anger. Squire began eating, avoiding eye contact with Brax.

Cali sensed immediate discontent. She offered her hand but abandoned the gesture when Squire continued shoveling food into his mouth.

Introductions turned out to be curt and superficial. Neither Brax nor Squire seemed to be men of many words.

Brax discarded a half-eaten lunch, sensing the early rumblings of indigestion. This would be their only appearance together inside headquarters as long as the operation was in motion.

Squire's cold listless hand—when he finally did bury his disappointment deep enough to go on—let Cali know he resented their meeting. The handshake had been purely perfunctory. Squire, Cali characterized, was one to wear his feelings on his sleeves.

"Squire's comm hub. Everything goes through him. *Everything*. He tracks all incoming intelligence and directs the relevant stuff to us. He'll set up your codes and channels. Use them. You make sure Squire knows where you are and what you're doing every minute of every day. One screw up and you're out. You get into trouble, he's your lifeline if you can't raise anyone else on the team. He can bring down the wrath of God if necessary. We operate with six standing emergency plans for every move we make. Make sure you know every one of them by heart."

Cali nodded. Brax's sharp words had a bite. For a moment she wondered what she had taken on. She wanted the best. Thoughts of her father cut off the words flowing into her ears. He was the best of the best. Something Brax had just said snapped her back.

"Where do I meet you?" Cali asked.

"I find you," Squire spat with a Rottweiler's snap.

Silence ensued while Squire finished his lunch. The silence suggested Cali's presence had driven a wedge between the two men. She took that as a cue to excuse herself.

The moment the cafeteria door closed, Squire slammed his fork down, lifted his eyes off his plate and leveled them directly at Brax. Anger seethed in those dark orbs, and the veins along Squire's locked temples pulsed.

"If you're going to fuck me, at least kiss me first."

"I know what you're going to say." Brax blurted out to diffuse Squire's erupting explosion.

"You throw me into that rotten sink hole twelve feet below the world of the living, and then you select a skirt to replace Jaffe. When is it my turn? When do I go out there to mix it up? I *am* part of the team."

"Squire, you're the best inside man we've got. I hand-picked you because of your inside talents. I need you right here."

"I'm *so* good that I get screwed out of fieldwork?"

"You're missing something we need on this one."

"And she has it? Yeah right. I don't have the experience, and I can't get the experience because you won't let me out of my room."

Brax had to refrain—even from Squire. For all his talents, he lacked two vital elements necessary for Wolf Pack to operate in the field. And if he knew what those two qualifications were, he would accept his inside role without retort. But some things had to be secret even from Squire. Inside he was safe.

Or so Brax believed.

"Squire, we don't know what's going on. Kano should have never soured. The hair on my neck is up. I need you, and what you do, inside. Especially now. You're the best digger we've got. You need to get a rundown on all ravens in flight. We have to know if someone knew of Jaffe's meeting. We're at risk and we can't abort now. This is too important."

Whether the words were the catalyst, or something deeper inside, Squire allowed his seething anger to subside, fully aware his superior was stroking him. Yet believing every word of what Brax had said to be true, Squire let a hint of a smile slip out. His way of apologizing for his callous demeanor. He was the best inside man in the Company. In his own right, he was a dangerous man with a keyboard and a video display screen. If information is power, then Squire had more clout than the DCI himself.

"You're vital to the mission. Don't let Cali's assignment shake your commitment."

Using the last bite of bread like a wipe, Squire cleaned his plate, his hunger for excitement far outstripping his appetite for cafeteria food.

4

> Arrangements secure. Family reunion
> on the fifth.
>
>   Brax

Silence consumed the white Sterling. Brax and Cali drove for hours in the lush Scottish countryside. Brax seemed guarded—a man content in the solace of his mind rather than his companion. All Cali knew for certain was they headed north and east. And before long they would run out of land. They had picked up the waiting Sterling after a flight to Glasgow from London, and Brax had circled the airport thrice before beginning their northward trek.

"Sorry to be late, Darling," he had said with an impeccable British accent before giving her a peck on the cheek when they rendezvoused at the gate at Dulles airport thirteen hours previous. That simple line provided Cali with sufficient information to establish the role she was to play. He hadn't spoken much since then.

Cali surmised they were man and wife, and she was to remain dutifully silent unless asked to speak. A role she would never stand for in real life. But as a player she had to execute her role exactly as expected. She concluded she must have performed in accordance with Brax's wishes, since he felt no need to prod her along with the ruse in progress.

Leaving the main coastal highway, Brax monitored traffic in their wake. In tourist fashion, he pulled onto the gravel shoulder twice, despite causing the autos following to swerve around him. When they raised a fist, he smiled politely and waved. During the respite they would stroll for a bit, snap a few meaningless photos, all the while appraising the surrounding terrain. Then they moved on.

A winding side road allowed them to skirt the northern coastal town of Wick, and once beyond, they turned east, choosing a graveled route running along the coast. Out their window, the sea spray washed over jutting rocks. The inviting blue-green water masked frigid temperatures and a current so fierce it would sweep even the able-bodied swimmers out to sea.

Cali absorbed the lush green splendor of the rolling hills and the occasional graystone rubble of what had many centuries ago been a castle. She imagined in her mind's eye the great turrets and spires that must have towered into the sky at a time when death was a way of life. The place rekindled memories of Ireland and her assignment in Belfast. She shut down the memory before it turned hellish.

"Few more miles," Brax offered, glancing at the mirror.

At last, he speaks, she told herself, knowing full well a comment like that could harm a budding professional relationship. Their silence came out of necessity rather than choice. Long range sophisticated eavesdropping devices could lock on to their car allowing anyone to capture every word they exchanged. And nothing could be left to chance. Nothing could be exposed to their enemies. Those were his first words in the past three hours.

The nearer their destination, the more Brax reconnoitered the road behind them and the flanking countryside. An absence of populous made a tail all the more obvious. Few had reason to travel this road. And anything out of the ordinary would be cause for suspicion.

Only when Brax felt absolutely comfortable with the security, did they exit the main road to take up a pair of ruts leading over a rise. From the crest, Cali got her first glimpse of their destination: a modest, thatched cottage with twin spires perched in the midst of a grassy sea, which ended at a rocky coast. It reminded her of an isolated outpost that could have been constructed a half century earlier to watch for approaching ships.

The front door's arched window had a curtain panel askew. Cali assumed that was the signal to proceed. Especially since Brax continued toward the cottage finally rolling to a stop at the door. Cali thought she detected a breath of relief slip from Brax's lips.

Cali waited outside the vehicle, both her hands clutching her purse like a nervous bride, while Brax removed the suitcases. She turned toward the residence at the sound of the cottage door opening.

A silver-haired woman, all smiles and welcoming arms, stepped excitedly into the fading sun.

"Oh Jackie, my boy, it's so good to have you visit," she chimed, throwing her arms around Brax as he set the suitcases down before the door.

He delivered a hug and a smile of pure plastic.

"Aunt Harriet," Brax said, sharing an embrace that lasted only a moment.

"And this must be Me-lang, your new wife. She is lovely, Jackie."

"Hello, Mrs..."

"McMurphy, it is."

"McMurphy," Cali said, offering the same embrace Brax had given the woman.

"Hurry in out of this damp. You must be tired after your trip. I've a cabbage pot on the boil."

Once within the safe confines of the cottage, the pretense vanished. The old woman retreated in silence to her kitchen, where indeed a pot of cabbage poppled on the stove. The charade having served its purpose, she attended her duties as if Brax and Cali were name-less boarders.

Brax tossed Cali her suitcase, motioning her to the stairs.

"Has Uncle Webley been by?"

"Yesterday, dear, on his way to Kilchurn. Trouble with clegs again, you know. Can't seem to keep the rutty little creatures out of our hair."

The words confirmed that the requisite sweep for bugs had been made. So Brax dropped his cockney accent and for the moment, let out a sigh of trust. Standing at the window, Brax took in the breadth of the area in a long, focused stare. For the present, at least, the place appeared sterile and usable.

"Pick a room upstairs, we begin as soon as the others arrive," Brax instructed, while he marched off in the direction opposite Cali's.

```
Arrived hotel on schedule. Looking
forward to hearing from you.
                              Brax
```

At the rear of the cottage, Brax tripped a secret lock that released a panel that concealed a descending staircase. At the base of the stairs, using what appeared to be a credit card, he passed it through a reader, and after the familiar soft click of an electromagnetic lock, he pushed open a windowless steel door.

Inside, a glass panel divided a conference room with seating for twelve and a small enclosed communications center. Brax settled into the comm center chair and switched on his computer. The screen immediately popped to life. A double pound sign prompt blinked insistently in the screen's upper left corner.

Brax logged in using a day-of-the-week password, an entry capable of being entered only twice incorrectly. A third incorrect attempt triggered total destruction of all data stored inside the machine. Only the Wolf Pack knew the correct password sequence, a sequence that never appeared in writing.

Seconds later, Squire acknowledged. The satellite data link between Langley and Scotland awakened from its sleep mode. Squire's cheerful greeting played across the screen initially as a stream of numbers, then a deciphering program converted the numbers into alpha characters like tumblers falling into place.

Brax hoped Squire had put aside the week-old clash in Langley. His only discernible character flaw: he could shoulder a grudge, though he never let it interfere with business.

Brax now had real time communications with Langley, and he immediately requested a full intelligence update. Intelligence gathering never rested. Fresh information was vital to the mission. Any report or incident, regardless how innocent it may seem on the surface, had to be scrutinized for a possible link to their prey. They had to be diligent, responding immediately to even the slightest hint of a terrorist threat. The bad guys never rest.

Flipping switches like a crazed scientist, Brax deployed the safe house monitoring net. Then he sat observing as, one by one, a dozen nine-inch black and white screens bloomed. Every angle of the outside grounds and every room in the above-ground cottage came under his scrutiny.

Brax lingered on the third screen. Cali set her suitcase on a chair and checked her bed by flopping down onto it face first.

"Naughty boy," she chided, waving a finger at the concealed camera, assuming he might be watching her. She had the sense to perform her own sweep of the room. Everything about her impressed Brax. He had resolved in his own mind that she was right for Wolf Pack.

Still, however, something kept him uneasy. Brax rubbed at his forehead, hoping to push it to the forefront. For all her efficacy, for all her talents, could she handle the assignment Housemother had offered her? How would she react when she learned the true parameters of their mission?

The explosion in Kano roared into Brax's head. He felt the heat and the force anew. Her being here suddenly felt wrong. He had to remind himself that it was her choice and not his job to protect her anymore than he would any other member of the team.

On the far right screen, in the kitchen, the old woman worked over her dinner preparations, while a hunched-over wrinkled man stopped to peck her on the cheek with a toothless pucker before departing out the rear door.

Brax synchronized his watch with the clock on the lower corner of his computer screen. Squire must have been about early preparing, since reports began filling the computer's memory less than a minute after his request. A counter clicked off the amount of memory in use and how much information had yet to be decoded. Brax wondered absently if Squire ever slept.

Anything on the Russian trace, Brax pecked in.

A cipher program scrambled the message then transmitted it to Squire in his sink hole below the CIA in Langley, where it then got unscrambled and displayed on Squire's screen.

A double pound sign blinked on Brax's screen; Squire had received the message free of interference.

Brax stole a moment to relax after flipping on a bank of switches on a panel beside the computer. These activated an overlapping net of high frequency white noise meant to neutralize any attempt to capture their conversations by the use of long distance ultra-sensitive listening devices. Inside the cottage they were as secure as modern wizardry could make them.

"Dinner smells fantastic, Mrs. Humphries," Brax said, entering the kitchen to find Cali at the table staring into a cup of steaming coffee. She took it black.

"Your favorite, sir. Cabbage rolls. Then I'll be leaving."

Cali said nothing, glanced out the window occasionally and in general remained patient. Her time would come to ask questions, and this time, get answers. However, the knots in her stomach tightened with each passing moment. They had traveled a long way to a place armored to the hilt to remain secure.

Two hours later the old man returned, jockeying the car into a narrow garage situated behind the cottage. A drowsy sun dipping below the horizon offered a washed out light, in which it appeared the old man had returned alone.

However, once safely within the garage, the trunk popped open, allowing a thirtyish Texan with a boyish smile as big as the hat he carried, to climb out. Lugging his bags with a furniture-mover's frame, he passed from garage to cottage between two nine-foot hedgerows that served to exclude distant eyes.

"Cody, Cali, Cali, Cody," Brax said, offering no more of an explanation than that to soothe Cody's upraised brow and interested eyes. Self-consciously, the Texan smoothed fingers through straw-colored hair.

"Hello, Darlin', I hope we'll be seeing more of you." Cody's smile resembled Cheshire cat's. A smile marred only by a slight chip in the left front tooth.

"I wouldn't bet on it," Cali said with thin straight lips pasted across her face.

"Settle in and unpack. Dinner's being brought down."

"Yes sir. Cabbage rolls again..." Cody muttered as he took the stairs two at a time.

Within minutes of Cody's arrival, a white, unmarked van rolled to a stop before the cottage. A man whose eyes and head remained hidden beneath a wool cap moved quickly from driver's seat to back doors.

While Mrs. Humphries held the front door open, Remy moved from van to interior lugging a carpet roll over his shoulder with his arm wrapped in such a way as to obscure his entire head. His other hand held a large tool case.

The team had assembled.

Once inside, the old man pulled himself into the blue overalls Remy had worn in, straightened a wool cap over his head and exited through the front door, taking over the wheel of the van.

Remy, a pure bred Brit for all his forty-eight years, shifted his tool case that actually contained his clothes to his left hand so as to offer a callused right to Cali as he climbed the stairs. She was descending.

"We haven't had the pleasure," Remy offered in his prim and perfect British pitch, expecting his gesture to halt Cali.

"Nor I expect we ever will," she said, pushing past him.

"Wait 'til Jaffe fills his eyes with her," Remy whispered as he watched her perfectly shaped behind sway with her walk.

Thirty minutes later, the team assembled in the conference room. Mrs. Humphries left dinner on serving trays at one end of the conference table, and took the car from the garage, leaving before the steel door locked behind the Wolf Pack.

For a long moment no one spoke. Without realizing it, Cali had taken what had been Jaffe's seat at the conference table. Remy's face fell slack. Cody worked his jaw back and forth in a clinch.

"Why do we have to eat these blasted things? Don't these fucking people know how to slaughter a steer?" Cody moaned, trying to avert the obvious. He smelled the cabbage rolls briefly before dousing them with American ketchup, which he produced from an ever present black leather bag.

Before sitting at the table, Brax checked the paper rolling off the comm center printer. He also monitored Mrs. Humphries' departure, and once she had cleared the perimeter, Brax switched on a network of seismic intruder sensors deployed about the grounds.

Back in the conference room, in a glance, he assayed the mounting tension at the table. He had dreaded facing this particular moment since the roar of the explosion diminished in his ears.

Cali surveyed the room, suppressing the wave of disbelief that washed over her. This was it? This was the entire team? She separated the cabbage from the meat, took a few bites, then pushed her plate away. She had suddenly lost her taste for food.

Remy and Cody exchanged looks that conveyed a melange of uncertain signals.

Remy worked his hands through his thatchy chestnut hair, hair sorely in need of a trimming, with the snowy edges falling over broad ears. Hardly the picture one would expect of a professional.

"Jaffe didn't..." Remy asked before Brax could speak.

"Nigeria soured."

"Fuck. Double fuck. Sorry. How?" Remy said. He had difficulty swallowing.

"What happened?" Cody asked.

Brax briefly recounted the incidents in Kano with the cadence one would expect of a subordinate reporting before a superior—carefully choosing words, offering short concise statements laden with facts. He omitted no important details, and at times, struggled to find the best words to convey meaning without heightening alarm.

Neither Remy nor Cody looked at Cali, who buried her surprise to a depth beyond detection. The thought of being blown to pieces sent her heart whacking against her chest. She had witnessed a bomb's destructive potency on human flesh at close hand one time in her life. It became an obstinate nightmare she carried with her always. *A replacement*, Brax had said in Langley. Her stomach convulsed as she listened.

"Jaffe leave any bastard children behind?" Remy asked after a protracted silence.

"Had a wife. Ex-wife. They never really divorced, though they separated a decade ago after a brief marriage. Other than that, he was alone."

"What's Housemother think? Are we compromised?" Remy pressed. He sought his answer not in Brax's words, but rather in his eyes. Eyes never lie. Eyes portend the truth.

"Can't tell right now."

Brax kept nothing from them. Remy trusted what he saw.

"What's this mean for us?" Cody asked. His jovial demeanor, present since his arrival, had been vanquished. His eyes glazed, though it became impossible to discern if those were actually tears.

"Squire's running traces on all known Ravens and active terrorists. We go on under the premise that Jaffe's death was an isolated incident by an out of control lowlander. Until confirmed otherwise, our covers remain intact. You two have any problem with that?"

"I most certainly have a problem with this. We're going after Leviathan. This isn't some intelligence gathering junket," Remy said. His face had paled; he shoved his plate away. Brax knew exactly what Remy was intimating.

Cody sat for a time staring at his plate.

"Cody?"

"I don't like it. If Ranzami's made us..."

"We need to assess the intelligence before we can determine if our operation's compromised."

"We gain anything before..." Remy asked.

"Jaffe transmitted that Mandigo had an incomplete list. It's possible Leviathan intends to enter by way of Nicaragua, then use a black route into the U.S."

"*If* you Yanks are Leviathan's target. What if it's London again?"

"Either of you dig up anything?"

Remy scratched guiltily at his prickly neck hairs.

"So far our IRA insider's blank. Near as we can tell, our target's steering clear of the Island," Remy said.

"Can we trust your man?"

"I trust him."

Brax turned to Cody, who was fumbling with a bottle of Tabasco.

"Nothing's coming out of the Far East. Two weeks ago, I tracked Shigeo out of Singapore. As far as I could tell, he never met with anyone we believe to be involved with Leviathan."

"Anything on a North Korean connection?"

"Shigeo went underground for a time in Seoul. Could have met with a North Korean Mud Gook."

"Who's Shigeo?" Cali pressed.

"Aum Shinrikyo. Aum on the streets. These bastards are *the* most vicious cults around. We believe Shigeo headed up a Kansai army of assassins before moving on to act as go-between for the group and the North Koreans. We think they're looking to finance something big. Anyway, nine months ago, a plant spotted him in the company of a double agent in Taegu, South Korea. We have since linked the double to one of Leviathan's known lieutenants."

"Can we play off the agent to gain intelligence on Leviathan?"

"Love to. But he got his throat ripped out before we could get to him. My guess is Shigeo. The man's got a propensity for sadistic murder. Down side to that is: the ugly shithead tends to leave a trademark on his kills. Gives us a chance to follow the trail of blood he leaves behind."

"What about money trails? We know large sums of money always move in advance of Leviathan's strike," Brax asked.

Remy and Cody shook their heads.

"May I ask a question?" Cali said, shifting forward in her chair, hoping to feel more like an insider. Not one of them would even address her.

"I'd prefer you didn't," Brax said bluntly.

"I say we put this on the table, now," Remy shot in, refusing to acknowledge Cali.

Brax ignored Remy's comment, instead he opened a file from a stack he removed from the comm center.

"Our hard target is Ranzami Abu Mabbas, codename Leviathan. He prefers to work with a small team; no more than four or five. He takes security as seriously as us. People get briefed on a need-to-know. He stays alive by keeping his people in the dark."

Remy and Cody redirected their interest to incoming intelligence. They had heard this spiel before.

"He moves efficiently; he moves quietly. If we can't neutralize him before the strike, our chances of getting to him after are slim. Ranzami sees himself as the general in his own new world army. And he kills to protect himself or his plan. Never underestimate this man. Also, he never involves himself directly. He isolates himself enough to make it difficult to nail him."

"How can we possibly track him then?" Cali asked.

"Minutia," Remy muttered more to himself than the others. The word, however, did not escape Cali.

"We have one ace. He is always close at hand when his attack takes place. He makes sure he's near the action. But never directly involved."

"Can we step out of the minutia and put this thing on the table," Remy said, setting an intelligence printout aside and dropping his reading glasses to the table for effect.

Cody, however, chose to steal glances at Cali like a kid plotting a raid on the cookie jar.

"Cody?" Brax said.

"Fine with me. I'm getting tired of standing knee-deep in minutia anyway. Whatever that is," he said, hands raised in supplication.

Brax yielded to Remy with a wave of the hand.

"Is there a particular professional reason why Cali here has been assigned as Jaffe's replacement?"

Cali inched forward in her chair. She gripped both armrests with fingers that quickly paled. This she had come unprepared for. She might have to defend herself, though she at present remained silent.

"I've no intention of coating this with ginger," Remy continued, though he did notice Cali's eyes burning into his right temple. "I'd rather suspect she hasn't received the full briefing."

"She knows enough."

"Enough? I'm very...uncomfortable with this. Women are, without retort, unfit for espionage, especially at this level. They're overemotional, oversentimental and just plain unreliable for this kind of assignment."

Cali rose with the grace of a diplomat's wife, while anger seethed beneath her hardened exterior. She had worked harder than any man to climb the rungs of the male-dominated Agency ladder. She studied harder, learned more, and exposed herself to greater risks than any of her male counterparts. She had the requisite brass balls, as these good old boys liked to chide, to work any assignment the DCI could dole out.

For a moment she remained silent while she organized her rebuff. The best offense right now, she surmised, might just be a sneak attack.

"Don't hold back, Remy. Don't soften it because I'm a woman. Hey, this is the nineties. You pompous limeys miss something? I'll hold my own against any of you. And who's caving in to his emotions now?"

Remy rose at the sound of Limeys to square off and stare directly into her eyes.

"This isn't surveillance, Betty. Can you slip a shiv into Leviathan's rib cage until it ruptures his stinking black heart?" The words marched out, measured and weighted for maximum impact.

Remy withdrew his switchblade. And with eyes still locked on hers, he released it to stab the tip into the table top next to her hand. He did it to emphasize the dire seriousness of their assignment.

Cali interpreted it as a challenge.

Neither looked at it.

In a frighteningly fast and fluid motion, Cali locked Remy's arm under hers, pulling him into her chest while she grabbed the knife and drew it across his throat just beneath the Adam's Apple.

The aggression so surprised Remy that he could do no more than remain rock still, feeling the sting of his own cold steel sliding against his flesh. He concealed any fear that might have invaded his mind.

Cody and Brax edged closer but remained clear of the two.

"I did my first kill at seven. He was North Vietnamese Regular. And that was before I learned how to kill. I don't think you want to fuck with me right now."

Cali released her hold on Remy's arm and shoulder. There was never so much as a single twitch in her muscles. Drawing the blade gingerly away, she stabbed it back into the table.

Without missing a beat, Remy added, "When the time comes, I need to know you can shove your gun barrel into Ranzami's temple and blow his sick freaking brains out?" He spoke as if nothing has occurred.

"Now who's wallowing in minutia? I'm sick of being tested."

Cali dropped back into her chair and wrapped her arms tightly across her chest. Inside she fumed. Outside she worked to maintain control.

"My kind of girl," Cody injected to break the tension smothering the room.

No one laughed but him.

Cali choked down the bile gagging the back of her throat. This was without a doubt the boldest move she had ever initiated against a comrade. But she had to be immovable. They had to know they could trust her. And besides, in the heat of the moment it was the most dramatic idea that came to mind. She said nothing, stared into Remy's eyes without flinching.

"Just give me the fucking gun," she added, her tone indicating finality.

"Then Brax informed you our mission is the expeditious demise of Leviathan before he can kill any more innocents. Did he tell you we don't exist? We operate unrestricted, outside our respective governments' knowledge. These very same politicians intend to deny any knowledge of us if we screw up. Did Brax also tell you a dozen governments will do *anything* to prevent us from achieving our target? There are places in this sick fuckin' world that make scum like Leviathan folk heroes."

"Her Company record's impeccable. I'm behind her on the team," Brax offered.

"I've a bad feeling about this. I wish there were something you could say to give me that same warm, fuzzy feeling," Cody said.

"We'll get only one shot at Leviathan. How can we be sure *she* won't muck it up at the last moment?"

"How can we be sure *you* won't muck it up at the last moment?" Cali snapped back, rising to level an accusatory finger at Remy.

"Or you!" she accused, shifting to Cody.

Calmly Cody responded.

"Because we've *been* tested by 10 years of this, and we're still here to be tested again."

Cali stood rock-still. Like bulls locking horns, for that moment neither would retreat.

"It's done. We go on," Brax said.

Cali returned to her seat and returned her arms across her chest with such tension that her skin paled from the cessation of blood.

"She's a top operations officer. She's capable of replacing Jaffe on this team," Brax added, maybe more to convince himself.

"Won't find a bird in the field for MI6, that's for sure," Remy said, satisfying his need for the last word.

Brax indulged him. That usually ended the matter.

"I just need to know she won't freeze at the moment of truth," Cody added.

"You want to dump on me, too, Cody?" Cali said.

At no time did Cali allow the slightest crack to emerge in her protective shell.

Cody raised his palms. "I trust Brax's judgement. If he says you're in, you're in."

Brax allowed the moment to linger. An undercurrent of fear had forced their emotions to the surface. Jaffe's death could mean the Pack had been marked. Any one or all of them could be next.

"As a precaution, I'm establishing new safe houses and meeting locations. Memorize the list, then destroy it. Under no circumstances revert to old locations. If Leviathan did make Jaffe and take him out, he may have also made one or more of us. For right now, Cali's the only one we can know for sure is safe."

"What about an insider? Another Aldridge Ames. Could one of ours have sold Jaffe to the Russians?"

"Squire's exploring that angle also. We've got to trust his talents. He may uncover something indicating the leak came from one of our own. If he does, we'll deal with it as necessary at the appropriate time."

For the next hour the team put Jaffe's demise and Cali's addition behind them. They focused on possible strategies to force Leviathan to surface on their terms instead of his own. The bastard moves invisibly through European countries. But sooner or later he had to surface. The team's objective was to anticipate and be ready when, and if, their moment came.

"For Cali's benefit," Brax started, "Leviathan works with only his most trusted. He subcontracts low level soldiers as go-betweens. No one really knows where he's at or what he's doing. However, we did intercept the word 'Landfill' in connection with him."

"What does that mean?"

"Don't know for sure. Could be the codename of his next target. It came from a foot soldier. So someone fucked up letting it slip into our hands. Normally only his top lieutenants get that kind of information. And he only contracts the best. We're not hoping for more leaks from his inner circle. He moves too quickly and quietly for that. And he does it for the profit. Rarely does he care to take responsibility for his destruction. Our best shot is to uncover a lieutenant and use him to get to the general. That could get us to a time and place where Leviathan will be. When we get there, he goes down...at any cost."

"How much progress has been made?" Cali asked.

"Very little. We were hoping Kano might yield our first break. We know Ranzami is always close at hand when the bomb goes off. Therefore, he needs a route into the U.S., if that's his target. I think without a doubt, he flips the switch. He won't be on the front line, but you can bet he'll be close enough to watch the action and direct his soldiers. He's also the one being handsomely paid to sound the charge in their revolution. The others are doing it for their own reasons."

"Who are the soldiers?"

"Black September, GIA, Red Brigade, HAMAS, and IRA. He's got the charisma to bring warring factions of a half dozen terrorist groups under a common cause. So there's no need for him personally to be on the front lines, he got scores of sacrificial lambs at his call, but you can bet he won't be far behind."

For three more hours, the team ran down everything they knew about Leviathan, hoping to catch a flash of inspiration. When a lull settled in over the table, Remy needing a stretch, took the turn of retrieving the latest sheets of Squire's intelligence reports rolling off the printer in the comm center.

In the meantime, Cali immersed herself in incoming information, trying to fit more pieces together for this operation. She found herself at a disadvantage, unaware of what the others already assimilated about their target. As a result, she kept silent and soaked up every detail. Like so many times before, she had to work twice as hard to keep up with the others.

"Scrimshander," Remy confided to her while he stretched behind his chair, staring at the ceiling only a foot above his head.

"Scrim what?"

"Scrimshander. Compromise code. In case Brax forgot to tell you. You get it, you bury yourself as deep as you can. We'll find a way to get you out."

Remy sat down.

A warbling alarm sounded. One of the seismic intruder sensors had triggered at the computer.

Guns swung into sight. Remy vaulted back to his feet. The team froze where they stood.

6

Need status of Summerfield resort
reservations.

                                    Cody

The team huddled around the control center. The cameras monitoring the perimeter automatically switched to night vision when the sun reached the horizon and now painted the landscape with a glowing green hue.

"The northwest quadrant seismic intruder sensor alarmed," Brax said, pointing to the third monitor in the row.

"Fuckin' coyot'," Cody said, narrowing his eyes to the screen.

"There's no coyotes in Scotland," Remy countered.

"I'm telling you it's a fucking coyot'," Cody insisted never straying from the display.

"You run the diagnostic on the sensors?" Remy asked.

"Doing it now," Brax said.

"Maybe just a dodgy sensor," Remy offered.

"These things are so fucking unreliable. Why do we have to buy this Japanese shit technology," Cody said.

"They're British. Made in Manchester."

"Why do we have to buy this shit British technology," Cody rephrased.

"Diagnostic passed," Brax said.

"Means one of us is going to have to go out there," Cody said.

All eyes turned to him.

"Why you looking at me? It's his shitty technology," Cody continued, leveling a finger at Remy.

"But the night vision goggles are you Yanks doing," Remy said in response.

Both Remy and Cody turned to Cali.

"No way are you two sticking me with going out there."

"Rock, scissors, paper?" Cody offered as a compromise.

No takers.

"I'll go. It's my turn anyway," Cody conceded.

Brax spread out the diagram showing the seismic sensor locations, marking the location of the sensor generating the alarm. While Brax, Remy and Cali watched on the monitor, Cody made a slow, methodical sweep of the northwest quadrant before honing in on the sensor that had triggered the alarm. Having to climb half way up a tree in the dark, cursing audibly into the small mike clipped to his shirt, he replaced the motion sensor with the new one he extracted from his pocket.

"Bet it was a fuckin' coyot'," he said visually sweeping the area once more through his night vision goggles before making the trek back to the cottage.

Relief swarmed over the team when they tested the sensor in the comm center. It had become defective. To celebrate, the team raided the icebox in the kitchen, emptying it of everything edible, before resuming the planning session. The incident had brought everyone back to full awake and now no one wanted to break for rest.

The sensor's false alarm exemplified just how much Jaffe's death had set the team on edge. Even the most sophisticated and carefully instituted security measures could be breached.

"Damn, shit, look at this," a blurry eyed Cody said two hours later without lifting his eyes from the paper. He slid it across to Brax, who cast aside everything to focus on Squire's latest report. Remy and Cali crowded around the table to view the material.

"Krovshankof surfaced in Benghazi forty-eight hours after you and Jaffe entered Nigeria."

"Where's that?" Cali asked.

"Geography not your strong suit, Cali?" Remy sniped. It was meant as a playful jab, though Remy couldn't discern if that was the manner in which it had been received.

"Coastal town in northern Libya. Qaddafi has a resort, if you like, for his Soviet consultants. Anything they want, if you know what I mean. Pretty gruesome bunch. Thanks to MI6, we've had a pair of eyes on the place for almost two years. We're hoping Leviathan shows his face there; that could give us a starting point to track him," Brax said.

"What's the chances Krovshankof was shadowing Jaffe's lowlander?"

"May be coincidence, may be Mandigo screwed up."

"Where does Krovshankof rank on the food chain?"

"Krovshankof's pretty near the bottom of the Soviet food chain. If I remember correctly, he did some sloppy clean up work for them in the late eighties. Nothing that I can recall of any great significance. I know the Company's got an extensive profile on him. Remy, you have anything on him?"

"Seems I remember Krovshankof having something to do with a Soviet operation in Bulgaria." Remy fell silent for a few moments while he rummaged through his memory.

"He ran up against one of my MI6 colleagues. I thought he had abandoned his operation and retreated back to the Soviet Union. They were attempting to assassinate one of their puppets at the time. Our man stepped in to warn of the impending attempt. Seems Krovshankof tripped himself up and revealed the party's intent prematurely. I figured that would be the end of the poor bastard. Usually, you fuck up before the party and it's off to the frozen tundra for good."

"For now, watch each other's backs, and make sure Squire updates you with fresh intelligence on any Soviets popping up where we're operating. Leviathan may be using ravens to beef up his organization.

Has Housemother approved expense
voucher? Please advise when to
expect funds.

Cali

April 9th. Ranzami entered Bonn by car from the
north using autobahn Route 59. His driver, a brawny
German with mean eyes and fiery temper, exited at
Augustiner to cross the Rhein and pick up Adenauer.
They stopped across from a tobacconist shop and
waited. Minutes later, a shaggy-haired man who
might easily be mistaken for a university student,
with scraggly moustache and yellowed teeth, exited
the shop. He paused to bring a match to his cigarette,
which he then discarded in the direction of the black
Mercedes.

Ranzami watched from the back seat behind
smoked glass as the smoker ambled off south down
the street. Ranzami checked his watch and returned
his gaze to the back of the smoker now almost out of
sight.

The driver's eyes moved methodically from rearview mirror to side mirrors with the regularity of a
sentry standing watch. Ranzami never altered his
position. He waited until the smoker reappeared and
pressed his half-smoked cigarette out on the heel of
his shoe.

Only then did Ranzami exit the vehicle with black
briefcase in hand, and stroll at a pace neither hurried
nor languid in the direction from which the smoker

had returned. Ranzami stopped at what appeared to be an unused warehouse, whose windows had been painted over in black and whose door showed the claw marks of numerous attempted break-ins. Leviathan found no need to announce his arrival with a knock, rather he waited while locks unbolted on the inside.

Willie Kirkhammer, a nervous little man, whose eyes perpetually gave off a sense of hyper-anxiety, answered promptly. He offered a toothy smile but stopped short of extending his hand to his visitor. He had been instructed by the smoker as to the protocol to follow when this visitor arrived. And he was to wait. Ranzami would extend his hand if he wished to shake. When he did, Willie shook Ranzami's hand limply, though he employed both his hands. His glance crossed Ranzami's dark hollow eyes. A thick well-groomed black beard hid the tightness in Ranzami's jaw. For a man approaching fifty, he could easily be mistaken for someone thirty-five.

Willie acted as if they were lifelong friends, despite having only talked to the man briefly at a meeting a year earlier. A meeting Ranzami carefully orchestrated. So much so, that Willie actually only heard Ranzami's voice; he never saw his face. Their business had been arranged almost entirely through an Asian, who approached Willie during a Frankfurt visit some eight months previous. A visit in which all the pertinent details of their arrangement had been exchanged. Willie never once glanced at the briefcase Ranzami carried. To acknowledge it would imply distrust.

Ranzami's slight frame ill-characterized this man who wielded an awesome power in his world.

Once Ranzami entered, Willie swept his eyes keenly from left to right, both up and down the street before closing the door. No cars appeared on the boulevard and no one could be seen standing in the vicinity. Willie observed nothing unusual about his street despite the significance of his visitor. Ranzami had approached alone and that sent a shallow wave of relief through Willie's suspicious brain. He had never expected to be receiving the man personally now. He felt honored, and at the same time pressured, since he warranted a personal visit from someone he knew only in legend.

Willie's own reputation had seeped through the European terrorist underground over the past three years, and his knowledge became prized in such places as Baghdad, Teheran and Tripoli. Even certain highly-placed persons in the South African underground had called upon Willie to pick his brain for some of the possibilities a man with his talents could offer.

The midday sun streamed in through the row of six southern facing, rain-stained windows, which made the light almost unbearable upon the eyes. Sensing Ranzami's discomfort, Willie threw a switch causing shades to drop quietly and without delay like eyelids over the eight foot windows. The loft's fourteen foot timber ceiling gave the space an almost reverent feel, as if one were moving down a cathedral aisle. With the exception of Willie's living needs and work area, which consumed only a third of the square footage available, the loft remained uncluttered.

Willie quickly dispensed with the expected cordiality afforded a man of Ranzami's stature—the honor of meeting him, the admiration for what he has done for the cause, etc. Then he led Ranzami to a workbench in disarray and heaped with every kind of device one could think of, including oscilloscopes, meters, electronic devices and a myriad of small tools that exhibited no accumulation of dust from lack of use.

"Everything I prepared according to your specifications," Willie said with a slight smile, while he avoided Ranzami's eyes. It was whispered that to stare into Ranzami's eyes was to reveal your soul to

him. Willie felt a sudden need to conceal from this
one his inner thoughts and the nervousness churning
inside. He had been given so little to work with. He
received nothing explicit in the specifications and
could only guess at exactly what Ranzami wished of
him. If he had failed, what would Ranzami think of
him? Ranzami was noted as a man intolerant of failure in himself and those around him.

Ranzami's smile was equally slight, almost perfunctory in nature. He disliked delays and meaningless chatter. He loathed disorganized, wasteful
people. Minutes, like money and men, were important
resources, not to be squandered. He settled onto a
stool, with the white paint worn off its seat and
scraped the legs along the floor to position himself
beside Willie. While Willie put things in order, Ranzami studied the array of gadgetry on the workbench
surface as if he knew exactly what he was looking at.

There was something scary in Ranzami's eyes,
and Willie sought to avoid them whenever possible.
Was it a portent of death and suffering that Willie
saw in those dark orbs? He detected no soul behind
the darkest hazel in Ranzami's eyes. Or was it that
the eyes were missing a sense of responsibility for
what he had come for and what he was about to do.
No conscience could be sensed from this one.

After a few more moments delay, while Willie
rearranged circuit boards and switch settings—he
now had everything in order on his workbench—he
proceeded to settle back onto his stool. Willie turned
his electronic gadget slightly and repositioned his
oscilloscope so Ranzami could see the demonstration
unhindered from where he chose to sit. Like a whiz-
kid student at the science fair, Willie preened his
project in the face of the judge...the ultimate judge of
his work...the customer.

A three by six inch circuit board held a collection
of electronic devices in a variegated array of shapes
and sizes. Prominent on the board were three small

light emitting diodes that illuminated like miniature Christmas lights and two one inch square metal devices whose metal pins protruded an eighth of an inch from the surface. The devices caught the eye as if they were at the core of the device's intent.

"I believe, General, I have interpreted your specifications correctly in designing this mechanism," Willie said with a voice as meek and unassuming as his appearance. He brushed his rust-colored hair from his face. His moment of truth had arrived. His smile beamed only on the inside.

Ranzami offered no comment, simply waved his hand expecting the demonstration to begin without further exchange.

Willie nodded. He could feel tiny beads of sweat forming on his forehead despite the lack of heat in the loft. He switched on his oscilloscope and another machine he positioned next to it. The second device displayed a digital counter that began offering up patterns of digits on its readout, much the way numbers appear on a scale when weight is added or subtracted.

"The device is remotely controlled with this," Willie said as he took up a small plastic remote with two surface switches and a small green light exactly like one on the circuit board on the bench.

"The left switch arms."

Willie pressed the switch to demonstrate. An amber light on the circuit board illuminated with a weak glow. Willie covered the board with a hand, darkening it to allow Ranzami to confirm that the light was truly on.

"Notice that I am right now emitting electronic noise from this generator in an attempt to jam the transmission of the arming signal. But the signal still gets through."

"It is then completely immune to electronic jamming?"

Willie felt the sudden pressure of a test question.

"Yes. The remote transmits a complex pattern of binary digits over the entire breadth of the frequency spectrum. Even if some frequencies are jammed, other frequencies will get through. Even jamming the sideband frequencies cannot neutralize the device."

"Where is the antenna?"

Willie paused to take in Ranzami's eyes for a brief moment. Had he assimilated what Willie had just told him? He detected a glint of satisfaction. His customer appeared so far to be pleased with his work. That fueled Willie's confidence, his voice grew stronger now. Much of what he had devised for Ranzami hinged on this next phase of the demonstration.

"This tape contains a micro-thin antenna wire embedded in it. You must place one end of the tape to this stripe here," Willie said, indicating what appear to be innocuous clear tape on a roll.

Ranzami seemed unimpressed.

"The tape must extend 25 centimeters outside any metal enclosure that the triggering mechanism might be fitted into. It becomes almost undetectable."

Ranzami's barely perceptible nod indicated his approval. Willie could proceed.

"At this point the device is armed. To detonate, depress the momentary switch on the right. I designed a twenty second delay into the remote to ensure that the device has been armed before the detonation code is deciphered.

Willie pressed the right button. A red light on the circuit board glowed in the loft's subdued light. Twenty seconds later, the triggers engaged. Like needles firing forward, the two small protruding pins snapped out silently and deadly to a half inch extension.

"Exactly as you have specified." Willie smiled for the first time with a sense of relief on his face.

Ranzami gazed at him with a frigid emptiness in his eyes. Was he not impressed? That look seemed to convey not pleasure but that he had expected nothing less from the German. Willie surmised that Ranzami had no understanding whatsoever of what it had taken to devise this thing Ranzami had requested.

"It is impossible to prevent the device from detonating by any means once it has been armed," Willie offered.

"And can it be disarmed?"

"No. If circuit power is removed, it detonates. A mercury switch here ensures that if any circuit devices are tampered with, it will detonate."

Ranzami, for the first time, touched the device on the table. It felt warm and powerful. It was if Ranzami needed to touch it to make sure it was real. He needed to know that it was not some fantasy dwelling only in his mind.

"I have also built a test switch into the circuit, so you may test it for proper operation before installing the...whatever is meant to contact the dual triggers."

"Explain please," Ranzami said.

"At any time before installing the agent, you may trigger the device. If the lights are illuminated just as you see here, then the device activated properly. To reset the device, press this switch here and hold for a second until the lights clear. At that time, the entire circuit becomes disarmed again, and you may install whatever agent you wish the device to control. This way you will be certain the device is operational when you install it."

Ranzami rose from the stool with little more than a hint of a smile across his thin colorless lips. He set the briefcase on the workbench whereupon he pushed it in Willie's direction. Their deal had concluded. He had met Ranzami's expectations.

Willie had been cautioned that the General gravely abhorred distrust. So, despite the gnawing urge to unlock the case and count the money, Willie simply set the case out of the way and removed an aluminum case from the shelf above his workbench.

"Oh, there is one more thing. This little green light on the remote will come on when the final circuit engages. You have asked for some way to confirm that the mechanism has detonated as designed."

"You have done well, Willie. I believe you will find our arrangement to your satisfaction."

Willie opened the aluminum case, fitted the circuit board, the tape roll and the remote device into precisely sized foam chambers and closed the case. After a brief consummating handshake, Ranzami mumbled his good-bye on the way down the stairs to the door. He left Willie's loft without further conversation or delay.

8

New relative uncovered in Brussels.
Monitoring.

Squire

The Dungeon. Squire worked in a paradox. His office was a windowless subterranean vault sealed from the outside world, yet he had access to every corner of the globe from that twelve-by-sixteen foot chamber. He had christened it 'the dungeon' for obvious reasons. Surrounded by state-of-the-art computer terminals, telephones, facsimile machines and the most sophisticated encryption scramblers technology could devise, Squire was never out of 'sight' from the rest of his team. At twenty-six, he wielded an awesome power. He could bring down the wrath of God if he had to, to save his team. He took Jaffe's demise personally, and spent a week of sleepless nights diligently backtracking to uncover his err and make certain it could never happen again.

Few had occasion to visit this place, and Squire by dictate, limited his contacts with others to a strict need-to-engage basis. No friends, no water cooler chats, no casual conversations. The less anyone outside the team knew about Squire the better. In desperation, he took to conversing with the only person he could trust absolutely...himself.

His undernourished frame and timorous smile made it an easy task to pass as a low level clerk or a Company errand boy. He vented the intense tension

that came with his job by employing his own necessary measures: downing pills from a small amber bottle, washing them down with coffee from a cup left
sitting from the previous night, and by biting down his
fingernails to mere nubs. What he couldn't bite, he
picked at like a nervous tic until he could no longer do
damage.

Squire found he could glean bits of information
by simply directing innocent questions to those he
passed on the floors. With a little finesse, he got most
to offer up tidbits that could in time be assembled
into cogent pieces of a larger panorama. In his six
years at the Agency, Sidney had become a master of
the game of questions and answers. He had a talent
for remembering everything that crossed in front of
his eyes and everything he heard, then he would later
connect those gleaned pieces of information into a
pattern. All life falls into patterns. Those astute
enough to recognize and exploit these patterns are
virtually guaranteed success at whatever their chosen
endeavor. Terrorist were no different than any other
human. They worked in patterns. Most often those
patterns would lead a field operative to a target. But
to really see the pattern, you had to open yourself up
to everything around you.

Sidney refused the credit for uncovering the Aldridge Ames leak, though he had drafted a report to his
superior at the time indicating Ames was by far the
most likely source of the information that had been
leaked. A lack of conviction in his intuitive reasoning
powers had kept him from insisting more diligently of
the validity of his results. That insecurity, a fallacy
Squire realized held him back in his career, had cost a
number of critical people their lives.

Sidney had to put it behind him and go on. The
Sidney Cook on the badge intimated no inkling that
the same Sidney was the inside comm man for Wolf
Pack.

Twice each day, all seven of them in a week, Squire received the marked-up newspaper copy that had previously been scoured by junior intelligence analysts on the second floor. These analysts identified anything even remotely connected with intelligence, espionage or terrorist activities. And though competent, most fledglings all too often missed bits of information that could be significant to Wolf Pack's target. Squire had to make certain nothing got by him.

As if an addiction, Squire read and reread every incoming intelligence report processed through the main Company computers. He extracted and maintained a huge and meticulously sophisticated cross-reference, and a secret database of information designed to help pinpoint their hard target. No one—absolutely no one—could be allowed to connect the Wolf Pack to the official Company channels. Therefore, all Sidney's information had to be isolated from normal Company channels. And no one could be allowed to monitor the traffic regularly routed through Sidney's machine. Another secret Squire was charged with safeguarding. But they even kept him in the dark as to Valentine's identity, the ultimate person in charge of Wolf Pack's mission.

Sidney had his suspicions, but as yet had been unable to make a solid connection. Everything the team knew about Leviathan had been carefully siphoned out of the routine data stream and stored on Squire's computer, and every six hours a special patch program, one Sidney authored himself with the help of a friend at Georgetown University, searched the database for indicators that someone somewhere had encountered the most vicious terrorist on the planet.

One of Sidney's previous assignments had forced him to acquire a discipline for programming as a way to solve complex problems. He now consumed his few idle hours devising a number of different patch programs—sniffers he called them—to help automate his chores. He liked sniffers because they monitored the net cops and their traffic on the inter-Agency network. He had figured out how to keep tabs on the cops whose job it was to keep tabs on him.

What made Sidney's sniffer programs special? Like computer viruses, they piggybacked themselves to his outbound message traffic on the Company computer network. At a destination, they detached themselves whenever the recipient user opened one of Sidney's files. Once free floating, the sniffer extracted the network hardware address and the recipient's login name on the host machine. It was like getting a person's name address and phone number without their knowledge. Information on the computer not normally made available. And it accomplished all that unknown to the computer user.

With those vital bits of information, the sniffer then returned home to Sidney's computer, where it offered up the data like a retriever holding a kill out for its master.

Armed with such information, Sidney now knew two significant things about where his file had been read: the physical location of receiving computer (network hardware addresses were assigned by location and a database in the Agency's main computer stored the physical location for each address assigned), and the computer identity of the person viewing his traffic. Squire couldn't actually determine a person's surname from his login name, but he could use various tricks to narrow down the possible candidates. For example, Sidney learned after a few test messages that Housemother's login name was legman and his computer was located on the protected side of the special operations firewall. Sidney had cataloged six different logins and computers that regularly scrutinized his message traffic on the Agency network. After lengthy investigative measures on his own, Sidney concluded all had legitimate reasons for becoming privy to the information he reported.

But a few days after Jaffe's death, one of his sniffers had returned a new login that had buoyed to the surface. Sidney had yet to confirm it for certain, but he suspected someone in the Congress had become interested in the information Sidney had to report. That meant the Senate Select Committee on Intelligence. Luckily, Sidney had disguised his sniffer well enough to escape detection. It became discomforting to think that someone outside the privileged circle had learned of Jaffe's death. And it was far too coincidental that someone started snooping around so soon after the incident. Because of this new *electronic* face in the crowd, Sidney began working on a more powerful sniffer that could confirm one way or the other if indeed a Congressional aide had tapped into his pipeline. This sniffer though would have to have firewall protections built in to prevent anyone from uncovering his identity.

Viewed individually and independent of any whole, much of the information passing Squire's eyes appeared insignificant. It was when those pieces were assembled like a jigsaw puzzle into their respective patterns that a broader picture of terrorist activity emerged. Every secret service organization of every free country devoted resources to monitoring terrorist activity and movement. Sidney had access to that network in the UK, France and Germany, though none of the participating agencies could know who was behind the keyboard. When their individual data gathering is combined and analyzed by one skilled in interpreting the subtleties of intelligence, a cogent picture emerges. To date, the picture has remained out of focus and snapped from a great distance. But each new scrap of information gleaned and placed beside the rest brought that picture of death and destruction closer and into clearer focus. Names, sightings, conversations and official field reports all funneled into one place: Squire's dungeon.

At any given moment, Squire could contact Brax anywhere in the world with the touch of a few buttons or the stroke of a half dozen keys on his keyboard. He also held the power to mobilize Company response teams to any location across the globe with direct authorization from Housemother.

One call could do it all. He literally could bring in the cavalry. Though everyone on the team knew help most often arrived too late in their business.

For a long moment, Squire turned his thoughts to Jaffe. He had let the team down. Fending off a shiver that ran all the way through him, he rose to pace the confined space, only to arrest his movement before a shoulder-length mirror, where he drew an imaginary gun from an imaginary shoulder holster, and fired an imaginary round into the forehead of his reflection.

"Die you fucking bastard!"

He saw not Sidney Cook in the glass but Leviathan. He wondered for that moment while he appraised his shooting acumen if he would be given an opportunity for a shot at their nemesis. As if the act somehow vented his anger and bottled-up tension, Sidney returned his imaginary gun to his imaginary holster and plopped back into the reality of his chair to attack the intelligence reports with renewed voracity. He would never allow that happen again.

Squire snatched up his mostly empty coffee cup, down another pair of pills from his bottle and settled back into the worn cushions of his chair. He swung his feet onto the edge of his table, allowing him to recline somewhat in his seat. While he sipped his coffee with two hands, daily reports marched up his screen with the cadence of a drill team in action. Most appeared routine and had nothing to do with their operation. There seemed to be a constant motion of agents and intelligence gathering going on around the world and a constant surveillance of targets' movements. They weren't people in this business. Any time a name appeared that could remotely be linked to a terrorist organization, Squire logged it into his secret database. People and events played key roles in tracking down Leviathan.

It was one thing to identify and track terrorist movement, quite another to prevent the destruction these vile creatures perpetrated against the innocent people of the free world. To date, the good guys' record remained quite dismal.

As he sat perusing the rows of words, Squire ventured he had a counterpart on the Russian side, one whose job it was to collect the movements of all known American agents aboard and feed that intelligence to the terrorist organizations they supported. No one in Wolf Pack held any doubts that the Russians were aiding the terrorists in their successes. Training, intelligence and most of all money flowed into terrorist hands from places like Russia, Iran, Iraq and Libya.

For a moment the screen paused as if it had to stop and think. The change snared Squire's attention. During periods of heavy traffic, the computer's controller paused to downloaded the overflow to the local hard disk. During such times the screen stopped momentarily.

When it restarted Squire settled back and returned to his pattern of searching for keywords on the screen. The key was to move rapidly against the flow of data rolling up the screen and lock on to those keywords and phrases that indicated a report might be useful. A second later he sprang forward in attention to stab the FREEZE SCREEN key on the keyboard with his index finger.

"What have we here, my pretty?" he said. His eyes narrowed as he focused on the important words.

A routine incident report passed through the London station originating out of an MI6 communiqué. The report detailed a Brussels police report concerning a raid on a suspected terrorist safe house in the outskirts of the city. The house had been traced back to a member of Black September, a particularly vicious group perpetrating violence against the United States. What snared Squire's curiosity on the report were the details of the dangerous chemical inspection accomplished as standard procedure on the house. Traces of Prussian Blue had been left behind by the fleeing terrorists. Those who escaped the raid remained at large twenty-four hours after the incident and had presumably by then fled the small country. Now it became strictly a local inquiry, but MI6 committed to shadow the investigation and report progress as it became available.

Squire banged another key to release the frozen screen and simultaneously divert the scrolling characters to a file for later retrieval and review.

Twenty minutes later when the inbound intelligence reports ended, Squire began going through a stack of newspapers he kept in a neat corner of his world. Failing to find the object of his search, he phoned the second floor to request all Brussels newspapers for the past ten days. Experience had shown that much of their intelligence came days after the news broke locally, and now Squire hoped the Brussels paper would offer more insight into the incident. If quantities of Prussian Blue were later recovered intact, and the suspected terrorists arrested, he could put the report to file and forget about it. But if they remained at large...

While he waited for the second floor to respond, Squire switched over to the Reuters news service, where he began prodding through the previous days' reports for information. Reuters posted no coverage in their database that Squire could locate, so he had to wait for the paper copy to funnel down to him.

By later that afternoon, Squire held the translated copy that appeared in the Brussels newspaper of two days prior. He gleaned that the house had been set up for some kind of chemical manufacturing, and that local police believed all inhabitants fled before they could get any kind of processing operation rooted.

But something bothered Squire about the local coverage: the newspaper made no mention of traces of dangerous chemicals being detected. That meant a quantity of Prussian Blue, unknown at the present, must have been inside the house and accompanied the fleeing terrorists. Historically, terrorists tended to abandon everything when they evacuate a site. That eliminated being taken by police with incriminating evidence in hand. The authorities were withholding the information regarding Prussian Blue from their people. The MI6 report stated it believed three of the inhabitants may have successfully eluded police. And that one of the dead had positively been linked to the Black September organization. The report concluded stating that fingerprints had been lifted and once identified would be included in a later communique.

Squire composed an encoded report apprising Brax of the Prussian Blue, concluding his message, as he always did, by adding he would monitor and report developments as they became available. And as a result, Prussian Blue now became the one hundred twenty-ninth topic on Squire's dangerous chemicals watch list, one he would monitor all news traffic out of Brussels, in the hopes of gaining additional intelligence.

As a cross check, Squire began probing earlier intelligence reports from that region to discern if any known ravens or other terrorists had crept into that area. The presence of other low level terrorists or Russian agents could provide a 'why' behind the presence of a substance like Prussian Blue.

For we seek not the worldwide
victory of one nation or system,
but a worldwide victory of men.
The modern globe is too small, its weapons
too destructive--they multiply too fast--
and its disorders too contagious to permit
any other kind of victory.

But difficult days need not be dark. I
think these are proud and memorable
days in the cause of peace and freedom.
We are proud, for example, of Maj.
Rudolf Anderson who gave his life over the
island of Cuba. We salute Sp. James Allen
Johnston who died on the border of South
Korea. We pay honor to Sgt. Gerald
Pendell who was killed in Viet Nam. They
are among the many who in this century,
far from home, have died for our country. Our task now, and the task of all
Americans, is to live up to their
commitments."

John F. Kennedy, January 14, 1963

9

Checking old records for father's
birthplace.

                    Squire

April 29th. Fucking bullshit! That's what it was. Bureau Special Agent Reggie Donley felt like he had been pissed on and kicked around by everyone higher than him on the food chain until he lay helpless in a pile of dog shit on the ground. A stellar twenty-six year career pissed down the toilet by that scumbag Commie Aldridge Ames. The Big Boys in the plush offices needed a scapegoat for the Ames debacle, and Reggie had been sent to the slaughter. He had studied the reports, considered the ramifications and some-how had arrived at the wrong conclusion. He never suspected Ames as the traitor, and now his punish-ment was to be banished to piss ant security duty. He had once held the number three man position on the Spy Catcher team, and one of his responsibilities two years earlier was to assess CIA profiles for a mole. Reggie had missed Ames. The bastard. Reggie never could figure out how, but he missed him and it cost him his whole fucking career. He missed him not once, not twice, but three friggin' times.

Word rippled through the chain that Donley was to be Agent-in-charge of overseeing security for the Statuary Hall wing renovation project. Talk about being butt-banged by the big boys!

He had screwed up royally to get this dumped on him. If they thought they were going to precipitate a resignation—they were dead fucking wrong. Reggie needed four more years, and he'd be damned if he would forfeit it over a slimy bastard like Ames.

At 9:00 A.M. on the morning of April 29th, Donley met with Captain Jason Lowery, the man assigned to manage the day-to-day security measures put in place to ensure nothing unusual occurred during the nine month renovation project. Nine fucking months, Reggie thought as he waited silently while Lowery droned on and on about security checkpoints and roving security routes. Reggie missed more than he heard. He could care less what Lowery said anyway.

Lowery was half his size, had a third the experience, and looked down his nose at Reggie because he was a bigot. Somehow having to report to a black man overseeing his security stuck in Lowery's throat. Too fucking bad. Reggie hated when piss ant security guards tried to act like real professionals.

"Who's overseeing the database?" Reggie asked at a pause, simply to demonstrate some semblance of interest in the project. In reality, he could care less who handled the shit. All he wanted was to get this shit-ass duty over with. Nine fucking months of this.

"We required every contractor to submit full backgrounds on each worker. The Secret Service and your people ran complete security checks prior to loading up the database. Even the Company ran checks. We allow only workers with badges verified against the database into the renovation area."

"You're fucking boring me again, Lowery," Reggie snapped. He had stopped listening. He knew down to the most insignificant detail how these candy ass operations worked. It must give Captain Blowhard a kick being able to sound important to the FBI.

"So?" Lowery asked.

"So? Sounds fine to me," Reggie responded hearing enough to approve the day-to-day operational plan for the project. He turned his thoughts toward the bar he planned to stop at as soon as he could get out of here. And lunch was still two hours away.

"Then you approve the security plan as I've outlined it to you?"

Nine fucking months of this.

Reggie wished like Hell for someone to get even with for this shit. Someone he could lash out at and beat the living crap out of—if not physically then verbally—until all the anger and frustration had been spent. There was no one...except maybe this Lowery jerk-off if he fucked up. And Reggie's six-foot-nine middle linebacker frame intimidated this little five-seven shit Lowery. Christ, with his black-rimmed glasses and wavy strawberry hair, this guy looked more like a grocery checker than a security chief.

"Our database contains over four hundred workers, and we expect to issue another hundred badges before the project's complete."

"Fucking computers gotta do everything for us. What the fuck do we need to be here for then?"

Reggie dropped his visions of vendetta; he realized he had slipped into a rambling bitch session like every other disgruntled employee he had crossed paths with over the last twenty years.

"How many roving guards will be involved?"

"You obviously weren't listening," Lowery said.

"Just tell me again."

Reggie had lost patience with the little weasel.

"We'll have six, split up over the twelve hours of work going on each day. Two more will man the construction entrance, and another two will monitor material movement. All in all, I expect this to be as routine as the west wing renovation I also handled six years ago."

"And you did a bang up fucking job," Reggie muttered under his breath.

Reggie was ready to leave; he had heard enough to know this was going to be one total shit detail that wouldn't go away by itself.

"I'll need regularly updated computer printouts of all workers cleared to access the building. And I want *full and complete* incident reports on any irregularity noted by any of your men, and make sure your people perform every routine inspection required." Reggie delivered his spiel with as much intimidation as he could muster under the circumstances.

"And they'll be looking for what?"

"Anything unusual or out of the ordinary. If it doesn't seem right, it gets reported. Is that going to be too difficult for your people?"

"You're the boss," Lowery said with eyes less than supportive and sincerity force fed into his voice. "I'll make sure nothing happens on my watch."

"I'm here to fucking make sure that's the case."

Reggie left the Capitol security office muttering over the indignity of handling such a routine security chore. He knew he was going to hate working with Lowery the dip-wad. *They* had made certain the next nine months of Reggie's life were to be a waste of his time and talents. Punishment that's what it was. He hoped like hell these hammer jockeys could finish the job on time, so he could get back to real life.

Before leaving, Reggie stopped at the construction entrance checkpoint designed by Lowery to minimize the disruption of worker flow in and out of the renovation area. He would rather have skipped this, but knew a perfunctory appearance would prevent the security morons from realizing he just no longer gave a shit about anything in this scum-sucking city.

He stood behind a meticulously-groomed security guard with a crew cut, who took every action seriously. Must be an ex-marine, Reggie surmised while he watched over the guard's shoulder as the man punched in the badge number for each of the twenty-two building inspectors in the line.

The computer quietly and efficiently verified each badge owner's security clearance, executing the instructions exactly as they had been programmed. Before passing an inspector through the checkpoint, the guard matched the picture on the badge with both its owner and the computer picture called up from memory. The process virtually eliminated the possibility of anyone unauthorized sneaking past security. But it also took an inordinately long time to retrieve one of these photographs from the computer's mass storage device.

Reggie watched as waiting inspectors shifted about to gesture displeasure at the lengthy delay the security verification process caused.

"Takes a long time..." Reggie commented while waiting for the computer to paint the screen with the photo of the inspector waiting to be cleared.

"Look, it's me," he grumbled with a mixture of impatience and sarcasm, when the guard seemed to be staring blankly at the screen.

The guard reluctantly drew his eyes from the screen, shrugging as if to exonerate himself of guilt.

"This is what I'm instructed to do. It's going to be a real problem when the workers line up in the morning. I'm listening for a better idea," the guard said over his shoulder without looking back at Reggie.

The entire process tied up the computer in excess of a minute, a long time when your waiting in line. Multiply a minute by sixty workers all waiting to get started, and you end up with an hour's worth of pissed off people. As a result, Reggie was about to make his first command decision.

He leaned forward as if to scrutinize the entire process splayed before him, pulled himself upright into a pensive stance while he rubbed at his chin for a moment then levied his decision.

"Verify the face with the picture on the badge. Call up the stored image when a discrepancy arises."

Done. Problem solved.

Reggie walked away with a smiling face. He had made his first contribution to the project.

Nine more fucking months of this, he thought.

One by one, inspectors passed through the checkpoint, producing badges and opening tool sacks to the curious eyes of the second guard stationed at the entrance. Since tools would move regularly in and out throughout the days from beginning to end, Lowery decided a metal detector would be cumbersome and ineffective. So, a guard would check the tools in as each worker passed through security. It made sense and kept the flow of workers moving. The guards at the entrance only performed more extensive searches if situations warranted. Those assigned the task of searching tool kits never asked what situations warranted more extensive examination.

Each project worker received the thirty-second briefing on how to move through security each time they entered the building. With their tools on the inspection table, the guard quickly waved a hand-held metal detector up and down, and after checking their tool boxes, passed them into the work area.

Drew Crandall shifted out of his place in the middle of the line to see what kept holding things up ahead. He rubbed his hand quickly over the bald center of his head. Sweat. It made him nervous. The air inside the Capitol had a slight chill to it, and still Drew had sweat rolling down his doughy cheeks. He listened to the sound of his own breathing, certain he was forcing the air in and out of his lungs. His heart raced as each minute in the line dragged on.

He transferred his canvass tool bag from his right hand to his left and resisted the driving urge to check his badge. He knew checking his badge would only draw attention to it. When his turn finally arrived at the guard station, he did nothing more than angle his body toward the guard, making the badge clipped to his shirt pocket visible. His eyes never left the guard's, who tapped in the characters of his last name on the keyboard.

It took all of fifteen seconds for Drew to pass the first checkpoint. He felt his breathing ease and the tightness in his chest dissipate. Smiling appreciatively, Drew filled in behind the line forming at the inspection table. He studied the guard checking the tool boxes, analyzing his every move. He detected nothing out of the ordinary, and nothing he hadn't been instructed to expect. The briefing he received from a nameless man in a rundown motel near the old navy ship yards had been accurate down to what the security guards would say.

The wait for tool inspection lasted more than five minutes. Something Drew hadn't anticipated. The guard seemed to be taking special interest in checking tool cases and scrutinizing the tools.

"What's this for?" Drew heard the guard ask the man two ahead of him. Suddenly Drew felt a fire burning in his stomach. He knew the sweat was beading on his forehead, but he also knew he could make no motion to wipe it away. One of the security men was watching him—a large black man with a face devoid of a smile.

When Drew's turn finally arrived, he set his tool sack on the table before the guard asked for it, and held his arms out away from his side while the metal detector roved over his one-hundred-eighty pound frame. He then opened his tool kit in anticipation.

The guard spent a long moment shifting around the assortment of screwdrivers, testing meters and inspection mirrors that Drew carried as part of his job. Before closing the sack up, the guard extracted a small rectangular meter. He turned it over in his hand quizzically, then returned it to the sack.

The urge to speak leapt into Drew's throat. But he knew to say anything now was to invite the guard's continued scrutiny. Instead, Drew smiled pleasantly and waited with his hands clasped in front of him.

The guard waved him through.

Drew zipped the case and ambled into the corridor just outside Statuary Hall. Each inspector had been assigned a specific area in which to perform a preliminary inspection that concerned a particular aspect of the renovation project. Drew's twenty-one year HVAC career earned him the chore of inspecting the existing ductwork and evaluating whether additional changes would be required beside those already spelled out in the project.

In reality, this, like a hundred other tricks, became just another method for contractors to bilk the government. They bid the job low to secure the work, then brought in inspectors who generated fancy reports advising that more work needed to be done than initially bid on. Drew had worked all the tricks HVAC companies used to jack up the cost of completing the work.

Within minutes, he strayed from the other inspectors to stroll casually up the stairs to the third level of the House wing. He paused when he arrived at a locked door at the end of a corridor. With quick glances, he checked behind him as causally as he could, then he removed a key given him by the same man who briefed him the day before, and used it to unlock the door. Drew knew better than to ask where the key came from.

Inside the four-by-four closet, a ladder secured to the back wall led to the crawl space over the offices, the Statuary Hall and the west wall of the House chamber. In the crawl space Drew would find the ducting used to move warm and cool air into the offices and the House Chamber.

Drew ascended the ladder cautiously, measuring each step so as not to generate unnecessary noise. He puffed like a two-pack-a-day smoker by the time he reached the top, despite having given up cigarettes three years previous. After tossing his tool sack onto the suspended transom, he pulled himself up and began the slow crawl into the darkened space.

A flashlight from his bag illuminated the transom ahead of him for at least five feet. He bypassed the ductwork for the offices and moved further into the space toward the House chamber. He knew exactly where he needed to go, having memorized the plans for the air disbursement into the House chamber from the government-provided plans. The man had told him in painful detail exactly where and what to do. All Drew had to do was follow the instructions.

At his current location, the main HVAC duct branched off to provide outlets for the Statuary Hall, now directly below him, then continued on to the House chamber, where it met a Y-junction and provided the main outlet for air flow into the chamber.

When he arrived at the location the man in the briefing had designated, Drew set his tool sack down, wiped the sweat away with a handkerchief already soaked through, and located a place just before the Y-junction in the ductwork where a sheet metal plate had been secured in place with a half dozen screws. Why it was there, no one knew, but the fact that it was, afforded Drew the ability to earn a huge chunk of money.

Lying on his side on the transom, Drew removed a power screwdriver from his bag and held his breath to steady his hand, while one by one, he removed the six screws. The magnetic screwdriver tip held each screw, preventing any from falling into the fluffy insulation below. Using his watch and a penlight, he noted the amount of time it took to remove the screws. Seventy-four seconds was too long.

The access plate concealed an eight-inch-square hole in the duct. Drew stuck a hand in and felt around. As expected, there had been no real purpose to having the access there. Wiping away the sweat that rolled down his face, and feeling a pressure against his chest that made breathing difficult, Drew removed four innocuous metal strips that he quickly assembled into a rectangular framework. Earlier, the guard had stared at the pieces without comprehending their significance.

Assembled as they were now, any guard would have become immediately suspicious and questioned Drew at length. The framework had small metal nubs in each corner and it secured four circular clips, two along the top of the framework and two along the bottom. Four quick fasteners were held in place in the four corners. It seemed an odd contraption to Drew, but he knew better than to question the man who gave him the pieces and demonstrated how each section mated with its brethren.

Drew stared at the finished assembly for a long moment. He tried to imagine its purpose...then he instructed himself not to think. Right now all that mattered was to accomplish the deed.

He suspected that what he was about to do was as bad as it gets, yet if he refused, they would kill his daughter.

Drew decided once this chore was done and his daughter free again, they would disappear. There were thousands of square miles of mountains in Utah, Colorado or Wyoming, where no one would ever find them nor threaten his family again. Well, what little remained of his family anyway. Widowed five years past, all he had left now was his daughter. And she abandoned him at eighteen for Peace Corp work in Senegal. They rarely communicated, but he would not abandon her now.

He never could figure out how they had singled him out and why, nor how they had executed such an elaborate kidnapping in order to force him here now.

For an instant, something inside urged him to smash the metal frame under his foot and withdraw now. But fear proved a stronger master than conscience. Would they release his daughter? Would they allow him to remain alive? His lack of answers compelled him to do as he had been instructed. He had to pray they intended on living up to their word.

The duct boomed into his ear when the blowers activated, forcing the four hundred cubic feet per minute air flow through the duct. The air escaping out the access hole across Drew's face refreshed him and dried the accumulated sweat on his craggy and now smudged cheeks.

But it also gave him another moment to contemplate his actions. He needed no college degree to know this frame would be used for something bad.

A minute later the blowers stopped. House Chamber voices drifted up to his ear. That minute afforded him time to convince himself to fulfill his obligation.

Drew applied two lavish rows of liquid steel adhesive to the frame runners before reaching in with the device. He attached it out of view on the near side of the inside duct wall, precisely as the man with the wire-rimmed glasses had instructed him to do. He even sounded ominous in the way he doled out instructions with an almost fanatic military crispness and precision. Drew coined him Liddy.

The adhesive held the frame securely in place on the duct wall. Within forty seconds, the frame bonded permanently to the sheet metal. Short of prying it off with a screwdriver, no one could detach the frame from its new resting place. Employing his inspection mirror and penlight, Drew scrutinized his job—precisely the way he had been instructed. The larger of the two sets of metal straps had to face away from the direction of the blowers.

Before leaving, Drew exchanged the regular screws holding the access plate with quick disconnect screws in each of the four corners. He left the last two screws off. The plate needed only four screws to be secure, and the quick disconnect screws allowed removal in under ten seconds. A tremendous improvement over the original and something the man had neglected to take into consideration. Drew had completed most of what they demanded he do. He felt like a spy. Then the very same thought turned his stomach.

Sweat stained his armpits and left a trail down the center of his shirt. It also shot chills under his skin with hypodermic efficacy as he descended the ladder and exited the closet. A preoccupied guard strolling the corridor took interest in the extent to which Drew had perspired, but only after he had thought to notice him. He slowed, seeking out the badge authorizing Drew as part of the renovation team and allowing him to be there. The guard then dismissed Drew's presence as part of the project.

"Hotter than a mother in there," Drew offered with a faint smile. He had been instructed to speak only when necessary, and draw no attention to himself. Drew didn't see any harm in what he had said.

The guard smiled and said nothing in reply, as if to imply he had no desire to change places with Drew, nor that he wanted to know him personally.

Drew released a breath when he and the guard were back to back, strolling away from each other in opposite directions. All that remained now was to return to his apartment, where the man would be waiting to record exactly where he had placed the frame on a computer generated layout of the ventilation system. Once done, he would receive confirmation that his daughter was free. The man assured Drew he would be allowed to speak to his daughter and know without doubt that she had been released unharmed.

Drew never would be allowed the opportunity to realize the task he had performed would, in the end, make him part of something far worse than the kidnapping of his daughter.

10

Weather stormy at home.

                    Squire.

A part of Brax refused to put Andrew's death behind him. Like a nagging child, it poked and prodded, unwilling to accept just any retort as an answer. *Why'd it happen? Why'd it happen? Why'd it happen?*

They had operated with meticulous care all the way up to the moment of the incident. Brax could uncover no rhyme nor reason for the meeting to run afoul the way it did. Andrew had done everything right. That had become one of Andrew's trademarks. He made no mistakes apparent to the naked eye. He had the depth of field operations experience to anticipate problems, and he knew how to escape them before a situation turned volatile. Could Andrew have let his guard down? Had he misread Mandigo? Was there a hidden side to the man that Andrew had failed to assess?

One throbbing concern swirled ominously inside Brax's mind. If Leviathan had made the team or the operation, that knowledge *had* to have come from inside the Company. A mole would have had to have access all the way to the top of the chain in order to know of the team's existence let alone the Wolf Pack members. But from where? All decisions hinged on keeping the team secure. All. If any move held the slightest chance of exposing Wolf Pack, it got recalculated, replanned or scrubbed. So few knew of Wolf Pack and their operation that suspicion had to fall on the highest levels of control inside the Agency.

Housemother buoyed to the top of Brax's thoughts. The only man above him was Valentine. Brax forced himself for a moment to consider the unthinkable. Then he dismissed it. Perhaps a mole had fed the Russians information about Andrew? Perhaps the Russians had Andrew disposed of for reasons other than the operation?

Brax's message to Squire seemed clear enough. If there had been a security leak inside, someone might have left a trail Squire could follow. It seemed more and more beyond coincidence that Andrew's death came from an out-of-control field operative. But none on the team would likely say or do anything to expose the nature of the operation and those involved, since exposure put them equally at risk.

Brax had to trust that Squire might unearth some scrap of information pointing to an internal security breach.

Squire spent the first few hours of the day in his hole reviewing the *dailies* funneled in from stations around the world. The overnights had been quiet; no new information had surfaced. The idle time resulting from the lack of new information gave Squire an opportunity to wander through a maze of disparate possibilities. Guilt rippled through him each time he considered what had happened to Jaffe. How had he missed the raven? If only he had picked up earlier on the Russian movement into Libya.

He knew Brax and Jaffe were meeting a Libyan connection. He knew any sudden Russian presence in the country became immediate grounds for aborting. Though he kept it internal, he felt like he had been the one who `fucked-up.' That he had put the two in jeopardy. Still, he had difficulty accepting such a meeting could have been compromised. Only Brax, Jaffe and himself knew of the meeting, unless....

A new thought stirred inside Squire's inquisitive mind. Jaffe had transmitted the message home detailing the essentials of the meeting. Standard procedure so Squire could set up emergency evac routes and back-ups. However, and this Squire suddenly realized became of penultimate significant, *that* message arrived hours later than expected. Normally, Squire receives notification twenty-four hours in advance of any meeting, so as to provide him time to assess local intelligence. He received Jaffe's meeting plan less than twelve hours in advance. Why?

Before leaving his warren, Squire entered a two-character command on his keyboard, which brought an update display of the team's positions on the screen. He relied more and more upon the silicon memory chips and disk files of his computer instead of his own memory. With nothing out of the ordinary, Squire left his dungeon. He formulated a loose plan as he rode the elevator to the third floor. There was one place he could look. It would be risky to try it, but he would never rest until he had confirmed it for certain.   If he wasn't already too late.

It took more schmoozing than he had ever attempted in the past, but Squire gained access to Housemother's secured files. Under the pretense that he had to verify information for Brax, and knowing Housemother would be unavailable in a Senate hearing, Squire began moving through the single file cabinet in the Deputy Director's office that contained only the most sensitive information regarding current operations. Only Squire had access to it outside the Deputy Director of Operations and the DDO's secretary. He could only access the file by having the DDO or the secretary unlock it. Files were never removed without being properly signed out and Squire knew any attempt to try to remove them would send off a barrage of suspicion. While going through the cabinet, Squire realized that what he was really looking for, or rather what was missing in the files, would probably be safeguarded in the DDO's office. He checked all drawers and still failed to locate what he had hoped to find.

"It's not in here," Squire muttered, just loud enough to distract the secretary at her computer.

"I can't find it."

"What are you looking for Sidney?"

"Calfield wants a report by the end of the day, and I can't find the file," Sidney said with rising frustration in his voice. "He gave me three files last week to study. I'm sure of it."

"From the cabinet?" the secretary asked.

"Yeah. Now there's only two. Could you tell me where the third file for Andrew is?" Squire persisted.

He had edged his way out onto that limb. Now he had to hope it held the strength to keep him from collapsing with it.

The secretary at first seemed too busy to answer and grudgingly pulled herself away from her computer screen. That was good.

"Anything you want will be stored in there."

"Well that's what I thought. But it's not here," Squire persisted on a ploy.

Finally the secretary abandoned her typing and swung her chair to face him.

"I'm sure it's in there."

"Look, last week I was in here and there were three files on Andrew. 1451, 9177 and I can't remember the third. Now's there only two. Can you tell me how come the file's missing without being noted on the charge sheet?"

He leveled his words like an accusation. If he could infuse guilt into the secretary's mind, he just might get past the DDO's human firewall.

"Have you spoken with the Deputy Director?"

"Yes. He asked me to finish this by the end of the day. Now I can't because someone misfiled one of the folders. And I have a real problem with this. No files can be removed without authorization and proper receipt."

Squire had turned the tables on the secretary, clearly implying that she had screwed up. Keep people busy defending themselves and they have little opportunity to question your motives. Besides, he had heard that authorization and proper receipt spiel from her so many times over the last few months that it felt good being able to dole it out her way for a change.

"The DDO may have removed the file. He kept one of the files on Andrew apart from the others," the secretary said in a way that implied she wanted Sidney to keep what he had been told to himself.

"I'm sure that's the file he gave me last week. I need a look at it so I can finish this report."

Sidney raised the meaningless stack of papers he had carried in with him to support his ruse.

"No can do without the Director's authorization."

"Why not?"

"I'm sorry."

"Look, I won't mention the file's unauthorized removal from the cabinet if you could just check to see if the file is in the Deputy Director's office."

The secretary hesitated for a moment to weigh the pros and cons. Sidney had done this before, going through files for the DDO and composing reports, so he wasn't asking for anything out of the ordinary. And Calfield did have a propensity for leaving files on his desk for her to refile at the end of the day. And Directors did severely punish subordinates for failing to annotate a file's movement. Even when the Director was at fault, a subordinate took the rap. If she had forgotten again to annotate the log, she would wind up in serious trouble.

"All right," she said finally, "Let me see if it's in the Deputy Director's office."

The secretary checked her watch, noting that lunch started in less than ten minutes, then she unlocked the door and disappeared behind it while Squire waited patiently at the desk. He never dreamed he could get this far with his flimsy scheme, and he realized fully that if he got caught, he was putting himself at risk with his superior. He would have one hell of a time explaining why he needed to have access to Housemother's personal files.

The secretary returned with file in hand.

Sidney swallowed, hiding the smile bursting to get out. Now he had to hope this was what he sought.

"This the missing one?"

Sidney had to flip it open before he could reply in the affirmative. He began reading as fast as he could. Before the end of the first paragraph Squire knew exactly what he had stumbled upon.

"I can't leave for lunch while you're here, so is this going to take long?"

"Only a minute," Sidney responded absently while he took in as much as he could.

Most who worked for the Company knew about soft files, most believed that at one time or another, a soft file would be opened on every Company employee. The Ames case had thrown the entire community into a frenzy of paranoia, and everyone in management developed a sudden urgent need to cover their butts. Soft files were the Company's way of keeping tabs on their own. The FBI spy catchers sought first to review a target's soft files before launching their own investigation into a suspected agent's activities.

Squire felt his back tingle as he quickly absorbed the salient details of the third page of the file. Inconsistencies had been noted in Andrew's last polygraph. The examiner identified a problem with Andrew's responses to a number of sensitive questions about contacts with foreign nationals. He, at the time, had recommended a more thorough interview take place to pursue those areas that left room for doubt.

Before moving on, Squire checked the report's date. The polygraph itself had been administered shortly before the team had been formed. However, the date of the examiner's evaluation report came months later. It appeared that someone had either intentionally or unintentionally delayed the report's circulation until after Andrew had been selected for the team. Squire wondered if Brax had been made aware that Andrew had been subjected to a polygraph, and did Brax learn of the inconclusive results.

A few pages deeper into the file, Squire came across an FBI investigation into Andrew's financial transactions for the period spanning three months in the year prior to his death. A significant number of deposits were recorded, all under the ten thousand dollar denomination limit and spread through a number of banks in six different states. The report never indicated any supposition for the source of the cash; only that Andrew had made a concerted effort to prevent detection of the money.

"Are you finished? I'm hungry," the secretary interrupted.

Squire paused. He realized his palms were sweating. The Company, it appeared, was building a case against Andrew one small piece at a time. Could Andrew have gone to market with his knowledge? But once he joined Wolf Pack he had so little access to sensitive material in the Agency. Jaffe saw only what Brax had authorized him to see. And Squire was the hub who viewed all the secret information and passed only the relevant stuff on to Jaffe. Jaffe had such limited usefulness to the Russians that the risk would hardly be worth the reward...unless....

"Just one more item I need to check," Squire offered without lifting his eyes from the pages. He sought to assimilate the information as quickly as possible and reply to the secretary at the same time. He feared he might miss something important. He also knew that anything more than a cursory glance would raise undue suspicions in the secretary.

"Just one more, then you can be off to lunch."

Squire paged through a number of routine surveillance reports that make his skin crawl. After the third, Squire choked down the bile that had backed up into his throat. Someone inside had been monitoring Jaffe in the field. Someone had to have known his movements beforehand to be able to set up a surveillance complex enough to fool a seasoned field operative like Jaffe.

Squire always knew where Jaffe would be and when. He, aside from Brax, was the only one to know all of Jaffe's movements. Could someone be monitoring Squire's traffic? Brax was beyond reproach. He would never jeopardize a team member for anything.

Squire flipped to the back of the file hoping to gain something useful before abandoning it back to the secretary. Had he informed Housemother of Jaffe's whereabouts around the time these last reports were filed? Two of the reports originated out of an FBI field office. A third was a Company-secret document.

Squire closed the file and handed it back to the secretary. She accepted it without a smile and left her desk to return the file to the DDO's office.

"Thanks," Squire called to her in the other office as he left.

In the brief time afforded him, Squire memorized as best he could the chronology of the paperwork. The polygraph had led the Office of Security for the CIA to run a financial check on Jaffe. They must have brought the FBI in afterward, since the surveillance reports were filed months after the financial check. He recalled that one of the CIA surveillance reports had come from overseas. These people wanted to keep a close eye on Jaffe.

Squire had to shake off the guilt swarming up inside. He had no idea how he could have betrayed his team member, but somehow the Company had monitored Jaffe's movements and it had to have come through Squire. Since Housemother had served mainly in a silent monitoring capacity, he could not have dictated where Jaffe would be to allow him to arrange for the kind of sophisticated surveillance a seasoned veteran like Jaffe would require.

Squire's thoughts drifted. There was no time to flounder. He focused his mind on what he had seen on the last page of the file.

An FBI investigation suspected Jaffe of breaching the Company's computer network. The report, though, lacked specifics on the how and when. But it stated conclusively that they had traced a login on the main computer back to Jaffe. That same last page had reported a second breach in computer security and recommended that a tag be placed on information Jaffe might have accessed.

Housemother had access to this file and knew of Jaffe's security violations. Did he have Jaffe... Housemother also knew, through one of Squire's reports, that Jaffe had made the arrangements for the meeting in Kano. Could Jaffe have gone to Kano to deliver information to his contact instead of receiving it? Could the Company have wanted Jaffe silenced?

Did they think Jaffe was meeting a Russian handler in Kano instead of a mole working for us in Libya? Squire turned the question back on himself. Could Jaffe have been meeting with a Russian to deliver information sensitive to our national security? Suddenly Squire had to consider the possibility that Jaffe had turned into a renegade rather than one of the good guys. Someone had to have known about the meeting. Someone might have been monitoring

Squire's communications with the team and analyzed
the message to determine the location, date and
Jaffe's presence at that meeting.

   Squire made his way back to the dungeon as
quickly as possible, all the time reviewing in his mind
how someone could have determined Jaffe's whereabouts. He began to consider how a mole inside the
Company could have monitored his transmissions to
Brax in the field. They relied heavily on computer
transmissions to pass information along. That meant
someone could have tapped into their message traffic
and intercepted it. A friendly computer could have
intercepted his messages.

   Squire decided it was time to place a more
sophisticated sniffer on his traffic in the hopes it
might return the login of anyone who had intercepted
his traffic before it left the Company. He knew once
his transmission left the Agency computer for the
network that it was virtually impossible to identify an
interceptor.

   It took well into the next morning before Squire
had debugged his new sniffer. After a few test runs,
he set it up to embed itself in every message moving
into the field. The tag would do nothing more that
capture the ID of the person who opened the message, then transmit that ID back to Squire even if the
traffic were intercepted outside the Company firewall.

   He had been running on adrenaline until now. All
he wanted was sleep, glorious sleep. But lives
depended on him. Lives that were the closest things
he had to friends since his forced exile to this abyss.
Instead of sleep he removed his little bottle from his
pocket, opted for two more of his little black pills,
which he washed down with what remained of cold
black coffee brewed the day before.

11

Alabaster roosting coastal after
short flight from southern shore.
                        Squire

Brax considered the implications as he read the
message. Alabaster was a low-level Russian mule. An
intel report from the French Counterterrorist Agency
in Paris a year earlier intimated a link between Alabaster and one of Leviathan's lieutenants at the time.
If Leviathan had used Alabaster then, he may be
employing him again. The Russians had little use for
Alabaster once the CIA had uncovered his real intent
in traveling regularly between Vienna and the U.S. As
a result, Alabaster had to increase his salability by
hauling for any terrorist group willing to pay. He had
been connected to the Hizballah during that time,
moving Russian pistols into France and Spain at regular intervals. Only a select few inside the Agency
knew of Alabaster's side job. Once turned over to
Wolf Pack, Alabaster became more than simply a target for surveillance.

Brax selected Remy to gather the intelligence. He
hoped Alabaster might in some remote way be working for Leviathan, and thus provide the team with a
link to the Devil himself. Mules were considered so
low on the food chain that they rarely afforded any
opportunity to the team. And Remy viewed his
assignment as more an irritant than useful duty.

Fierce rain backed up landings into Boston's Logan airport, forcing Remy to endure a two hour circling ordeal before finally touching down. It reminded him all too much of home, which only served to gnaw at his mind more now that he was doing surveillance in the States. Being attached to MI6, he operated outside the United Kingdom. Only the MI5 branch of the British Secret Service conducted operations inside the country. That having been said, Wolf Pack however, was prepared to violate any directive that stood between them and their hard target. Remy felt without doubt Leviathan's next strike would come in Britain. And he would be letting his own government down if he failed to do everything in his power to save lives. By the time Remy left the airport he seemed able to bury his personal feelings and focus on the target at hand.

He drove directly to the Concord Hotel in the downtown area near the harbor. California or Florida would have been a better choice, but Alabaster, it seemed, had no interest in cooperating. A phone call to Squire while still on the airplane had gotten Alabaster's accommodations. The man made no effort to disguise his identity or where he was staying.

Remy completed his first task of setting up surveillance on the man by taking a room in the hotel across the street from the Concord. From his perch, he would patiently watch and wait for that moment when he might uncover something useful. If there were even something useful to uncover. The room proved adequate for Remy's needs though he would have preferred more luxury than the Lexington had to offer.

Remy disliked working single-handed, it complicated the task of shadowing, and left opportunities to miss important incidents. However, Alabaster was so low on the scale that there was little chance they might gain anything useful from this sycophant-faced scumbag. Nevertheless, Alabaster was another of those slimy rocks needing to be turned over just in case.

Three hours after settling in at his window with camera, listening parabola and assorted groceries, Remy left it behind to fall in Alabaster's wake as he began what seemed to be a leisurely stroll down the street. He stopped frequently to take in sights and eventually settled in at a restaurant for dinner.

Remy's stomach rumbled but he had to wait until he could grab something without compromising his surveillance. Alabaster had taken a table well inside the restaurant—and despite that, Remy confirmed Alabaster had chosen to dine alone. Remy remained outside until his target reemerged, well fed and watered with wine. That fact Remy had determined by the two wine bottles left at the table when Alabaster rose to leave.

Alabaster had a twenty-four hour head start in Boston over Remy, so there was a chance that he had already fulfilled his purpose in coming to this place. Remy guessed Alabaster would likely remain no more than forty-eight hours before moving on. Rarely did mules stay put for more than a couple of days. Sooner or later someone might take notice. If, and Remy knew the ifs were mega-ifs, if Alabaster were on the move for Leviathan, he would make his contact, pick up or deliver promptly, then clear out. If and when he did, Remy wanted to assess the significance without delay.

After dining, Alabaster strolled back to his hotel and remained in his room for the remainder of the evening switching between the radio and the television set. Both of which drove Remy to absolute boredom.

From his location across the street, perched one floor higher than Alabaster's, Remy adjusted his listening dish. The parabolic synthetic resin dish was the latest technological advancement to arrive from the Japanese. The XFC16's sensitivity range was so great that when aimed at the target's window twenty meters away, it captured and amplified the vibrations of the glass resulting from conversation inside the room. With the focal point beamed toward Alabaster's window, Remy listened to silence in his headset. He fine-tuned the amplifier until he began to pick up the movement of air in and out of a sleeping Alabaster's lungs. It helped that Alabaster's cigarette habit forced his breathing to be significantly labored, making it easily captured and amplified.

Remy could tell by the creaks when Alabaster moved on his bed, listened to the splash while he relieved himself in the Loo with the door open, and switched on the TV to catch up with the news from CNN when he couldn't get back to sleep.

So far there had been no ringing telephone, no gentle raps at Alabaster's door. All remained quiet, and after setting up his camera with telephoto lens, Remy settled in for a lonely, dreary night.

At forty minutes past nine, however, things changed. The telephone rang.

Remy snapped forward in his chair and notched up the volume.

"Give me something good," he murmured.

Alabaster spoke briefly, succinctly, saying he would try to get together with the caller before he left. Remy notched the volume down when he detected the phone's return to the cradle. The conversation seemed innocuous; Remy recorded it nonetheless. He replayed the tape three times, analyzing every syllable, searching for a clue that might reveal some kind of code.

"*...I'm on my way back. Just here for the night...*"

Remy rewound, listened again.

"*Got in yesterday...no haven't' had a chance...*"

It seemed insignificance.

"*Too bad the Red Sox aren't in town...*"

Remy dialed.

"Are the Red Sox in town?" he posed to Squire.

A second later he got an answer. The Red Sox were in Atlanta.

Growing restive and bored, Remy scanned his directional microphone across other windows, hoping to snare a bit of excitement.

"How long do you have," a lovely seductive voice said. Remy held on the room for a moment, no answer came. He conjured the vision of beauty that would match such a lovely voice. Then he moved on.

A shadow passed before Alabaster's window. The target was off the bed and moving. Remy swung the mike back to his window.

The door opened.

"Come in," he said.

"Fuck," Remy muttered.

He had missed the knock, maybe more.

"How much?"

"What do you want?"

"Around the world."

"Two hundred."

"Two hundred! Sophie said you'd cut me a deal."

"You want a deal? I send you to the moon for three hundred."

"Fuck you...a deal."

"Fuck you. This is expensive. You want it or not?"

"That's it, you tell him, honey," Remy said as he listened. He shifted his camera hoping to peer in through a crack in the window curtains. But even with the powerful lens, the sliver of opening between the curtains proved too formidable to get a peek at Alabaster's caller.

"Sweetheart, when I'm done, you'll be offering me two hundred for more," Alabaster said in his boastful way.

"Okay, stallion, let's see the cash," she said with a sardonic ring.

"You don't take credit cards?"

"You a comedian by profession?"

"You don't trust me?"

"I trust only cash."

"You got a certificate?" Alabaster asked.

"I'll show you mine; you show me yours."

Silence smothered the room.

"Sure glad I packed extra clothes if we're going on a trip around the world," Remy joked. He settled back into his chair and sought the diversion of a two month out of date Combat Handgun magazine. He checked his watch to mark the time.

He had listened to this kind of stuff so much in the course of his twenty years with the service that he afforded little attention to the actual lovemaking instructions the two issued each other while they performed on the bed...then on the floor...then on either a table or bureau by the heavy wooden thumping. From the racket, they made it more a contest than an intimate exchange. The encounter lasted under two hours. Then Alabaster sent the woman on her way.

"A hundred bucks an hour," Remy muttered as he shook his head. He listened to Alabaster stretch out on his bed and surf through the channels on the television.

Remy diverted his camera to the street below, waiting in anticipation for the tart who had just taken Alabaster's money. Minutes passed. No one exited the hotel.

Remy scratched his head. Why?

An inside hooker? Or maybe she had other johns in the hotel? Remy continued to mull over the situation. The telephone rang again at exactly eleven forty-five.

Alabaster answered, but said nothing and hung up a minute later. Remy deduced from the clinking sounds that Alabaster had pulled on his pants and the noise had come form his belt.

"Okay, you've eaten and gotten your rocks off. What else could you want?"

Remy listened. Something was up. He locked his room, raced down the stairs taking two and three at a time, so as to arrive at his hotel front door just before Alabaster came out. He could see glimpses of Alabaster in the hotel lobby as he emerged from his elevator. That left Remy less than ten seconds to slip unnoticed to a vantage point to take up his surveillance.

A few seconds following, Alabaster exited the Concord, this time to stroll north against sparse pedestrian traffic, which forced Remy to allow a greater distance between he and his target. But Alabaster didn't stray far. He stopped at a pay phone inside a sports bar and restaurant one block off the main drag.

"Damn," Remy muttered all the while trying to come up with a vantage point. He pulled his jacket collar up to partially obscure his face before pausing outside the restaurant to read the menu taped on the inside of the glass next to the door. He leaned an ear to the pane separating he and Alabaster.

Despite the background noise, Remy picked up that Alabaster spoke in German, having to raise his voice to be heard over a passing trio of men who exhibited all the signs of inebriation. The interference obliterated parts of the conversation, but Remy distinctly heard Frankfort, tomorrow and the fourteenth.

The next few words came as fragments. Remy pieced them together, probing for significance. Unfortunately a pair of drunken assholes slurred over Alabaster's conversation just before he hung up.

Remy stuffed a hurriedly wadded handkerchief into his left shoe, forming a heel lift and forcing him to walk with a limp. He placed his back toward Alabaster during his exit, hoping Alabaster had failed to notice him standing there during his conversation. Once Alabaster passed, Remy moved off across the street with his limp just to cover himself in the event any of Leviathan's goons were keeping an eye on their mule.

Alabaster never once looked back for a tail, which indicated he felt secure or comfortable in the knowledge that no one was watching over him.

Remy turned down a blackened alley and raced to the other end, where he removed the heel lift, turned his jacket inside out, taking it from a dark blue to a tan, then resumed his normal gait with his target within his sights.

The entire telephone exchange took less than two minutes, and the contact was important enough to exclude clandestine listeners. It also indicated that if Alabaster were leaving for Germany tomorrow, he must already have whatever he had been tasked with picking up, or completed his delivery. In the latter case, there was nothing Remy could do now. In the former, he had to get inside Alabaster's room long enough to find what had brought the mule to Boston.

During the walk back to the hotel, Remy reassembled the pieces of the conversation in his mind. If only he could have positioned himself closer to the phone. Alabaster returned to his room and returned to his television set, laughing more in a giggle than an outright laugh at an old rerun of The Dick Van Dyke Show on some obscure cable channel.

Back in his room, Remy contacted Squire to get an update on Alabaster's itinerary prior to Boston. A response to his request came with the dawn after five hours sleep.

"FBI tracked him through Philly, Baltimore and Arlington. I show him booked on a flight from Boston to Paris."

"He's going to Frankfort."

"Hang on," Squire said. Through the phone, Remy could hear fingers tapping at a keyboard with the rhythm of elevator music. It was like listening to Jeopardy.

"There's a Frankfort flight departing twenty minutes before his ticketed Paris flight. He's going to pull a switch at the last second."

"Who's in Frankfort?"

"Hang on a minute."

The minute lasted ten.

"Bingo! I've got a last seen on Yullenlander in Frankfort…five days ago. He's PKK." Squire let his excitement ring.

"I'm guessing our friend picked up something before Boston. I'm going in."

"I'll inform Brax. Give me an all clear as soon as you can." Squire hung up.

Willie exited the tobacconist shop, whistled as he strolled across the street to the flower shop to purchase a bouquet of daisies. Tonight he would ask Annalise to marry him, and if she agreed, they would fly to Monte Carlo, get married and then continue on to a Caribbean honeymoon in the Cayman Islands. It was a place Willie had read much about and now wanted to enjoy with the one woman he felt he truly loved. He had researched travel brochures as carefully as he researched his specialty and knew the Caymans would be the perfect place to start his new life. In twenty four hours, all would be behind him.

Annalise was more than just a lover. She understood him and shared in his cause. Together they could overcome anything. Willie's face alighted when he envisioned her look of surprise and admiration when he showed her the money he had earned. Enough to make a new life in a new place; enough to put his past behind them and never again have to worry about watching over their shoulder.

The cause no longer glittered like gold. Killing innocent people no longer served to solidify their beliefs. For Willie, it was time to abandon the ideals and root his feet in reality. Governments are corrupt by their very nature and killing innocent woman and children will never force an end to corruption. He intended to become co-opted into the very same system he fought to destroy.

So caught up in his thoughts was Willie that he nearly overshot his loft apartment. He chuckled to himself as he juggled grocery sack and flowers to unlock the door.

Dinner would be her favorite. He would prepare everything just the way she liked it. The wine would intoxicate her, their lovemaking would intoxicate them both.

Willie climbed the stairs two at a time with his mind relishing the gentle ocean breezes of a place over three thousand miles away. Inside the loft, the windows allowed granite blocks of sunlight to paint the floor, forcing darkness to crowd the corners. Enough darkness that Willie never saw the human shape perched motionless beside his workbench.

Willie grabbed his remote, leveled it at his stereo and fired, bringing the great force of Pavarotti to six four-foot speakers. Music masked the sounds of movement out of the corner. Willie's back remained to the windows while he unloaded his dinner necessities on the table in the portion of the loft where he took his meals. Everything had to be market fresh, the way Annalise liked it.

Shigeo appeared like a specter out of thin air. He narrowed his dark eyes as he descended upon his unknowing prey with the swiftness of the hawk and the lethal destruction of the viper. His fists became hammers, poised to reek bloody havoc upon his victim.

Willie turned to put the greens next to the stove.

Shigeo's right hand cracked Willie's jaw with the force of brick. So precise had been Shigeo's strike, that it tore the mandible loose, causing it to dangle as blood sprayed from the gaping rictus of Willie's impotent scream.

Willie stared aghast into the dark assassin eyes, empty and pitiless.

There could be no force in Willie's desperate scream since blood began backing up into Willie's throat. Even if he could scream with force, the music would drown out the sound. Willie's terror-stricken eyes never strayed from Shigeo's demon eyes. No feeling, no emotion. Eyes that killed with without conscience. The man who had arranged the job with Ranzami. The man who had set him up to earn the money to make his life livable again.

Shigeo struck again, executing the mechanization's of killing before Willie could get his hands up to defend himself. In that moment, those fists of fury completed the task of dislodging the jaw until it hung limp and useless from Willie's face. Blood covered him as if it had been painted on. Those deadly hands were in constant motion, battering Willie's face until the blood spurted across Shigeo's cheeks.

Willie mustered the inner strength to overcome the fierce pain and launch a feeble strike at his assailant. Annaliase's face flooded his mind. He wanted to live to see her again. But he knew he would not.

Shigeo seized Willie's clumsily outstretched arm and snapped it in two with a driving kick. The agony of his beating disappeared from Willie's eyes. He could make no sound other than the chortling of blood in his throat each time he attempted to suck in air. He knew the man had come to kill him. Death became inescapable. In that last moment before death took him, Willie tried to form Annalise's name on what was left of his lips. It never came.

Shigeo had toyed with his victim enough. While Willie teetered on the verge of collapse, Shigeo took Willie's head between his hands and with one sharp snap ended his suffering.

Silence filled the loft. The compact disk player randomly sought another track. Shigeo searched the entire loft from end to end until he uncovered the money Ranzami had given Willie. The money was inconsequential to Ranzami's purposes. It was Shigeo's bonus for accomplishing the job asked of him. Willie posed a security risk to his plan. That had brought Shigeo to this place.

His assignment complete, Shigeo washed his face and hands at the sink, tossing the bloody towel he used to wipe himself into a trash can, which he then doused with a cleaning fluid he found on the workbench. Before igniting it, he slid the can beneath the bench to ensure the flames would catch the wood. Seconds later, amber tongues licked the underside of the workbench. Black smoke churned up over the edge.

As easily as Shigeo had slipped unnoticed into Willie's apartment, he likewise vanished. In a matter of minutes all evidence would become charred rubble. Willie no longer posed a risk to Leviathan. Or so Shigeo thought....

12

The Devil's on the move.

                              Squire

With the dawn came an offering, an offering almost too good to be true. Chevanovich was on the move. As Brax read the communication from Squire he felt his heart race with the fury of a tempest. Nikolai Adriandrov Chevanovich. A master of chemical weaponry, the Company had codenamed him Dr. Doom during Afghanistan. Chevanovich had orchestrated the deployment of the chemical weapons against the Afghan rebels.

Back in '90, with Desert Storm imminent and the concern paramount for what U.S. troops might face in Iraq, the president called upon Brax to assemble a three-man team with one crucial objective: Eliminate Dr. Doom if he made any move out of the then Soviet bloc. Chevanovich wielded the kind of power free world governments fear most. The ability to deliver mass destruction. Brax and his team—codenamed the Sentinels—had painstakingly monitored every move the good doctor made inside the Soviet Union. Not an hour elapsed when the doctor escaped the eyes of the Sentinels. For this operation, Brax had positioned himself at the point of greatest risk. The one exposed to the enemy. But in so doing, he became the one most likely to make the kill should Chevanovich even hint he might aid the Iraqi cause. He accepted from the beginning that his position would be suicidal. Had he been called upon to make the kill, there became virtually no chance of escaping the country. Nikolai never realized how fortunate he was when he remained in St. Petersburg during the conflict. This man was considered *that* dangerous.

It didn't take great deductive powers to reason that if Chevanovich were moving, there was a reason to suspect he might be migrating toward Leviathan. His work in Afghanistan earned him international recognition in the intelligence community. Every free world watcher knew Chevanovich's face and complete profile. For a time after Desert Storm, the Company and MI6 developed a joint offensive to put him out of commission for good, but the bureaucracy and the politics kept anything from growing into an operation.

Brax maintained a meticulously detailed profile of the man and his capabilities, and he cautioned every president that Chevanovich was far too lethal to be left alone. But the British Prime Minister at the time felt compelled to inaction as long as Chevanovich remained in St. Petersburg.

Now Chevanovich had reason to leave his soft, comfortable home in St. Petersburg; he was en route to Berlin via the rail. No one for one minute believed Berlin to be his final destination. Berlin served as the gateway. Russians, along with terrorists, moved easily in and out.

"What's the status on Remy," Brax asked Squire over the secured phone.

"Still shadowing our mule. Do I pull him," Squire replied.

Brax thought for a long moment. He needed full strength to watch over Dr. Doom. But something Remy had reported about Alabaster urged Brax to stick with the surveillance. He trusted Remy's instincts on this one.

"Communicate to Remy to remain with Alabaster until he boards the plane in Boston. Contact the Frankfort station chief and get a man on Alabaster when he arrives. We'll cover the good doctor until Remy can rendezvous with us."

The team minus Remy would assemble in Berlin to devise a hasty plan for tracking Chevanovich's movements. All they knew at the moment was Chevanovich left St. Petersburg by train, stopping overnight in Karastan in the south, then continuing on to Berlin. Thanks to Squire and a trio of Air Force fighters, Brax, Cali and Cody could be on the ground and positioned for the doctor's arrival if nothing went amiss.

Sleeping beneath headphones made a deep sleep impossible. Remy felt more fatigued now than when he laid down. But sounds of Alabaster crawling into the shower alerted him. Remy shifted to the window to monitor his target.

Shortly after the water went silent, clad only in a towel around his neck, Alabaster opened the curtains and stretched before the window.

"Put something on, you scum," Remy said sourly. He found the very thought of viewing naked men repulsive to say the least. Why didn't these people use more women? That would at least make the watching more interesting. Especially since Alabaster now stood there scratching at his Artemus Dooley.

The target retreated from the window to dress in the background of the room while watching a morning news show on the television. Remy watched as Alabaster's darkened form moved in and out of the light shed by the television screen, which forced Alabaster to appear like an apparition in the room. After checking his grooming in the mirror, Alabaster scooped up his wallet and keys from the bureau and prepared to leave.

"Thank you, thank you," Remy whispered with a smile broader than the sunrise.

Minutes later, Alabaster strolled out the hotel doors, spoke briefly to a barrel-shaped doorman, then strolled off in the direction he had taken the night before. As soon as Alabaster was away, Remy dashed into the street, zigzagged through the traffic and marched at a determined pace into the Concord. He surmised he might get thirty minutes or possibly more if Alabaster had gone out for breakfast. His intent was to be in and out in under ten.

With briefcase held in both hands across his front, Remy rode a deserted elevator to the fifteen floor, walked quickly and quietly down the stairs to the twelfth, where he located Alabaster's room. It took twenty seconds to pick the lock and slip inside. He could do better, he thought, once safely inside. Arthritis in his hands had caused them to lose their touch.

"So this is where you showed that little philly a taste of Heaven," he murmured while he methodically went through each of Alabaster's bags. After working each bag in the room, Remy came away with nothing that might contain information. He wasn't even certain at this point what he hoped to find. He just had a feeling that this mule was hauling. And information, Remy figured, was Alabaster's purpose in coming to Boston. Some type of sensitive information, papers, documents, photographs, something.

Remy snickered when a realization came to him. He returned to the first bag.

What did Alabaster mean by he has it? Remy pondered for a long moment, longer than he should have. Then he checked the time and pondered some more. He had a few more minutes. Too soon to abort and scurry for cover.

Remy searched the pockets of Alabaster's suits inside the hanging bag. In the left breast pocket of a richly-tailored Italian double-breasted tweed jacket, he withdrew a stack of crisp hundreds. Remy inspected one in the harsh light from the window. Iranian counterfeits. Good enough to escape an untrained eye. But not good enough to evade scrutiny by someone trained. As much as Remy hated to, he had to abandon the cash. Some poor snooks were going to get taken. The Iranians theorized they could help the terrorists organizations by feeding them American counterfeit, and at the same time work to destabilize the currency of their enemy.

In the other breast pocket Remy found a Diner's Club card.

Bingo! Something out of place.

He grabbed his cell phone and dialed.

"Run this right away,' Remy said, then slowed his words as he read off the card's number without having to repeat it.

For a moment he waited, staring at the plastic.

"It's bogus," Squire reported back.

Remy hung up, unlocked his briefcase and opened it to a compact electronic device that looked like an adding machine that had gone through some kind of freak mutation. He set the card's magnetic strip into a slot and forced it to the right side. He watched a digital readout panel whir with an unending stream of numbers scrolling like a watershed.

The mutant device read and stored every type of magnetic media, be it tape, disk, or credit card strips.

"Yes!" Remy chimed as he watched the digital display race out of control. "Sonofabitch, he must have a book on here," he added when the string finally ended.

A numeric reading of the amount of memory used up by the information off the card blinked on the display. Forty-four thousands bytes of data. This was no credit card. Someone was transporting sensitive information via bogus credit cards, and using a mule to get the information out of the country. The credit card, to an untrained eye, could easily escape detection. The secret lie in the fact that the card could not be used in a transaction. Ergo, why Alabaster left it behind in his suit pocket.

Remy closed his briefcase, carefully returned the credit card to the pocket from which it came and meticulously rearranged the clothing and the bags to the precise way he had found them. It took great measure to contain the excitement boiling over inside. The trick now was to make certain Alabaster would not become suspicious of a compromise. Whatever Remy had uncovered, he hoped it might somehow relate to their objective.

An exhilaration consumed his mind as he slipped back into the corridor occupied by only a cleaning lady three doors away.

"Good morning sir," she said politely with a smile that offered gold caps on her front teeth. "Are you enjoying your stay?"

"No!" Remy shot back gruffly.

He continued on, disappearing into the stairwell.

Arriving at the elevator on the fifteenth floor, he wiped away the sweat with a handkerchief that reeked of dirty socks. Unconsciously, he whistled while he rode the elevator back to the lobby.

Alabaster strolled in as Remy strolled out. Neither offered eye contact. Remy continued his whistle even when he realized he was whistling a British tune. That might have raised an eyebrow in the States. However, stopping suddenly would have certainly snared Alabaster's attention.

Back in his room, Remy sat at the table, sucking down a cup of tepid instant coffee and listening to Alabaster moving about the room.

For the next two hours Alabaster watched television, then rechecked his bags and rang the desk for his bill. As far as Remy could tell from the sights and sounds he monitored, Alabaster had no suspicions that his room had been sacked.

Against another gray Boston day, Remy relaxed and took in the sights while following Alabaster to the airport. And as Squire had predicted, Alabaster boarded the plane bound for Frankfort at the last possible moment, thereby abandoning the bags checked in for the flight to Paris. But he did have the hanging bag over his arm when he boarded for Frankfort. The Paris ticket had been a ruse that, as far as Alabaster was concerned, had worked.

Remy said his good-byes as the 737 pulled from the gate. He had accomplished what needed to be done in Boston without incident. Now he crossed the airport to board the next hourly commuter flight to D.C. He needed to turn the information over to Squire and move on. An Air Force jet awaited him at Andrews AFB.

But above all, what this Congress can be remembered for is opening the way to a new American revolution--a peaceful revolution in which power was turned back to the people--in which government at all levels was refreshed and renewed and made truly responsive. This can be a revolution as profound, as far-reaching, as exciting as that first revolution almost 200 years ago--and it can mean that just five years from now America will enter its third century as a young nation new in spirit, with all the vigor and the freshness with which it began its first century.

Richard M. Nixon, January 22, 1971

13

```
Arrived on time. Advise on Uncle
Cadre
                    Cody
```

Chevanovich disembarked in the old East Berlin station with a single bag and a gait that clearly marked him a military man. The sparse hair that remained on his head resembled fine strands of white cotton neatly trimmed and ordered. His bag appeared sufficiently large enough to hold clothes for no more than a week away from home. Then again Russians always traveled with only bare necessities.

Cali fell in behind the doctor as he strolled amidst the crowd. She allowed him a dozen paces and used various bobbing heads between her and the doctor to prevent him from getting a look at her face should he glance over his shoulder. With a scratching finger to her right ear, Cali signaled Cody, who was stacking cartons intently across the station with a cap pulled low over his face. The target acquired, surveillance began. Few could fathom the kind of exhilaration the team felt. If ever one man was pivotal to a mission, it was Dr. Doom. Cali's eyes never strayed from Chevanovich's head as he strolled leisurely on; now a couple dozen paces ahead and to her right flank. He turned to profile when he stepped off the train, facilitating positive identification. He also made no attempt to disguise his appearance, nor zigzag his movements in the hopes of exposing a shadow.

Chevanovich made the first stage of their surveillance—target acquisition—easy, maybe too easy, since he did nothing more than browse in a gift shop for thirty minutes. However, Cody determined that as time wore on, Chevanovich increased the frequency with which he checked his watch.

"He's timing a move," Cody whispered in his button mike. All wore listening devices that fit unobtrusively in their ears.

"I'm positioning for embarkation," Cali said.

She glanced to a man on a bench in the rear of the waiting zone. Brax adjusted the bag he carried on his shoulder to acknowledge her transmission. He had set himself up as a rear guard, watching for signs to indicate that the good doctor had a friend watching over him from a distance. If the friend spotted a tail he would signal the doctor who might then board a train returning to the Russian territory.

"Cody, make your move, I've got the target," Brax whispered, when the old woman beside him rose and strolled off in more of a hobble than a walk.

Twice during the last minute Chevanovich glanced up at the station clock across the mezzanine. His eyes methodically swept the crowd flowing back and forth through the main lobby. None of the team ever made eye contact with the target. Even the slightest sign of recognition might spook their subject. Clearly, the doctor intended to time his next move with great precision. The team had anticipated the doctor's actions.

Cody knew from studying the schedule there were two trains departing at the same time, each on a track in close proximity to the other. The problem would come when Chevanovich moved to board a train for his next destination. Cody risked a moment to study the doctor's eyes. Chevanovich would look at neither before making his move. But Cody surmised, the first train Chevanovich locked on with his eyes would be the one he intended to board. That was an old weakness few had the discipline to overcome. Cody bet Chevanovich was too old and too weary to think about the subtle psychology of his actions.

Cali observed Chevanovich from her corner. He checked his watch with greater frequency as the thirty minute wait drew to a close. The good doctor must refrain, wait until the absolute last second before revealing which train he would board. Then he must observe who boarded the same train after him.

Travelers moved through the open expanse to board the two trains as Cali watched the targeted tracks. The lines waiting to board dwindled to but a few dawdling riders before Chevanovich made his move. In a glance, Cali swept the crowds hoping to detect if someone were passing a compromise signal on to the doctor. It seemed the doctor had been left alone for this leg of his journey. Cali spotted no Russian shadow interested enough in the doctor to watch over his movements.

Then she spotted him. A lean, bespectacled man of maybe forty years, rich black hair and a beard neatly trimmed, who slung a jacket over his shoulder. He rose from a bench situated not far from the gift shop and paused to gaze through the shop's window. Cali surmised it to be more than coincidence that he stopped directly in Chevanovich's line of sight and shifted his jacket from one shoulder to the other. The signal spurred the good doctor to reshelve his magazine and collect up his bag beside his feet.

As Chevanovich ambled out of the gift shop with only his bag in hand, Cali had to abandon her surveillance and yielded to Cody, who took over. Cody had guessed correctly. Chevanovich glanced first at the train on the furthest track, then he ambled directly toward the other, only to alter his course at the last second. The doctor boarded the train bound for Switzerland. Cody had positioned himself to slip unnoticed on board the train one car ahead of the doctor.

Cali fumbled with her papers as if confused then dashed to board last, slipping into an aisle seat at the rear of the same car as Chevanovich.

Shortly after Cali found her seat, Cody walked through the car and continued on into the next car back, never once looking over at either the doctor or Cali.

As the locomotive pulled the eight cars into the bright sunlight, Cody settled into a seat just inside the door, where he leaned his head back against his rolled-up jacket. He feigned sleep until the first stop, which came two hours and twenty minutes into their journey. At Nuremberg, Cody left the train to contact Brax and report their location. It seemed the doctor was enjoying his trip. He chatted with the woman occupying the seat beside him. He seemed at ease now, never looking over his shoulder to inspect those occupying the same car as him.

Later, when the train chugged out of Heidelberg, Cali left the car to be replaced by Cody, who seemed preoccupied with reading about the various castles accessible to tourists throughout Germany. Twice Cody spoke to the man sitting across the aisle from him using impeccable German, even down to the subtle inflection attributed to the region they happened to be traveling through.

During this six hours passage, Chevanovich browsed a magazine he removed from his bag and seemed content to sleep when the countryside lost its luster. Cody used his book to mask an inspection of a small map of Switzerland, which indicated with red dots those cities the where train would stop. One of them might be Chevanovich's destination? Or he might exit this train only to board another. The more he maneuvered to expose surveillance, the more Cody believed their surveillance had a chance of a pay off. Chevanovich was certainly high enough on the food chain to warrant a personal visit from Leviathan. As Cody checked the map, he felt his heart quicken.

Months of nothing now could be behind them. He thought of Jaffe. Jaffe would have wanted to be a part of this. They could be positioning themselves to achieve their ultimate objective.

Brax and newly-arrived Remy waited in a car at Freiburg, positioning for a swap when the train entered the station. They would replace Cali with Remy. Cali and Brax would then drive on to the next stop and maintain a defensive posture for the team.

For a time after train came to rest, Chevanovich appeared that he would remain on board, then in a flurry, he quickly gathered up his things and headed for the exit. The action caught the team momentarily out of position. Chevanovich stopped at the door to look back into the faces of the other passengers for what seemed an unending moment.

Cody trained his eyes on his book, never once succumbing to that driving urge to bring them up to meet the doctor's. However, he remained no more than five steps behind as Chevanovich stepped onto the station platform. But Cody couldn't risk it; he had to abandon his plan and remain on the train. The risk of exposure became too great for him to disembark.

Cali had wisely positioned herself three cars to the rear of the doctor's and straddled the doors waiting to confirm that Remy made it on board before departing herself. Remy had the good presence of mind to abort the moment he saw Chevanovich rise from his seat. Cali then had to delay her move a few seconds with her door still jammed open and the train pulling away. She held up until Chevanovich turned away before she made her jump to the platform and disappeared amongst a crowd funneling into the station.

As Chevanovich emerged through the double doors of the Freiburg station, a car honked and a smiling young man clad in tie and jacket waved to gain the doctor's attention. He looked like he had been cast from the mold of a thousand students from the university greeting a grandfather, though it seemed few words were exchanged as Chevanovich slid into the car's passenger seat.

Remy and Cali dispersed out of Chevanovich's sight. The good doctor, however, had the presence of mind to study the faces of those near the car as they merged into the station traffic.

Only after the black Mercedes sped away did the two converge to be met by Brax in a silver Saab.

"Close call," Remy muttered as he slid into the rear seat while the Saab forced its way into traffic. "Good thing I kept eyeballing him. I'd be on my way to bloody Switzerland now."

"He's being very careful," Cali reported, pointing toward the Mercedes, though Brax already had it in sight and maneuvered to get within three cars of its gray curling exhaust.

They followed Chevanovich to the next town on the highway, twenty kilometers from where he disembarked, and during which there seemed to be no attempt to uncover a shadow or any maneuvers meant to shake anyone interested in the doctor's movements. However, in Basel, Chevanovich left the car in a hurry and scampered to board another train, this one pointing west and destined to cross the path with the one he had just left.

Only Remy succeeded in boarding the train without risking exposure before it pulled out of the station, and he had boarded the last car while Chevanovich had boarded the first. They could no longer risk Cali in the surveillance, since her somewhat markable appearance on this train would certainly signal a shadow to the good doctor.

For now, Remy flew solo surveillance. He would contact Brax as soon as he knew where Chevanovich would leave the train. From the Saab's passenger seat, Cali contacted Squire with the station name. It took Squire two minutes to rattle off the trains next three stops like he was a computer. Excitement began to crowd the car. Brax barked commands. Cali relayed them to Squire over the phone. Chevanovich had fallen into a standard Russian routine to elude surveillance. Undoubtedly, there would be someone on that last train charged with the sole task of determining if the good doctor had picked up a shadow. If so, this one would issue an abort on the rendezvous.

It was up to Remy now to uncover the watcher and keep his cover intact. Brax had to hope one of Leviathan's lieutenants had been assigned to shadow Chevanovich the remainder of the journey.

Unfortunately, it became impossible for the team to be waiting when the doctor again decided to disembark. The train sped out of sight, and Brax had to rely on Remy's contacting Squire with an update.

Brax toyed with attempting to plant Cali on the train at the next stop, but he quickly abandoned it. A mistake now could be costly. Remy had the job.

Even before Brax could fully consider other alternatives, the secure telephone in the Saab rang.

"Go," Brax said.

"I just picked up intelligence that a large sum of Krugerrands is moving north out of Baghdad," Squire said from his vault in Langley.

"Damnit, it's starting to pour down on us."

It was start of day in Washington, and the message had come in from the overnights. An analyst had routed it to Squire the moment it was decoded.

"Who's the courier?" Brax asked, slowing as he watched a train moving parallel to him on a trestle jutting out the side of a craggy mountain. It wasn't the train with the doctor. This one headed in the opposite direction on a different track.

"I'm running that information down now. We know it's Devrimci Sol sanctioned. The latest intelligence believes the money will move under tight guard over land to Ankara. You going in?"

"Send a message to Thesseo. Instruct him to try to find out where the transfer will take place. But under no circumstance is he to risk compromise. Make certain he understands that. Update me the moment you ID the target," Brax said then hung up.

He checked his watch. An overland route from Baghdad to Ankara might give him just enough time to get a military flight to Turkey and position himself for an intercept. Iran and Iraq funded a significant portion of the terrorist activities in the West. Chances were good that any large sum of money moving out of Iraq would end up in terrorist hands. The fact that these were Krugerrands meant something, but exactly what at the moment eluded Brax.

"When it rains it pours," Cali said. "You want me to go after it?"

Brax fondled the idea for a short time. If Cali had been with the team longer, he might have bit on the idea. He decided instead to use a local to track the money north, and report hourly to Langley, where the fresh intelligence could be fed to Squire and then relayed to him en route.

"What's the plan, boss?" Cali asked when it seemed Brax was consumed in thought.

"Either target could take us to our man. You'll have to assist Remy. Don't let the doctor out of sight. I'm going to Ankara to track the money. It may be a handoff to someone linked to Leviathan."

"And if it's Leviathan himself?" Cali asked with an edge of concern to her words. "You're alone."

The master strategy behind Wolf Pack was to take on Leviathan en masse. One on one had never been factored into the plans.

"I save you from watching Doctor Doom."

Brax abandoned his pursuit of the train, turned the Saab over to Cali and tasked Squire with securing a ride to the nearest airport, which turned out to be less than an hour away. The car arrived fourteen minutes later with a German driver. For now time was on his side, and he knew it.

14

Lost Uncle Webley in Nottingham.
                                    Remy

Rommel waited. Carpenters and painters snatched up tool bags and trekked from the parking lot to the construction entrance. There appeared a lethargy about their movement, the kind apparent in people loathing the chore of having to show up for work. Rommel had arrived early but chose to park in the corner furthest from the Capitol building's manned doors. He rubbed his sweating palms out of habit, rehearsing his instructions by rote in his head. If he followed the man's instructions, everything would go off without a hitch, that's what the creepy guy had said repeatedly during his briefing. Rommel prayed in Tagalog, reverting to his native tongue unconsciously. Something he had avoided for many years.

While he waited, he reflected on what he was about to do. He nervously rubbed the badge given him by the man, and he checked it for the forth time in as many minutes. Then he clipped it to his shirt pocket. That would buy him access to the renovation site. The man had cautioned Rommel repeatedly against looking or acting any way that might raise a flag of suspicion. In his younger days, Rommel had fantasized of being a famous actor. Now he would find out if he housed any of that innate ability to act.

"*The guards are butthead assholes, and if you don't fuck up, they'll pass you through without a second glance,*" the man had said.

Every footfall had been planned and rehearsed to the *n*th degree; he should encounter no difficulty completing his task, the man offered Rommel just before leaving.

They say money forces men to evil. Not always. Sometimes family can be the demon that forces men to evil, Rommel preached to himself as he watched the congestion at the door build.

Watching a crew of three Hispanic laborers slog in two-by-six scaffolding, followed by an irresistible female carpenter in painted-on jeans, Rommel knew his moment had arrived. Her hips and jutting breasts across the tight denim workshirt would distract the eyes of even the most conscientious. Rommel moved quickly, snapping closed his tool chest while he walked, and falling in a stride behind her.

Rommel sucked in a breath moving through the doorway, smiling as he held the door for the pretty señorita. She must go before him, to distract the guards.

As briefed, the entry guards appeared neither rushed nor particularly organized this day. The renovation project had been in full swing for two months, and the clearance process now became so routine that passivity in operations had already settled in.

Rommel ran his fingers through his crewcut black hair. It masked his attempt to remove the sweat beading his forehead. When the line stopped, he presented his affable smile, and knocked his badge with a swipe of his hand to reaffirm that he had not lost it on the way in. *Nothing out of the ordinary*, the man had cautioned. The urge to check his picture on the badge one more time overwhelmed Rommel. But he fought it down and stared at the guard sitting before the computer screen. *Eye contact, always make eye contact with the guards.*

As Rommel had hoped, the tight feminine ass moving to the metal detector checkpoint held the guard's eyes steadfast. Slowly, reluctantly they returned to Rommel and their assigned task. The guard flashed a guilt-ridden smile, realizing Rommel understood exactly what churned inside the guard's brain. The guard raised an eyebrow, indicating his approval of her shape, then scanned down to Rommel's badge.

Rommel rotated his upper body, but only slightly, presenting his badge in such a way that the guard could see it, yet imply that security should be streamlined and not impede getting the job done.

The guard, however, extended his hand, expecting Rommel to remove the badge and set it in his waiting palm.

Rommel hesitated. *It would be routine*, the man had said. *Butthead assholes*, the man said. Rommel suddenly realized the guard had not asked for the badges of those ahead of him in line. Had he somehow screwed up?

"I can't read it from there."

"Sorry," Rommel said, his smile slight and apologetic. He unclipped the badge from his pocket and handed it over to the guard, who read the number off and tapped it into the computer.

"Is it pronounced Rommel, like the general, or Rom'mel?"

"Rommel, like the general," Rommel replied, swallowing the 'sir' he almost tagged on to his response. The words came out weak and ineffective. Rommel scolded himself inside. Be strong. Let him hear your voice, he instructed himself in the same sharp manner as the man who had briefed him.

Rommel waited. The guard clung to the badge rather than return it. A bad sign, Rommel thought. The urge to look back at the door swarmed through him like an adrenaline rush. He resisted. Instead, Rommel forced his hand to his side, refraining from reaching up to wipe the sweat trickling down his doughy, tawny cheeks. Even when the wait exceeded the expected minute, Rommel neither shifted nor altered his position in any way.

What was happening?

Rommel resolved that at the slightest hint of trouble he would bolt. He needed to breathe badly, but he waited, letting air slip silently out his slightly parted lips.

Finally the guard nodded and offered the badge back.

Without even a sigh, Rommel advanced to the tool inspection station. Sweat rimmed his hairline. He could feel it. He also knew he had to let it roll down his face. One more checkpoint to negotiate.

When his turn at the table arrived, he set his metal chest gingerly down, though it weighed easily thirty pounds with all the tools packed inside. He lifted the lid as if he had performed this routine a thousand times. With one hand he rotated the case, positioning it so an effortless inspection would be required on the part of the guard.

Using his pen like a prod, the rotund, scabrous-faced guard nudged screwdrivers, pliers, wire cutters, wire nuts, electrical tape, and an assortment of electrical test gear. Nothing deserved more than a cursory glance; nothing appeared out of the ordinary for an electrical worker assigned to work this project.

Rommel received the perfunctory nod. He was in. The guard's head followed Rommel into the work area, while with his hand he motioned for the next in line. His interest came not from the short Filipino, but rather he, too, succumbed to that intense male craving for another eye full of the tight jeans strolling into the discord of carpenters.

Without looking back over his shoulder or glancing side to side, Rommel buried his smile and continued on. He passed the security process—the most difficult part. Everything got easier from here, or so the man had said. While Rommel strolled through the Statuary Hall, he felt for the impression of a key in his pocket. He knew exactly which door lock it fit, and when and how he must use it to get inside.

He held just enough knowledge of electrical work to pass for a legitimate worker if questioned, though he had no intention of touching the wiring inside this wonderful historic edifice.

With the noise and commotion of the project behind him, Rommel proceeded in the wake of a trio of painters, who laughed at some crude joke as they ascended the stairs to the second floor. At all times, Rommel offered the appearance that he knew exactly where he was going and what he had to do. Once on the second floor, though, he veered off from the painters, waiting near an office door with an 'UNDER RENOVATION' sign taped to the glass until a roving guard completed his tour at the opposing end of the corridor.

No one questioned his presence, nor inquired as to what job he had been assigned to complete. Just as the man had instructed him. Rommel had sharp, crisp answers ready just in case.

Rubbernecking the silent hall in both directions, Rommel confirmed that he, for the moment, was alone and could continue. He walked at an unhurried pace right to the access door, unlocked it after fumbling nervously with the key, then slipped inside. He paused for a long moment, his head resting against the door, his hand still clutching the door handle to allow the weakness in his legs to fade.

Before making his ascent, he gazed up the ladder at the dark open expanse hovering at the crest. With one hand slinging the tool chest, Rommel climbed using the other. He carefully placed each foot on the rung; he must avoid a mishap that might bring attention to him. He imagined his crashing tool box sounding the alarm and bringing guards swarming into this little closet. He could have left the tools behind—he would need only a few items from amongst the many, but the case cemented his persona. And leaving something as important as tools behind could alert someone to impropriety. Arousing suspicion at this juncture could be fatal.

The man had insisted Rommel abandon the task at even the slightest possibility of compromise. That afforded Rommel an out should he lose his nerve before completing his assignment. However, failing to complete the task meant he would only receive a fraction of what had been offered. Successful completion brought the big money. And Adriele, his daughter deserved every opportunity for a life better than the one Rommel had thus far made for himself.

Rommel paused at the top rung to confirm he was indeed alone. Then he swung the tool box onto the transom. The thud and shudder traveled like a great wave in the otherwise tranquil air. He checked below for some kind of reassurance that he had locked the door after slipping inside. Did he forget? That tinge of doubt muddied the waters of his confidence. Should he descend to check it? The indecision tied a knot in his stomach. Surely he must have locked the door. Go on, he instructed himself.

Rommel opened the chest, positioning a penlight in his mouth to light his tools. First came a flat-bladed screwdriver, then he lifted out his real purpose for being in this place. The heat trapped inside the vacuous cavity of the crawl space began to settle upon him in full force, causing rivulets of sweat to run down his neck. One by one, utilizing both hands to prevent losing any of the screws, Rommel extracted the two screws holding the rear panel of an electrical meter in place. His breathing heightened as he lifted the panel off.

The moment tightened around his heart. He was about to cross the line. He agonized. Adriele's sweet face bloomed across his mind.

He had come this far. Something inside urged him to stop. At this moment everything changed. He was crossing the line that separated innocuous from perilous. Once here, he would never be able to go back. Never be able to undo what he was about to do.

After removing the meter's back panel, Rommel eased the electronic circuit board out. The colorful array of components contained three small red lights and two sets of metal rings with locking clips. The apparatus meant nothing to him.

Only the most inquisitive might have deciphered the circuit's true intent. What he held was not integral to the electrical meter, nor was the meter even functional had anyone attempted to employ it for its designed intent. The man had very cleverly disguised the device where it seemed perfectly suited.

Rommel collected up the roll of clear tape provided with the circuit board, tucked both into his breast pocket and clenched the screwdriver before collecting up his tool box and proceeding on hands and knees down the transom. Like a strict teacher, the man had observed Rommel as he rehearsed the next steps until both felt certain Rommel knew exactly where he was going and precisely how to accomplish his task.

Initially, Rommel tracked his beam not on the ductwork that consumed much of the crawl space, but rather on the wall, hoping to locate some electrical junction box with which to justify his reason for being in this place. A lack of electrical paraphernalia could arouse suspicion if Rommel were discovered here. He knew exactly where he must go, but under no circumstance was he to approach the location unless absolutely certain nothing could threaten his assignment. The man had made it sound so clandestine.

Sweeping the light across the duct, Rommel located the metal access plate. As was given him, four screws held it in place. He should be able to remove them in ten seconds. He would need only another thirty to install the device and re-secure the opening.

The tinny muffled voices of Representatives in the house below involved in lively debate drifted up through the ductwork and seeped into the crawl space. The human side of what he was doing began to gnaw at him. Something Rommel had failed to account for when he accepted. That put him on edge; he withdrew from the target area. But a moment later, his inner voice forced himself back.

On the floor below, carpenters pounded out rhythmic reverberations that masked some of the voices amplified by the effects of the sheet metal.

Rommel felt his heart hammer at his chest in sync with the work going on below. He shifted his full attention to the plate on the duct.

Something stopped him. He didn't know what or why, but something inside urged him to withdraw now and protect his cover. Heeding that cautious voice, Rommel turned toward a covered junction box on the wall. Just as he did, a head popped up at the top of the ladder and two eyes stared along a flash-light beam directly into his.

"You AC," the gruff voice called.

"No electrical...safety inspection on some of this old wiring," Rommel responded, removing his screw-driver and fidgeting with the screws holding the junction box cover on.

Damn my brother, Rommel thought. Why did he have to become involved with that sparrow unit in the New People's Army back in Manila? Why does he force me to become involved in this?

The man, puffy-cheeked and weighty as much as he was overbearing, climbed on to the transom, mut-tering vulgarities as he stepped around the open tool chest. He approached at a rapid clip hunched over, since he stood far too tall to be on the transom any-way.

"Sorry, about leaving my tools," Rommel said, "I didn't think anyone else would be up here."

"Yeah, sure," the guy muttered, breathing heavy as if walking was taking everything out of him.

At that moment Rommel realized he had left the back off his electrical meter; now he worried this guy might have glanced into the box and noticed the incongruity.

Rommel felt for the circuit board in his pocket while he feigned intense interest in the rat's nest of wire and tape snaking around inside the junction box. Then he closed the box, attached a phony inspection tag to the junction box and made his way back to his tool chest.

"Hotter than a motherfucker up here, ain't it," the man whined as he waited for Rommel to pass him on the transom.

"Hate coming up in the summer," Rommel said.

"You think those clowns do any good?"

Rommel stopped.

The man indicated the voices filtering into the crawl space from below.

Rommel laughed, an uneasy laugh. He neither agreed nor disagreed with the comment, and without offering eye contact, he snapped his tool box shut.

"Glad I'm done up here," Rommel said wiping away the rolling sweat coming off his cheeks. His heart raced a thousand beats a minute while he fumbled to get the pieces back in his tool chest. He realized he still had the electronic circuit board in his pocket and decided to leave it there since there would be no security inspections to pass through on his departure.

His opportunity now completely shot to hell, and knowing he had no chance of returning while this one was lurking around, Rommel retreated down the ladder.

"Have a nice day," Rommel squeaked out as he descended. He received no reply.

He must now wait at least a week before another attempt. His employer would be disappointed, but not angry, as long as Rommel made certain his position had not been compromised.

The team reassembled in a Geneva safe house. The past twelve hours had proved disastrous for them. Brax sat in a threadbare overstuffed chair while Cali spoke to Squire on the phone. Remy paced ferociously before the window.

"I don't have a fucking bloody clue how he slipped me! I picked up his vehicle outside the train station and never once allowed it out of my sight."

"Are you certain he even got into that car?"

"Absolutely. Fuck, maybe he didn't. Maybe they switched cars to shake me. I watched someone get into that bloody car."

"Squire get anything on the vehicle?" Brax asked over his shoulder to Cali.

"A local reported it stolen a week ago. Probably put on ice for the good doctor's arrival. How important is this Chevanovich?" Cali asked. She turned the mouthpiece upward away her lips while she waited for Squire to return to the line.

"If anyone could have warranted a face-to-face with Leviathan it was our Dr. Doom."

Brax ruminated over the statement. Leviathan could be in Geneva right now meeting with Chevanovich. They could be close.

"I'm not making excuses. I'm sorry. I let the team down. Been up forty hours to get here. But it's still no excuse for failing."

"Don't beat yourself up. Dr. Doom's movements had been carefully orchestrated. For now, we assume our good doctor's in Geneva. Cali, have Squire tap into the Swiss and Austrian intelligence banks and start digging. If Chevanovich has business here, then other familiar faces are bound to turn up."

A rap on the door drew guns. Remy retreated from the window and Brax moved to the side of the door.

Cody had finally arrived.

"Horseshit fucking transportation in this God for-saken country," was all Cody said before dropping onto the sofa and kicking his feet up.

"I take it from the glum faces, we lost our tar-get?"

"Gave me the slip at the train station."

"Fuck. Anything come out of Ankara?"

"Thesseo set up to shadow then vanished. Last communication to Langley confirmed a courier had arrived. Nothing I could do once I got there. No trace of the courier, the money, or Thesseo."

"You think Leviathan's setting up his next deal?"

"If he is, why Krugerrands?" Brax asked.

"Remy, anything come out of Boston?" Cody asked.

"Bloody well may have. Alabaster had a credit card loaded with information bound for Frankfort."

"Anything useful to us?"

"Don't know yet. Damn stuff was PGP enciphered. The one code we haven't broken yet. Squire's got your people working on it; I've got a bloke in MI6 lending a hand.

"Fifty pounds say our boys break it first," Cody offered with his boyish grin.

"You're on. We've been doing this a lot longer than you yanks."

"Where do we go from here, boss?" Cody said.

"You and Remy remain on station. I need to get back to the States for now. Cali, follow-up on Ankara and see if there's anything we can gain from the sta-tion chief."

Fourteen hours later, Brax deplaned in San Jose, where he fell into Kevin Chambers as easily as if he were changing into an old comfortable sweatshirt. He felt a pressure building as each day passed and the team found themselves groping blindly for information. He could feel Leviathan's clutches tightening around him. They were running out of time, and still they knew little about the who, what, and where of his next terrorist attack.

As the Beemer crested the summit of the Santa Cruz mountains, Brax decided to force business into his subconscious and let it massage the data in hopes of uncovering a revelation that seemed to consistently allude his conscious efforts.

Rather than proceeding directly home, since he knew Suzanne would still be at work for another forty-five minutes, he detoured to the school, checked in at the office, and strolled down the still hall, stopping outside the third grade class. From his vantage point, he watched Suzanne as she leaned over a table, helping one of the children with some kind of craft project. Giggles and chatter came in rapid bursts. It seemed more like play than work.

She is so beautiful, he thought, watching her operate in surroundings so calm and peaceful. Her approving smile brought excited clapping from the delighted student. Small achievements that must seem monumental to an eight year old.

Suzanne was both happy and content with her children. She loved her career and felt no stress in the role she had taken on in life. Despite the clamor of a handful of children surrounding her, Suzanne never once demonstrated anything less than a patient smile.

Would marriage disturb this? How far would Suzanne be willing to go for him? Brax decided he must tell Suzanne the truth before they marry. She should know all the dark sides of his life before stepping into that kind of a union.

When Suzanne returned upright, she turn to catch a glimpse of Kevin out the corner of her eye. At first she sought to ignore his presence, but she had been without him for weeks and she ached to make love. By the time she reached her desk, she felt the excitement stirring inside. It took but a minute for her to surrender self control; she knew she must go to him.

"Miss Masters has a visitor in the hall. Each of you work on your project *quietly*. Can we do that?"

"Yes, Miss Masters," twenty-four children chimed in chorus. Those nearest the door stretched to the limits of their seats, hoping for a glimpse of the mystery guest. One of her students actually left his desk without permission, went over to the glass pane of the door and waved to Kevin.

Kevin waved back, which brought a frown from Suzanne. His action encouraged inappropriate behavior, something Suzanne worked daily to discourage in her classroom.

"Jimmy, please return to your desk. Now everyone be very quiet and no one is allowed out of their seats," Suzanne cautioned in tone absent of the stern demeanor of discipline.

Once outside with the door closed, and having him so near, Suzanne wanted so bad to kiss him; instead, she brushed his cheek with her fingers and moved so close she could indulge herself in his body heat. She wished to wrap her arms under his and work her body against his. None of this, of course, was proper, so she settled for slipping her hand unobtrusively into his.

"When did you get in?"

"Couple hours ago."

"You'll be home when I get there?"

Each time she spoke, Suzanne inched closer. Yielding to a desire raging out of control, she pulled him beyond the window's range, quickly checked both directions in the corridor and kissed him while easing him back against the wall. That one moment had to stay her passion until they could be together.

"God, I missed you," she whispered, withdrawing quickly to make certain no one had witnessed their endearment. Suzanne risked a serious violation of the school's cardinal rules, but Kevin was worth the risk and any possible punishment.

"When can you get home?"

"Give me half an hour. I'll skip the staff meeting, say I'm not feeling well."

Suzanne risked another kiss, realizing from the sudden rumble of chairs and erupting chaos that she must return to the classroom lest pandemonium break out. She could spare no more time to the man she loved so dearly.

🔫

Kevin pulled into the garage then proceeded immediately to his den, where he switched on his computer and entered the command to download secret files from Systech Software Solutions. The files originated out of Langley, having been sent by Squire over the previous twenty-four hours. They contained the latest intelligence funneling in from the field. Brax was anxious for word out of Ankara.

Bits and pieces of disparate intelligence on terrorist activities and unfriendly agents, someone had to sift through it all and uncover who had been slated to die for no reason at all. Somewhere in that mass of movement and clandestine meetings, Leviathan was honing his next attack. Brax had to figure out where and when.

Kevin waited, working his marble through his fingers while sophisticated software deciphered the encrypted messages. What appeared initially as financial reports and product sales projections, once decoded, became a broad picture of known Russian movements and shadowed terrorists throughout Western Europe and the Western Hemisphere.

However, useful information to date had been scant, and for the most part, of little value. No Leviathan sightings had been reported, nor any of his high level officers. Leviathan worked with only a select group, and none so far had surfaced. He also kept security tight, thereby safeguarding his own freedom.

Kevin transmitted an encoded message to Squire requesting updates on anything new regarding Andrew's death. A minute later, Squire acknowledged the message, promising something in the next twenty-four hours.

Next Kevin requested an update on the team's activity in Zurich. Before he could receive a reply, the front door opened and Suzanne called from the foyer.

The lack of relevance in the information already scanned prompted a decision to shut off his computer and let Squire transmit new data when it became available.

Suzanne pushed open the den's door with an outstretched infer, unfurled her hair to allow it to fall to her shoulders and peeled open her blouse. Her milky flesh held Kevin spellbound while she unzipped her skirt. Her prudish classroom visage dropped with her clothing.

Within thirty seconds, they were naked, locked into embrace and making love on the sofa positioned before the great glass wall overlooking the Pacific. From where they lay they viewed the rushing water, though neither had any desire at the moment to watch it.

Kevin forestalled his pleasure for the sake of Suzanne's and still she craved more, refusing to release him once they had both been spent. His kisses, soft and inviting, kept her in want of more.

Kevin's clothes cluttered his desk, while Suzanne's panties hung off a corner of the computer monitor. Her bra obliterated most of the keyboard's keys.

Kevin carried Suzanne from the den to their bed, where their passions continued to glow like hot burning embers until the sun no longer glistened in an untainted ocean-blue sky.

When neither could muster the energy to make love a fourth time, despite a desire for more, they retreated to a pristine white living room, adorned like a giant shell plopped on the sand and welcoming the sea, staring out the windows as the moon glittered off the waters and a gently pounding surf lulled them.

"When should we set the date?" Suzanne asked, interlocking her fingers with his. Her head never strayed far from his still naked body.

For a moment Kevin remained silent. Not a good sign.

"The date?"

"Kevin!"

"Oh, The Date! When do *you* want it to be?"

"August. Can you get time off? It doesn't have to be anything fancy. We could just have our immediate families and your friends." Suzanne began to rattle off all the words bottled up inside during Kevin's absence.

Slowly it began to sink in to Kevin how difficult it would be to get married. The impulse to ask her had neglected to work through all the details that came with acceptance. How could he plan a honeymoon if he had to run off at the least sign of Leviathan's presence? How long would they have together before he might have to dash off to thwart a terrorist plot? How could he possibly keep something like that secret from her?

He suddenly reached over, pulled her into his arms, and kissed her lips with an arresting urgency.

The fireball had returned, sucking the life out of him. Holding Suzanne became his lifeline, his link back to the world of the sane. He clung to her the way a frightened child clings to its mother.

"Would you be upset if I wanted to wait until late in the fall?" he said drawing away from her. He wasn't even sure why he said it. Would a few extra months make a difference? A dark shadow lurking in the corner of his mind taunted him with the notion that he may not survive to make a Fall wedding.

"Oh," was all Suzanne could say, studying beyond his eyes for some hidden meaning in his request. Was there uncertainty there? Was there a need to reconsider?

"Certain deals in motion could make it difficult to give you the time you deserve for a wedding and honeymoon."

"But the Fall would disrupt my class schedule. I don't understand what you mean? Can't you just take a vacation and let some of your subordinates handle the business? You do have subordinates don't you?"

"It's not that simple. Some decisions must come at the moment of opportunity. I'm the only one who can make them."

"How about over the phone...or by fax or something?"

Suzanne checked herself; she was pushing, and she hated to sound like a shrew. She also detected something in Kevin's eyes that cautioned her to back off. It had something to do with that side he kept from her. *Patience.* In time he would confide in her. And they had a lifetime now in which to share.

"I'd like to meet some of your family before the wedding. I don't want to be introduced to them as your new wife. I want them to know me before we're married."

Kevin's hot kisses forced Suzanne to forget all about his family, people she knew nothing about and had never seen even in pictures, and anything else that might have been wandering around inside her head. As he moved between her parting legs, she let everything else but him slip from of her mind.

15

Can you provide status for
subsidiary in Turkey?

Brax

While Kevin slept uneasily, falling into a shallow slumber after Suzanne had fallen asleep beside him, Brax went to work inside his head. So many things raced through his mind that he found it impossible to clear it enough to relax. Krugerrands kept pushing to the forefront. Why Krugerrands? Leviathan had never used gold before. Perhaps the money was meant for some other purpose.

Finally, exhaustion drew Brax into a dreamless sleep. But his subconscious refused to rest. Something buoyed to the surface and refused to subside. Within hours Brax began reliving those minutes in Kano. Andrew's mike had cut out during their check. Why did he allow the meeting to proceed? The right thing was to abort, go back at a later time. Guilt fondled his mind the way an overindulged child needles its submissive mother. Kevin bolted awake when the fireball exploded over the roof tops.

He bolted up in his bed, awake, dripping. He spun chaotically. For that brief moment he had forgotten where and who he was. His breathing came in gasps and his heart thumped in his chest. But this time, Brax refused to bury the horror of that moment. He had to face it squarely. Something swimming below the surface had jolted him awake and for the first time since that day, he forced himself to re-examine the intimate details. Was it therapy, or was there something crucial he had missed?

Brax sat in his bed a long moment, motionless, focusing not on the explosion but rather those minutes preceding it. Andrew had said something. Something about the watch list. No, it was Mandigo who mentioned the watch list. Andrew had instructed him regarding the names to watch for—names linked to Leviathan. Leviathan's real name, Ranzami, surely had not been on the passport list; Andrew would have transmitted that immediately. The very thought sent shivers down Brax's spine.

Why did the watch list keep nagging him?

Brax returned to his mattress and closed his eyes, knowing sleep would remain furthest from his mind. Had Andrew said anything important just before... Piece by piece, Brax forced himself to reassemble the details. Their discussion in transit had been strained. Andrew exuded his usual confidence. Nothing could go wrong.

I know how to handle these Africans, he had said. Then he joked during the mike check. Once inside, Andrew insisted Mandigo's list was incomplete.

Could their earlier intelligence have been wrong? Maybe the Libyan passports were a red herring.

No, Squire confirmed information through a source close to a high ranking member of the Jihad. A list existed in the minister's safe of those who had received the passports.

"The watch list," Brax said aloud. Then it struck him. Mandigo had started a name when the microphone cut out. The first syllable was floating out there. Brax ransacked his memory with a ferocious fervor. What had he heard?

So much floated to the surface. Andrew's words. What Mandigo had fired off in anger. It was all about trust. Mandigo felt betrayed. Wait. He said he memorized the watch list just as Andrew had instructed. The name on the list was....

Brax's recollection ended as if someone had lopped off his memory. He closed his eyes. In sleep, he feared the fireball would return. In sleep, he hoped his subconscious might extract the name that Mandigo had started. A name that might be vital to finding Leviathan.

Brax washed the anger from his mind. Anger only destroys. Sleep finally overtook him.

Brax awoke to the dim glow of a predawn sun. He checked his watch.

Five A.M. He had been allowed only three hours sleep.

"Lon..." he vaulted as if the syllable were an involuntary eruption. Brax rolled out of bed and grabbed his unsecured phone without dressing.

"Squire, search everything out there for a terrorist whose name begins with Lon. If you find something, look for any kind of link to Leviathan."

A new exhilaration filled Brax. Andrew's death had *not* been in vain if that one syllable could be linked to a terrorist. A terrorist that traced back to their hard target. Brax felt a watershed of guilt leave his body. He had reconciled in himself that something had come out of that botched meeting.

Within hours, Squire returned with information. One was Malacky Lonigan, an IRA lieutenant with a file in the British Intelligence's MI5 computer for suspected terrorist involvement in Austria in 1991. The second, one Glaston Lonahan, seemed to be a new arrival to the IRA. Bits and pieces had been compiled on him, though nothing linked him directly to terrorist activities at the present.

"I think Lonahan is too new to the underground to be trusted. My money's on this Lonigan. He's definitely got the temperament for killing," Squire reported.

Suzanne had gone off to school allowing Brax to concentrate fully on their latest revelation. Squire was in the process of gathering both men's complete profiles. Lonigan's name did end up on the watch list because he had been reported in Amsterdam near where a Leviathan sighting had been reported eighteen months earlier. What appeared most suspicious was Squire's follow-up that Lonigan literally disappeared off the face of the earth after that sighting. Despite MI6's best efforts, no one had gotten a glimpse of the man since.

The British agent who submitted the original MI5 report had included names of all persons coming into close proximity with the man Ranzami contacted in Amsterdam. The team always ruled out coincidence.

Now the only question remaining was: Did Mandigo say Lonigan at that meeting? Brax tasked Squire with running an analysis on the same databases for any and all vocal derivations of the Bra sound.

Before signing off at his computer, Brax instructed Squire to put out a broadcast to all agencies worldwide for assistance in locating Lonigan. Included in the message were to be instructions that under no circumstance apprehend or acknowledge interest.

Squire also sent a security flash to border patrols in states bordering Mexico to be alert for Lonigan's illegal entry into the U.S. The Libyan passport would get him safely onto the North American continent. He would need additional help infiltrating the U.S.

16

Any test results to report from Dr.
Delano?

                    Cali

Three days of sitting in a Geneva safe house put
the team on edge. They had become restless from the
inactivity, snapping at each over small inconve-
niences, while Remy continued to batter himself over
the loss of Chevanovich.

They spurned those insidious urges to place
blame. Shit happens. Humans are fallible. People die.
Remy shouldered the responsibility for his country-
men. That's life in their world.

Cody began to question the wisdom of bottling
the team up out of sight. Twice he sent messages to
Brax requesting permission to disperse onto the
Geneva streets in the hopes of making something
happen. Chevanovich could be long gone, or he could
be shopping the Boulevard. They would never know if
they remained holed up. But Brax had to weigh the
risks of exposing their faces prematurely. If they had
been marked, Leviathan's men could be waiting to
take them down one at a time or en masse.

Tension drained like a watershed when Remy
decoded Squire's latest message. Dakarov, a procurer
for a small faction of Black September in Switzerland
had been spotted emerging from a hotel lobby in the
downtown streets of Geneva.

Cody and Cali jumped on it. They acquired the target within three hours, using a local in a delivery ruse to confirm they had indeed locked on the right target. Using a system of alternating surveillance, where one dropped off to allow the other to fall in, they tracked Dakarov from his room to various innocuous stops throughout the afternoon. At no time did Dakarov appear to be moving with pattern or purpose. Instead, he browsed, he lunched on a terrace overlooking downtown Geneva, and he idled away time reading the local newspaper. He met no one, talked to no one and delivered no clandestine signals to indicate he was there for a meeting.

Cody reported hourly to Remy, who relayed the status to Brax, who was en route and scheduled to arrive in three hours. Each time, Remy attempted to link Dakarov's movement with some location in Geneva where he might anticipate a rendezvous with Chevanovich. But as the sun began to drift out of the sky, Dakarov's movements took on direction and purpose. He became intensely aware of his surroundings and performed a Russian-trained zigzag pattern designed to expose surveillance.

Twice Cali had to break off, slipping out of sight at the last moment to prevent detection. Each time she feared she had been too late.

If Dakarov detected their shadow, he would immediately abandon his unorthodox movements and proceed away from any prearranged contact point. And since it appeared he still ran his evasive maneuvers, Cali believed they were at the moment secure.

An hour later, Cali and Cody observed Dakarov strolling into a somber open-air drug market in a park nestled between the Rue De Lausanne on the west and Lake Geneva on the east, isolated from the main shopping district. Needle Park, the locals called it. He progressed from junkie to junkie in a friendly fashion, conversing casually with the druggies that lingered in the hopes of making a score. Dakarov seemed to take an intense interest in these Forgotten Ones, in this place where only dealers and addicts could feel safe. These discarded youth of the nineties rebelled against everyone and everything. Known as trash cans in the drug subculture because they were indiscriminately strung out on heroin, cocaine or any other substance they could swallow, smoke or inject. Here their actions, though illegal, were ignored by authorities. If these foolish youth harbored a death wish, then why should government expend precious dollars attempting to prevent it?

Again Dakarov gravitated to a cluster of trash cans and struck up a conversation. Cody and Cali were much too distant to overhear, and try as she might, Cali failed to read Dakarov's lips. He passed something from his pocket to their hands, doling out whatever it was the way a paymaster hands out money. It might have been drugs, but Cali couldn't confirm it from her location. Yet if it were drugs, no money came back from the recipients.

Regularly now Dakarov glanced over his shoulder. He scanned the faces in the park. He appeared more agitated—insecure. When he left that cluster of six, he stopped to talk to no one else. He continued from that point on oblivious to the others.

Thirty meters further into this place, he stopped in woody hollow with a paved road winding through it. Standing with his back to the wind, and also to Cody and Cali, he lit his cigarette and sucked in hard. He seemed to be waiting.

"Something's going to happen," Cody reported over his button mike to Brax and Remy, who sat waiting in a white Mercedes safely out of sight three streets from the park's north entrance. The moment Brax had arrived they deployed to back up Cody and Cali.

Cody played down the rush in his veins. He signaled Cali, who altered her position to keep a closer eye on the road leading into the hollow.

Over the next twenty minutes, with the sun almost completely gone and darkness crowding in over the grounds, one by one, those who Dakarov had spoken with earlier began to collect.

Cody remained sheltered behind the bole of a majestic oak, where he transmitted an update to Brax. Something was beginning to happen.

"We're moving closer. Cali be ready to move on my command," Brax said.

Dakarov said little. He acknowledged those who joined him with a welcoming nod and a relaxed reassuring smile. The variegated gathering of a dozen seemed agitated, expectant. A few of the youths spoke to Dakarov more than once while they waited. In the dim light, the glow of cigarettes marked their location.

When it seemed the gathering was fully assembled, and no one appeared to be forthcoming, Dakarov placed a call from a cell phone that lasted so briefly that only a few words could have possibly been transmitted.

"Brax, something's happening," Cody reported. A double click in his ear piece acknowledged his transmission. Cali signaled Cody with a slight wave that she would begin moving back toward him.

"I've got a blue, unmarked windowed van moving into the park," Cali whispered into her button mike after placing her back to the group. She positioned herself less than twenty meters from the gathering, using the cover of near darkness to cloak her presence. She was so close she could discern Dakarov's eyes move immediately to the vehicle.

"It's for the target and his people."

"We're moving now. Two minutes away," Remy transmitted over the air waves.

"Van's stopping," Cali reported from her vantage point in the trees.

"Cali, pull back to rendezvous for pick up. We're coming in via the north entrance."

Cali held her position long enough to observe the young people pile in one after another. Then she slowly and unobtrusively backed out of the hollow. Every seat got used. Smaller women sat on laps to fit. The last few knelt just inside the sliding door.

"He's hauling a full load," Cody reported.

"Is Dakarov getting in?"

"Not yet. Negative. He's closing the door. What do you want me to do? What a minute. He's taking the wheel now. Driver's leaving on foot."

"We're one street from where the van went in. We'll pick you up the moment we're clear," Remy said.

The moment the van departed the hollow in the trees, Brax and Remy pulled in. A running Cali and Cody jumped into the back seats as the Mercedes sped away to regain the ground it had to give up to the van. The team kept their distance as the van left the streets of Geneva and fell into the darkened roads of rural Switzerland heading north on Route 1 in the direction of Rolle.

"I counted a dozen in the van beside Dakarov," Cody said as all four maintained constant sight of the van's tail lights.

At irregular intervals, Brax doused his headlights and allowed the van to gain distance on them. He hoped Dakarov would think the car behind them had turned off and after a while another had come up behind him.

The desolate countryside remained a blanket of darkness, save for the occasional rectangles of farmhouse lights near enough to the road to be seen. After twenty minutes, it seemed the van might be traveling without destination.

But then the van slowed, taking the turn off for St-Cergue. The new road snaked into the pitch of rolling hills, forcing Brax to alternate his speed almost constantly to maintain their surveillance without raising suspicion. Within thirty minutes of traveling the route, Remy pointed out lights flickering through the trees from an isolated warehouse at the end of a long descending road leading away from the highway. The van took up the rutted path without showing its brake lights.

"I think we've just made their destination."

Ranzami listened with the stoic silence of an indulging son as Chevanovich explained the myriad of technical details behind what he had planned. Ranzami cared little for the details. He trusted the good doctor. He wanted to view the results. Details were for smaller men.

"Using your specifications, I carefully calculated the dispersal rate to maintain a near constant one hundred ten parts per million concentration throughout the duration of the expulsion. You understand that it is only the combination of the gases I have chosen that provides the exact results you seek."

Ranzami nodded acceptance, more interested in proceeding with the demonstration than taking in the spew of technical jargon Chevanovich served up. He cast his eyes toward the monitors situated on a control station before them. Yet he could see by the glint in Chevanovich's eyes that the doctor took great relish in his latest accomplishment.

"Based on volume and population you indicated, I have planned this demonstration on the same scale. The monitor on your left displays exactly how my inhalants are delivered. The trigger is based on the data you've provided.

"How much longer?" Ranzami asked with an edge of tiring patience in his voice. He checked his watch.

"Few more minutes. I must make one more calibration to make certain our flow rate is correct."

On a monitor at the right side of a central console, Chevanovich and Ranzami watched headlights approach. A blue van stopped at the prearranged door under the glow of a amber overhead light, and one by one, people unloaded. They gathered in a huddled mass near the door, with only one taking notice of the security camera capturing the nervous flutter. A faceless man in black emerged from the warehouse door to wave them in, barking orders with a military cadence that the kids seemed to understand and comply with.

In the lamp light, Dakarov's face became distinct. He smiled with smug assurance as he looked into the surveillance camera.

All was proceeding as planned.

Dakarov shifted nervously, scanning the woody groves behind him that swallowed up the road, while he waited for the last of the gathering to stretch their legs. All except Dakarov had now left the chill night air for the relative warmth of the warehouse interior. Then Dakarov waved to the camera and slid into the front passenger seat. The faceless man, who had exited the warehouse on their arrival, closed the warehouse door and took over the driver's seat. The van pulled quickly away into the night.

Ranzami and Chevanovich watched their monitors from their concealed perch as the twelve youths filed into a lavishly furnished reception room measuring thirty meters square. On one side of the room, a table dressed crisply in white damask linen and laden with cheeses, fruit, crackers and sliced meats, along with a dozen open bottles of wine welcomed their guests. It took only a moment for the visitors to find their way to the refreshments. Most appeared emaciated under the bright light, and they grabbed the food as if they had not see any for days.

While they coagulated around the table, a silent electromagnetic lock bolted the door. Designed to withstand the bludgeoning of a ten kilogram sledge hammer, the door could now only be released from the control room where Ranzami and Chevanovich stood.

"Our number corresponds in scale to the number you specified," Chevanovich said with an even, unaffected voice. The hint of a smile broke on the corners of the doctor's lips. His moment had arrived. After six tedious months of planning and experimentation, he was about to leave an indelible mark on the world. Black though it may be, it would be unequivocally Chevanovich's mark.

For a moment Ranzami and the doctor listened. The young people dispersed from the table fragmenting into smaller knots more evenly distributed in the chamber.

"That is good," the doctor commented, motioning on the screen to the way they had evenly distributed about the room.

But their guests grew quickly restless. A few asked about, inquiring as to what was expected in order to earn the promised offering. Shrugs came in reply.

One became suspicious, and as Ranzami watched, he meandered over to the door, where he gave it a slight tug. However, he kept his findings secret and began searching along the ceiling seam. Ranzami could see his face go from pleasant to concerned to frightened. This one now wormed through the others to reach the wall opposite the door and the concealed camera.

"When do we get our fucking stuff," he said looking directly into the lens. This one exceeded expectations. He proved superior to the others still munching the cheese and quaffing down the wine. A pity for him. Then he swept his eyes across the room in search of the man who had brought them here.

"He's not in here with us," that one said just above a whisper.

He sought the safety of others huddled in a corner and engorging themselves with food from plates.

"Please, my friends, indulge yourselves. There has been only a slight delay. In a few moments one of our proctors will lead you all to the testing center," Chevanovich said over the intercom.

All heads titled upward to stare at the speakers in the ceiling.

"When do we get the fucking stuff we came for?" someone said.

"What fucking testing center? What kind of test is this?" another suspicious one asked, moving without alarming the others toward the door.

"In just a minute on your watches," Chevanovich replied. "Let me assure you that you will receive everything we promised. You need only complete a simple test."

Chevanovich switched the intercom off to return his attention to the center three screens on his console. They afforded those in the control booth with a complete view of every participant in the room.

"Open the intake ducts," Chevanovich ordered an assistant clad in a camouflaged jumpsuit. "I'll need another minute more," the doctor continued as he zeroed a large clock above the center screen. The hands snapped back to the twelve o'clock position and waited.

🔫

"What in bloody hell do we do now?" Remy asked. They watched as the van pulled back onto the highway with Dakarov in the passenger seat.

"Hundred pounds says Dr. Doom's in that warehouse," Cody said.

"A bloody suckers bet that is," Remy replied without taking his eyes off the van's shrinking tail lights.

"I take it that's a no, then?"

"Whatever's going on inside that warehouse, Dakarov's completed his job for now."

Without any lights, the Mercedes crept along the rutted dirt path to get as close to the building as possible before having to resort to foot travel. The warehouse lights flickered as trees swayed back and forth.

"If Dr. Doom's really in there, those people won't be coming out," Cali muttered more to herself than the others.

Stopped in a densely packed grove of oak and spruce that ended twenty meters from the edifice, Cody and Cali checked their Desert Eagles in the back seat, while Remy went to the trunk to withdraw the Uzis and a dozen extra clips. After paying them out to each, he made certain his own weapon contained a full magazine. For a time they stood outside the car, watching and waiting.

"We could risk a compromise, if we go in and we're wrong," Remy cautioned. He stared for a moment at the two-story outline, formulating what might be their best chance for breaching the building.

Brax said nothing.

"I say we blaze the place. This isn't rocket science. We've got a confirmed sighting on Chevanovich, and now a scumbag terrorist wannabe delivers a dozen bodies to an isolated warehouse. Something's going down, and I'll bet our hard target's involved."

As Cody spoke he handed over a pair of night vision goggles to Remy. After a careful scan along the building's perimeter, Remy swung upward toward the top row of windows.

"I've got one with a submachine gun over on the left standing sentry, and another gazing out the second floor window, there."

"Bingo! I'm telling you our bastard's inside. I'll go two hundred pounds."

"What do you want to do, Brax?" Remy asked.

Brax returned to the trunk, where he removed black ski masks, Russian Makarov PMs and Russian Stechkin machine pistols.

"Dump your arms in here. We cover up. Both going in and coming out. If those people are at risk, we free them and disappear. If our hard target's in there, he and all his kin never leave the building. Any questions?"

Remy glanced over toward Cali. It was an instinctive response, that he realized afterward sent a message of ill concern over her.

The Uzis and Desert Eagles remained behind in the trunk. If any of the Pack went down inside and had to be abandoned, the Russian armament would keep the authorities guessing, at least for awhile.

"If Ranzami's in there, he's got an escape plan contingent upon our advance," Remy said.

"Great, now we've got to discuss this in committee. Did you want me to phone the place to ask if he's in there?"

Cody grew restless. Inaction only ground away at them. But Brax had to weigh the risks. The innocents inside were secondary to their hard target.

"Let's just nail the scum fuck before he can escape."

Cody wanted to move, to get the operation going. The anticipation of a fire fight gnawed away at all their nerves. He could see in Cali's eyes that she was struggling to maintain her steel face.

"We approach from the side away from where the van stopped. We can use those windows. That thicket should conceal us until we're upon them."

"I'd rather we reconnoitered the backside before we breach," Remy offered. "Could be Leviathan's anticipating us and has more in there than we can oppose."

"You always have to pull logic into this, don't you? Can't you Brits just once go on your gut?" Cody remarked.

"My gut's saying there's more in there than we think. Leviathan wouldn't hesitate to kill those people for a shot at eliminating every one of us."

"I say we go in the way Brax suggested and locate Leviathan or Chevanovich or whoever has reason to take a dozen street loungers into that warehouse."

It was time for Brax to make the command decision. There could be no more discussion.

"We go in together. Remy, once inside, assess their egress possibilities and work to shut them down. Cody, you and I go right for the core. They'll be under lights until the firing starts, so we gravitate toward the light and hope we've gotten lucky."

"And me?" Cali asked, feeling as if she had for some reason been intentionally slighted. There was no mistaking the fear overrunning her eyes.

"You cover all our asses and make damn sure we can get the hell out of there alive."

Cody scrutinized Cali before they started out on foot. She was the new kid, the unknown variable in this. Could she handle a fire fight? He stayed within two paces of her during the trek. They paused to reassess as the first flickers of the light over the side entrance broke through the trees.

"Can you handle this?" Cody asked, seizing Cali's arm.

Cali hesitated, but only for a moment.

"We need to know that you've got our backs."

Cali flicked the Stechkin's safety to the top position. Full automatic. She tightened her other hand around her supply of magazines.

"You make sure you take out the target. I'll make sure there's a safe corridor out of that building."

If there were any way Cody could think of to keep her out of the fight, he would have used it now. Something sent a wave of nausea into the pit of his stomach. That same nebulous feeling set the hair on his neck on end, but he failed to pin down exactly what had brought it on.

Brax motioned for Remy to take the point and guide them through the lightless woody maze to the warehouse. Ahead blocks of window light flickered through the trees like beacons.

No one spoke. Every one of them hoped they had stumbled on to something big, something that involved their hard target.

Ranzami edged closer to the screens as Chevanovich flipped the guarded switch on his console. With a leveled finger, he directed Ranzami's eyes to the left screen, which showed two aluminum canister's about twice the diameter of a thumb mounted on a metal framework. Attached to a framework an electronic circuit board lit up with red and green lights. It also contained a pair of firing pins. Wires snaked from a connector on the circuit board, disappearing off the screen to the right.

As the green light illuminated, the two firing pins stabbed into valves mounted on the canisters. Smoke drifted slowly out of the canisters, filling the duct.

"Green indicates detonation. We're simulating the blowers, since we're unable to know for certain the cubic feet per minute moving through the duct at the actual time of detonation."

"Fine," Ranzami responded. His eyes remained fixed on the thick fumes crowding the duct until the canisters and the frame became hidden behind the cloud. Only the faint glow of the green light remained visible on their monitor.

Chevanovich slapped down a second switch.

Rushing air swept the vapor cloud away in an instant. Both men shifted their intensity to the three monitors locked on the dozen occupants in the reception room.

"Notice disbursement is completely beyond detection," Chevanovich said with a smile of great accomplishment.

For what seemed an unending moment, the crowd appeared perfectly at ease, even jovial, indulging in banter amongst themselves, chugging goblets of wine in a kind of competition. After all, they need only participate in a simple test to receive in exchange for their participation many weeks worth of heroin or cocaine, whichever they might choose.

In the control booth, safely isolated from the experiment, a heavily armed attendant stole Ranzami's attention with a harsh, insistent whisper and a hand to the forearm.

"General, four advance from the forest."

"How much time?" Ranzami asked without flinching. His men had prepared for every possibility, even this one.

"We can delay them maybe three minutes," the attendant said.

Ranzami looked to Chevanovich.

"Sufficient. Look," Chevanovich said. A almost childlike quality took over his face.

The moment distracted Ranzami. He turned to his guard. "Allow them to breach. Alert the helicopter. We will need sufficient time to egress."

Ranzami returned his attention to the screens. He wore no smile, no signs of elation, only the face of a man deeply involved in a business transaction.

A slight sickly twentyish woman, no taller than five foot suddenly lurched from her seat. She retched the whole of her stomach in a long projectile stream. A moment later, she toppled into her own mess.

The laughing and jocularity ceased in an instant.

Screams erupted. Screams so blood curdling they would stop even the coldest heart.

Two more vomited violently. They clawed at their throats while blood erupted from within. While another heaved, those remaining victims barged their way for the door, where they pounded with the force of sheer terror.

Ranzami and Chevanovich patiently listened to their outbursts of rage and vulgarity, only to be replaced in a moment with screams of utter panic. Chevanovich switched off the intercom and checked the number on the clock.

"One minute forty-two seconds," he announced with an exaltation. He had achieved his objective. Goose flesh rose upon his arms as the last of the dozen victims fell lifeless to the floor.

"General, it is time," his soldier cautioned.

"I trust you approve?" Chevanovich asked now with no trace of a smile on his face.

"I do."

"They're here, General," a guard injected from the control room door. While he checked his Uzi, the other soldiers who had been silent in the rear of the control booth joined his side.

Chevanovich calmly removed an aluminum briefcase from a locked cabinet beneath the console monitors, opened it on the console and turned it so Ranzami could inspect the contents. Inside gray foam enveloped two polished steel canisters the diameter of a fist and the length of a hand.

"The correct pressure and dosage for your specifications. You can expect the same results within three minutes of dispersion."

Ranzami handed the doctor a weighty black satchel that one of his soldiers had held in the background until this moment. Their bargain had been consummated. Ranzami got what he ordered and Chevanovich received the amount he had requested.

"Do we engage?" the soldier asked.

Ranzami withdrew his Russian Makarov and blasted the monitor displaying the device in the ductwork. He, along with Chevanovich and two armed guards, evacuated the control booth through a rear door. The first shots rang out as Ranzami slipped away down the rear stairs of the warehouse.

Before leaving, Chevanovich armed the clock on the center monitor, resetting it to three minutes. It began counting down one second at a time.

Brax breached the window first. Cody kicked in a second window and dove through a second later. Three simultaneous bursts of staccato gunfire sent the team scrambling.

Cali dove through the window in Cody's wake, rolled into a tight ball until she came up beside Brax, who was on one knee returning fire at the flashes of saffron light emanating from an open staircase across the warehouse floor.

Cody sprayed the base of the staircase, emptying a full 30-round magazine in a three second burst at a shooter wedged behind a row of chest high crates.

Remy somersaulted through the window last after first eliminating the sentry, who had rounded the corner spraying Uzi fire. Remy's precise shot to the forehead guaranteed a kill even if the man had been wearing Kevlar.

A second barrage of gunfire from the crates sprayed harmlessly over the heads of the team as they scattered to penetrate deeper into the building.

Brax pounded out a dozen rounds at the staircase forcing the shooter to retreat. When he stopped he scanned for his team. They were moving toward the stairs. But the return fire had completely stopped.

Brax motioned Cali closer to him and signaled for Remy and Cody to advance to the staircase. They darted a dozen paces and waited. No fire rained down from the top of the stairs. They advanced and waited.

Silence.

The team continued to hold their positions for a matter of seconds, and when no fire came, all simultaneously rose and sent a fusillade of bullets into the area of the crates adjacent to the stairs.

The lack of return fire hoisted a warning flag. Slowly the team penetrated deeper into the warehouse with Cody moving along the outside of an enclosed windowless chamber positioned at the warehouse's southern wall. It resembled a giant freezer complete with two sheet metal ducts entering from the top. Yet there appeared no entrance door.

"Nothing left," Cody transmitted.

"Clear right," Remy transmitted to the team.

Brax signaled to close in, and they moved cautiously up the steel stairs to a loft above the warehouse floor. Brax kicked the door open while Cody sent a burst of Stechkin fire into the control booth.

Nothing inside moved.

Brax led the team in and froze, staring at the three monitors on the console. Only one remained intact and functioning. But it displayed more than enough. A dozen squalid bodies populated the screen in a larger-than-life fashion, most with faces frozen in a gaping rictus and blood filled eyes bulging from their heads. The gruesome horror mesmerized them. No one on the team moved.

"What the fuck happened to them?" Cody muttered, unable to draw his eyes from the screen.

"Brax, they let us in here," Remy said, suddenly alarmed. "They abandoned the fight."

The *whomp* of helicopter blades knifed through the eerie silence, snaring the team's attention.

"They're moving out," Cody said.

"They wanted us to see this," Cali commented.

"Why?" Brax asked the room.

Cali leveled her gun barrel at the clock counting down. Even before she could speak, Brax analyzed the indication and deduced its meaning.

Thirty-three...
"Those poor people never had a chance."
Thirty-two...
"Everyone out, NOW!" Brax commanded.
Thirty...
As the last one to leave the control room, Brax glanced back at the clock readout.
Twenty-six...
The team jumped over the cast iron banister, free falling the fourteen feet to the floor in order to preserve precious moments otherwise expended pounding down the stairs. Remy landed poorly, wrenching his right ankle and struggling to regain his feet. Cali's hand went down in instinct to pull him up and forward. They raced across the warehouse expanse, Cali under one of Remy's arms, while Cody shouldered the other. Brax held back a few paces to cover their backs until the team could escape out the windows.

The first percussion from inside bellowed as Brax came somersaulting onto the ground. He rolled back to his feet, spraying gunfire skyward while the team dashed clear of the building. Cody and Cali raked the trees with gunfire just in case a shooter had remained behind to ambush them.

The explosives inside the warehouse had been concentrated in two areas. Most of the C4 had been placed on the ceiling of the reception room, where the bodies were located, the second concentration having been placed in the control booth.

The first explosion rocked the building, blew out every window in the structure and sent a mushrooming fireball out every orifice. It also eradicated every scrap of evidence of Chevanovich's work. The searing flames ensured no examinations could be performed on the victims to ascertain cause of death. Without cause of death, no one would know how those twelve had died, and likewise, could have no way of uncovering Ranzami's plan. Only three people knew.

The second explosion sent debris in a spout over-head. Corrugated sheet metal and century-old timber rained down upon the team as they egressed. It also eliminated every piece of equipment Chevanovich had used to prepare and perform his deadly demon-stration for Ranzami. Even the most talented investi-gator would find it impossible to piece together what had been used in that warehouse.

As the helicopter reared skyward, rolling safely to the west, diametrically opposed to the warehouse, Ranzami watched the building transform into a bril-liant orange ball of flames.

"That should eliminate Wolf Pack," he said with a smile to Chevanovich, who sat beside him watching the night sky return to black as they left the flaming building behind.

Below gunfire popped like firecrackers. The action forced the helicopter to climb too quickly.

"Keep firing," Brax commanded. "Force them high enough for radar to paint them."

Cody and Cali continued to spray bullets into the night sky while Remy, propped against the car for support, covered the surrounding woods. They relented until all their magazines had been spent.

In a moment, Brax had Squire on his secure phone.

"Tap into Geneva air route traffic radar and get a vector direction on a helicopter climbing out thirty to forty kilometers north/northwest of the city. We need to know where that bastard's heading."

"He was in there," Remy muttered while he fired, "Leviathan was in there."

With the Soviet Union we seek peaceful understandings that can lessen the danger to freedom.

Last fall I asked the American people to choose that course. I will carry forward their command.

If we are to live together in peace, we must come to know each other better.

I am sure the American people would welcome a chance to listen to the Soviet leaders on our television--as I would like the Soviet people to hear our leaders.

I hope the new Soviet leaders can visit America so they can learn about this country at firsthand.

In Eastern Europe restless nations are slowly beginning to assert their identity. Your Government, assisted by leaders in labor and business, is exploring ways to increase peaceful trade with these countries and the Soviet Union. I will report our conclusions to the Congress.

...These moves have not ended the aggression, but they have prevented its success. The aims of the enemy have been put out of reach by the skill and bravery of Americans and their allies, and by the enduring courage of the South Vietnamese who, I can tell you, lost eight men last year to every one of ours.

Lyndon B. Johnson, January 12, 1966

17

Jacques Pierre opening the window
from the fourth

Squire

Sleep eluded Brax. He lay in his bed back in the Geneva safe house staring at the ceiling. Cody and Remy remained awake at the table reviewing Squire's latest intelligence. No one had spoken on the drive back from the warehouse. Was Leviathan in there? The pack had cleared the area cleanly well ahead of any emergency vehicles being called to the scene. Most likely an explosion in such an isolated area would burn itself out long before sufficient firefighting equipment arrived to extinguish it. That meant all evidence of the carnage they had witnessed would also be lost. The team had to relinquish all interest in the event and rely on Squire's intelligence gathering to provide them with information the locals would collect from the charred remains.

The faces of the dead haunted Brax. Chevanovich had to have masterminded the mass murder. It was far too coincidental that Chevanovich travel to Geneva and now a dozen young people die. The explosion certainly covered their tracks.

Brax switched his mind off when a soft rap came at his door.

"Boss, a communiqué from Squire. He alerted the French Counterterrorist Authority after analyzing the radar data from the Geneva Air Traffic control. The helicopter crossed into French airspace within an hour of taking off, then it dropped out of sight. What do we do now?"

"Squire get a vector reading on their direction?"

"A vector direct for Paris."

"He needs underground support to escape the country. Paris is the hub for France's terrorist network. If Chevanovich wants to get anywhere, he's got to go through Paris. People there can make sure the good doctor remains under wraps until they could move him out of the country. They've got safe houses, transportation and heavy artillery."

"So we move on it?"

"Pack it up. You and Remy head for Paris. Cali and I will hold back here just in case our good doctor doubles back via ground transport to Geneva. Let's hope someone spots that bastard before he can get underground."

Chevanovich arrived by train into a bustling mid-day Paris, where he collected up his bags from the porter and wormed his way through the crowded Gare de Lyon station to the street. Railway was the preferred passage, since crowded stations increased the difficulty for FCA agents to make identifications. Never once did he allow the black satchel he carried to leave his side. His French was so rusty he feared using it might arouse suspicion. His English was better, but decidedly European trained, and he worried using it might attract undue attention to himself. He could never pass for an American if he had to converse for any length of time with the locals. The French distaste for English and Americans made faces easier to recall when they came from behind the American language. He knew to avoid his native tongue at all costs.

As a result, he spoke only when absolutely necessary, stumbled behind butchered French and frac-
tured English, which brought smug replies from the
natives, and as much as possible he avoided contact
with anyone crossing his path. He hid the inevitable
confusion and uncertainty in his eyes while he waited
outside the station, but he must have failed, since a
roving policeman asked if he required assistance.

"My driver has become thirty minutes tardy,"
Chevanovich said to the authority. He checked his
watch with the regularity of a nervous tick.

The policeman offered an empty smile.

"Good morning, Doctor," a bearded face offered.
The man made his approach the moment the policeman had moved on as if he had been lingering in the
background. His hand went immediately for the bags,
though Chevanovich had mistaken the gesture for a
greeting and shifted his satchel clumsily between
hands to offer his right.

"My car delays traffic," he said in English laden
with the desire for French.

Chevanovich offered a slight smile in forgiveness.
He was far too important to be exposed the way this
imbecile had left him. The doctor expelled his relief,
dabbed the sweat from his face with his handkerchief, all the while tightening his grip on his black
satchel.

The driver led him through the crowd with the
adeptness of a rugby player and loaded one bag into
the trunk while fending off jeers and verbal assaults
from other motorists angered by his lack of consideration.

"Arrangements have been made," the driver said
in a strained mix of French and English.

"You will be handling my return?"

"I am only the driver, Doctor. I do as I am told."

Within the safe confines of the Peugeot, Chevanovich siphoned off the pressure churning within.
He knew the French authorities maintained a com-

plete dossier on him. The British would wet their knickers if they could get their hands on him. Chevanovich fully understood the risks of traveling outside the eastern bloc. But what he held in his black satchel made the risks more than worthwhile.

He tightened his withered fingers around the black leather. All he could think about was the contents and what he could do with it.

"I must make the alternative plan now. It is not good that a policeman spoke to you."

"Why did you force me to stand?"

"Traffic," was all the driver offered.

Chevanovich wished to use his native tongue, wanted to know when he would be home, how the transportation had been arranged, and how long he would have to wait. Waiting kept him on edge. He hoped his time in Paris would be measured in hours rather than days. In his youth he would have relished a trip to Paris. Now all he wanted was to go home.

As they drove in what seemed an aimless route through the clogged Champs Elysees of Paris, the driver checked his mirrors like a bad habit. He circled Notre Dame three times on the quai de Bercy before continuing on. Once comfortable with the traffic in their wake, he doubled back using the Peripherique to pick up the rue de Vaugirard and returned to the Champs Elysees.

"No one took an interest in you at the station, did they, Doctor?" the man asked after a long period of staring into the mirror.

"No. When will I leave Paris?"

The driver offered no answer.

As they reached the end of Ave de Clichy, the driver turned into a narrow cross street and stopped.

"We must alter our plan again. You are certain no one monitored your passage on the train?"

Chevanovich shrugged answer. A knot tightened inside making breathing difficult. He turned to look out the back window.

"Do not show your face, Doctor," the driver scolded. He had noticed that another police car had fallen in behind and followed for the last ten minutes.

The driver worked his way back into the traffic clogs with patience, all the time watching a white sedan now insistent on keeping pace with him. He saw his opportunity ahead. A truck had just started its right turn onto the tight confines of a street reserved for deliveries.

"Grip something," the driver warned. He whipped the car onto the walkway and blared his horn to scatter pedestrians out of the way. In a few seconds, he swerved around the truck and watched his rear view mirror.

"Is good. We safe for now. But it is wiser if I turn you over to another. When I stop the car, you must exit and proceed directly to Napoleon's tomb. There another will pick you up."

Chevanovich knew better than to question the driver's judgment. Ranzami had assure Chevanovich that his return to St. Petersburg would be arranged in a manner befitting one of the good doctor's stature. All caution would be observed to prevent Chevanovich from falling into the authorities' hands.

The driver roared through street after street until he came to the Invalides, a vaulted stone building at the end of a boulevard. As soon as he stopped, Chevanovich threw open the door, and clutching satchel with both hands, marched away at a determined pace, blending in with the crowd entering the arched doors at the apex of a dozen stairs.

In moments the Peugeot disappeared.

Remy and Cody watched from a distance as the Peugeot screeched to a halt at the side of the boulevard. As they expected, Chevanovich fled the vehicle for the safety of the crowd entering Napoleon's tomb.

"You are too good. How'd you know?" Cody said.

"Believe it or not, they pulled this same stunt two years ago. One drops the target off at the tomb and another takes him out the other way. Trick is you've got to keep your eye on the target or the crowd will swallow him up."

As soon as the Peugeot pulled away, Remy roared to a screeching stop at the front entrance where moments before Chevanovich disappeared.

"Go get him, Cowboy," Remy said with a thumbs up. The moment Cody departed Remy winced from the pain lingering in his ankle.

Cody followed the path Chevanovich had taken a few moments earlier, working his way patiently through clogs of tourists funneling into the vaulted entry hall.

Once inside it took Cody a few minutes to locate the doctor and fall in a safe distance behind.

Chevanovich ensconced himself within the group as they meandered down the great hall. He paused when they paused, resumed when they resumed. When the gathering came upon the tomb of Napoleon, the good doctor eased his way to the rear of the crowd.

It was there that Chevanovich let slip his intentions. After a short time, minutes on the watch, the others began to drift on, but Chevanovich remained, appearing as if he waited to be approached.

Cody had to back out of the hall, yet still maintain a vantage point over his target. However, his wait lasted less than a minute. A tawny-skinned, barrel-shaped man with scraggly black goatee and closely-trimmed hair thinned to a widow's peak approached Chevanovich. Cody watched as they spoke. His lip reading skills weak, he succeeded in collecting only fragments of the conversation, which he determined took place in English.

"I must get you off the streets. There is a safe place nearby where we may sleep for the night," the man told Chevanovich.

Chevanovich nodded, but there was no smile on the doctor's face. No sign of relief that someone had been there to meet him like he had been told. Suddenly he felt at risk. Vulnerable in this place.

"Then I go home?"

"No," the man said sharply as if irritated by Chevanovich's question. "I must deliver you to another house where you will remain safe until I receive new instructions."

"Why? You are to see me safely back to my homeland!"

Chevanovich spoke too loud for this place. Others might overhear. The man refused to look back, only continued his determined stride for the door with Chevanovich and his black satchel in tow.

The man marched out of Napoleon's tomb at a side entrance, opposite the one the doctor had used to enter.

Chevanovich hoped his harsh response hid the terror rising in his throat. Something had gone wrong. He risked glancing over his shoulder. He detected no one moving to the entrance they were moving through. He disliked being shuffled around by these people. They were Ranzami's foot soldiers, and something inside Chevanvoich warned him to remain vigilant. But of more concern now was the possibility that someone had taken an interest in his movement. He suspected his shadows were not the Israelis, since they would have taken him right on the street without regard. The British and the Americans were more likely to move quietly and without fanfare. They would find a secluded time and place to arrest him. If anyone followed, Chevanovich guessed it would be the Brits.

"I know not why, doctor. I am told. I follow orders," the man said after they had left Napoleon's tomb and settled into his red fiat with broken side view mirror and cracked windshield. A tear in the passenger seat upholstery made sitting uncomfortable for Chevanovich.

Cody had just enough time to memorize the vehicle's license number before running around the building to rejoin Remy at the front. Remy surged forward the moment he saw Cody round the corner. It took three minutes for them to re-locate and fall in behind the doctor's car.

Chevanovich tightened his grip on his satchel. He wanted the safety of the Russian border as soon as possible. Only there could he feel secure against his Western enemies.

"Ranzami assured me one of my own would escort me home," Chevanovich probed.

"Yes, Doctor, a Russian courier arrives tomorrow. He will stay with you until you are safely back to your home."

Just hearing the words sent waves of relief through him. Chevanovich settled back but could no longer resist the urge to glance out the window behind them.

"Please refrain from that, Doctor. I watch. You relax. You are in the best of hands from now on. We have a friend behind us who will make certain any one interested in us is delayed. Right now we are free of any tail."

Chevanovich forced a slight smile. It sent a clear message of concern. Who had taken an interest in them? Who besides Ranzami himself knew of his journey from Geneva to Paris?

They drove the Latin quarters in a seemingly dis-interested circle until the sun finally fell beneath the horizon. Then the driver set a determined course, driving the doctor to a small three-story building that turned out to be a clone of a dozen others on that stretch of street distant from the lights and the cafes of central Paris. So tightly packed were the buildings that even a sliver of light from the street lamps found it difficult to penetrate between the dwellings.

The man parked the car in a rear garage and led the doctor to the third door from the end. The blanket of night over them made identification from a distance of more than five meters impossible.

They trekked up stairs littered with refuse and filth to a second floor apartment, whose windows overlooked the boulevard. Rats scattered from the sudden intrusion of half light filtering in from the corridor. Inside, the apartment mirrored the corridor. The vile stench of human waste and decaying food stuffs assaulted Chevanovich's nose the moment he stepped inside. It reminded him of Afghanistan, where a like stench came as a result of his craftsmanship. For a brief moment, he relived in his mind's eyes the death and suffering he had masterminded for The Party. It had been a day he would carry with him the rest of his life.

Chevanovich flinched when the driver kicked garbage aloft so he could move to the window unencumbered.

"Is the best under the circumstances," the man said, monitoring the traffic on the street below. "You important?"

Chevanovich peered into a side room, hoping to find something better than where he now stood.

"Important? No."

The man shrugged.

"Someone thinks you are. This is the third time a Volkswagen passes this building. I suspect the two men inside are searching for you."

"Are we safe here, then?"

"For now. The men in the car will continue to search, then they will move on."

Chevanovich crossed to the window, abandoning the side room as a suitable place for the night.

"They gone now. For tonight you can sleep without worry."

"And without comfort. Did they not inform you who I am? This is unacceptable," Chevanovich demanded.

"Sorry, Doctor. Your safety is more of a concern to me than your comfort. Only for one night anyway."

The man retreated from the window, seeking to clear a place in the corner of the room furthest from the windows.

"Am I to be alone?"

"No. I remain until I can deliver you to the place where you will be safe. Tomorrow we go to a house more suited to your station."

While Chevanovich sought out a place to sleep in another room in the three-room apartment, he listened to the driver speak to someone on a cell phone. The man spoke only French, and all Chevanvoich understood clearly was that they were out of sight and safe for the night. The driver expressed his confidence that they had eluded the shadow that the driver had detected. It sounded as if someone would be joining them in the morning.

18

Can you recheck reservations. We
seemed to have lost our paperwork.
                              Remy

"We bloody lost the bastard, again," Remy spat
into the phone as he and Cody sat at the entrance to a
lightless brick alleyway in the Latin quarter.

Brax listened but said nothing in response. Two
times the good doctor had succeeded in eluding
them.

"At least we know Dr. Doom's in Paris."

"Where do we go now?"

"I've got Squire getting the FCA to provide us
with a list of all known terrorist safe houses in and
around Paris."

"Cody thinks they'll put Chevanovich on ice until
they're sure they can move him out safely."

"Then we may have a chance at getting to him."

"I figure they'll have to move him out by car. Airports and train stations are going to be crowded with
FCA now that we've alerted them to Chevanovich's
presence."

"He's going underground until they can arrange
transportation for him back to his country. Remy, any
sources we can draw on?"

"One. Goes pretty far back. But I'll see what I can
do."

Chevanovich awoke with a start to blocks of morning light crawling the floor. Something scurried into a heap of garbage, forcing Chevanovich to draw his legs up under his buttocks. He'd gotten only a few hours sleep in the corner of the bedroom. The slumber came as a result of sheer exhaustion. Many years had passed since duty forced him to such sacrifice. Throughout the night hours, insistent scratching of nocturnal scavengers foraging among the rubbish kept him from taking a restful sleep.

Despite a lingering exhaustion, Chevanovich felt exhilaration at the feel of his satchel beneath his arm. Since arriving here, he harbored an uneasiness about this place. As a precaution, he had slept with his hand tightly caressing the 9mm Beretta Brigadier he secreted inside his coat. He placed little trust in the words of a terrorist, and he thought for sure they intended to rob him then disappear.

For most of his sleepless hours, Chevanovich tried to convince himself that he would not allow himself to die amid such squalor, the way his parents had died a half century earlier.

From his corner, he listened. The driver moved about in the other room. Chevanovich listened to the sounds of the man urinating in a place so near the doorway to his room that Chevanovich though he could feel the splash.

The long night was over. His driver had not deserted him nor attempted to rob him of his satchel. Chevanovich released his aching hand from the grip of his gun. He pulled himself off the floor calling upon weary muscles now angered by the torture of six hours against a floor. When he emerged from the bedroom, his driver was zipping his pants.

"We go now," Chevanovich said, more in the tone of a demand than a request.

"When he arrives."

Chevanovich could choke off nature no longer, and he, like the driver, found a place to relieve himself.

Minutes ticked away. A famished Chevanovich waited in filth. Unlike the doctor, the driver seemed at ease in these surroundings, almost at home among the misery. Perhaps it rose out of the difference in their reasons for being together in this place. Chevanovich had his money; the patriot had yet to achieve whatever victory he sought.

"When will he arrive?" Chevanovich badgered.

"Soon," he received in reply.

"I wish to eat, can't you call him?" Chevanovich said a minute later.

"Soon," he received in reply.

Finally, shortly before noon, a young man of no more than twenty with floppy hair that obscured his eyes, strolled up the boulevard, approaching the building. No other pedestrians had even noticed this place. He wore meticulously coordinated clothes—out of place in these surroundings—and he carried himself in the manner of a statesman. He scanned the area furtively before making his approach, though to an untrained eye, his mannerisms remained beyond detection. He climbed the stairs with a sort of easy comfort, entered the building and rapped lightly on the door to the apartment where the two men had holed up.

"Welcome, Doctor," the man offered in English with a leaden Russian slant. "I will see you safely to your home."

"Now we shall eat," the driver said.

No names were exchanged. But Chevanovich knew the addition had to be the promised Russian agent. His eyes elicited a hardness that planted assurance in Chevanovich's heart. He was a comrade. He could be trusted, Chevanovich thought, though they had exchanged only a few cordial words.

"Soon we go to St. Petersburg," the new man said on their departure from the apartment.

Those were the words Chevanovich longed to hear. Those words sent a warm rush inside the doctor.

"I wish to leave on the hour," Chevanovich commented once they were inside the car.

"Soon," was all Chevanovich received in reply from the new man, who now occupied the back seat beside the doctor. He also made certain Chevanovich noticed the Russian Makarov PM strapped beneath his jacket. The same weapon Chevanovich had strapped at his waist in Afghanistan.

For a moment Chevanovich breathed easier. One of his own would watch over him. He had never trusted the French with their arrogance and condescension. Only another Russian could be trusted. Only another Russian would care deeply enough to guard over him.

The three drove for two hours before stopping at a cafe off the tourist path of the busy Paris streets.

Chevanovich spoke little during the meal. His Russian escort said nothing beyond ordering from the menu. After dining, they waited while the driver made a number of phone calls. But this time he chose a public phone across the street instead of the cell telephone he kept in his pocket.

"We go now. All is arranged," he said upon returning. His smile was businesslike. He offered no more than that.

But Chevanovich wished more information. *Where* were they going? What arrangements? When would he leave the country? He remained vulnerable outside his native land despite having a Russian agent beside him.

The driver offered him nothing.

Nervously, Chevanovich quickly scanned the surrounding faces. Had one of them reappeared from the day before?

Against a cloudless sunny afternoon, the car left Paris, traveling south and east for the better part of two hours. Chevanvoich grew uneasy at the sparsely populated surroundings. Isolation could be his ally, or his enemy. He wanted the bustling congestion and relative obscurity of the city. Traffic and people could hide him, make him invisible to those who sought him. Alone in the seclusion of the French countryside he felt exposed. He needed motion and activity. He didn't want to be isolated.

The car turned off the main highway in favor of a two lane stretch through a small town that seemed to sprout up in the midst of grassy fields. The driver left that road shortly there after for a rutted path that led ultimately to a small house on the fringe of the last cluster of houses for the town. The house they chose offered some strategic qualities. It appeared unapproachable without detection, and could be easily evacuated at a moment's notice. Two sides of the surrounding field had been cut back to fifty meters and maintained in an almost manicured fashion. Any vehicle approaching up the road from either direction came quickly under the scrutiny of the house's occupants through the front and side windows. There could be no surprises from the Brits.

"Here is where we wait until I receive the arrangements," the driver said. He motioned for Chevanovich's bag, but the doctor refused to allow it from his hand.

The Russian agent swept the surroundings in a focused glance that missed nothing. He must have concurred with the French plan, since he raised no objections on the walk to the front door.

Inside, two more French patriots joined the three. On the floor in the television room sat the bag Chevanovich had become separated from in Paris.

The two men brandished Glock 17 pistols in shoulder holsters like medals of valor. Czech Skorpions and Chinese Type 80 automatic machine pistols littered the living room like carelessly placed bric-a-brac. The Skorpions delivered the fire power of the Uzi, but proved more lethal at close range. The Chinese Type 80 machine pistols came cheap to the GIA and Black September terrorist groups. Chevanovich inventoried the armament lying about, capable of holding off a full scale frontal assault by the French Counterterrorist Authority itself. Perhaps that was its intended purpose?

The Russian agent did no more than raise a brow at the fortifications, as if to indicate that he expected nothing less for the doctor. He offered a smile meant to praise, though in reality, it aroused suspicions about the very need for such an arsenal. Safe houses were meant to be just that—houses safe from the authorities. Havens for terrorist safe in the knowledge that the authorities were unaware of their locations.

"You are safe here, Doctor. These men are under our charge," the driver said. Then he issued commands or instructions to the two. Chevanovich became confused which, since the driver issued them in French, spoke very quickly, and his words generated reluctant smiles on the comrades' faces. They could have been merely instructions, but the force with which he barked them made it seem more like commands.

However, Chevanovich's escort appeared to accept the situation. He removed his jacket to parade his own weapon, flopped down on the threadbare damask sofa in the television room, and closed his eyes while leaning his head back against the cushion. They understood.

For the first time since departing Geneva, Chevanovich relaxed the muscles in his hands clinging to his satchel. For now he felt in capable hands. He inquired about his room, and found it to be comfortable and more fitting to his station than their previous night's lodging. His was the room upstairs, facing the rear of the house and overlooking a wildly overgrown field, again cleared back to a distance of fifty meters from the house.

For a time the doctor sat on his bed, taking in the frolic of birds fluttering about in raucous flight in the trees outside his window.

Then after locking his door, Chevanovich opened his satchel beside him on the bed. Krugerrands filled the space, causing the satchel to be a weighty load to bear. Having reassured himself the money remained in his possession, for first time in days, Chevanovich strayed from his precious satchel. But even now he refused to stray from his weapon.

Only gold could suffice as payment, he had instructed Ranzami. And only Krugerrands would be acceptable to move the gold through Europe and back to his homeland.

The bed proved most comfortable and within the hour Chevanovich fell sound asleep. His boisterous snoring drifted out the window to be heard by any passersby. Downstairs, the guards laughed at the clamor, then they realized they must sleep amongst that same racket.

At eight sharp, the Russian rapped at Chevanovich's door to inform him dinner awaited.

Throughout the meal the two guards spoke strictly French and laughed boisterously as if exchanging humorous anecdotes. Both Chevanovich and his escort seemed unable to comprehend the humor. They ate in silence. In a crude English, one asked Chevanovich how he liked the food and frowned when the doctor said his sensitive stomach convulsed from the food the French were fond of preparing.

The French translated that to mean French food made Chevanovich sick. So, they refused to speak to him for the remainder of the meal.

With dinner finished, the two consumed three bottles of wine, while both Chevanovich and the Russian agent politely declined. Their excessive drinking made Chevanvoich uncomfortable. A drunken soldier is useless and more a liability to those around him than an asset. Chevanovich tightened his jaw when one of the guardians became agitated and had to be restrained by his partner. Guns and alcohol were a volatile combination, more deadly than an armed fool with a patriotic cause, Chevanovich thought to himself as he sat in the television room while his guardians cleared away the dishes and washed them in the sink.

"Afghanistan," the agent said with a glint of recognition.

"Yes," Chevanovich responded proudly. His eyes became alight as he waited for more.

"You were there...against the rebels. That is where I have seen you before."

"You were there?"

"For a time. My team provided intelligence. In a sense we worked together."

For a long moment there was silence. Chevanovich relived memories he had buried after leaving Afghanistan. He never allowed himself to reason over the things he did. He never allowed himself to debate the right or wrong, the good or the bad. He did what he did for reasons far less rewarding than money.

"I witnessed the aftermath of what you had done," the agent said with a tinge of sorrow in his words. He left the room and climbed the stairs, never once looking back at Chevanovich, who remained in his chair staring at the night outside the window.

Chevanovich retired at eleven to the warmth of a down mattress with clean stiff sheets and a goose feather pillow. Much more to his liking than the previous night's surroundings. He made certain he locked his door before tucking his satchel beneath his blanket and clutching his gun under his pillow.

Determining the identity of the man who met Chevanovich at the train station gave the team at least a chance of determining where he might have been taken. Brax no longer held the hope of linking Chevanovich to Leviathan. What he did hope for was that under interrogation the good doctor would reveal what he knew of Leviathan's intent. They also knew they had a window of opportunity of maybe forty-eight hours—if they were lucky. A man of Chevanovich's reputation would not likely escape the vigilant eye of the Israeli Secret Service nor the Americans for long. That meant the doctor would move through Europe by car and avoid airports and places where intelligence gathering organizations frequented.

If prior arrangements had been made, Chevanovich may already be arriving back in Russia, and they would have forfeit any chance of taking him for interrogation. But moving the doctor to Paris seemed to indicate that no one had set up a prearranged return route for the doctor.

The Wolf Pack had to determine if Chevanovich had become involved with Leviathan. They had to learn if the doctor played a role in Ranzami's next terrorist assault. The faces of the dead in Geneva supported the supposition that Chevanovich had devised some method of mass murder for the terrorist. Given that as a fact, who, where, and when became questions requiring urgent answers.

On the other hand, the possibility existed that Chevanovich had to be holed up somewhere near

Paris while the mechanizations were assembled for transporting him back home.

Brax had authorized a great risk when he allowed Chevanovich to roam free in Geneva. A dozen young men and women paid for his gamble. Now he had to make that gamble pay off.

So far it hadn't.

Had Chevanovich led the pack to Leviathan, they could have taken them both out with one swift surgical strike. Two monsters in one swoop. Quietly and efficiently the Wolf Pack could have eliminated the threat Ranzami posed. But again too many variables to control. The terrorists always have the edge. Now the team was scrambling to salvage at least something for their efforts.

The situation unfolding forced Squire to remain in his warren around the clock. He left no outlet untapped, no chit uncalled. He poked and prodded the Chief Operations Officer for the Paris office, who worked with the FCA, and through their combined efforts, established a list of three possible terrorist safe houses in and around Paris.

Remy knew better than to rely on the French. They loathed the Americans and the British, and would do nothing to aid them in any intelligence operation. So, he called in his prized chit. One he had secreted away for more than two years. A chit he acquired by saving the life of an Israeli agent who had become compromised in Budapest. It was one of those rare instances when Remy had killed someone.

As a result of that chit, Remy gained the locations of two additional suspected terrorist strongholds in the area. But he reported back with anything but a smile across his face.

"One's a Black September house uncovered three months earlier," he reported to the three other anxious members of the team. Then he hesitated.

"And the other?" Brax asked.

"I've got good news and bad news on that."

"The good news is?"

"It's a GIA location."

"And the bad news is?" Cody asked.

"It's a GIA location."

The Armed Islamic Group, GIA to Counterterrorist operatives, had an almost fanatical loathing for the French, the British and the Americans. Any encounter with GIA always resulted in bloodshed and carnage. Both strongholds the Israelis kept secret from the FCA. Even the FCA could not be fully trusted. Terrorists had ways of infiltrating even the most secure organizations. Terrorists used money or terror if need be, to gain intelligence about those tasked with destroying them. Remy placed more trust in his Israeli than the French Counterterrorist Authority. The Israelis dug deeper and worked harder than any other nation to keep tabs on any and all terrorist activity. They had good reason to.

Meanwhile in Paris, the French grew immediately uneasy about divulging knowledge they kept otherwise secret from the CIA and MI6. Until now it was something they had all to themselves. It took Housemother's intervention to force the information to the table. Squire heard rumblings that we were paying dearly to access that information. Sharing made the French feel less superior. Housemother, it appeared, still wielded significant clout in the international arena. More than Squire had given him credit for at least.

As long as the French remained ignorant of the two locations Brax now knew about, the Pack felt secure they could go in without French involvement or counter-involvement. Using proper channels now would only delay the operation and possibly put the Wolf Pack at risk. The team would then have little choice but to abort rather than compromise their hard target.

Brax chose to go in with full force, in the event they encountered an active safe house prepared to resist. If they had to, they would take Chevanovich out. Whatever deaths came as a result would have to be smoothed over by the State Department with the French government.

The team opted to reconnoiter the latter two first, since odds favored the notion that the doctor would be moved to a safe house secure from the French. And if the Israelis had uncovered them, the team knew the intelligence would be fresh and accurate. That's how the Israelis worked.

By late afternoon, Remy's surveillance determined the Black September safe house closest to Paris proper went unused and exhibited no signs of occupation in the recent past. While Cody watched over the surroundings, Remy went in through a side window and within three minutes had made a silent and thorough sweep. A lack of rations and armament indicated no visitors were imminent. Low-level mules generally stocked safe houses prior to an arrival and emptied them immediately upon departure. The lack of anything left behind, no trash tossed out, no food bits left about, supported the theory that no one had used the place in the past twenty-four hours. Even the most meticulous unwittingly left behind telltales signs of recent occupation.

The second house—the GIA house—was located more than two hours drive outside Paris, and though it seemed a likely candidate, and time was critical, Brax opted to go in fresh after a few hours sleep. He had to weigh the risk of possibly arriving too late to snare their prey versus being at less than their best if they encountered GIA resistance. Brax knew a man of Chevanovich's stature would never be left unprotected. And Leviathan maintained a general's mindset—always. He would fortify the location to protect his assets.

The team dispersed to separate Paris safe houses with a 2 A.M. rendezvous. They intended to reach their second target with the coming of the dawn.

19

Have located a respectable doctor.
Will advise to nature of operation.
                              Brax.

As his second day drew to a close, Chevanovich began to feel safe among the men given the task of protecting him. When a sedan of unknown origin turned onto their street, the guardians quickly brandished their Skorpions in his defense. He no longer doubted their efficacy or their worthiness. As the car closed on the house, they hustled the doctor into a basement room and ordered him to remain there until told to come out.

Chevanovich had obeyed without question. Whether their efforts were sincere or merely a show, Chevanovich could not know. But they seemed genuine in their responsibility for his safety.

When after a short delay, Chevanovich returned from the basement room, to learn the car carried the driver of the previous day. Chevanovich learned to his elation that all had been properly arranged. They would leave at noon the following day, and drive without stop to Berlin, where Chevanovich would board an express to St. Petersburg.

Chevanovich breathed a sigh of relief when he had heard those words. The sooner he returned to St. Petersburg, the better. Home was the only safe place for him now. The driver handed him a set of papers sanitized to get him into Russia without arousing

199

suspicion by German authorities, who would be certain to check his papers at the train station.

But all the news was not good. Before leaving, the driver left them with some disturbing developments. It seemed some Americans had taken a sudden interest in the FCA, and that could only mean Chevanovich's presence had raised a rather serious flag in the counterterrorist community. An insider had leaked word to the terrorists that an American agent would be arriving at the end of day tomorrow. That escalated Chevanovich's planned departure to ensure he would be clear of their country before the American arrived. Whoever this American agent was, he would find the trail to the good doctor cold when he stepped off the airplane.

Already many of the suspected terrorists around Paris had dispersed into the countryside to confound efforts by the authorities to round them up. The driver also assured Chevanovich he would be home sleeping in his own bed before anyone could determine that he had been here.

As the doctor crawled into the bed, safely ensconced inside his room at the top of the stairs, he checked his money once more and fingered his gun under his pillow. The rewards had made the risks worthwhile. Soon he would be away from these cold, arrogant people and back with his beloved Russians. Soon all this would be over and he would be safe. Soon was less than twenty-four hours away.

His stomach rumbled in rebellion to the ingestion of so much food rich in animal fats. The doctor contemplated going downstairs for something to relieve his stomach. But by midnight, his cramps had subsided and he fell fast asleep. His rhythmic snoring cut through the night still.

The Wolf Pack left the deserted Paris streets behind, heading into a flat countryside splashed with the silver light off a gibbous moon. They traveled south and east, all the while maintaining surveillance in their wake. It seemed for the time being, their presence had escaped the FCA's detection.

Remy's charge was to deliver the team to the location in a timely manner. Cody took responsibility for reconnoitering the location and providing an operational assault strategy should it become necessary. Cali's task was rear guard and working up a counterassault strategy should they need one.

For two hours no one spoke. Each focused on their individual task. Each assumed responsibility for the rest of the team's survival. Terrorists were all too quick to engage an enemy, believing dying for the cause led to martyrdom. That made them more dangerous than other enemies. Suicide was acceptable, even exalted, in their minds. A man who can successfully shed his fear of dying will relent without reservation, regardless of the odds stacked against him.

A red-rimmed sun peeked over the horizon as they pulled into the town of Bouilly. Remy oriented himself to the lay of the land before beginning an earnest search for the location of the suspected safe house. As they approached the west side of the small town, he at first thought he had bungled his assignment. Then he saw the street sign they sought. His friend had been on target so far.

Chevanovich awoke with the first inkling of dawn seeping through the cracks in the shade over his window. A fresh morning breeze luffed the curtains as it swept across his face. It reminded him of home, with the sea breeze greeting him in the morning. Today he was going home. He wanted to turn over, to go back to sleep for a few more hours, but a nagging voice inside his head urged him out of bed. At first he failed to comprehend the why, only that going back to sleep seemed suddenly a very bad idea.

Something was wrong.

Yet he was at a loss to put his finger directly on it. He felt for his satchel. It was gone. He calmed himself when he felt it at his feet. During the night it had worked its way down to be stopped by the foot of his bed. In a moment, the weighty sack was back in hand. He need not open it, its heft assured him it remained undisturbed during the night.

So what was it nagging at his brain this morning? What was so different that it snared his attention?

Chevanovich pulled on his pants and slipped into a shirt, but he left it unbuttoned and his feet bare. His corns had ached since Geneva and the more he went shoeless, the better his withered old dogs felt. He would buy Italian loafers when he returned home. Then his feet would ache no more. For all he had given to The Party, the least they could do was offer him in return shoes with the comfort of those made in Italy. He would have a dozen pairs. He could afford everything he wanted now.

He would partake in every luxury. The Party cared only for their own. People like Chevanovich were meant to be used until they were all used up then discarded.

It wasn't until Chevanovich reached the bottom stair that he realized what had jolted him from a sound sleep. An utter silence shrouded the entire house. No one about in the kitchen preparing break-fast, though in previous days, one of his guardians had always aroused with the dawn to cook breakfast. *That* was what had nagged him so in his bed. He smelled no aromas of an imminent breakfast.

Perhaps they, too, were indulging themselves a little, realizing they had nearly completed their assignment for the general?

Chevanovich froze at the kitchen entrance. His face went slack; the blood left his cheeks. The back door had been left open—not unlocked—wide open.

Chevanovich said nothing. Breathing became difficult. He hurried through the rooms and threw open the door to the first floor bedroom.

Empty.

Nothing was amiss. The room was empty, the bed untouched. All clothes were gone.

"Where are you!" he screamed so loud that anyone passing on the road would have heard.

Then he realized...he had left his gun under his pillow upstairs. *Get the gun*, raced through his mind. For a long moment his feet remained rooted to the floor. He was alone, wasn't he?

Slowly, he crept up the stairs, stopping at each step to listen. No sounds other than his heightened breathing and thumping heart came from anywhere in the house.

He had to reach his gun.

They had deserted him.

Chevanovich had to get to his gun.

Pausing at the last stair, he glanced back down to take in what he could see of the first floor.

Nothing moved.

Why abandon him and leave the money behind? Surely they had to know he carried a large sum of currency by the way he protected his satchel.

Sweat raced down the doctor's face. He inched toward his bedroom door, which he had left ajar. Or had he? Something urged him to come about and run at full pelt from the house. That sixth sense of fear demanded that he *not* return to that room. Normally, he trusted that sense without question. But both his weapon and his money were inside that room.

He eased the door open. The satchel appeared on his bed, just as he had left it. The sun's rays grew intense, spreading light throughout the room.

He would grab his money and gun and flee quickly and quietly.

Seeing his case exactly as he had left it eased the mounting terror. He must be alone. But why would they leave? Any confrontation would have awakened him if they were forced to flee in a rush. Then why leave him behind. They were here to safeguard him, to get him safely back to his country.

Chevanovich dashed for the bed. He scooped up the satchel with one hand, groped back and forth beneath his pillow with his other. His gun was gone!

Terror seized him. Chevanovich straightened.

A fiery piercing jab invaded the base of his neck, paralyzing every muscle in his body. His shoulders and head trembled out of control, his eyes fluttered, his arms quivered. He emptied both bladder and bowels where he stood. Every muscle had gone into wild uncontrollable gyrations.

Unable to do anything, Chevanovich stared at the reflection in the window's glass. He knew that face; had seen his killer before. The dark form lurched over him. Suspended by his neck, Chevanovich felt like an animal on tenterhooks. He couldn't fall despite legs that had become rubber. He felt the warm sticky blood stream down his back, but he remained helpless to defend himself.

Invading from the lower ridge of Chevanovich's peripheral vision, a gloved hand clasping a glinting object came around to locate the center of his chest. Then the fire of a second piercing jab below his rib cage spread throughout. Death came before his next breath.

20

Have surrendered the tickets. Need
new travel arrangements.

                              Brax

Remy stopped the car just long enough for Cody
to exit at the end of the street. Cody would approach
from the rear, working his way close enough for a
risk assessment. He moved efficiently through the
back field and paused one house from the target. The
open rear door raised an immediate flag. Had they
learned the Americans were coming? Had they fled in
such a rush that they left the door unsecured? His
eyes roved the vicinity, seeking a reason to justify the
unsecured door.

For long tedious moments he waited. Nothing
outside moved. Only rustling window curtains inside.

Cody advanced; he readied his Glock. He considered his response in the event an unsuspecting terrorist emerged. They needed only to determine if
Chevanovich was inside, not get into a fire fight with
a band of holed-up crazies.

After a few more minutes of intense scrutiny,
Cody concluded no one was about inside the house.
He assessed his chances of a clandestine penetration.
A barking dog snared his attention. Cody hesitated.
He updated Brax, requesting back up before attempt-
ing to breach the target.

A minute later Cali eased up behind him with her
weapon concealed beneath a jacket. When Cody

moved forward, she stopped him with a hand to his forearm, pointing to an upstairs window where the curtain rippled in the breeze.

Cody stayed on the window but detected no movement from the inside.

"I don't like this," Cali whispered. An open door with no one around to account for it meant something was wrong. Cali urged Cody to back off.

"I'm going in," he whispered, "cover my ass if I come flying out in a hurry."

Cody read her eyes. Something about this situation sent a shudder through him. The sinking feeling he had experienced in Wick, Scotland during their heated debate over her efficacy had returned. The moment might be at hand when he had to trust her, *really* trust her. He thought he could go through with it, now he wasn't so sure.

Cody picked his way toward that open door. He relied more on his ears than his eyes to alert him to changes in the house's interior. Anyone moving around inside should send off sufficient noise to warn him and provide time to abort.

It took two agonizing minutes to reach the door. And during that time, it plagued him that someone would leave a door unsecured. Maybe they were at the wrong house. Innocent people would be at risk if he went in with his gun ready.

For a long moment a stationary Cody stared in through the slit in the kitchen curtains. The red and blue print fabric obscured his view, but the slit gave him a slice of the interior. Enough to indicate no one sat at the kitchen table a few paces inside the door.

Cody readjusted his Glock. The sweat played havoc with his concentration. Terrorist safe houses scared the living shit out of him. Always heavily fortified and equally heavily defended. He could encounter three or more zealots with fingers on the trigger of Uzis or shotguns.

Cody dropped to his belly to slide up to the doorway like a snake emerging from high grass. From his
prone position, he could gain an interior view before
his head became visible to anyone inside.

His initial reconnaissance indicated an unoccu-
pied kitchen, so Cody returned to his feet, his weapon
always directed inside the house, and he slipped
inside. He paused and listened while he trained his
Glock on the entrance to the television room.

Nothing.

No snoring, toilet flush, nor sounds of any kind.

"I'm in," he whispered.

Four quick steps took him across the kitchen and
he scanned an unkempt television room. A ruffled
blanket and pillow lay on the battered sofa. Cody
swept in search of the bathroom. Whoever had slept
on the sofa could be in the john.

The absence of fire power issued an alarm to
Cody's brain. So much so, that Cody dropped to a
knee, leveling his Glock. He thought he picked out a
sound. Something upstairs? Or was it just his nerves?

He waited. Nothing moved. No new sounds crept
down from the floor above. To his left, he spied the
bathroom's open door. He took the time to suck in a
deep breath and settle his nerves. He wanted to transmit that the place was empty, but knew he had to
clear the upstairs before issuing an all clear.

He suspected the house had been abandoned,
and he transmitted those suspicions to Brax, informing him that he had not cleared the upper floor.

Brax ordered a full breach, and while Cali came
up to the back door, Brax and Remy moved from their
vehicle toward the rear of the house. Remy's tightly
wrapped ankle only slightly slowing him now. Cody
held his position in the television room with his
weapon trained on the top of the staircase.

One by one, he climbed the bare wood stairs. His
eyes bounced back and forth between the two doors,
which were both closed. His weight on the last stair

before the top caused a creak that froze him in place. His Glock bounced back and forth anticipating one of the doors opening.

Cody shed relief when he glanced over his shoulder to Cali poised at the base of the stairs with her weapon trained in his defense. Her stern face and unflinching eyes reinforced her capability in Cody's mind. He no longer doubted her willingness to put her life on the line for him. She had just better be good with a gun.

Cody chose the left door and waited while Cali made her way silently up the stairs. She over-stepped the creaky one near the top.

Slowly, Cody turned the handle. Without a sound, he eased the door open until the bed came into view. It had been slept in, but he saw no one in the room.

Closing that door, Cody crept to the other and eased it open. As the bed came into view, he caught sight of a splay-legged mass on the floor beside the bed. A small pool of blood collected at the neck.

Before advancing, Cody swept the room with his weapon. The body on the floor was the only sign of occupation, though Cody knew the body was dead.

"All clear," he transmitted.

Cali entered the room at his side and lowered her weapon when she saw the body. They could hear Brax and Remy moving in below.

Cody advanced the few paces to inspect the body, stopping well short of the pool of blood.

Cali remained just inside the door, using the wall for support. She knew even without seeing the face who they would find beside the bed.

As Brax and Remy entered the room, Cali retreated to her position outside the residence. Her responsibility now shifted to making certain no one could launch a surprise attack on the Pack.

Brax and Remy went directly to the body, stopping so they could get a clear view from the side.

"Chevanovich," was all Brax said.

The three stared at the body for a long moment. They were stunned, confused by the presence of such an important figure to the terrorist underworld dead. Had the Israelis gotten here first? Had Remy's contact betrayed them? Brax surveyed the surroundings carefully before moving in closer.

"Wasn't shot," Remy said, taking a position on the mattress so as to inspect the body without disturbing the scene. From his perch, he began an examination. Employing a pencil from his pocket, he worked it beneath Chevanovich's chin. No throat wound. Then he closed the Russian's unseeing eyes.

"Cali, we clear outside?" Brax transmitted through his button mike.

"All clear," came back

"How'd he die?" Cody asked.

"Nasty death. Look at this," Remy said to Brax, pointing out the base of Chevanovich's neck.

Brax moved in close to inspect the findings.

"Warm blood," Cody injected. He wiped his tainted finger on his pants.

"Killed within the last few hours," Remy said.

"Get a look at the chest," Brax told Remy, who stretched across the bed and shifted to ease in closer.

"I can't get closer without disturbing the scene. Why? I've got a puncture at the base of the neck."

"Wasn't the cause of death. Meant to debilitate. Look for a puncture at the base of the breast bone."

"I'll try."

Remy shifted through a series of five different positions before he found one allowing him to tilt the body sufficiently to scrutinize the chest. He needed to inspect the area then reposition the body close enough to its original to preclude detection. Above all else, they had to prevent French authorities from learning they had been here and discovered the body.

"Damn. How'd you know? Right there at the base of the breast bone," Remy said as he leaned forward resting his fist on the night table to steady himself.

"The neck stab holds the prey; a second pick to the chest ruptures the heart," Cody said.

"Double ice pick," Brax murmured with recognition.

"And that means?" Remy asked.

"That means we back out and cover our tracks."

As they retreated down the stairs, Cody monitored their wake to make certain nothing remained behind to indicate American presence.

"Weapons?"

"Clean," Cody responded.

Outside the sun inched off the horizon. Daylight washed over their return as if someone had installed a giant Klieg light to follow every step of the way.

"What's it mean?" Cody asked again once they were inside the car. This time agitation rose to the top of his voice.

"Not sure. There's something I have to do. We disperse back to safe ground and keep our eyes open."

"You think Leviathan's erasing his tracks?"

Remy grew worried over Brax's sudden silence. He could see the mechanizations of Brax's mind going on beyond those steely gray eyes. What was the significance in the way Chevanovich died? What did Brax see that set him on edge?

For the present, Brax had to keep his suspicions silent. Soon they hoped they would learn the meaning behind the murder.

"Someone made damn sure Chevanovich can't tell us if he's working for Leviathan," Brax commented absent-mindedly.

On the drive to Orly, the car was held in abject silence. Each boarded a different flight to a separate destination. Remy boarded a London commuter. He wanted to check on the information he had lifted from Alabaster. All had much to think about now that a vital link to their hard target had been eliminated.

21

Looking for lost relative. Return
home on Tuesday.

                              Brax

Sitting behind the same scratched and marred
desk that his grandfather sat at struggling to decipher German codes a half century ago, and positioned beneath a window to allow the cool night
breeze to wash across his face, Remy stared vacantly
at the pages of deciphered data MI6 had successfully
extracted from Alabaster's credit card. It was the first
time in a month that he had slept in his own bed in
his flat on the north side of London.

For the longest time he saw nothing. A series of
lines running parallel for a length then angling off at
a near right angle only to change direction again by
ninety degrees. He had been playing 'what if' for
hours with no progress. What if they were electrical
lines? or natural gas lines? He concluded early on that
what he held was a small part of some larger picture.
The only markings deciphered that seemed significant were a series of dashed lines at one of the turns.
Those dashes had to indicate something. But what?

Remy switched over to another tactic. What possibly could be Leviathan's target? If he assumed the
courier intended to deliver the information to Leviathan, then this information became integral to Leviathan's plan. After midnight, Remy switched off his

work table lamp, stored the information into a locked desk drawer and crawled exhausted into bed.

Sleep came immediately, though his slumber lasted no more than an hour. In the midst of the pitch, Remy jolted up in bed with a start. He fumbled about the unlit room for his clothes. He dressed haphazardly, eliminated the socks, underwear and sweater in the interest of time and raced through the deserted London streets to reach his headquarters building.

His identification got him through the requisite checkpoints to gain access to the central records facility for MI6. In the subbasement, he moved up and down the aisles of files until he came to the target of his sleepless obsession.

Remy's clearance gained him access to virtually any file he requested, save for those files that required verbal authorization from the chief himself. Remy had no immediate interest in those files anyway.

Like a kid with copy of Treasure Island, Remy opened the file he sought and began scanning even before he got to a well lit table in the corner. The file offered no answers to his inquiries, but it did direct him to another set of files stored three aisles away. Remy clutched those files tightly and returned to the table. There he spread the contents to consume the entire breadth of the surface.

"Damn you, Leviathan," he said between clinched teeth.

The files he stared at, the thoughts that jarred him from sleep like a terrifying nightmare detailed the construction for the newly opened tunnel traversing the English channel. The drawings that most captured his attention laid out the ventilation ducts installed as part of the tunnel.

The earlier file that directed him to these plans had been the Terrorist Risk Assessment for the tunnel spanning beneath the English Channel.

"You bastard," Remy whispered to himself as he realized the significance of an attack on the tunnel.

But Leviathan was not one who easily subscribed to the kamikaze mindset made popular by the Japanese in World War II. Leviathan liked to strike hard but lose few or no men in the process. Dying was for the fanatics and zealots. Leviathan wished to reap the rewards of his terror.

Remy focused on the drawing and sought to connect the fragments of the computer file locked in his memory to some portion of what lie before him.

By five A.M. he abandoned his quest. Nothing he could identify on any of the Chunnel drawings quite matched what he had seen on Alabaster's coded card. In the midst of deep ruminations he absent-mindedly returned the files to the attendant. If the tunnel were Leviathan's hard target, they had an excellent shot at preventing it, if they could uncover more information about the how and the when. Most important right now was to make sure Leviathan remained unaware that his plan had been compromised.

For the first time in days Remy felt the inkling of a smile on his face. His stride down the stairs into the first weak beams of a newly brightening sun reflected his renewed spirit.

As he approached a rusted black Sterling parked with its right front tire cocked half over the curb, he glanced per chance into the rain-dappled window glass. In his faint reflection, the ominous red dot of a laser targeting beam traced up his chest.

Remy dove.

Crack!

The first shot popped like a car's backfire. The round whizzed past Remy's ear, narrowly missing his head by but a few centimeters. Remy flattened on the pavement, mashing himself as best he could beneath the vehicle parked along the street. A second shot pinged off the car, continuing on to shatter the window glass of the flat behind him.

Remy rose to firing position on one knee, leveling his Glock over the hood of his car. He sought to nail anything that so much as flickered. The sun had yet to climb sufficiently to shed full daylight. In the half light Remy searched, his eyes missing nothing.

As quickly as the attack came, so it vanished. Nothing moved. Remy surmised that the shots must have originated on the rooftops across the road.

Before entering his car, Remy checked beneath the frame and under the hood for signs of an explosive device. Though he had no more than an hour's sleep, he was sure he would be awake for the remainder of the day. Very possibly another piece of Leviathan's plan had fallen into place and brought the Wolf Pack one step closer to ending his deadly reign of unchecked terror.

Remy transmitted a message to Squire reporting what he had pieced together and what had occurred outside the MI6 research building. He requested the Wolf Pack meet to appraise the possibilities of his newly formed theory and to collect on his wager with Cody. Squire reported that the CIA code breakers had yet to decipher what Remy had turned over to them.

🔫

Cody and Cali arrived in Bonn, where they met with an MI6 operations officer assigned the task of providing clandestine access to the crime scene.

Willie Kirkhammer's death had caused little if any stir among the people of Bonn. He had lived a quiet, unassuming life and except for close friends and relatives, no one much cared that he had been murdered.

The three arrived at Willie's loft at dusk. They waited until nightfall had settled completely in before making their approach on the building.

Cody picked the lock in under thirty seconds, blamed the delay on poor lighting, and without disturbing anything, Cody and Cali made their way up the stairs without benefit of light. The MI6 man suggested he remain outside and out of sight across the street, to run interference if anything went awry. Police had very little patience with people who disturbed their crime scenes, and the last thing Cody and Cali wanted was anyone knowing why they were interested in the Kirkhammer killing.

Inside, they moved quickly up the stairs, used penlights to illuminate small expanses of the loft that caught their attention and eventually ended up at the workbench. The left half of the bench was charred black from where the fire had been started. However, someone had arrived in time to extinguish it before it could gut the building.

"What makes this guy worth our time?"

"Lockerbie," was all Cody said. He locked his light across the loft to the workbench.

"Okay."

"Kirkhammer's a detonation man. He rigs the timers used to detonate the terrorist bombs. We believe he's the one who set the bomb to blow on the 747 over Lockerbie."

Cali quickly assayed the loft's living space, and turning up nothing of any consequence, moved to the markings on the floor where the body had been discovered.

"We may owe somebody big time for this," Cody said, "they must have gotten the blaze out before the whole place went up. Bring your light over here."

Raking their lights in sync across the surface littered with electronic components, wires, and various other electronic gadgets, Cody and Cali collected a quick inventory as best they could of what lay scattered about.

"A lot of this stuff is used for detonators," Cody said, inspecting some of the components falling under his light.

"What kind?"

"The very sophisticated kind."

Cody grabbed Cali's light and holding the two together, he swept very slowly over the surface.

"What are we looking for?" Cali asked.

For a time Cody said nothing. He seemed consumed in his search. He shifted the light to the shelf, where he ran his hand over the surface. The beam fell on four small plastic circuit packs. Cody snatched them up and turned them to read the numbers in the light.

"These," he said as if he had uncovered a revelation.

"What are they?"

"I don't know, but I know they're not your typical detonation variety. We'll get our lab boys to check them out."

They continued their sweep of the loft apartment, but turned up nothing else that might be useful and exited.

"We need to get a look at the police file on this crime," Cody commented once they were back in the car with his MI6 contact.

"Could be a problem. We've never turned over any intelligence on Kirkhammer to the German government. Our agreement with them calls for full disclosure. Far as they know, Willie had no connection to any terrorist organization. We start asking questions now and they're going to accuse us of violating the agreement."

"Any way to bypass channels?"

"I can pay off one of the lieutenants, if its that important. How's your German?"

"Good enough."

"Then I will see what I can do."

Seven hours later, in the Bonn police headquarters, and passing themselves off as a couple related to Willie, they were met in the lobby by a lieutenant and escorted into a private room on the third floor. No other explanations needed, Cody and Cali opened the official police file on the Kirkhammer murder.

Cody's suspicions became immediately aroused when he saw the way the body had been brutally taken apart. Willie had not been shot, nor stabbed. He suffered a terrible beating and from the splay of his arms and legs, many of his bones had been broken. The contusions suggested he endured a vicious beating before his neck was snapped. The killer wanted Willie to suffer. Yet Cody could uncover no telltale signs of Leviathan's handiwork.

"Says here the chief inspector on the case believes the death to be drug related. Yet no drug arrests or drug activity are detailed in the file."

"Wing chun," Cali said softly, staring at the graphic photographs of the crime.

"Sadistic murder, I'd call it."

Cali spread the pictures out to view all of them at the same time. The close-up of the head, though, offered up what she based her conclusions on.

"Anything missing? Fingers, genitals, anything missing from the body?"

"No. Why do you ask?"

Cali shrugged.

"Not a ritual killing then."

"Nor drug related. According to this, Willie had no priors."

"He was killed with wing chun," Cali said after they had returned the file to the lieutenant and exited the police station.

"And that is?"

"A rare discipline. Uses six kills. The one who killed Willie is a master. He took out the jaw to neutralize a counterattack. He wanted Kirkhammer to suffer before dying."

"Leviathan likes to trademark his kills. One guy we came across who betrayed Leviathan had both little fingers removed and shoved down his throat. Found another with his testicles in his rectum. Either Leviathan's changing his ways, or this guy was done for reasons independent of the man we're after. Though I must say, I've never seen one like that before."

"I have. Leviathan use Koreans?"

"I tracked one for a couple of weeks in Singapore. Never made a solid link to Leviathan though."

Cali's face paled as they returned to their car.

"If he's recruiting Koreans with those talents, we're going to need bigger guns.

Brax checked himself in his rearview mirror, straightening his conservative navy tie, shifting black-rimmed glasses and in general making certain nothing appeared out of place before entering the Madison Casualty and Life building in the thriving downtown Madison square. That is if one could ever call eight square blocks of retail and office buildings a thriving metropolis. The sign neatly engraved in gilt letters against rich oak grain read, "MADISON AVIARY PRESERVATION SOCIETY."

"Good Morning," a pleasant voice said as if she were anxious to talk to anyone who happened into the office, even if it were by mistake. "May I help you?"

The young woman's plain face and rounded contours could not detract from the pleasant smile she wore. She sat behind a reception desk positioned before a closed inner office door with remnants scattered about of a job that carried with it little responsibility. A romance novel with curled back pages sat near her right hand and cuticle tools happened to be spread before her like surgical tools.

"Yes, I'm sure you may, Ms. Winegart, is it?" Brax started as he shifted his briefcase and purposely looked over his glasses at the gold name plate with the receptionist's name in black letters.

Ms. Winegart appreciated that he had expended the effort to address her by name. Most never went beyond 'Miss.' Seemed nobody took the time to learn names anymore.

Brax delivered a business card from his breast pocket to Ms. Winegart's hand. He felt foreign in the suit and hoped his discomfort would remain buried.

"Yes. And you are?" Ms. Winegart paused while she inspected the card, "Mr. Edwards. How can we help you?"

"Well, you see, call me James, Ms. Winegart," Brax said, revealing his most unguarded smile for her. "I represent a philanthropist who is considering your society for one of his donations."

"That's wonderful. How can I help."

"My client is rather persnickety. He requires that I provide him with a complete report on the, let's say, distribution of donations by any charity he expresses an interest in. So, before I can recommend your organization, I must know a little bit about it."

Ms. Winegart, seeing this as her opportunity to perform in some measure for her employer, was quick to withdraw from her side desk drawer a six-page four color brochure that described in illustriously vivid detail the variety of winged waterfowl the Society worked diligently to protect.

"Our Congressman from Madison has a bill before the Congress to include three additional names to the endangered species list."

Brax noticed that Ms. Winegart seemed overly careful to prevent him from getting a glimpse at the contents of the desk drawer.

"This is all well and good, but I would need to speak to your president," Brax paused, searching the brochure for the name. After many long empty moments of silence he continued, "Mr. Dennis McVickers. Is he available to meet with me?"

Brax stared at a black and white corner photo of a silver-haired gentlemen with a politician's smile and instantly compassionate hazel eyes. This Mr. McVickers was easily in his sixties.

"I'm afraid it's impossible to see Mr. McVickers without an appointment. He spends most of his time working directly with our state government."

"I understand. But we are talking about a sizable donation here."

"Exactly how much?"

Ms. Winegart seemed to slip easily from airhead receptionist to interrogator.

"I'm afraid I'm not at liberty to disclose the amount." Brax paused for a moment to heighten the dramatic effect and set the hook. "However, let me assure you that any six figure donation is certainly worth Mr. McVickers' time. When might I see him?"

"I'll have to check his schedule."

Brax waited, surveying the office that offered an ample display of wildlife photography adorning the walls, a half dozen conservation magazines sprawled neatly on the small table in the corner, and sufficient live foliage to provide the necessary oxygen to sustain a family of four indefinitely.

Ms. Winegart shifted to her computer on the corner of her desk. The screen was angled in such a way to prevent Brax from catching a glimpse of the information appearing on it without making an attempt obvious.

"I don't suppose Mr. McVickers would have time for me right now? I only require five minutes. There are a few details my client requires before making a final decision."

"Maybe I can help with the details?" Ms. Winegart was quick to inject.

Brax glanced at the closed office door.

"I would need to see your society's non-profit registration with the Internal Revenue Service."

"That I have," she said.

"A historical record of the organization's work over the past five years."

"That I can get."

"And full disclosure of all executives in the organization, their annual salaries, and a breakdown of how each dollar is distributed by the society."

That stopped Ms. Winegart in her tracks.

"I'm sorry. Only Mr. McVickers can release that information."

"When is the earliest I might see Mr. McVickers?"

Ms. Winegart rotated back to her screen. As she did, Brax shifted his weight so that his hand came into contact with the corner of her desk. With a slight pressure, he affixed a button mike to the underside of her work surface.

"Friday's the soonest, at two-thirty."

"Friday? Dang. I was hoping to wrap things up today or tomorrow at the latest."

"I'm sorry. Mr. McVickers is unavailable until then."

"Perhaps I could meet him for a cocktail at the end of his day. Five minutes is all I would need. And I did come a long way to see him."

"I'm sorry, Mr. Edwards. Mr. McVickers is completely unavailable until Friday. Shall I pencil you in for his two-thirty."

"Well, I guess. Could you see that Mr. McVickers has the requisite paperwork available, so we may get through it with time enough for me to catch a flight back to New York."

"I certainly will."

"Then thank you very much, Ms. Winegart, and I look forward to seeing you and Mr. McVickers on Friday."

Brax said nothing further. He exited the office, and once in the corridor slipped the ear piece in place. He hurried to get to the men's restroom and from there tuned what looked like a Walkman cassette player until he could pick up the sounds of Ms. Winegart.

For the first few minutes he detected breathing, paper rustling and foot falls. Then as he descended the stairs back to the lobby he caught an earful of dial tone so loud it forced him to notch the volume down.

His heart surged. He hoped he might have triggered something with his ruse. The mike turned out to be so sensitive it allowed Brax to count the rings on the line.

"Hi Rick, sorry to cut you off. No, just some dick head wanting information. Can you believe it? Somebody came in looking to make a donation. You didn't shoot off while I was gone, did you? You were just about to slip your fingers between my legs when I had to hang up. No start over from the beginning. I was just starting to get creamy."

Brax settled in behind the wheel of his rented Taurus with the sinking feeling that this Madison trip and the ruse to scrutinize the Madison Aviary Preservation Society was going to fizzle.

Ms. Winegart did more cooing than talking. Brax tuned out the dialog, since it had nothing to do with his purpose for being there. It took her nearly thirty minutes of non-stop phone sex to finish her business with Rick and finally end the call.

In the meantime, Brax dialed up Squire to put him to work digging up information on this McVickers character. If the guy checked out in Washington, then he would just wrap things up here and rejoin the team.

Regardless of what he told himself, Brax just couldn't quiet that nagging feeling that something was amiss. The double ice pick kill was something Jaffe had liked to use. Silent, torturous, and professional. Only two people that Brax knew of used that particular method for silent killing. One was dead and the other....

After Ms. Winegart hung up with Rick, Brax listened to shuffling and the click of what sounded like the door locking. A few minutes later footsteps returned. She punched numbers on the phone and must have dialed up a female friend, who chatted almost non-stop for thirty minutes and covered such a myriad of subjects that anyone would find it impossible to keep all the information straight without writing it down. None of the conversation dealt with anything remotely significant to what Brax hoped to learn.

He remained out of sight in his car until five fifteen, a bit surprised that Ms. Winegart had not exited the building promptly at five with the herd that moved out the double doors to the side parking lot. Part of Brax wanted him to abandon the investigation and rejoin the team. Another part urged him to cling to the threads of inconsistencies that kept him wondering about what he had just seen. Was there only a single brochure in that drawer? Is that why Ms. Winegart was so careful to keep him from seeing inside? Could McVickers really be unavailable until Friday? The brochure mentioned no other names than the president's.

He drew forward when the telephone rang.

"Madison Aviary Preservation Society," Ms. Winegart said. A pause filled the air while she listened.

"Yes sir, a man. This morning. He came in wanting information. I'm sorry sir. I paged the moment he left. Five-seven. Dark hair. Yes thin. No si..."

Dial tone.

The conversation ended before Ms. Winegart could finish. Brax's hands clutched the steering wheel. A moment later, Ms. Winegart exited the building in a rush. She scanned the street in a way that drew suspicion to her as she hastened to her parked car.

Brax grabbed the phone.

"You turn up anything on McVickers?"

"Nothing. He exists. But only for about the last four years. Brax, there's such a clean paper trail that it looks like a Witness Protection operation."

"Stay with this. Something smells bad. Real bad. I'm coming home to meet with Housemother."

"Remy wants a meeting."

"Why? What's up," Brax asked. Something about the way Squire said the words raised the hair on Brax's neck.

"His boys decoded Alabaster's data. He's got a theory on our hard target."

"And?"

"Someone took a shot at him at home. He's not certain whether it was a random attempt or if he's been marked."

22

News forthcoming. The man you asked
about has been located in the
computer.

                                    Squire

August 28th. Tommy Whitison squandered a
pampered childhood with dreams of wheeling an
Indy car into the winner's circle of the famed Indianapolis 500 race and hoisting that Borg-Warner for all
to admire. He literally spent every month of May from
age 8 to eighteen sitting at the Indianapolis speedway
watching two generations of Andrettis, Unsers and
Foyt put their cars through the paces. Forget alcohol.
Forget drugs. Forget sex. Speed was Tommy's addiction. But a foolish mistake behind the wheel of a
winged Sprint car at an Indianapolis dirt track at age
twenty permanently deformed his right ankle and
right wrist, and as a result dashed any hope of fame
and glory.

For a time Tommy fought the inevitable, returning to winged Sprint cars at the Indianapolis Raceway
Park, hoping he could overcome the disability. But he
soon realized his deformities prevented him from
maintaining control of his car, and thereby, endan-
gering future hopefuls in the sport.

Now at forty-nine, the closest Tommy got to the
fame of the winner's circle was owning an Indy car
team and vicariously reliving the dreams of his youth
through Marta Guliadomo, his young, sometimes over
zealous driver. He substituted fortune for fame, and

in retrospect, realized the inner satisfaction felt nearly the same.

The four hundred mile exhibition race in Cosenza, a picturesque village in the south of Italy, arranged by CART/PPG in its never-ending quest to generate more revenue, needed a hefty purse to lure the Indy cars across the ocean. As it turned out, this was Tommy's last hope. Fortunes are slippery little devils as he learned trying to keep his car on the track. Few believed the Italians could ever become as excited about Indy cars as they were for Formula One. But CART decided to test the waters for an international circuit anyway. Australia, years earlier, had proved a financial windfall.

CART now hoped for a repeat performance. So much so, that they footed the freight for transporting cars and crew across the ocean. Tommy had little to lose and much to gain in making the trek.

In the nine years he owned his car, he participated in sixteen races with only one finish. And that was a twenty-first finish in a field of twenty-four. The only three cars he outlasted had dropped out with mechanical failures.

Most of Tommy's starts ended prematurely in crashes, two of which so completely demolished his car that his sponsors one by one had abandoned him. His remaining non-finishes were from the plague of mechanical anomalies ever present in the sport. Only Tommy's flare with the drama of racing had kept his remaining backers behind him. Now they were all gone. His money dried up and if he finished out of the money here, it was all over. Only the top ten finishers in Cosenza drew cash. So Tommy knew exactly where he had to be when the checkered flag dropped.

There was one thing that kept Tommy from sinking into that black pit of depression. He had one more ace he could play...if he needed it.

Race morning dawned with Tommy jumping around his garage with his crew after only two hours sleep, putting the final setup on the car. The practice laps had gone well—extremely well—the previous day, and while number 99 secured the fifteenth spot in the field, it remained close enough to the tenth in the field to spawn in Tommy the illusion that he could pull in the money he needed for a run at Indianapolis in the Spring.

Tommy nurtured a conservative strategy focusing on his driver just keeping the car off the concrete for the complete eighty laps, then through simple attrition, he could come away in the money.

Ninety-nine started the race cramped in the middle of the field and for a time it gingerly picked its way around the faster cars to seventh place. Tommy swallowed any premature excitement threatening to take root. After forty laps and two excellent pit stops, his car held seventh place and threatened a move for sixth. They had to hope for a caution flag to drop and give them the opportunity to close the gap.

Tommy timed the laps, updated his driver with the same regularly, and crossed his fingers so hard his knuckles paled. We don't have to win, he told himself a thousand times. Just stay in the top ten. Tommy was sweating, hoping and praying.

On lap fifty-nine, Tommy's wish came true. The twenty-four car spun out after a love tap to its rear wheel. Open wheel race cars are most vulnerable there. It skidded along the wall for a hundred feet. Ninety-nine moved in behind the sixth place car as the field crossed the start/finish line and a fervently waving yellow flag.

The pit crew readied for the next stop. The next time around, his car screeched to a stop into their pit. The driver flipped Tommy a thumb's up, and Tommy thought for sure they could make a move around the sixth place car within five laps.

The roar of ten cars all rocketing out of pit row at the same moment proved deafening. But Tommy could hear over the radio that his man slipped out just ahead of the sixth place car. Tommy Whitison now controlled sixth.

They had a way to go to catch fifth, but at this point it was possible that Tommy's car could capture fifth before the end of the race and lock up a piece of the big money.

For the first time in six months on the circuit, Tommy let a sprout of excitement escape to surface on his face.

But three laps later, the Messenger of Doom had slipped into Tommy's pit to deliver a package without warning. Ninety-nine was creeping up on fifth when the forty-seven car, two laps off the pace lost it, overshot a turn, and plowed into Ninety-nine, forcing it into concrete.

Tommy never saw the crash, since it occurred on the back stretch. His pit crew deflated when the announcement blared that the Ninety-nine car had kissed the wall.

Four minutes later Tommy watched his crumpled dream being towed off the track and into the garage area. He never heard how it happened, though his driver tried to explain a half dozen times. His dream had been flushed once more.

As the sun left the sky and the other owners, drivers and crews celebrated at a banquet in their honor, Tommy remained beside his wrecked car, replacing one piece after another to return it to racing shape. Somehow the act of fixing it kept the depression of the loss at bay. He sacrificed a marriage, two kids and his own sanity for this dream. Twelve years of sacrifice and saving sat in a crumpled heap of fiber glass in the corner.

Ten o'clock came. As promised, a man in rich Italian leather shoes and slicked back black hair stood in the open bay doorway.

"Luck is more difficult to hold on to than it is to catch," Ranzami said, withholding his smile out of respect for another whose dreams dominated his life.

They shared much in common. Now they would have one more thing to share.

Ranzami made no attempt to enter the garage until Tommy rose from his chair and approached with a welcoming hand.

Their contact was brief, and afterward Ranzami strolled around the car like a shopper looking to buy.

"It appeared you had a chance this time, Whitison," Ranzami said.

Silently Shigeo appeared in the doorway. He showed no interest in the car nor its owner, and he remained at the fringe of the garage in a seemingly mannequin stare.

"Then we have a deal?" Ranzami said with a coldness in his eyes that could chill even a warm Italian night. It also sent shivers up Tommy's spine.

"One hundred thousand now; two hundred thousand more back in your garage in New York."

"As we agreed," Tommy responded in a defeated voice.

Tommy offered his hand not to seal the deal but to accept the first payment. And yet he knew not why Ranzami was paying him. He believed that for whatever reason, it had to be illegal. But desperation had numbed his sense of value. Desperation had kept him from asking questions. Desperation had made wrong now right.

"You're certain this is safe?" Tommy asked, growing suddenly nervous.

Shigeo advanced into the garage to hand Tommy a cashier's check drawn on a New York bank and made out to him. Tommy stared at the check for a long moment in disbelief. He felt the spark of his dream returning to life as he verified the number of zeroes.

"Now you must resume your ambition to take this car to Indianapolis in the Spring. And we have work to do. You will excuse us," Ranzami said.

Tommy understood. He left the garage, never looking back as the door came down with the two men inside.

An almost funereal stillness hung in the Statuary Hall after so many hours of banging hammers and power tools. It was an ungodly hour of the night to be in this place. Shortly before two A.M. the team of six moved through the construction area as if they had entered a hot zone. Two German Shepherds led the way, sniffing the air as if they were honing in on fresh meat. Clicking claws along the marble floor shattered the still, their leather leashes hung slack at their handler's sides.

Donley briefed the team an hour earlier. And though each man had his own expertise in counter-espionage search and destroy, Donley, standing at the entrance to the hall, reiterated once more for the record exactly what had to be accomplished. And most importantly, it had to be completed and the crew out before the first renovation worker arrived with the dawn. Above all else, no one could know the extent security went to uncover tradecraft.

The six member team consisted of an uncomfortable composition of four Company professionals and two Bureau 'Spy Catcher' experts. Donley knew the Bureau boys personally; they offered a grim reminder of what his life used to be. The Company boys he knew only by reputation and recommendation from his Agency liaison. Beneath the surface, a fierce competition raged between the two organizations. The Bureau had a problem any time Agency personnel worked inside the U.S. The Company just had a problem any time they came into contact with these particular members of the Bureau.

The identities of Bureau Spy Catchers were no secret to CIA personnel. Though, the two Bureau team members had gone to lengths to present themselves more the novice than the expert. The Company viewed Bureau people the same way a beat cop views Internal Affairs. Spy Catchers were there to watch over Company Operations Officers. The Ames case had put everyone in the Agency on edge.

Each group represented his organization in this operation and each took failure personally. Since Ames, promotions and jobs hung in the balance. While they bantered back and forth lightheartedly during the briefing, all humor ceased the moment they entered the Capitol building. Counterespionage was business...serious business. Any time a target came away clean, they felt as if they had failed in their responsibility. They didn't need to be told that the Russians would do anything to get monitoring devices in a place like this.

The German Shepherds, on the other hand, could care less about electronic eavesdropping devices. They were there to sniff out the presence of eight different kinds of explosive matter in quantities as small as a quarter ounce, even if someone buried a bomb inside six inches of concrete. And the animals wasted no time in commencing their work.

With the hounds sniffing at every crack and crevice in the construction zone, the remaining four members donned a collection of headsets, and each tuned the assortment of sophisticated electronic monitoring equipment designed to reveal the presence of listening devices.

Each piece of equipment had its own specialty. Combined they could detect the presence of almost any monitoring device the Russians could plant. Using a sophisticated algorithm of electronic frequency generation, the equipment detected hidden microphones by forcing them to resonate, thereby causing the little bastards to emit a telltale electronic signature that the investigator could hone in on to locate the bug. The sweepers focused their attention on the second floor offices in the House wing and worked painfully slow, methodically covering every inch of each office before proceeding to the next one.

One device could be tuned to seek out the presence of any transmitting devices that might have been installed and awaited the addition of a microphone.

The only devices capable of eluding sweeper detection were the sleepers, those installed and put to sleep, with the intent of awakening them after the security crew had completed their inspections at the end of the job. These bugs might lay dormant for months after the project's completion. The Company knew the Russians liked to plant their sleepers in groups of three, activating the second or third devices only after the first or second ones had been discovered and removed. If the team could detect the presence of one sleeper, they would know to seek out the other two before blessing this place.

Knowing that, Donley requested the best the Agency could turn out to sweep for sleepers. The highly complicated task required broadcasting a wide band of high frequency waves into the walls, then listening for the electronic response as the transmitter devices reflected the minute radio waves. Sort of like reading a polygraph, hunting down sleepers was more an art than a science. The pro Donley brought in cut his teeth on the American embassy in Moscow. He could bring a sleeper to the surface when all the others swore the place was clean.

The sleeper detection method, however, had one shortcoming—it generated an unusually large number of false readings around metal. Therefore, the Russians had taken to enveloping sleepers in metal shells to elude the American sweepers. The metal lessened the sleepers effectiveness, but it did allow them to escape American detection.

After three hours of intense effort in the House wing, the team reassembled in the center of the Statuary Hall to report their findings. All came back empty handed. No devices had been uncovered and the team concluded none could had been planted in the renovation area.

During the same three hour inspection, the dogs gave no indication that they had detected the presence of any dangerous substances. Donley expected the place to be clean, attributed it to his role in overseeing security and left for breakfast satisfied that he had performed to the letter of his supervisor's dictate.

He offered to buy the team breakfast—the Bureau members accepted; the Agency guys just wanted to get back to their offices. Donley sensed they viewed the effort as a failure and were less ready to accept that no attempt had been made to penetrate the Capitol.

We superpowers also have the responsibility to exercise restraint in the use of our great military force. The integrity and the independence of weaker nations must not be threatened. They must know that in our presence they are secure.

But now the Soviet Union has taken a radical and an aggressive new step. It's using its great military power against a relatively defenseless nation. The implications of the Soviet invasion of Afghanistan could pose the most serious threat to the peace since the Second World War.

The vast majority of nations on Earth have condemned this latest Soviet attempt to extend its colonial domination to others and have demanded the immediate withdrawal of Soviet troops. The Moslem world is especially and justifiably outraged by this aggression against Islamic people. No Action of a world power has ever been so quickly and so overwhelmingly condemned. But verbal condemnation is not enough. The Soviet Union must pay a concrete price for their aggression.

This situation demands careful thought, steady nerves, and resolute action, not only for this year but for many years to come. It demands collective efforts to meet this new threat to security in the Persian Gulf and in Southwest Asia.

Jimmy Carter, January 23, 1980

₿

Dick and Jane sitting on the stoop.
Cody

September 19th. Brax's hunch had been dead on the money. Squire's broadcast message had returned a hit on an IRA lieutenant going by the name Lonigan. A surveillance on a suspected Fuqra black route into Texas revealed a fair-haired man in his twenties being brought across the border with a truckload of Mexicans. An albatross amongst ducklings, Lonigan became easy to ID. Seemed the Fuqra's current contribution to terrorism in the U.S. included aiding and abetting. After a history of assassinations and fire-bombings across the United States during the '80s, most of the radical members had been convicted and imprisoned. Those remaining loyal to the sect of Pakistani cleric Shaykh Mubarik Ali Gilani had gone underground. *Until now.* The FBI immediately took control, setting up the surveillance of Lonigan's movements, and at the same time dissecting the mechanizations of exactly how flesh moved through the states.

Only on strict authorization from Washington could either the border patrol or the FBI shut the operation down. For the moment, Housemother wanted to gain every bit of knowledge possible. Knowing the how behind terrorist infiltration into the states could give the Pack a very deadly edge.

There was one very grave risk involved in allowing Lonigan to move about the country. He could elude at some time surveillance and disappear, only to surface at the moment of a terrorist attack. But they had to live with that risk. This man could be a link.

The FBI performed much of the necessary groundwork for Cody and Cali, tracking Lonigan up through Memphis, Cincinnati, Detroit then finally via Greyhound into New York. At no time were the Bureau ever more than a few yards from their prey. Once Lonigan settled in New York city, they set up an observation post to maintain a constant surveillance. For the first day, Lonigan maintained a low profile, occupying a single bedroom apartment on the east side of Brooklyn. A building situated just two miles west of a known Russian safe house that had gone unused for the past nine months. The FBI had been keeping tabs on the safe house, so they had to scramble to the new location when Lonigan chose an alternate. Perhaps this one was not operating under Russian sanction. The fact that Lonigan avoided the Russian house could have meant the Russians were unaware of this one's visit. Or they were being very careful about their movements. The situation smelled of Leviathan, and Cody and Cali were already moving in to take over control.

The two agents assigned were none too pleased to receive immediate vacate orders so soon after settling in. So much had been so delicately manipulated to protect their surveillance that they took the order as a slap in the face. Without knowing exactly who had issued the directive, they deduced it had to be Company linked. The New York Bureau Chief instructed them to abandon the observation post without delay.

From their secure position, Cody and Cali monitored the two exiting the apartment building. They loaded black cases into the rear of a non-descript windowless van, then scanned the surroundings from inside before departing. Cali, being anxious, moved prematurely toward the building. Cody's grab held her back.

"Wait. Let's make sure those little weasels clear the area. I don't want us being made by the Bureau."

Cody approached first, entering the building from a rear entrance. Cali followed ten minutes later shouldering two bags of groceries. They had to hope their sensitive operation hadn't already been blown by bumbling bureau agents tipping Lonigan off to surveillance.

Within the hour, Cody and Cali had assessed the target location and completed their move into the observation station. It took three trips spaced over a thirty minute period to bring in their equipment, since hauling up everything at once might had attracted unwanted attention.

"Those Bureau assholes are such pigs," Cali remarked staring at the toilet, while Cody set up the camera and took aim on Lonigan's window. "How's our boy doing?"

"I've got a lock on the target."

"Then we're off and running. You think they'd at least clean the damn toilet before leaving," Cali commented. She broke out a bottle of toilet cleaner, waving it in the air as if she had scored some kind of victory with it.

"It's a man thing," Cody commented. He remained focused on the viewfinder, making final adjustments. Even with an intense glare of the afternoon sun pouring through Lonigan's window, Cody easily penetrated the apartment as if he were standing just outside the window.

"What do you think?"

Cali stopped her cleaning to cross to the window to verify the camera set up.

"Looks good to me."

While Cody checked in with Squire over the secure phone that never left their side, Cali began inventorying the listening devices. Cody opened the surveillance log file on Lonigan by noting the precise time of target acquisition.

"Call it in the air," Cody said after hanging up the phone.

Cali intercepted the coin at its zenith.

"Heads, I win," she said.

"Well that's just fine. You figure 'cause you've been to sound school, you're better qualified than me? You know I could've went to sound school. It's not that I'm stupid or anything like that. Damn mule! Kicked me in the head when I was ten. Since then I *canst* hear out my right ear."

His rendition of a down-home Okie failed to raise a smile on Cali's face.

"I'll handle the phone, you plant the bedroom," Cali replied. She wasn't amused.

Cody watched through tripod-mounted binoculars as below Cali crossed the street, weaving through the blockage of traffic to make her way to Lonigan's building. His mind filled more with thoughts of Cali as a woman than a partner or team member. The crystal blue in her eyes captivated him, and though he buried his interest deep enough to prevent detection, he knew sooner or later she would excavate that long suppressed desire.

After she disappeared, Cody opened his own bag of equipment to peruse the devices, deciding which he would use to wire Lonigan's apartment. A single bedroom meant one well-placed bug could score complete coverage, though he would plant a second as backup. He figured he could be in and out in less than fifteen minutes.

While Cody waited for Cali's return, Squire phoned in an update from the two agents who previously watched over their target.

"So far we're in luck. Guy's a real homebody," Squire reported, "seemed he only leaves the place to eat and stretch. Hasn't had a contact yet."

"Good, then we're the only ones who'll know who and what he does. How did he get to New York?"

"Black route into Texas, Fuqra sponsored. Not sure exactly on the details. Border guards tipped us off. This guy made certain nobody shadowed him."

Cody signed off to return to his window. He clicked a half dozen shots on the camera capturing Lonigan as he crossed the window then receded back into the murky interior of the room. There was no mistaking Malakey Lonigan. Dark baggy eyes. Pale lifeless skin beneath a scraggly beard and profusely receding hairline, and a face that seemed troubled even when he had the rare occasion to cast a smile.

Cody's heart lurched. They may have finally come up with a link to their target. Cody quieted visions of a meeting between Lonigan and Leviathan in New York. They were lucky, but they would never expect things to go that easy. He knew their target was too cunning to make their job easy.

"Okay, you stinking bag of cow shit, lead us to the scum who pays you."

Cali returned to catch the tail of his words and witness him biting off a chunk of chew. With each chew he searched for the outlet he would soon need.

"Oh no. No chewing. I ain't putting up with the spit," Cali said.

"Damn, woman, you're worse than a wife," Cody moaned. He hesitated before finally seeking out a waste can to empty his cheek.

Cali settled in at the table and extracted headphones that she fitted snugly over her ears. Throwing a master switch illuminated a red light on her panel, indicating her bug had power, and after adjusting a few dials, she shot Cody a thumbs up to confirm that it had become fully operational. The monitor, which filled a briefcase, consisted of a voice-activated cassette tape recorder the size of a Walkman and capable of storing twelve hours of voice on a 4mm cassette, and a sophisticated array of filters and sound clippers. With patience and persistence, she could tune out almost any unwanted sounds to focus in on the one she wanted. She double checked the equipment with meters, then settled back in her chair with a smug smile intended for Cody.

"I would have been in and out in under four minutes," Cody said from window.

"Yeah, so?"

"You took eight."

Cali shrugged off the remark.

For the next four hours they sat, listened, and stared.

"I've got dial tone," Cali vaulted as the tape began to move slowly and silently. She listened while Lonigan called a restaurant to inquire as to their dining hours and menu selections. He asked so many annoying questions that the voice on the other end was glad to be rid of him. Does anyone really care if the garlic is roasted in olive oil rather than butter?

It seemed by nine o'clock that Lonigan had no intention of leaving to afford Cody his opportunity to get inside to plant his devices.

However, a little after eleven Cody watched the apartment lights go out followed a few minutes later by Lonigan's undernourished form appearing on the street. Cali took the first surveillance, lagging half a block behind her target as he strolled north.

Cody's turn to infiltrate. He grabbed his tools and dashed across the street, disappearing into Lonigan's apartment building through the front door. The lock on Lonigan's apartment door succumbed to Cody's touch in under ten seconds. So much for deadbolt security.

Inside, Cody wasted no time planting the two listening devices he had earlier selected for monitoring. The Japanese KC9 series devices were the best he had with him, more than adequate for his needs. Checking his watch, and feeling unpressed for time, Cody installed a micro-miniature camera in a ceiling light fixture over the bed. With its fish eye lens, they could monitor Lonigan's movements throughout the breadth of the apartment and detect the slightest anomaly in his actions. Cody knew installing the camera was overkill, but he just couldn't resist.

The CIA's best intelligence up to this point indicated Lonigan more prone to one-on-one killing than mass murder. But he did have one incident to his credit that made him a potential soldier for Leviathan. So Cody risked spending an extra minute searching for Lonigan's assassination tool kit. He expected to locate it, clinched a fist when he found nothing and vacated without compromise.

When Cali returned more than an hour later, they listened as Lonigan relieved himself. Cali shot Cody a smile and a thumbs up.

"You plant that little sucker behind the toilet?" she said, surprised by the clarity of the signal they received.

"No!" Cody replied, taking her comment serious.

"I'm just kidding."

Lonigan's sudden flatulent release brought laughter in the room.

"Is it real, or is it Memorex?" Cody asked jokingly.

Their work done for the time being, Cody settled into the chair facing the target's apartment while Cali took the first sleep shift on the single bed. So far, Lonigan had been a good boy and simply retired after returning from a routine solitary, late night dinner.

"You asleep?" Cody asked after an only hour by himself.

"Not now," Cali said. She turned over to face him.

"Why'd you get into this?"

"You mean why did I, a woman, get into this? Or why did I, an Amerasian, get into this? Or why did I, Cali, get into this?"

"Well all three, actually."

"I guess it's what I'm good at. How about you let me get some sleep."

Cody settled into his chair, covered his face with his hat and closed his eyes, taking in Lonigan's whimpering snores through his headphones.

The following day passed without incident and only the sounds of the television and Lonigan's regular movement were trapped by the bugs.

Cody backed off with Cali. She sent a pretty strong message in response to him prying into her life.

"I was recruited out of Oklahoma University," he said as he lunched on chips and a roast beef sandwich, while Cali picked apart a tuna salad laden with mayonnaise.

Cali smiled but showed little interest. Instead she browsed through a stack of intelligence reports she had collected while passing through Langley a week back.

"When I was a kid, my daddy used to bring home road kill for stew three days a week. Liked the armadillo the best."

"Really? I lived on beetle larvae until I was six."

"No Shit. You too? Your momma stir fry 'em? Mine liked to deep fry ours."

"You soft Americans. We'd just dig 'em out of the hole and pop them buggers into our mouths. They wiggle all the way to your stomach."

Cody dropped his sandwich to the plate and pushed it away, surrendering to Cali.

"You win. Where'd you go to school?" Cody asked, he couldn't stop himself.

"Sac State in California."

The conversation died there. Cody could tell his questions had begun to ruffle Cali.

Lonigan never spent one moment alone, unbeknownst to him. Each time he left the apartment, one of them followed at a safe distance. They altered their routines and dress as much as three times in a day to minimize the chances of being exposed in their surveillance. While one followed Lonigan's every move in the neighborhood, the other constantly watched for signs of a contact. They suspected many of Lonigan's little trips had been set up to unmask surveillance, since he roamed the neighborhood without destination only to return a short time later. They had to be cautious that another of Leviathan's soldiers might be watching from a safe perch to determine if anyone had taken an interest in Lonigan. Once compromised, Lonigan would simply leave the country.

Neither could tell how many more little trips Lonigan would have to take before his contact became comfortable that he was indeed alone.

Lonigan must have felt reasonably free of surveillance, since he performed his rituals less and less as time dragged on seemingly without purpose.

His regular anti-surveillance activity heightened Cody and Cali's interest. When Remy heard of Lonigan's pattern, he, too, concluded they have snagged a gem. Sooner or later Lonigan would lead them to their target. Only Leviathan went to such great lengths to protect himself and his operation.

Only after Lonigan himself was absolutely certain it was safe would he proceed with his real reason for being in New York. The fact that he lingered day in and day out without meeting a contact could mean one of two things: his contact was still unconvinced a meeting would be absolutely secure, or Lonigan had already been compromised and the contact had aborted and evacuated the city.

With the end of the fourth day, came concern. Concern that Lonigan might be a decoy deployed to keep surveillance agents busy while Leviathan met with another.

As a result, Cody began updating Squire every two hours, who in turn kept Brax apprised of the surveillance. But for the eighteenth consecutive report,

there was nothing to indicate Lonigan had any con-
spiratorial intent. Behind the scenes, the New York
Bureau office was suddenly growing short on
patience; they wanted Lonigan taken into custody.
Midnight phone calls were made, secret meetings
were held in seclusion. However, a single phone call
from Housemother silenced the local Bureau.

That night both Cali and Cody followed Lonigan,
confident the sound-activated recorder would trap
anything that occurred inside the apartment while
they were gone. Cody watched for changes in neighboring windows that indicate a contact's signal. Over
the past twelve hours, Cody had become restive from
the arduous long hours of inactivity and needed the
movement to work off his pent-up energy. What he
really needed was a few days away from the rigors of
hunting down a master terrorist, or a night with a
woman. He'd take either, the latter preferred.

Lonigan took the subway and rode aimlessly,
switching in Manhattan to another train which took
him into the city's flesh district. Mostly, he just
stared vacantly out the window while he rode. He
never once scanned the bystanders as he waited for
his connecting train. Throughout, he spoke to no one
and occupied the first available seat at the door
through which he boarded. After exiting, Lonigan
browsed from shop to shop under the bright neon of
pseudo-flesh for sale. The peep shows, book shops
and nightclubs attracted his eye, but he walked on
without entering any of them.

Normally, Cody and Cali would switch off surveillance, following him in and out of establishments,
but Cali would draw obvious attention if she showed
up in a nude dance club or porno bookstore alone,
and coincident with Lonigan.

Cody remained unshaken in his surveillance. He
switched patterns and routines frequently to safeguard his mission. For a while it seemed to Cody this
would be an ideal place for a contact or a rendezvous.

A casual passing, someone exiting a video preview booth just before Lonigan entered. Information could be left in a movie booth or a private dance booth, where for those willing to pay, a woman performed for an audience of one down to complete nudity while safely separated by a pane of glass.

Cody rehearsed the response he would employ should he detect a contact as Lonigan walked shoulder to shoulder through some of the crowded night spots. It had to go down hard and fast if they had to intercept whatever brought Lonigan to New York.

Lonigan's venture into the slime lasted less than two hours. Afterward, he made his way back to the subway and finally to his apartment. On the return ride, Cali occupied a car ahead of the target while Cody stood at the windowed door at the car just to the rear. At no time did they allow Lonigan completely out of their sight. It seemed like the excursion had been nothing more than a diversion from the television in the apartment. Lonigan never even purchased a souvenir to take back with him.

Back at their observation post, Cody took the first sleep shift while Cali made herself comfortable on the chair. From there, she listened to Lonigan's snoring through the headphones.

But his sleep lasted only a few hours. At three, he dialed and exchanged words with a soft erotic voice. Lonigan had requested a visit from a personal counselor and agreed to pay a hundred for it.

"Counselor," Cali laughed as she listened.

A few minutes after Lonigan hung up, the telephone rang. Cali recorded the caller's number that appeared on her ID display.

"Love that caller ID," she remarked in a whisper so as not to disturb Cody.

The same soft voice confirmed a counselor but for a two hundred dollar price tag. Seemed Lonigan must have had a reputation with these girls.

Cali waited in the darkened room. She flipped back and forth between waking Cody and letting him sleep. Could be a hooker...could be a contact. She sharpened her camera's focus on Lonigan's window. A dim light filtered through the drawn curtain, but this time the narrow slit prevented Cali from getting a clear view of the inside.

Twenty minutes later, a cab pulled to a squeaky stop before the apartment building on the otherwise deserted street. A sleek shape in a white skirt that barely hid her V slid out. Platinum hair, ample breasts and fish net hose became visible under the scrutiny of the light over the door. No panning nor pausing, the counselor marched inside.

Cali had delayed as long as she could.

"We've got something," she said, awakening Cody.

He jolted awake and bolted upward out of a deep sleep. For a long moment he stared through the darkness at Cali as if confused by his surroundings.

Cali returned to the window, pointing down to the cab that had pulled over to the curb, extinguished its headlights and waited.

Coincidence? Or a short time. Two hundred was a pretty steep price for a short time.

"What's up," Cody said finally, comprehending finally what Cali was pointing out.

"Lover boy called in a visitor," Cali said. She moved left to allow Cody to assess the situation.

"Fuck. Why didn't you wake me sooner?"

"I wanted to assess the situation before disturbing you."

"Look, goddamnit, just disturb me. You think we've got something?"

Minutes of silence passed while Cody listened on the headphones. He laughed. Then he went to his briefcase, removed a six-inch television monitor and set it on the table.

"Shall we," he said with a smile.

"You didn't?"

"I did."

He connected a black box no larger than a cigarette pack to the rear of the set and turned a dial very slowly until a snowy picture materialized on the small screen. The next tweak of the dial brought the picture in clear.

The bird's eye view of Lonigan's apartment showed Lonigan sitting on his bed masturbating.

"I love this job," Cody muttered.

The buzzer brought Lonigan's hand off his member like a schoolboy caught by his mother. After slipping his thing away, Lonigan moved out of the scene to answer the door.

"The least irregularity we pick up the contact when she leaves the building," Cody instructed.

"Two hundred, right," Lonigan confirmed with the visitor, who remained out of the range of the surveillance camera.

"You are one sneaky devil," Cali said, rummaging through a mostly empty grocery bag for something to munch. She pulled open a bag of chips and settled in.

"She looks legit," Cody said when Platinum followed Lonigan to the bed.

Cali let a sigh slip silently away. At first she thought she might have blown the surveillance.

"Sound or no sound? I like this stuff better with the moaning," Cody said. His eyes remained on Platinum, who began slowly peeling her clothes away while Lonigan went back to his masturbation on the bed.

"What are you going to do?" Lonigan asked.

"Anything you want, honey. Anything you want."

Even before she could get on the bed Lonigan had filled his hand with her breast. She gently removed it and leveled her hand.

"Business first, honey."

Lonigan complied. He filled her waiting palm with what appeared through the camera to be two hundreds.

"I'll bet he's passing Iranians," Cody chided.

"She deserves it then for being stupid," Cali offered.

In a Pavlovian response, Platinum took hold of his member and began working it in earnest, gently biting his nipple while he stroked her flowing hair.

"You must be real horny," she cooed pulling her lips off his chest, drawing her conclusion from the speed with which he sprang to readiness.

Her efforts forced Lonigan to stroke her hair with greater vigor. Then he got real excited. He yanked the hair back, forcing the wig from her crown.

Cali and Cody laughed at a pinned back head of hair half bleached blonde and half grown-out chestnut.

"God, she's getting uglier by the minute," Cody remarked.

"Easy, Honey, don't want to mess me up," Platinum offered as she returned the wig to her head.

Lonigan eased her head down along his stomach and positioned her so she could easily acquire his member. The positioning put Lonigan's head in between the camera and the action.

"Men are such scum," Cali commented, tossing the bag onto the table and reaching for something new. "We need pop corn. I should have gotten some."

"I don't see anything here to indicate she's passing information," Cody said with a smile.

"I'll make sure that gets in the report."

Lonigan, tiring of her oral efforts, motioned her to move to her knees on the bed. Like a schoolboy, he began fondling her mound even before she slid out of her remaining garment.

"If you're going to be up, I'll grab some sleep. Nothing on television worth watching anyway," Cali remarked.

"I'll keep the sound down so as not to disturb you," Cody said, waving her off with his hand.

Lonigan's voyage into sexual ecstasy lasted less than thirty minutes. Then it turned ugly. The sharp claps of his open hand against her face snapped Cali out of bed.

"That fucker," she said, watching as Lonigan slapped Platinum with unrestrained force. He muffled her screams by ramming his other hand into her gaping mouth.

"You bite and I cut your fucking tongue out, you bitch."

Lonigan levied a knife with its point jabbing Platinum's reddened cheek.

"Where'd he pull the fucking knife from?"

"Must have been under the pillow. I looked for his kit but came up empty."

"Jesus Christ, he's going to kill her," Cali said, her voice rising in panic.

"No he's not. How's he get rid of the body?"

"Like a freak like that thinks about those things."

Cody and Cali watched as the blade moved from her cheek to her throat, then down toward her unprotected crotch. Platinum's eyes had turned so white with terror they dominated her face. Tears found their way down her cheeks, mixing with the blood oozing from a cut inside her mouth.

"You fucking whore. You don't deserve to live anyway. You'll fuck anybody. You're a fucking whore!"

Lonigan pommelled the woman to the floor, and standing over her, tossed the knife to the bed.

For a brief second, Platinum stared at the blade. She never moved, not even to wipe the blood drooling from the corner of her mouth. It was as if Lonigan was taunting her, begging her to go for the blade, so he could rip it from her hands and stick her.

"Get your fucking clothes, and get the fuck out of out of here, before I change my mind and cut your fucking whoring cunt out of you."

Silence fell upon both apartments.

By sunrise, Cody had studied the audio and video a hundred times. Could the exchange have been an act? A way for information to pass from Lonigan to Platinum or vice versa? The blood and fear on Platinum's face had been so convincing that Cody concluded Platinum had been nothing more than a sick release for Lonigan and not involved with any terrorist organization.

"How's our little fucker this morning?" Cali said, pulling sleepy eyes open and turning toward Cody sitting at the window behind binoculars.

"Sleeping like a baby."

"I'll bet."

"You should have it easy. He'll sleep 'til noon now."

And Cody was right. One o'clock came and went before Lonigan awakened and switched on the television. He surfed the channels, finally settling on a Brazilian soccer match on a cable sports channel.

Cody went for hot sandwiches in the afternoon, five hours sleep seemed ample for him, and while they sat and listened to the game emanating from Lonigan's apartment, Cody dispatched another report to Squire. Aside from the sex and violence, the surveillance could bore even the most dedicated to tears.

In Squire's return message he passed on Brax's concern that Lonigan might be a waste of time and resources, since to date he displayed no overt signs that a meeting or contact was imminent. But patience was the call of the day; they knew it as did their nemesis, and they had to hope sooner or later someone somewhere would slip and deliver them Leviathan. They just had no idea how much time they had before the bastard struck again.

In late afternoon, with the shadow of their building painting Lonigan's, Cali sat dividing her attention
between Lonigan's window and the foot traffic below.
The man's phone almost never rang. Cali wondered
whether this surveillance would pan out. Maybe
Brax's recollection was flawed? Maybe they were
watching a nobody, with no link whatsoever to Leviathan, or any other known terrorist for that matter.

"Our boy's in the shower, doing himself again,"
Cali reported. She stretched out on the bed, allowing
Cody to take over at the window.

"Not even a sign?" Cody asked.

"Nada." Cali closed her eyes, hoping to drift off
to sleep.

Cody sat at the table flipping cards in such a way
so as to allow him to watch the apartment, the street
below and play out a poor attempt at Solitaire,
though at times he couldn't help but want to watch
Cali.

"Why'd you join the Company?" he asked, probably more out of boredom than curiosity.

"Why do you want to know?" she said, her eyes
still closed.

"Just wondering."

"Wondering why a woman would want this business?"

"Wondering why a beautiful woman like you
would want this business."

Cali shifted. Compliments made her uncomfortable. Maybe Cody was getting horny from watching
Lonigan doing his thing?

"Company helped my father get me out of Viet-
nam when I was eight. Why'd you join? You a
patriot?"

"Just a Joe with a talent for...."

Cali popped off the bed. A dial tone silenced
them. Lonigan was making a call. She watched the
digits appear on the display and stared at the slowly

moving tape in the cartridge. The phone rang a dozen times, still Lonigan hung on to the call.

In a second, Cody was on the secure phone matching a name to the number. Cody jotted down a name and address on his notepad. Was this a signal? Was the party there and expected to let it ring? Or was Lonigan calling for another whore?

Finally the telephone picked up. No voices. Instead a series of warbled tones and high-pitch squeals.

"Fuck," Cody muttered stretching full length to reach the briefcase and slap down a switch that put their telephone bug to sleep.

"Damnit. They're sweeping," Cali said, an instant behind Cody's hand.

"Fuck! I hope we got to it in time." Cody's face had turned to stone. He grabbed binoculars to sweep Lonigan's apartment.

They had it! The first sign that Lonigan might be involved in something. The Russians regularly employed sophisticated detection devices that caused telephone bugs to resonant and echo back a radiated signal to a super sensitive receiver tapped into the telephone line. Someone had just checked the line for bugs. Only Leviathan and the Russians might exhibit such extreme caution. The smaller terrorist groups spent their funds on explosives rather than tradecraft.

Silence returned to the apartment. Lonigan received no other phone calls. Nor did he seem to alter his pattern in any way.

Had they shut down the bug in time?

Cody and Cali now had to wait and wonder if they passed the test. If the contact had detected the bug, he would abort any planned meeting with Lonigan. If he hadn't, he might sweep again to be absolutely sure before making an approach. At least, Cali and Cody knew now they had the right man. If they passed the test, Lonigan would be expecting a contact and soon.

At eight, Lonigan left the apartment. Cali and Cody remained within fifty yards at all times. Lonigan walked to the subway and transferred once getting off in midtown Manhattan.

Cali was relieved. This appeared not to be another flesh trip. She could do without that.

Lonigan walked for awhile, moving in and out of the lights, watching people pass and pausing at intervals just to stare at the windows. He was obviously using reflections to locate shadows.

After a few more blocks, he entered a shabby-faced bar off the beaten path.

Cali continued past the location and turned down the next block. Cody, who had been trailing from across the street, entered the bar first; Cali was to follow five minutes later.

Country music blared from a DJ's alcove in a sparsely populated dance hall. Cody scanned the interior, his eyes moving over Lonigan's as if he were just another face. He took a stool at the center of the bar like he had just come in off the range, then he motioned for a drink. His Texas drawl came naturally.

He wished now he had worn his hat and boots. On the street he would have stuck out. In here he blended. The down home music seeped under his skin and within a minute he was tapping to the beat. When his beer came, he shifted to the right just enough to catch Lonigan in the mirror behind the cash register. Lonigan took a corner booth, sat alone, and quaffed down a beer in three gulps.

The current of the atmosphere only fed Cody's desire to get away from the pressure and let his hair down. He needed to get back to Houston, even if only for a weekend. New York had to be the world's most densely populated outhouse as far as Cody was concerned.

Cali timed her entry to the establishment behind a trio of young ladies in hats, boots and western blouses, complete with tassels and western embroidery. Aside from the dress, Cali appeared to be one of the group. Her maneuver allowed her to fade off from the others and find a seat in a corner away from Lonigan. She could see him, but he couldn't see her.

Cali and Cody's eyes never met, though they had exchanged a signal to acknowledge coverage of the target. The spin jockey liked to smooth his wavy jet black hair back beneath a wide-brimmed hat—he performed the operation at least three times during each song. And he strutted what seemed to be an authentic Tennessee drawl. He started the music with more than a little fanfare, and Cody turned from his bar stool to check out the ladies parading past him with more than just a passing glance.

Over the course of the next thirty minutes the place doubled in population. Off and on a few couples wandered out to the dance floor. Nothing like down home, Cody thought, wouldn't find enough room to stand a broom on end at his favorite haunt.

Cali nursed a wine cooler, checking the door frequently in a ruse that she expected to be joined at any moment. For the most part, no one offered her more than a passing once-over. And that was the way she wanted it. The last thing she wanted now was some cowboy wannabe putting the make on her. She already had one of them to put up with.

Throughout, Lonigan did nothing more than suck down beer and enjoy the music. When Lonigan went to the john, Cody was right behind, standing at the mirror to comb his hair while Lonigan took care of business. No one approached the target, nor did he talk to anyone other than the barmaid, who returned regularly to keep his glass full.

"Want to give this thing a whirl, cowboy," a sweet, chesty blonde proposed, her finger beckoning Cody as he emerged from the restroom. She must have planned her approach, since she pounced within paces of his exit. The words caught Lonigan's attention. He turned from his booth in Cody's direction.

Cody swallowed the young lady in his arms and swept her onto the dance floor, where he led her around like a man who had been two-stepping since age four.

"I'm Katie," she said.

Cody missed her name. He scanned to make sure his target remained where he was a few seconds earlier.

"Oh sorry, Clete."

"And you're from?"

"Amarilla, darlin'. Ever been there?"

Seconds later the music ended, much to Cody's delight. He abandoned the young lady on the floor and returned to his bottle at the bar. By now, moving was a squeeze and it took an outstretched arm to retrieve his long neck. Like it or not, he had given his stool to a luscious red head with a smile as sprawling as his home state.

Dancers flowed on and off the floor with the changing of the music. The true lovers of country music stayed on the floor. The crowd seemed evenly split between line dancers and couples. Most were competent, a few even good by Cody's standards, though it was obvious they were without the refinement of dancers in Texas. Some fumbled back and forth just trying to catch on to the steps while trying to avoid turning the place into a mosh pit.

Cody meandered through the clusters, never allowing more than a few seconds to elapse without checking on his target.

"May I," he asked, setting a hand out.

"I don't do that," Cali offered under her breath in a genuinely innocent expression of surprise.

Cody winked.

Cali smiled, took his hand, and let him lead her to the crowded dance floor. Was this such a good idea?

She wondered. Lonigan could place them together now.

Cody's grace and rhythm seemed paradoxical for a man of his size. He moved effortlessly around other couples, never missing a step and never once stepping on Cali's feet, even though she jerked them around trying to make it look like she knew what she was doing. His gently guiding hand corrected her mistakes and made it easier for her to follow. Just the way he held her wove an intoxicating spell over her. By the end of the second dance, she found herself actually getting the hang of it.

Like two strangers, they spoke little while they danced, and when the music stopped, Cali remained beside him in a clear signal of interest, hoping another song might start before having to part company.

From their vantage point they could easily view Lonigan. No one approached his table. No one sent him a signal from anywhere in the room that they could detect.

To Cody's wishes, Garth Brook's 'The Rodeo' started. He put his hand on Cali's hip in instructive fashion and took her hand in his other. When Cali moved closer to him, he motioned her away.

His boyish innocent charm held her under its spell until the song finished. Cody didn't need to talk to captivate a woman. All he had to do was look at her with those playground eyes and impish smile. The steps were more difficult in this dance, but Cali had caught on and by the end moved in unison with him.

Cali's palms were sweating more than she wanted. She had to force herself on occasion to draw her eyes from his. Touching him, having him close began stirring up things deep inside. Things she told herself she would avoid at all costs. She wondered if he could somehow feel her heart racing inside her chest.

"I really should sit down," she offered in a whisper.

Whether Cody had planned it or not she couldn't know for sure, but when the song ended they were left standing three feet from Lonigan's table. He took no notice of their presence—seemed more interested in something at the bar.

Cody tracked Lonigan's line of sight but the place had become so packed with country dancers and onlookers lining the bar that any one of about thirty could have attracted Lonigan's interest.

Yet having said she should sit down, Cali made no move to leave Cody's side. In fact, she kept her hand in his and prayed another song would start before they became obvious.

Another song did start, a George Strait favorite, and she was quick to place her hand around his waist to allow him to lead.

About halfway through the music, Cody spun Cali around in a move that seemed out of place with the song and his so precisely choreographed dance steps. Lonigan's booth was empty.

"He's gone," she said.

"I know," Cody responded drawing her in close to press her body against his. Having realized his dream was about to end, he relished in their one last embrace.

As if it had been some grandly orchestrated maneuver, Cody positioned her in time with the music to observe Lonigan a few strides from the door. Cali's instinct ordered her to break away.

Cody brought her back close.

"Too soon. Let him get out," Cody whispered next to her ear. He filled his lungs with her heady perfume. He agonized over having to release her. Their eyes met for an instant. Cody read more in hers than their assignment.

Their lips were inches apart. Cody wanted to kiss her, to thank her for the pleasures of the past hour.

But he had to allow the moment to dissipate. Their target was on the move.

Once the door closed and Lonigan had past the neon-emblazoned front window, Cody and Cali wormed their way through the crowd picking a direct path for the door. Cody clung to Cali's hand more out of need than any other reason.

Upon reaching the door, Cody realized his error. Had a plant been in the bar to cover Lonigan's back? If there was one, the two of them were now exposed and their surveillance compromised.

Mistakes happen—even to the best. Cody had let Cali's scent and softness distract him. In a profession intolerable of human frailty, Cody had let his guard down, if only for a moment. Now it could cost them dearly.

24

Working to remove the impasse. Will
advise new agenda.

                         Brax

All Cody and Cali could do now was go on and
hope for the best. Lonigan walked for a while, changing direction in an aimless wandering. He ended up at
an X-rated movie house, forcing Cody to follow and
slip unnoticed into a seat in the third row from the
rear. The sparse crowd heightened Cody's risk of
exposure. Something maybe Lonigan had intended. If
Lonigan had marked him in the bar and now
observed him again in the theater, it was sure to compromise the surveillance.

The situation forced Cali out of sight across a
deserted street. From her vantage no one could exit
the theater unobserved. Even if they chose the side
fire exit. It was after midnight. An occasional car
passed. Each time headlights approached, Cali
receded into the darkness of a doorway until the
lights faded.

She checked her watch. The last place she wanted
to be was standing alone waiting for some pervert to
get his rocks off in a smut show.

Forty-five minutes passed uneventfully. Cali
waited, silent, unmoving, invisible in the surroundings.

Inside, Cody slouched in the seat, covered the
lower half of his face with strategically placed hands

and kept one eye on Lonigan. While this setting seemed ideal for a meeting, no one approached Lonigan while he sat near the front of the theater munching popcorn and sucking down soda. While Cody ignored the movie, Lonigan seemed unable to pull his eyes from the screen. A screen crowded over with bronzed feminine flesh in an uninhibited assortment of sex acts involving couples, lesbians and gay men.

Outside, Cali became restive, shifting in and out of a weak light falling upon the crevasse between buildings from a street lamp twenty yards distant. She played the dim light off her watch to check the time.

Footsteps approached. She turned to face a lanky black figure throwing off an alcoholic stench and advancing with staggering gait.

"Hey mama-son, you give blow job, I give five dollar," he slurred, offering a smile of carious front teeth.

"Just keep it moving," Cali said. Her eyes never once strayed from the black, who slowed his stride as he came to within a few paces of her.

Cali prepared.

"Fuck you, bitch," the man said with a voice as clear as sobriety could make it. His blade glinted in the marquee lights from across the street.

"Asshole," Cali muttered as her left hand seized the bladed hand in a blur so fast the man had no time to respond. Her right hand fired off three pulverizing lightning jabs to the man's face, breaking his nose, knocking his jaw askew and splitting both upper and lower lip.

Inky blood spewed from his nose and mouth. But Cali had not finished yet. She delivered an excruciating kick to the inside of the knee, which toppled the assailant to the pavement. A sharp, compassionless chop to the Adam's Apple forced him to gag for air.

While he writhed in pain, Cali cracked his wrist back, forcing him to surrender the knife. As she did, the blade sliced into her palm.

"My next one puts junior out of commission," Cali said with eyes ablaze and breathing seized.

So petrified was the assailant that he never once attempted to break free. Cali watched as he wet his pants while splayed on the pavement.

"You want to live, Fuckhead? Drag your black ass out of here, RIGHT NOW!" The words had been delivered with such restrained force that they assured the man's full attention.

Cali slid his knife dangerously close to his groin while he scooted along the walk to crawl clear of her. In the next step, he worked back to his feet and hobbled away as fast as his one good leg could take him.

Cali slipped the knife into her pocket, discovering only then the slice she had taken to her palm. While she waited another twenty-five minutes for Lonigan's exit, she worked to stop the bleeding and clean away the blood as best she could. The last thing she needed was a wound or blood to draw attention to her. The nearest subway station was a three block walk to the south.

Cali fell in behind their target immediately while Cody lingered in the theater lobby until he could be assured they had disappeared well down the street. He took up a secondary position, allowing Cali to control the surveillance.

Lonigan returned to his apartment without incident.

Cali, though shaken, remained diligent on her surveillance until she had put Lonigan to bed for the night. She wasted no time removing the bloody clothes and slipping into a black thigh-length jersey. Cody returned to find her bent over at the sink, rubbing vigorously.

"Shit. What happened?"

"Some scumbag bled all over me," Cali said.

Cody cupped her hands to check the cut. The action brought Cali face to face with him.

"Poor dumb asshole," Cody said.

Cody inched closer. He could feel her warmth radiating over him. The low cut V of the jersey revealed the delicate white lace of her bra against her Asian skin tone. The supple flesh of her breasts spilled over the material in a way that excited Cody.

In the faint light falling into the apartment from the street, Cali's eyes sparkled like polished gemstones. Her slick lips asked for him. On impulse, Cody bent forward to cover her lips with his in a hungry kiss, unsure of how she might react. He sensed indecision in the way her facial muscles tensed. Her hands reflexively moved from his.

"Cool your jets, Bond, this isn't a movie," Cali said when their lips at last parted, but she made no move to arrest his advance. Nor did she embrace it either. There was hesitancy and a lingering uncertainty that stuck in the front of Cody's mind. They both knew they were crossing a line. A crossing that would change everything. However, the subtle seduction woven into her voice contradicted her words.

Cody kissed her again. His probing tongue parted her lips to accept him. Cali consumed the excitement their contact radiated. A contact that was causing him to swell. She surrendered to him, wrapping her arms around him, wanting to engulf him with her passion. He slid his hand along her shoulder, then down her back, slipping inside her jersey to release the clasp of her bra. His very touch sent shivers coursing through her body.

"I don't think this is right," she said when he released his kiss. But part of her had to hold on to him. That dark corner of her mind surging to break its restraints refused to push him away. Even as his hand unzipped her slacks, Cali found herself incapable of stopping him.

"I love the smell of blood after a kill," he whispered.

His soft caresses upon her breasts fanned the smoldering heat of her rising desire. She worked her fingers into his hair at the nape of his neck. The moan that erupted from deep in his throat only fueled the heat raging inside her. Still she had to be the stronger one. She had to resist.

"I think you let the dancing get to your head," Cali said. Yet she made no effort to push him away. Nor did she adjust her shirt to remove the temptation.

Cody's hand slid inside her slacks to ease them over her slight hips. His index finger wormed inside the waist band of her panties to begin its descent.

A dial tone stopped them. After a single ring, a female voice answered. They listened as Lonigan requested another counselor.

Cali abandoned all resistance when Cody's hand slipped inside the front of her panties to find her pleasure spot. She worked her pelvis closer, wanting more than he was at present offering. His petting was masterfully soft and gentle, teasing her in a way that made her need more. Her body responded to his, despite orders from her left brain to resist. Logic be damned. Her emotional need bottled up for decades seized control. He pressed her against him, sliding his hand around to caress the roundness of her cheek—she wanted desperately to feel all of him inside her.

Against the sound of a soft rap on Lonigan's door, Cody undressed Cali slowly, removing first her jersey, after which he paused to kiss each dark nipple that had grown erect under his fondling. Then he advanced to peel her panties down over her hips and allow them to slither to the floor. The heady scent of her state of arousal filled his nose. He relished the sheer joy of caressing her heated flesh. But before proceeding further, Cody shifted Cali's position slightly, the same gentle way he had maneuvered her earlier on the dance floor, so the dim light falling in from the street lamp beyond the window could paint her body. Cali made no effort to conceal anything from him.

"You are beautiful," he whispered, then kissed her again.

For a moment Cali didn't know how to react. She had buried love's passion so deeply that she had thought she would never feel this thing again.

In the background they could hear Lonigan's clumsy and feeble attempt at managing small talk with his counselor. Within a few minutes he abandoned it completely in favor of describing for her exactly what he expected.

While Cody stood with hands at her sides, Cali slid her fingers inside Cody's shirt, raking teasingly across his hairless chest with her nails before spreading the garment full open to allow it to drop from his well-defined shoulders. Cody shivered an acceptance, which brought a smile and a delicious kiss from Cali.

Neither had the power now to stop what consumed them. Neither wanted it to stop.

Cody remained perfectly still, not guiding her, nor rushing her in any way. She needed no instructions on how to excite him. He allowed himself to experience Cali without doing or saying anything that might destroy what was building between them. Words now could only dampen the moment.

Without groping or fumbling, Cali found his belt, unclasped it and peeled open his jeans. In so doing, she brushed the tips of her fingers ever so slightly across him as she moved the slacks over his hips.

"Going commando, are we?" she cooed in a playful way. Cody had nothing left to be removed. In a stilted maneuver that required a steadying hand to her shoulder, Cody stepped out of his pants and shoes in one motion. Cali offered her support by taking his athletically tight buns firmly in hand.

Cody could no longer restrain himself. He slid his hand around the back of her neck, brought her lips to his, and with his other hand, pressed her body against his.

Their gasps raged out of control. Passion had allowed them, if only for a brief span of time, to forget who they were, what they were, and what lie in their futures.

After easing her onto the bed, Cody stretched alongside her, stabilizing himself with a hand to her thigh while he worked his way onto the sliver of mattress that remained. The power of his touch electrified her. The bed barely accommodated one body; and two, despite Cali's petite frame, seemed to be courting disaster.

Cody employed his lips and fingers with the softness of a feather to quell any last resistance Cali's left brain could mount to oppose what they were doing. When he brought his body over hers, supporting his weight on his hands to spare her from having to endure his girth, she parted her legs to accommodate him.

While Lonigan moaned into the moving tape, Cody and Cali began their own lovemaking at an unhurried pace on the single bed. Cody's own deep moan that escaped the moment he penetrated her became lost amongst Lonigan's.

Cali held him there, wanting the pleasure swarming over her to last a whole lifetime. The lurid background noise from Lonigan, however, kept tugging at her brain.

"I can't make love listening to that," Cali whispered.

In the background, Lonigan instructed his whore in graphic detail as to how he expected her to perform. The vile voice and words were destroying what Cody sought patiently to create. He hated to evacuate her at this moment when everything was beginning to reach critical mass. But he had to do something or risk losing her.

So, Cody scrambled off the bed, flicked off the speaker and returned to Cali's body. She spread her legs anew—this time as an invitation for his hand to begin back at the beginning.

"You can't shut it off. What if he says something important?" Cali released through gasps that told Cody he had better come up with something quick.

Without retort, Cody scrambled off the bed once more, fitted the headphones over his ears, and returned to the bed, where he wrapped his arms around a waiting, and now totally ripened Cali. This time she guided him atop her, letting him know she wanted him inside without further foreplay. Despite the disruptions and annoyance of the situation, his entry was unhurried and gentle. He displayed as much a concern for hers as for his own pleasure.

Cody's loving diligence with his lips, hands and member brought her tenderly to the pinnacle of her excitement. Her head swam in the throes of her own pleasure while he held her there for what seemed an eternity. She heralded her joy into the night when he took her over the edge before reaching for his own ecstasy. Only then did he slowly abate, bringing her down from her high without haste, careful to afford her a lasting climax that would fade over the ensuing minutes of cuddling into a glowing ember as they lay clutching each other on the narrow bed.

Morning found the two asleep in each other's arms, Cody still in headphones connecting him to the monitoring machine.

"Oh Jesus," Cali whispered when she felt Cody's body molded to hers. His arm blanketed her, his hand cupped her breast while he slept. He stirred when she attempted to slip away.

Cody lifted his eyelids with great reluctance, and for a long moment, they stared at each other in disbelief.

"Hi," she said with guilt writ across her face.

"Oh no, I'm deaf," Cody chided. He could think of no funnier line at the moment. He refused to take his eyes off Cali's.

The laugh they shared seemed forced. Neither certain of how they should react. Cali removed the headphones and kissed him as if they were long time lovers. No guilt, no remorse for what they had done. They had just filled needs in each other.

"I'd love to buy you breakfast, but we have to wait until our little pervert decides to arouse himself from his bed."

"So how was it?" Cali asked as she slipped out of the bed and scrambled for her clothes. Cody grabbed her hand to bring her back beside him. He smoothed his hand along the low side of her belly while kissing her breast. She did nothing to oppose his playful petting, found herself getting lost in his touch all over again.

"I love that," she cooed.

"I know. I was paying attention last night."

"Well, how was it?"

"Fantastic."

"I meant listening to Lonigan last night."

"That's what I thought you meant."

They shared a laugh that released a bit of the tension the union had created.

"Same as before. But he only hit the girl once that I could detect and nothing about a knife or killing her."

Cali kissed him, succumbing to her more carnal impulses, and slipped elusively away into the bathroom.

"I assumed the other was fantastic. Your watch. I'm going to shower."

Cody sat bare-chested at the window, his hat atop his jostled hair, staring at Lonigan's apartment, yet seeing nothing. His mind became steeped in the night before. She was the best lover he had ever been with.

What was he doing?

He made love to another member of the team. And now all he could think about was slipping into the shower with her, and kissing every inch of her body all over again. He wanted to take her back to bed and make love again. In the next moment, he saw himself standing at a rocky cliff in extremely dangerous territory. Then he swallowed the guilt and anticipated the opportunity to sleep with her again.

"Our boy up yet?" Cali asked, stepping out of the bathroom fully clothed. Clearly a sign that the time for business had returned.

Cody had hoped she might come to him naked, give him a sign that she felt the same about him.

"Snoring like one of the seven dwarves," Cody said with a stone face masking the excitement roaring up inside him.

"I'll get breakfast. You call in a report."

The afternoon passed in silence—in both apartments. Lonigan slept well beyond his usual one o'clock, and Cali spent her time catching up on the steady stream of intelligence coming in from Squire. She needed to fill in a plethora of gaps in her knowledge that the other team members had over her. She still had an unclear connection between Lonigan and their hard target, though she trusted Brax knew what he was doing.

Cody seemed restless, unable to focus on anything for more than a few minutes. Though he said little, Cali could sense their passion had agitated him.

"You really kill someone when you were seven?" he asked after a while.

Cali detected something unsettling in those eyes. They offered up a glimpse as to what was in his heart at that moment, revealing to her that to Cody what they had shared in the night turned out to be more than just pent-up tension. Despite the tenderness and pleasure he gave her, she remained uncertain of her feelings for him. What they had shared was wrong.

Loving anyone in this business created insurmount-able obstacles to oppose any measure of happiness.

"After the bastard raped me, I got to his Soviet pistol while he was busy pulling his pants up. Then I blew his brains out the back of his head."

Cali uttered the words in such a measured fash-ion, it was as if some other voice had taken over her body. A voice completely devoid of human compas-sion and mercy. Her eyes avoided Cody's, choosing instead to fix on the apartment across the street.

There was something in the way Cali said the words that forced Cody across the room to touch her. His eyes now held hers. He wanted to kiss her but refrained. Instead he let his hand gesture transmit to her what he felt in his heart. For him, it was incom-prehensible what she had endured then.

Cali fought down a rush of tears. Tears she had buried in her village in the Vietnamese jungles more than twenty-three years ago. She rose to curl into his arms. She felt warm and safe against him. A night-mare from so long ago had wormed its way back to the surface. A horror that tore at her soul relentlessly during moments of intimacy.

She vowed she would never let a man love her.

"I'm sorry," he said in a whisper. Cody stoked her hair with an almost imperceptible touch.

But her granite heart had suffered it first crack.

With the dusk, Lonigan awakened and lounged about the apartment. He had a pizza delivered, and consumed it while staring at television in a seemingly unending stream of old movies on cable.

"Why is he here?" Cali asked as they sat in the dark, watching out the window, eating greasy ham-burgers for the umpteenth time since their arrival in New York.

Cody fought down the recurrent urge to kiss her. She had shown no overt signs of intimate interest, and now he wondered if he harbored regrets over what they had done.

"Only he knows, unless you've picked up something."

The secure phone rang. As Cody spoke to Brax, shades of guilt crossed over his face. He updated him on the surveillance, though there was little new to report. Lonigan made it obvious his visit was not for pleasure, nor it seemed was it for business. Brax agreed that someone had tried to sweep his phone for bugs, and he shared their hope that Cody had put the telephone bug to sleep before the tones detected it. Maybe it was just taking a long time to get the business going. Leviathan was a careful man. He would wait until he was sure it was safe before making a contact. *If* Leviathan turned out to be the reason Lonigan had come to New York.

After taking in a string of instructions that lasted no more than a few minutes, Cody hung up.

"He's coming in tomorrow," Cody said. There was an edge of dejection in his words as if it signaled an end to their intimacy.

"I guess that means we may only get one more night together," Cali said. She came to him, slipped her arms snugly around his waist and surrendered her lips to his. Closing her eyes, she let herself become part of him. Another crack erupted in her granite heart.

Brax arrived with the dawn to find Cody and Cali awake and listening to the dormant void of Lonigan's apartment. In the past day, Lonigan had made no calls nor any trips from his apartment further than a pharmacy and a liquor store three blocks away. The report turned out to be so barren of suspicious activity that Brax wrestled with the notion that the team had wasted valuable time watching this one. Yet, his sixth sense told him Lonigan was a deadly player in this game and not to be discounted.

"Our operative in Ankara turned up three days ago. Well, his head did."

Silence hung over the table for a long moment.

"We set him up. I mean he's linked to Wolf Pack."

"I know," Brax said. His eyes seemed to be looking past Cody.

"Only the four of us knew about him. You tell Remy?"

"Yes. He thinks it's a sign. He's concerned somebody's got our scent. Very possibly Thesseo had to roll us over before he died. Now somebody's closing in on us."

"You think whoever they are, they might have been expecting one of us to meet with Thesseo?"

"Our intelligence sources suspected the PKK organization of intercepting our man before he could get to the target."

"Leviathan recruited a PKK lieutenant two years ago. They could have somehow tapped into our network?"

Cali watched Cody's eyes narrow. They darkened a shade or two when he got this way.

"Can't know for sure right now."

Brax left the table to wander over by the window. They had to switch off the past and concentrate on the present. Nothing could be done for Thesseo now. Clearly they had tortured him before silencing him for good.

"How do we move this Lonigan situation off this impasse?" Brax asked while standing at the window looking through the camera lens.

He saw nothing.

"We need to determine if he has a link to Leviathan here," he continued, moving back to the table.

"We can run a gag, see if he bites," Cody offered.

"How about a honey trap?" Cali offered.

Cody shot her a fired glare laden with more than a hint of displeasure in his eyes.

"He's into whores. I can go in, see if I can loosen him up."

"I don't think that would work," Cody was quick to inject. "One wrong word and you compromise the surveillance."

"You saying you think I can't do it?" Cali rose out of her chair. She was legitimately angry.

"No. I didn't mean it that way. Well, I did. All you have to do is say something out of sync and he might take off."

"I think I know that."

"I'm not opposed to that," Brax added calmly.

"We let him pick me up in a bar. Make him think he scored one on his own. Seems the only way this creepy scuzbucket can get laid is if he buys it."

"That's better. Cody, you think it's workable?"

Brax studied Cody's eyes during that moment of silence while Cody appraised the plan. Brax sought something other than Cody's answer.

"Absolutely. Risky but workable."

"Okay. We go for it. If he doesn't move before then, tomorrow night. Remy comes in and works the trap with you, Cali. Cody, you and I remain out of sight to move in if anything sours."

Cody swallowed his urge to object. Knots choked off his stomach. He hated the idea that Cali would use herself to get close to Lonigan. He wanted her as far away from that shithead as possible. But he had to hide that from Brax. She was just another team member, doing what it takes to get the job done. He buried his burning obsession and had to go along with it. If Brax ever uncovered they were lovers, he'd yank Cali or him from the team immediately.

"Lonigan's got a reputation. He likes to slap around his dates."

"I'm well aware of that," Brax said. "I read the report. But we have to risk it."

Twelve hours later, Remy replaced Cody in the apartment. Cali and Remy began working through the myriad of details required to make a short notice honey trap work. Normally weeks of planning and regimented execution went into a honey trap. They had less than a day to put one together. The objective was to get Lonigan interested enough in Cali that he might reveal how long he intended to be in New York, and why he had come there in the first place. After a few drinks and an equal number of hours of unbridled passion, men babbled incessantly, doling out all sorts of information they hoped might impress a new found love.

Cali and Remy rehearsed the lines back and forth for hours. Every possible question Lonigan could ask had to be covered. Every answer had to be timid. shy and flawless.

They decided Cali had to initiate the contact, convince him she was genuine and trustworthy, then get him to open up. Cali knew the trick was to offer him just enough to get what she needed without having to give away too much. But the objective was information, and she had to go into this trap willing to give whatever it took.

After working meticulously through a dozen scenarios which included three emergency escape signals, both agreed the honey trap was as ready as it could be under such conditions.

While Cali showered, Remy reviewed notes he had written to himself.

"Can we pull this off?" Cali asked, emerging from the bathroom with hair in a towel. She dressed in tight slacks and a top that accentuated her small breasts. She had not the best accoutrement for the job at hand. But she knew what men wanted and how to seduce them if it served her purpose. For a long moment, she stared vacantly out the window at Lonigan's apartment. Lonigan's insatiable sexual appetite could easily be turned against him. Cali contemplated her position and what she might have to offer up to achieve their objective. She convinced herself that any measure of sacrifice had to be accepted. Her father and the Koji master had instilled that in her. She embraced without reservation the teachings and disciplines of the warrior. In honor of her father, she would never abandon that.

"Absolutely. Just stick to your cover and trust that we're right here to help you out if anything goes amuck."

Cali wasn't listening.

"Cali?"

"What?"

"He's a demon with a blade. You smell even the slightest scent of steel, and you issue the abort. I'm not going to let anything happen to you."

Cali crossed to the table where Remy sat, looking over things he had jotted on a pad.

"I know."

She set both hands on his shoulders. Looking back at her, Remy covered her hands with his in reassurance. While his eyes left Cali with no doubt as to his sincerity, his clumsy smile betrayed the uncertainty that comes with any such operation. Not every variable can be controlled. Not every move can be perfectly scripted.

Their brief contact reignited fond stirrings buried deep inside Cali. Memories of moments she shared with her father before he died. The way Remy looked back at her just now was exactly the way her father gazed at her during those last days.

"I know," she said before returning to the bathroom to dry her hair and affix just the right dressing of cosmetics for the night's operation.

15

> The Rooster has taken to a nest.
>
> Remy

The 747 jet configured to haul cargo and carrying the twenty-two Indy race cars returning from Italy received its landing and taxi instructions to proceed to the staged cargo area of LaGuardia airport. There it awaited the usual customs inspection and clearance. The doors remained sealed until a customs inspector arrived to perform his routine inspection. Nothing moved until customs gave the okay.

Tommy Whitison lounged in the terminal, pouring coffee down his gullet one cup after another while he waited. He had his people standing by, ready to transfer the car to the enclosed trailer for the drive back to his garage in Rochester, once the cars were released. The delay, however, gnawed at Tommy's nerves until he thought he might explode.

The remainder of his payment hinged on the car being released from customs and returning intact to his garage. He checked his watch for the third time in five minutes. The wait droned on and on. Something inside warned of impropriety. So much so, that Tommy left his seat to pace before the glass windows. He could see the plane across the tarmac and observed as an offical-looking open bed truck pulled up to the front.

He had no idea as to the cause of the delay, nor what the mysterious man had used his car for; he only knew his deal was to allow the man secluded access to his vehicle before the trip and after its return to the United States.

Tommy studied the pair of inspectors accompanied by three German Shepherds with handlers. They climbed the stairs to enter the plane through the front door. It had to be a standard drug search, Tommy surmised, though the man in Italy assured him no drugs would be transported using his vehicle.

Every five to ten seconds Tommy checked his watch. He signaled for another cup of coffee, though his cup remained nearly full.

"Tough luck in Cosenza," another owner said. He came up to wait beside Tommy. He also stared at the plane.

"What a shit deal. The losers get bumped for a week before getting hauled back. Tell you, you ain't got the name, you don't get shit from CART."

The customs people were in there a long time. How long these inspections took Tommy had no idea, but he figured they had been in there too long. Any moment now Tommy would bite his tongue from the tension.

Twenty agonizing minutes later, the inspectors emerged out the side cargo door. The dogs sniffed their way from the plane to the K-loader that had eased up to the cargo door. They rode the loader down to the ground, springing happily into the back of the customs pickup truck.

"Gentlemen, I've just been notified that your cars have been cleared. If you'll instruct your men to stage their trucks in the offload order you've been given, we'll have you out of here within the hour," the steward said.

Tommy felt his heart restart at the sound of the words. He could only hope no one took notice of the release washing over his face at that moment. Had a customs inspector witnessed such a display, he would have immediately re-inspected Tommy's car.

Number 98 was seventh in the off-load order. His crew made the transfer from plane to K-loader without incident then to the waiting trailer. Not a screw appeared out of place on the body, nor were any questions asked about his or any other vehicle on the flight. All had been exactly as the man had said: routine.

The drive back to Rochester afforded Tommy time to speculate as to what use his vehicle had served for the man. Whatever it was, it had successfully slipped through a customs inspection. When they arrived back at his garage, Tommy unloaded the car into the stall and uncharacteristically, if not a bit mysteriously released the crew, despite their obvious eagerness to begin the tear down process. He said he wanted them rested up before the next round of fervid preparations began. Tommy withheld that he was drained of cash and would be saving his newly acquired stash to make the Indy 500 run in the Spring.

Perched on the roof of an idled manufacturing plant four hundred yards north of the garage, a pair of Asian eyes scanned Tommy Whitison's building and the surrounding entrances and exits. Shigeo reported any and all activity even when it seemed unrelated to the garage and its occupant.

Alone Tommy waited, standing at the open bay door. The hour was late, the sun had sunk below the skyline and Tommy needed a few drinks to help him put this day behind him. He hadn't slept more than a few hours anticipating the customs inspection. The delays only intensified his anxiety.

Ranzami arrived precisely as arranged, and only advanced after receiving Shigeo's signal that all could proceed. He dispensed quickly with the formality of transacting his business.

"Everything went as smoothly as I had said?" Ranzami asked with his perfect English diction. His smile was more perfunctory than genuine.

"Fine. Customs went fine."

"Is good."

Ranzami waited, restraining impatience, while Tommy counted out the stacks of bills to verify his remuneration. Once checked, he returned the stacks to the briefcase and offered a hand to Ranzami.

Ranzami saw no need to accept it.

"A win-win arrangement. I look forward to watching the ninety-eight car in the Indy 500 next year. Perhaps you will even win."

"This will certainly help," Tommy said. His smile was nervous and slight. His stomach felt like a bottomless pit. Whatever he had done, he knew it had to be bad to warrant this kind of pay off. No one parts with the kind of money contained in that briefcase for anything legal. Tommy wanted nothing more to do with the reason for Ranzami's presence.

"Lock up when you're done," Tommy said, more in jest than in instruction.

As he strolled to his black Viper, he swallowed the bitter guilt creeping up the back of his throat. What had he done? Then he told himself to forget it, go forward and never look back. One of the traits of a winner.

Once Tommy cleared the garage, Ranzami removed a hand-held radio from his pocket and switched it on. His eyes followed the Viper as it sped off.

"All clear?"

"All clear, General." Shigeo's voice came through free of distortion.

Ranzami waited with the patience of a man who had scored some great victory until Tommy's car cleared the garage parking lot, then he lowered the bay door. Alone in the garage, he removed the quick disconnect screws holding the right side body cowling in place. There, secured to the underside of the exhaust manifold, he removed the two cylinders he had planted in Italy.

Ranzami held them in his hands before transferring them to the aluminum case he had carried in with him. They represented the very soul of his plan. Only a few more details required his attention.

Customs had been looking for contraband or drugs, never for the deadly cargo he was importing. The most precarious part of his cabal had gone off without a hitch. The price he paid was a mere pittance for the service Tommy Whitison had unwittingly performed. And only Ranzami knew precisely what each cylinder contained, and how he would be put them to use. For that reason, Tommy Whitison would be allowed to live to race another day.

On Friday night, the day after Remy and Cali's plan had been finalized, Lonigan finally chose to leave his apartment, whereupon he took the subway uptown to exit in a glitzy section of Manhattan.

Cali and Remy maintained a secure distance during the subway ride, while Brax and Cody followed above ground in a station wagon. Remy, using a button mike sewn into the thick roll of his sweater's neck, reported their location at regular intervals. Brax and Cody remained always within a mile of the target.

Unexpectedly though, Lonigan left the subway at a stop different from the others he had taken before. He walked down 71st street with his head hunched. He never looked over his shoulder, either not suspicious of a tail, or confident a tail would gain nothing in the way of intelligence.

Cali walked alone far enough behind Lonigan to prevent her detection, while Remy kept close tabs on the target to prevent him from slipping away.

Remy stopped when Lonigan entered a club on the north corner of a poorly lit intersection. A few others entered the establishment just after Lonigan. A single neon sign touted beer inside and the windows had been blackened over.

"Rooster taken to a nest. Here we go," Remy whispered.

Remy shifted his jacket, signaling Cali for the operation to proceed. Afterward he positioned himself across the street and out of sight while Cali made her entrance.

Cali checked herself one last time before she strolled up and opened the door to the throb of rock music. After one measured look inside, she pulled back from the doorway. Scanning her flanks she marched quickly across the street to disappear into the dark alley. There she remained in the shadows until Remy could clandestinely make his way to her.

"What's the matter?"

"We have to switch," she said.

"Switch? What are you talking about?"

Cali pointed to the bar just as two men, hand in hand, exited. The shorter nuzzled his head on the other's shoulder and wrapped an arm around his companion's waist in an unbridled amorous exchange.

"A fucking gay bar? Fuck. Brax, you copy?"

Cali waited; Remy took in the instructions.

"There's a hundred guys in there making googly-eyes at each other. I may have blown the operation," Cali offered.

Remy waved her off.

"What do you want to do?" he transmitted a second later.

They waited.

"You have to take my place," Cali insisted.

"I'm not going in there," Remy insisted, "Brax?"

Cali watched the front door as two men entered.

"What's he saying?" she asked.

"What's our chances of success with this new twist."

Cali took her eyes off the entrance.

"Don't ask me. I figured him for straight. He had a couple of whores at his apartment," she offered.

"Okay. No. Yes," Remy replied to something Brax, himself and Cody were aware of. Only Cali was being kept in the dark.

"We go with the alternate. I'm going in wired and we hope for the best. Fuck, I hate this," Remy said, staring for a long moment at the building's front.

All over the world, even after the Cold War, people still look to us and trust us to help them seek the blessings of peace and freedom. But as the Cold War fades into memory, voices of isolation say America should retreat from its responsibilities. I say they are wrong.

The threats we face today as Americans respect no nation's borders. Think of them: terrorism, the spread of weapons of mass destruction, organized crime, drug trafficking, ethnic and religious hatred, aggression by rogue states, environmental degradation. If we fail to address these threats today, we will suffer the consequences in all our tomorrows.

Bill Clinton, January 23, 1996.

16

Heaven's gate open. Will advise.
                              Brax

An hour and twenty-two minutes after going in, Remy held the door for Lonigan, whispering something only Lonigan could hear as they stepped out of the bar. Both men smiled at each other as if to acknowledge some level of desire. Remy never dreamed he could pick up another man in such a short time. Remy's words brought a laugh that diverted Lonigan's attention from the street outside. Remy filled in intimately close behind his catch so as to block the opening from the patrons inside the bar. Lonigan never saw the club that rendered him unconscious two steps onto the pavement.

Cody caught the toppling mass, and with Remy's aid, whisked Lonigan into the back seat of the station wagon. Brax tromped the accelerator the moment Cody fell into the front seat. Taking the canister Brax handed over, Cody leaned over the front seat, doused a cloth with Ether and covered Lonigan's nose and mouth.

"That should keep the little cretin out until we reach our destination."

Even if stopped by police, they'd just explain that their friend had overindulged and they were merely driving him home.

Remy disappeared into darkness to rejoin Cali, who was waiting in another vehicle staged across the street. She held her position to let the station wagon progress more than a street ahead. Both unlighted vehicles sped away, careful of their speed.

"We clear?" Brax transmitted

"All clear," Cali radioed back.

No one had witnessed the abduction.

An hour later, in a dimly lit alley behind a collection of row houses battered by neglect and apathy, Brax and Cody transferred a sleeping Lonigan through the rear door of the last building on the row. It was three A.M. and pitch enveloped the alley, thanks to Cody's excellent rock toss the day before. Actually, it took four attempts to put the lamp out, thereby minimizing the chances of unwanted eyes observing the body's movement.

Lonigan awakened with a jolt, groggy and disoriented in total darkness. The air reeked of raw earth and garbage. He struggled against unyielding straight jacket straps imprisoning his arms. He had also lost all this clothes. His thighs and butt cheeks went numb from the time spent curled on the cold, crumbling concrete slab. He shivered uncontrollably. But he knew better than to cry out for help. Instead, he curled himself into a tight ball in the corner, set his haunches on his ankles to keep them off the stone, and moved back and forth vigorously using the rough canvass to generate friction against his skin, thereby warming his body.

Upstairs, Brax and Cody observed Lonigan using an infrared monitoring camera.

"He won't be easy," Cody commented after witnessing the calm reserve their prisoner displayed.

"That's what makes this fun," Brax offered.

His wink indicated a readiness to begin. Allowing Lonigan to stew in isolation would have little positive impact on their interrogation. The Company's profile indicated Lonigan to be a totally committed terrorist, a true believer in the cause, and therefore one who nurtured a formidable resolve to make the team's task more than merely difficult.

But Brax and Cody had prepared for even that eventuality.

Cody leveled his Makarov while Brax unlocked the door to the cell. As the light falling off a sixty watt bulb flooded in, Lonigan hid his eyes. He opened them only slightly to Cody pulling him to his feet by grasping what hair he could and yanking.

"Get the fuck moving," Cody commanded in a voice right out of the Bronx. A glaring light from across a large open expanse washed over Brax and Cody's and backs, preventing Lonigan from getting a good look at either of his captors.

"I have no money, if that's what you're after," Lonigan said in a voice as meek as a choir boy's. He knew they had no interest in money. He knew exactly what they sought.

Brax and Cody knew well Lonigan's enthusiasm for killing in cold blood. Neither bought into the false staccato voice Lonigan chose to engage. When Lonigan cleared the doorway, Cody snared him by the strap secured near his collar bone and yanked him along into the hastily arranged interrogation room. Lonigan made no attempt to fight his captors nor to attempt a dash for freedom.

"What can you hope to gain? I have nothing."

Cody hammered a fist into Lonigan's head, forcing him to carom off the table then fall into a battered wooden chair beside it. His ankles brushed against leather shackles secured to the front chair legs. When he struggled to rise, Cody slammed his face into the table and yanked him back upright.

"Just so you understand how we feel about you, Lonigan," Cody said, the name coming out like spit.

They locked eyes the way rams lock horns before a fight. Lonigan ransacked his memory to recall the bastard now inches from his face. He had seen that face, but now failed to remember where.

"Stay the fuck down, or I ram my fist down your fucking throat!" Cody ordered with a meanness that left no margin of doubt as to his sincerity.

Lonigan crossed his legs out of protective instinct, being naked except for the straight jacket, and he stared vacantly into the harsh light emanating from behind Cody and Brax.

"We know what the fuck you really are, Lonigan."

Lonigan's face suddenly took on an empty demeanor, as if he had just disconnected himself from this place and time. He abandoned his mild Lonigan identity after its usefulness expired, replacing it with a vacant menacing stare.

"Who is your contact in New York?"

"I have no contact in New York."

Cody emerged from the darkness, lowering his face to within inches of Lonigan's.

"We're not here to fucking play with you, jag off. Tell me who you came to New York to contact."

"No one."

Cody pummeled Lonigan's face into the table again. This time Lonigan came up with nose and lips split and bleeding.

"You can beat me all you want. I have no other reason for coming to New York than to visit a relative whom I have not seen in more than a decade."

Brax entered the light. He stared for a long moment into Lonigan's eyes before settling into a chair strategically positioned directly across from Lonigan. A barren tabletop separated them. Brax detected a glint of recognition in those green eyes. He knew that Lonigan realized who he was and why they were together in this place. For all of a minute, neither exchanged more than cold hard stares.

"We know why you came to New York. We know how you entered the United States. We know who you are and what you do," Brax said calmly in a British accent even the queen herself would have difficulty detecting flaws in.

While Brax spoke, Cody retreated into the darkness of the interrogation room. But he did not leave.

"What we don't know is who your contact is here. If you'd be willing to tell us, we could avoid anything unpleasant."

"Let's not fool each other," Lonigan started, "you must also know that you'll get nothing out of me. And if I am not at a certain place at a specific time, my contact will know I have been compromised."

Lonigan issued his words with the calm, measured resolve of a man confident nothing could shake his steel exterior. He chose to lock on to Brax's eyes and never stray.

"You MI6 fools will get nothing for your trouble."

Brax flew from his chair over the tabletop and clamped his fingers around Lonigan's throat. He squeezed with a demonic glint in his eyes until Lonigan's face turned ruddy and his eyes bugged out almost to the point of popping from their sockets.

"June eleventh, 1994, a bomb went off in the North Harwich train station shortly before 8:45 in the morning. Nineteen went to hospitals, four went to the morgue. Three survivors fingered your gruesome fucking mug as the man leaving the car shortly before the explosion. Why do you think that is, Lonigan?"

"Fuck you, asshole, fuck you and fuck your whoring mother!" Lonigan struggled to eject. Blood sprayed with his words.

"I need to know who your contact is."

"Fuck you!" Lonigan forced out while trying to suck in enough air to keep from passing out.

"Listen, you shithead scum, no one knows you're here, so no one will know we've killed you."

Lonigan laughed.

"Killing me will do nothing to help you. Killing me will prevent nothing."

At that moment, Cody re-emerged with a black box in both hands. He set it gingerly on the table close enough for Lonigan to watch as he removed an electrical plug from inside. He stared at the plug before fitting it into the side outlet of the overhead dangling light fixture. He wanted Lonigan to see the nickel-sized paddles attached to six inch probes that he removed next from the box and plugged into small receptacles on the side. He wanted Lonigan to watch while he fitted the rubber gloves, adjusting one finger at a time.

"You can tell me the name of your contact right now, or you can beg me to stop later. Which will it be?" Brax said surrounded by an eerie calm.

"You think you frighten me?"

"You bet ya. Lonigan, when we're done, every time you piss, you're going to wish we had killed you instead."

Lonigan's smug laugh vanished. His face fell slack. Cody flipped the switch on the black box. A high-pitched squeal erupted. The terrifying sound lasted the span of a minute.

"To help you over your stubbornness, we're going to tickle your balls with twelve thousand volts of electricity," Cody offered in a plaintive voice. His eyes never strayed from Lonigan's.

Yet Lonigan's eyes displayed an equal resolve.

Cody brought the two paddles to within an inch of each other. At that separation, a blue arc snapped across the gap with the rasp of meat searing on fire. Once discharged, the machine began its ominous whine anew, preparing its next deadly emission.

"Who's your bloody fucking contact in New York?" Brax hammered out.

Lonigan sprang from the chair, dashing feebly toward the far side of the room, where he prayed a door might be. Brax snared him from behind, threw him face first against the nearest wall, then yanked him back by his binding.

For Lonigan, the full weight of his vulnerability settled over him...unable to prevent what was about to happen. Without actually facing it, no man can possibly fathom the terror that seizes every muscle in the body during the moments preceding imminent torture. For one who has delivered it, so should he now face it.

Then Brax forced him back into his chair.

"Who is your contact? Who are you to meet in New York?"

Cody jerked Lonigan and the chair back from the table, allowing him to stand directly in front of his prisoner. When he did, he kicked Lonigan's legs out so as to wedge himself between them. While Cody held Lonigan in that position, Brax bound each leg in the shackles at the sides of the chair, securing the ankles so tightly around the wood that it became impossible for Lonigan to protect his genitals. To further restrain Lonigan from squirming about, Brax secured Lonigan's chest to the chair back using hundred-pound-test nylon rope.

"You breath okay, Lonigan?" Brax said in a calm measured voice. "I want you to be able to scream."

Jerk and strain as he might, Lonigan could no longer protect his most sensitive areas from these monsters.

With a face of stone, Cody positioned the paddles to either side of Lonigan's genitals. Then he waited.

"Who is your contact?"

Lonigan began to mewl.

Cody pressed the button without fanfare.

Lonigan's scream curdled blood. He reared with such violence that his shoulder joint tore loose from its socket.

"You motherfuckers! I will kill fifty for this."

Brax yanked Lonigan's head back by the hair.

"You've already killed fifty," Brax said in a subdued voice.

Brax released Lonigan's head to hang limply forward, tears of agony gushing down his face.

"Who is your contact?" Brax asked again.

Lonigan slumped into the chair like a useless bag of bones.

"Please, I beg you. No more..."

Sitting in a darkened room one floor above the interrogation room, Cali and Remy watched a black and white monitor as Lonigan screamed and squirmed in his chair.

When the next jolt went through Lonigan's genitals, Cali reached across to tighten on Remy's forearm. She witnessed Lonigan's pubic hair catch flame only to sizzle and burn out a few seconds later.

"First time?" he asked casually, skimming reports downloaded from Squire and scrolling across his laptop.

Cali chose not to respond. She knew anything she might say would only confirm for Remy that he had been right back in Scotland. That she didn't have the stomach for this kind of work.

"Brings back bad memories. Cong forced me to watch while they tortured my older brother and a cousin."

On the screen, Cody hit the recharge switch. The machine whined, accumulating the twelve thousand volt charge on the paddles. This time Lonigan fought with all his will to prevent Cody from placing the paddles on his burning scrotum. He screamed when his efforts failed.

Cody hit the button.

Lonigan spat blood and a slur of obscenities.

"That's got to hurt the old Artemus Dooley," Remy said, lifting his eyes off the laptop screen long enough to get a good look at Lonigan's suffering. "He did do it, you know," Remy offered, a part of him needing justification for what was happening.

Cali regained her composure, allowing her to remove her hand from Remy's forearm.

"Did what?"

"Set off the bomb in Harwich. We had good intelligence on him, but he escaped the country before we could nail the little scum-shit bastard."

Back in the interrogation room, Cody backed away, with Brax replacing him before Lonigan's face.

"I can double the voltage. Your balls will sizzle like a bead of water on a hot griddle. Give me the name of your fucking contact, or we keep it up until your goddamn terrorist balls turn black and fall off."

"No more," Lonigan said, crying, actually crying from the pain. He mustered the strength to spew obscenities to block out the whine of the machine recharging once more.

Despite his defeated whimpers and pleas, Cody retook his position over Lonigan's genitals. The smile that shone from Cody's face assured Lonigan that Cody had no intention of yielding to compassion.

"Ranzami's my contact," Lonigan surrendered.

His entire body went slack; he whimpered more from his betrayal than the searing fire in his genitals.

"Why?" Brax charged.

"No," Lonigan said with terror in his eyes. "No. please. I don't know why. Oh God, please believe me. I don't know why."

Lonigan reverted to crying like a child now.

"Not good enough, Lonigan. Why were you sent here to contact Ranzami?"

"I don't know. All I was told was to wait at the apartment. He would initiate a contact."

"How? How was the contact to be made?"

"I don't know…please believe me, I don't know," Lonigan said between whimpers. "Please, not again."

Brax and Cody retreated, leaving Lonigan bound and babbling. The machine remained ominously on the table illuminated by the cone of light above.

In the upstairs observation room, Cali and Remy rose when Cody and Brax entered. Cali appeared shaken from the experience and extremely grateful she had been spared from having to participate.

However, she maintained a stone visage when Brax and Cody looked at her.

"I think he's telling the truth," Remy offered matter-of-factly, watching Lonigan on the monitor.

"I agree," Cody added, "nobody holds out after a second ball buster."

"Reckon it will be long time before he gets another Merry Andrew. So, where do we go from here?" Remy said.

For a moment no one spoke. Lonigan's whimpers still bled through the television even though Cali had lowered the volume nearly to silence after Lonigan's first scream.

"Turn the little fucker on his master?" Remy promoted.

"Maybe the best shot we're going to get. He might give us one of Leviathan's lieutenants. I can't imagine him saying no to anything right now," Cody said.

They watched the monitor in silence for a few minutes. Could Lonigan lead them to their target? Brax had to weigh the variables before reaching a decision. They must proceed with extreme caution. Lonigan could expose them to Leviathan if they employed him as a stooge and erred in execution.

"How do we eliminate the possibility of him tipping Ranzami off?" Cali asked.

"That's the problem. We can't," Remy said, "but do we have another choice?"

"I guess not," Brax said, at last removing his eyes from the screen. "Let's go offer him a deal he won't have the balls to refuse."

The Pack returned Lonigan to his apartment, but this time Remy slipped in under cover of night. Out of view of the outside world, Remy waited for that all important call. Lonigan burst into a crying fit every time he had to relieve himself and worried his swollen genitalia came as a result of some festering infection. Watching Lonigan suffer brought a tear of joy to Remy's eye. Nothing could ever undo the deaths in Harwich. Poor Lonigan could sleep only on his back and remained in such all-consuming agony that he left the apartment only when absolutely necessary.

On those occasions when he did venture out, Cali or Cody picked up the surveillance and tracked his every move. Lonigan was never out of sight of one of the Pack. And Lonigan played his role perfectly, never looking around for his tail, never gesturing in any way that might betray those shadowing him. He had good reason to play the role. If Ranzami smelled a compromise, he may kill Lonigan just to prevent the trail from leading back to him. Lonigan knew *that* all too well. His best chance now to remain alive was to cooperate and hope like hell his handlers captured Ranzami.

Through tears of real agony, Lonigan begged for, and received, sufficient Demerol to ease the pain in his groin. He swore a half dozen times that his testicles were about to fall off. Without the drug, the pain was unbearable. Brax assured him his testicles weren't about to fall off; as a matter of fact, in time his genitals would recover and life would return to normal. Though he will most certainly never produce a family.

Lonigan refused to believe Brax. He was certain he'd never be able to get an erection nor have sex with another woman or man again.

"Like I give a fuck, you shithead weasel," was Brax's response.

"You don't stop your whining, I'll whack them off," Remy added, indicating the butt of his Glock would be the method of choice.

On his third day back in his apartment, the phone rang. From across the street Cali monitored the line through her headset. As instructed, Lonigan waited until the third ring to pick up the call. That gave Cali sufficient time to set up the trace circuit. Lonigan answered, listened then hung up. His eyes told Remy he had just received *the* call. They were to meet tonight at a gay bar on the upper east side. Lonigan knew the place, had frequented it many times on previous visits to New York.

"We're on, midnight at Saliantro's," Remy said into his radio.

Brax and Cody were on the receiving end. They had four hours to prepare, though they felt like they had been preparing for this for the last eight months. If they were careful, if they executed flawlessly, they might get their shot at Ranzami.

A crowded bar was the last place they wanted to take on Ranzami. No doubt there would be soldiers there to protect the general, and the place would be reconnoitered carefully by one of Ranzami's trusted aides. Brax and Cody worked out a series of plausible assault scenarios. Everyone of them had the same single objective. Take the general down at any and all costs. Civilian casualties played heavy on Brax's mind. He consulted Housemother via a secure phone conversation and both agreed they had to bear the cost. Valentine would remain uninformed to provide him with deniability. If it went down, Brax and the Pack would take the sole responsibility. Everyone else remained outside the need to know circle.

```
Arranging to meet with local legal.
Will need all the necessary
paperwork immediately.
                              Cody
```

Cody fired off an encoded message to Squire providing him with only the most vital details. Squire responded with a request to join the Pack in the field. He wanted to be there. He wanted to be part of the climax.

Brax denied the request; he couldn't risk an internal leak now. Just before they encountered their target, Brax would transmit a full message providing Squire their location and situation. Until then Squire would have to stand at the ready in his dungeon and react to whatever situation arose. Housemother would be on site with Squire, to make immediate decisions and coordinate with Valentine should unforeseen circumstances arise.

Against a night made even darker by an ominous overcast sky, Lonigan left the apartment at eight, dined at a local Chinese carryout and returned to his apartment with a brown bag. He ate only half his dinner; the other half went to Remy.

From Cali's vantage point, she detected no interest in Lonigan's wake either coming or going. So far, Brax had no reason to believe their operation had been compromised. At eleven, Brax issued the signal for the operation to proceed. Each team member deployed to his prearranged position like actors on a grand stage. The performance was about to begin.

At exactly eleven twenty, after downing a double dose of the Demerol, Lonigan emerged from his apartment to enter the second cab he flagged down, the first being a decoy just to be safe. Cody had the wheel when Lonigan entered. Brax turned onto the street a full block behind the cab, and Remy and Cali rendezvoused at a black Taurus parked two blocks away.

The curtain had risen. They were in motion. Brax's heart thumped out of control as he watched the cab move slowly down the cluttered street. Their hard target could be less than thirty minutes away.

"All clear so far," Cody said just loud enough for his button mike to pick up the words. His was to be a totally one-sided conversation. The team could not transmit back to him. Therefore, Cody had to rely on instinct to alert him to possible peril. A visual abort signal had been arranged to safeguard Cody in the event something went amiss.

Brax maintained his distance. Remy and Cali followed along a parallel track, arriving at the bar ahead of their stooge.

When the cab stopped a few paces before the bar's door, Lonigan hesitated before getting out. In his nervousness he had to be reminded to pay for the cab ride.

Cody had to sweat through that few moments of hesitation. While counting the money, his eyes appraised the scene clandestinely. He saw no reason to abort.

Lonigan left the cab and marched into the bar without so much as turning his head to once-over his surroundings. The picture of a man confident he moved unshadowed.

A minute later, Brax cruised by while Cody pulled the cab from the curb and fell in behind. When he turned the corner, he ditched the cab in an alley and switched to a waiting Escort. The cab could be collected up later, after the operation had completed.

Brax himself would shadow Lonigan into the bar, concerned that Remy could be made since he approached Lonigan in the bar three nights earlier. Cali also would appear too out of place in a gay bar, and Cody had been used to get Lonigan to the rendezvous.

When Brax entered, he gravitated toward an open stool at the corner of the bar. He waved to the bartender as if they were old friends, and the bartender nodded in acknowledgment, though he had never seen Brax before. Unconsciously, the bartender had played his part perfectly.

Thin streaming layers of gray cigarette smoke and clusters of men either sitting or standing together clogged the lounge. A few scanned in Brax's direction, one held his eyes more in an overtly amorous interest than intrigue.

Brax ordered a beer and tried to blend with the foliage. Not an easy task in a place where many of the eyes were on the prowl. If he leaned slightly to the left, he could observe Lonigan in a corner booth near a neon-lit jukebox. Brax never looked directly Lonigan's way, felt confident he could maintain his surveillance indirectly using reflections in the mirror.

Lonigan studied his drink and the smoke curling out of his ash tray. It wasn't until his third drink that someone approached him. The man chatted, standing at Lonigan's table. He made no move to join Lonigan nor did Lonigan make any move to invite him.

Brax studied Lonigan's lips; he could only decipher conversation appropriate for two men in a gay bar. Abandoning Lonigan, the man scanned the crowd languidly, ending his sweep well before reaching the corner Brax occupied. Lonigan had been instructed to discourage contact of any kind with anyone other than the man he was to meet. If he felt threatened in any way, he was to break into an uncontrollable hacking and make his way to the restroom. Brax would then take on the task of getting Lonigan out of the situation.

Lonigan downed another drink.

Brax accepted another beer from the bartender, wishing to avoid attention swinging his way by abstaining in a bar.

"You alone," a roseate-cheeked fellow ventured from his bar stool three away from Brax.

Brax refused to answer at first.

"I'm expecting someone," he finally said.

"Too bad. I'm Sweet Cheeks," the man offered with a wink that came out more like a tic than a gesture of interest.

Brax offered a glint of an interested smile, for what reason he had no other idea than maybe to cement his cover.

Sweet Cheeks ordered another drink and motioned the bartender to refill Brax's glass. Once done, Brax raised his glass in appreciation. Sweet Cheeks misread the response. He slid from his chair to take the stool beside Brax.

Just then Cody's arm came to rest on Brax's shoulder.

"You mind if I take this seat," Cody said, bearing down on Sweet Cheeks with venom in his eyes.

Brax shrugged.

"I said I was waiting for someone," Brax replied.

Sweet Cheeks abandoned his play to return to his stool. However, he did not remain there long. He drifted from his stool into a cluster huddled around the center of the bar.

Cody slid in close to Brax and leaned so Brax could watch over his shoulder. Sweet Cheeks ended up drifting away from the gathering, eventually end-ing up at to Lonigan's table.

Brax felt a sudden knot constrict around his heart. His stomach convulsed until bile backed up into his throat. Something felt wrong about the exchange. Was it coincidence that Sweet Cheeks just went from him to his stooge?

Lonigan laughed, motioning for Sweet Cheeks to join him. They kept conversation low and intimate, and neither motioned the bartender for more alcohol.

At that moment, a blaring warning went off inside Brax's head urging him to abort the operation. But the chance that this might lead him to Leviathan kept his tongue in check.

Sweet Cheeks covered Lonigan's hand in a ges-ture intimating it was time for them to leave together. Sweet Cheeks led, Lonigan followed as they snaked their way through the expanding crowd to get to the door. They waited just inside, allowing a jovial three-some to enter before they exited. It might have been a measure to allow Sweet Cheeks to detect anyone else suddenly interested in leaving the establishment.

"They're on the move," Cody whispered to the waiting team members.

Cali and Remy stood by outside waiting to attach themselves to the surveillance.

Once on the street, Lonigan waited while Sweet Cheeks disappeared around the corner for his car. A red Miata with the top tucked away roared up sec-onds later. A bad sign since the night chill seemed too oppressive for a starlit drive. Lonigan hesitated a moment before jumping into the passenger seat. Then the car zoomed off, turning the corner before Cody and Brax exited the bar.

Cali and Remy fell in a half block behind the sportster while in their mirror they could see Brax and Cody scrambling for their vehicle.

Remy called out the streets they passed until he heard from Brax, who now narrowed the gap between them to one city block.

"They're snuggling like a couple of Faggi-annies," Remy retorted.

Cali maneuvered in behind a Jeep Cherokee, using the opportunity to hit a cutoff switch for the right parking light. The next time they reappeared behind their target in the darkness, they would look like a different vehicle.

After twenty minutes in their wake, the cars switched. Cody and Brax took up behind the Miata, with Remy and Cali falling out to follow a parallel course. Cali returned the right parking light to operation.

"What's lover boy doing now?" Cali asked.

"Wandering aimlessly," Brax reported.

"There's something wrong," Cody reported a short time later when the Miata cornered in a squeal and began to double back.

"We're breaking off! We're breaking off! Pick them up going north on Ninth Avenue," Brax transmitted and continued straight. Once through the desolate intersection, Brax tromped the accelerator and shifted to the left lane.

"We're in trouble," Remy shouted, a few seconds after they would have intercepted the target. The Miata had side-stepped their surveillance.

"He's dumped! He's dumped!" Remy called out.

"Break it off," Brax ordered and roared around the block to rendezvous with the others.

Cali and Remy squealed into an alley. As they stopped their headlights fell on the Miata's rear just as Lonigan's crumpled mass toppled into a refuse heap. His blood soaked shirt glistened in the headlights. His eyes bulged white with terror.

"Fuck!" Brax screamed.

The cars halted one behind the other. Remy's headlights washed over Lonigan's body. The four came up beside their stooge, their guns leveled into the darkness. The Miata's two tiny red lights at the end of the alley were all that remained.

"Bastard! He's not dead," Remy said, checking the body.

"We got to go, boss, there's nothing we can do now. They made us. He was toying with us from the get-go," Cody said.

"We can't risk leaving him this way," Remy persisted.

Brax looked at Remy. Remy looked back at Brax. Both knew Lonigan could roll them over if he lived.

"*Coup de grace* is our only choice."

Brax had but a single moment to reach a decision. A distant siren spilled into the alley.

"I'll clean up," Remy offered.

"No," Brax said. He seized Remy's arm before he could withdraw his Beretta. "I have to take care of this. Full abort. Abandon."

The team dispersed. Remy returned to the vehicle to begin backing out of the alley. Cody backed the first car out and sped north. Cali disappeared on foot to the south.

Brax leveled his Glock to Lonigan's temple. A single pop and a flash ended his suffering. They couldn't risk Lonigan living long enough to expose the team. It had to be cleaned up. Afterward, Brax fled on foot into the darkness.

The Wolf Pack returned to square one.

Every realist knows that the democratic way of life is at this moment being directly assailed in every part of the world--assailed either by arms, or by secret spreading of poisonous propaganda by those who seek to destroy unity and promote discord in nations still at peace. During the sixteen months this assault has blotted out the whole pattern of democratic life in an appalling number of independent nations, great and small. The assailants are still on the march, threatening other nations, great and small.

Franklin D. Roosevelt January 6, 1941.

28

The rapier has fallen.

Squire

Three days had passed since the debacle in New York. No news reports surfaced on Lonigan's death. That should have blared a warning to Brax and the team, but it didn't.

Only Squire and Brax were privy to the whereabouts of the others. They hid from everyone, including Housemother and the other members of the Pack. The hours dragged on. Squire lived on his little black pills in his dungeon, pouring over intelligence and information funneling in from every official channel in New York.

Sleep came for Brax only through exhaustion. Sweet Cheeks had made the team. Brax knew it as well as he knew their hard target. Ranzami had chosen to eliminate the security threat rather than risk a compromise. Brax wanted that to mean the U.S. had become Ranzami's next attack. But such a conclusion now, if they were incorrect, could keep them out of position for the real strike when it came.

The secure phone beside Brax's bed rang shortly after eleven in the morning. Brax had grown sick of the television and the radio. He hoped Squire had good news to convey.

"Message came in from a Alejandro Fuentes on the secure line. I'm quoting. Your number is no longer unlisted. Contact immediately."

"He say anything else?"

"That was it."

Brax took no time to think or assess the information. Someone had taken an interest in his private telephone number. He used it to contact only two numbers. Someone was picking away at his cover.

"Squire, dig around for any sudden Company interest in Santa Cruz."

"Gotcha, where will you be?"

"I'm off line. We may have a problem. Have the team re-deploy in search of new leads."

"Where will you be?"

"I'll be contacting you."

Brax raced to the Newark International airport. He was helpless until he could get on a westbound plane. Once in the air, he phoned Suzanne. He got the answering machine.

After landing in San Jose, Brax again tried Suzanne, and again listened to her innocuous machine message. It was after ten; he was dead tired. Sleep was impossible on the flight. So many things to think about that putting them out of his mind became an insurmountable effort.

Fatigue forced him to take the drive over the hill slower. He watched his wake for signs of a shadow, which was something he never had to do in the past, and if all remained clear, he would crawl into his bed and meet with his telephone company contact the first thing in the morning. Exhaustion began to muddle his thinking, which forced him to greater effort to realign his mind into the role of Kevin Chambers.

Suzanne stepped out of the shower refreshed and excited. She never heard the telephone's ring over the rushing water. All she derived from Kevin's brief message was he was flying in tonight, and they would sleep together. Sleep never entered her mind. Unfortunately, Kevin failed to leave her the flight information in his message, so she had no idea where he was flying in from, nor what time to expect him. But that was Kevin. He always doled out only minimum information about his travels and grew silent when queried about any of it.

As she sat at her dressing table in Kevin's sweats, combing out her wet hair, she considered what life would be like after they married. Should she still teach? Of course, for a while. They both wanted children but talked about waiting at least another year or two before starting a family. Suzanne had sufficient time, she could forestall the family a few years before having to keep tabs on her biological clock. She just didn't want to wait too long. But in the end she agreed with his logic that waiting would be wiser.

With his frequent traveling, she would need something to fill her days before their first child arrived. Besides, she loved having twenty-one children to care for. Even if it was only six hours a day.

Part of her wanted her hair dried before climbing into bed, another part told her to let it go and crawl beneath the blanket. A yawn slipped out. She scolded herself and reminded herself that she must not fall asleep on him tonight. She relied on the excitement he would stir inside her to counter her fatigue.

With her hair mostly dry, Suzanne settled into the bed, switched on the small television set on the bureau across the room and channel surfed, hoping to find an old movie to help her remain awake until

Kevin returned home. It was after eleven and she figured she had only another hour to hold on.

Thirty minutes into an old Bogart movie,
Suzanne's eyes slipped closed despite her efforts to
keep them open. She thought she heard a door opening, so she decided to switch the television off, feign
sleep, and allow Kevin to wake her when he entered
the bed.

A few minutes passed and nothing. No footsteps
climbing the stairs. She concluded she must had been
mistaken. Maybe the television made her think Kevin
had arrived? She recalled setting the house alarm and
only Kevin knew the combination to disable it after
entry. In the still, she opted to leave the television
and lights off, and allow herself to drift off to sleep
while she waited.

Fifteen minutes later the sounds came again. It
had to be Kevin. Why was he lingering downstairs?
Fear crept up her spine, but Suzanne reassured herself that she was safe as long as the alarm was active.

Finally, footsteps arose coming toward her room.
She quickly turned away from the door and closed
her eyes.

The bedroom door opened. Through a narrow slit
in one eye she could see hall light falling across the
bedroom.

She listened as Kevin kicked off his shoes,
slipped out of his pants, then a moment later slid
into bed beside her.

His kisses gently graced the nape of her neck. She
turned with a smile brighter than the gibbous moon
falling in through the skylight.

"I've been waiting up for you," she said, reaching
to take hold of him under the blanket. "I've missed
you so much."

"I love you," Kevin said, finding her breast while
his lips devoured hers.

Their breathing marched in sync with their passion. Suzanne opened herself up when Kevin worked his hand into her sweat pants.

"What took you so long?" she whispered.

"I flew in from Florida. That takes a while."

"No, I mean downstairs. I heard you come in twenty minutes ago."

Kevin flew from the bed like a rifle shot, pulling Suzanne from the mattress to the floor.

"Grab something, now!" Kevin blurted in a harsh whisper. He was already at the closet door and searching.

The first burst of gunfire ripped through the bedroom door. Splinters rained down upon the carpet and the bed.

Kevin grabbed a gun he kept concealed in the closet and returned a fusillade of bullets, reaching out at the same time with one arm to grab Suzanne before she could scream. Kevin continued to fire into the door while he pushed Suzanne out onto the balcony and crawled into sweat pants.

Below, the water raced to the sand at the bottom of the thirty foot cliff outside their house.

Suzanne, too terrified to speak, too stunned to even know what to do, clung to Kevin.

"Over the railing!" he yelled. Another staccato burst of gunfire erupted into the bedroom. Kevin emptied another clip back into the darkness.

Suzanne jumped, landed squarely on her right ankle, wrenching it. Kevin came down a second later, landing flatly on both feet at the same time motioning to a rock foothold jutting out of the face of the cliff.

"We're going down."

Kevin angled his return fire through the balcony floor so the bullets would enter the bedroom and force the perpetrator to remain inside the house until he could disappear over the cliff's edge.

But no return fire left the house. The intruder, or intruders, had backed off.

Kevin worked a terrified Suzanne onto his back in a fireman's carry and held her with one arm while he moved down to the second foothold a few feet down from the ledge.

"Hold on tight! No matter what!" he commanded. He had to let her go. He needed both hands to negotiate the rock wall.

Kevin had scaled this sheer precipice a hundred times in the dead of night preparing for this very moment. He had set up two escape routes so carefully, never realizing that if he had to use one of them, Suzanne might be required to make the descent with him.

In the moonlight, he saw a paralyzing terror consuming her so totally, that she could think of nothing but clinging to him like a helpless child.

Kevin braced against the wall when he felt the initial wave of the explosion that ripped through the first level of the house above. He had just enough time to swing Suzanne in under him and hang on to the rock before the wave of burning debris rained down. The explosion sent a fireball over the cliff's edge, but the flames dissipated well before reaching them. Plastic explosives, Kevin thought from the color of the fire and the speed with which the flames dried up. Not a gasoline fire. Knowing that fired terror inside him.

But the tremendous wave of heat that washed over them sucked the oxygen out of their burning lungs. Neither dared breathe during that moment. And as soon as they felt the surge of cooler ocean breeze rising up to wash over them, Kevin scrambled the remaining ten feet to the beach. Navigating through the scattered debris, pulling a terrified Suzanne in his wake, they breached the water.

"What's happening?" she cried above rushing waves lapping at their bare feet.

"Into the water," was all Kevin could bark.

The two disappeared into the frigid surf and swam down the coast a distance of at least two hundred yards. The endeavor drained every last ounce of strength either could find. And it seemed to take forever. Kevin kept one arm under Suzanne at all times to keep her from going under. He pulled stroke after stroke with a strength he thought had dissipated long ago.

Emerging from the crashing surf, Suzanne's teeth chattered; she shivered out of control. Kevin wrapped her arm around his waist and helped her through the sand toward a timber walkway ascending off the beach. To their left flank, flames licked the night like beacons against the lightless coastline.

Suzanne needed to stop. She wanted Kevin to wrap both his arms around her. She couldn't stop shivering. Instead, he pulled her up a cleft in the rocky wall.

"Kevin, stop! What's happening?" she cried over the rush of waves.

"Come on!" he snarled with a caustic bite that could have drawn blood. His voice became granite. He tugged her up a set of timbers and returned his arm around her to fight off the cold seeping to the very core of her being.

Suzanne breathed in gasps. No sooner had they returned to the top of the cliff when Kevin jogged through the trees with Suzanne in tow. They at last stopped behind a stucco garage detached from an A-frame house secluded from both the road and the cliff.

Suzanne caved in to her panic and began crying, though only her sobs were detectable. Tears remained masked by the water dripping from her saturated hair.

Kevin fumbled to mount a two foot high rock, using it as a step ladder to dig around under the roof shingles. He had secreted a key under them. The rock had been positioned intentionally for that very purpose.

"What are you doing?" Suzanne stammered while trying to control her chattering jaw. A rising cloud of smoke gathering above the trees held her eyes. Approaching sirens broke the night.

Kevin finally uncovered the key, unlocked the garage door and slipped inside with Suzanne clutching the back of his sweat pants. Without the benefit of light, they climbed into a waiting Porsche 911 turbo and Kevin ran through a quick checklist. The Desert Eagle he lifted from beneath the driver's seat took on the dimensions of a canon in the darkness. He hit the remote door opener. As soon as the engine fired, Kevin rammed the accelerator and the Porsche fish-tailed wildly as they flew down a winding drive and spun in a cloud of smoking rubber onto the street.

Without headlights, the Porsche sped off in the direction opposite the oncoming fire trucks.

Only after they were blocks from the scene did Kevin switch on the headlights. He slapped the heater control over to full heat, all the while negotiating the winding road at a speed that put them on two wheels.

"Kevin, goddamnit! What the hell is happening?"

"I can't explain now. We've got to get safe first."

"Safe? Why? Who's trying to kill us?"

"I'll explain it all. Right now I have to get us out of here. They won't believe we were still in the house when it went up."

"Kevin, who? Who won't believe we were in the house?"

"I don't know who!" Kevin was yelling. "Just get close to the heat and let me drive!"

The Porsche roared onto the access ramp for Highway One North and hugged the left lane at ninety. Kevin slowed only enough to make the transition to the ramp feeding Highway Seventeen. He took it at seventy.

Suzanne screamed as the car careened across both lanes before Kevin regained control.

A desolate road lie ahead. Not so for the lanes behind them. Kevin dared not slow. He caught a pair of headlights creeping up his rear view mirror. He had lived this escape plan in his mind a hundred times. He knew by rote everything he must do to remain alive. There was no time to even contemplate who wanted them dead. Now was only survival.

Suzanne slipped low in her seat and remained quiet. The rush of hot air coming over her quieted her shivers. However, her wet clothes kept her from truly warming up. The frigid ocean must have dropped her body temperature at least five degrees, even though they were only in it less than fifteen minutes.

It took all the will she could muster to stave off the flood of tears pushing to get out. She had never before in her life even contemplated death. Now she was facing it head on. It took a moment for her to fathom just how close she had come.

Kevin took the incline of the mountain at a running start, weathering through a pair of cars puffing to keep their speed on the six degree incline. The headlights in his wake disappeared for a short time as they twisted and climbed toward Summit Road only a dozen miles ahead. Kevin knew he needed nine minutes at his current speed to reach the Summit and what he hoped would be safety.

Suddenly the headlights reappeared, roaring up the mountain at a speed defying any vehicle's ability to hold the pavement.

"Fuck. Hold on, this could get hairy," Kevin shouted, moving to the outside lane and praying no slow moving vehicles were around the next bend.

"Oh, like it hasn't already?" Suzanne tried to inject.

Two more winding treacherous miles until they reached the Summit Road turnoff.

A shot rang out.

The Porsche's rear window shattered, spilling behind the seats; Suzanne screamed. Kevin locked his fingers to the steering wheel and swerved to make them harder to hit. That kind of firing accuracy meant there had to be more than one in the car behind them.

Kevin mashed the pedal to the floor, employed both lanes to make a sharp left to cling to the snaking grade and gunned the engine to put more distance between them and the shooter.

"Hold tight, lean forward, and put your head to your knees," Kevin ordered as they rounded the turn. The lighted exit sign for Summit Road came into view.

Suzanne's crying rose above the roar of the engine.

Kevin doused his lights, slammed the brakes just as the Porsche hit the off ramp and slid into the woody darkness off the highway.

The Porsche screeched to a halt, and Kevin leveled his weapon out his open window.

Seconds later as Kevin watched, a pair of headlights roared past and continued on the highway, turning and climbing toward the peak of Highway Seventeen.

Kevin dropped his gun between his legs and rammed the shifter into first. He accelerated until they moved on to Summit Road, then switched his lights back on. He took the winding grade as quickly as he could in the darkness and watched his mirror for signs of the car's return. He knew when the pursuit car missed the off ramp, he had gained at least three to five minutes on his adversary. Three minutes was enough time for them to become lost on the mountain roads.

A few minutes later, Kevin coasted off the road to take up a rutted dirt path that ended at a secluded lightless cabin.

"Key's under the planter," Kevin said. His eyes never left the road leading up to the cabin.

Suzanne ran to the door, located the key and disappeared inside. Kevin opened the garage door, eased the Porsche into the dark haven then took up a defensive position amongst the gathering of trees with his Desert Eagle ready. He had a full magazine in the weapon and more in the cabin.

Minutes melted away. The road remained dark, silent. They were safe...for now.

Suzanne threw herself into his arms the moment he closed the cabin door. Despite his need to keep her close, he pushed her away, and dropped before a wood pile beside the fireplace situated in the center of the back wall. He removed another gun and a box of shells.

Suzanne crossed after him in a rush, grabbed both his arms with such force that her nails dug into his skin. Her face had turned to rage.

"Goddamn you, tell me what is going on!"

She refused to release him despite his attempt to pull free. For the first time since falling in love with him, Suzanne saw fear—real fear—in those otherwise gentle and loving eyes. Behind that granite face and rock solid muscles, a frightened boy peered through.

As if some terrible burden had been lifted from his shoulders, Kevin let his arms fall. His face shed a wave of relief.

"I work for the government," he started. He felt his fingers relax around the grip of his Desert Eagle. Suzanne's grip began to soften.

"How? What do you mean?"

"CIA."

The words hung there for a long moment. A mask had come off Kevin's face. Now a completely different person emerged.

"You're a spy..."

"I'm sorry. I know I should have told you before I asked you to marry me."

"You're sorry? YOU'RE GODDAMN SORRY! Somebody fires a machine gun into our bedroom, and while we're climbing down a goddamn cliff, they blow up our house, and you're fucking sorry!"

It took all the strength Suzanne could muster to suppress that driving urge to scream until all her pent-up rage had been expunged. But she contained herself, somehow amid all this she found her sense of balance, and released Kevin's arms.

"The toughest problem I've ever had to face was one of my students running around crying she couldn't hold it long enough to reach the bathroom. Or maybe one of the girl's screaming that a bug had crawled upon her shoe. Now you're telling me someone is trying to kill me?"

"Not you. Me, Suzanne. Someone's trying to kill me."

"Yeah, well I guess you forgot to tell them you just happen to be living with someone."

Kevin tucked his desert Eagle in the elastic band of his sweat pants and loaded the 9mm Beretta he had removed from the wood pile.

Without speaking he crossed to a dresser and pulled out neatly folded sets of clothes. He moved about almost mechanically, like none of this mattered to him. He threw a shirt and pants to Suzanne and began shedding his wet clothes.

"They're too big for me," she said, holding them as if she had the freedom to refuse.

"Sorry, I didn't think to plan for you. It's all we've got right now."

"I guess you didn't think about me. Oh, maybe I should tell my fiancée that somebody might want to blow me up. Damn you. I'm a third grade teacher. How could you do this to me?"

Suzanne's mewls turned into unrestrained cries. Kevin, sensing Suzanne's imminent collapse, raced across the room to catch her just before the fall.

"Suzanne, I love you, and I need you now more than ever. I need you to help me now."

Suzanne stared at him through eyes distant and strange.

"What are we going to do?"

"I've got to get you to a safe house. There's a place where you'll be safe for now."

Kevin set Suzanne on the sofa, then drew the shades before lighting a hurricane lamp. He settled beside Suzanne before the fireplace, all the time tuned to the night for the sound of any approaching vehicles.

"What do you do...for the CIA?"

"I can't tell you. All I can say is innocent people will die if I fail. What I do is not like the movies."

"Kevin, this is crazy," Suzanne started then stopped. What was his name? Who is this man she fell in love with. "After loving you for three years, you're telling me you're a spy. And somebody wants us dead because of that."

Kevin kissed her, hoping to divert her mind from the fear that must be swelling out of control inside her. He could see it in her eyes and feel it in her voice.

"I love you, Suzanne. I'm sorry you got dragged into this. I'm sorry that I have to do what I'm about to do."

"What do you mean?"

"You can't go back."

"What does that mean?"

"That means there's no returning to the school. You can't go back to Aptos."

"I'll stay with my mother in Sacramento."

"I can't risk that. Someone may have tied you to me. You're vulnerable now. I'm vulnerable now."

"So what's going to happen?"

"We'll deal with that tomorrow. For now just get some rest. We stay put until tomorrow night. I have almost everything we need to get you to a place of safety."

"Then what happens?"

"I find out who tried to kill us tonight."

Neither Suzanne nor Kevin slept. In the morning Kevin walked to a nearby cabin and thirty minutes after his return, Orienda showed up at their door.

Despite brave attempts, she failed to conceal the concern in her eyes. She came with clothes that fit Suzanne and papers. Papers hastily assembled, papers giving Suzanne a new identity with which to travel.

Before leaving she kissed each of them on the cheek and drove off in the Porsche, leaving her Suburban behind.

"I don't get it. How does Orienda fit in?"

"I saved her a long time ago. In Bulgaria. She said she would be eternally grateful for what I had done. This is her way of repaying the debt."

19

Mr. Cavendish has arrived. Uncle
Webley arranging to meet.

                              Squire

October 30th. Suzanne could do nothing more
than stare vacantly out the cabin window at wooded
rolling hills and a scummy pond less than fifty paces
from the building. She had been alone for over a
week, and she received no calls from Kevin in the
past three days. Knowing who he really was made the
burden only slightly easier to endure.

She picked up the phone for the fifth time in the
last few hours. She wanted so badly to dial her
mother and let her know that she was all right. By
now everyone at school must have given her up for
dead. The newspaper would have reported the house
explosion. And with the house so completely
destroyed, everyone would have concluded that Kevin
and her both perished in the ensuing blaze. How
could she ever hope to explain her disappearance to
her friends? What friends, she thought. Would she
ever see California again? Would she ever leave this
prison of a place?

Nights without Kevin became unbearable. Even
though she saw him just as much now as she did
before...she needed him more now that she became
sequestered in this woody prison.

She never missed a news broadcast and fell
asleep at night to the monotone voice on an all-news

radio station. She hoped to hear something, anything that meant whatever Kevin was involved in was over, and she could return to the way her life with him had been. The hellish nightmares of that night hounded her in sleep. The rapid burst of gunfire played over and over inside her head. The thundering explosion while she clung precariously to Kevin on the cliff, and the remains of their house lying scattered like flotsam along the beach. The visions tormented her. Fatigue brought fear, fear of the nightmare, and fear that someone would break into the cabin while she slept to put a bullet into her head.

Kevin was to blame. He involved her in this. He said he loved her; he said he wanted to marry her. How could she marry someone like him?

And if she went through with the union, could they ever go back to the way it was? How could she face life with a man who conceals his identity from everyone around him, even those he claims to love?

After a dinner of macaroni and cheese—generic, not the good stuff—Suzanne walked the grounds, never straying beyond sight of the cabin and always hopeful that a car might come down the dirt road. To have Kevin behind the wheel might be too much to hope for, but she prayed for it anyway.

She even began to think like one of them, planning escape routes on foot if someone came after her. She paused along the ridge of a dried up shallow ravine, not to admire the late season wild flowers still in bloom, but rather to seek out a crevasse or opening she could force herself into if she had to hide.

But in a strange way she felt safe in this place. No houses nor people as far as she could see, no traffic to be nosing around. She felt totally isolated, but safe. How could anyone possibly find her so far removed from the rest of the living world?

As the last rays of the sun dwindled amongst the trees, Suzanne trekked back up the hill to the cabin to prepare herself for another night alone in a cold bed with only two television stations and a radio to ease the loneliness inside. She tried focusing on a couple of books collecting dust on the shelves over the fireplace, but reading and concentrating became impossible. All Suzanne could think about was what had happened in Aptos, and when she might see Kevin again.

When she caught the grumbling of an approaching car, her heart beat furiously. Was it? Then terror swept through her. What if the men who bombed the house had tracked her down to this place. She was alone. What if they...

She dropped, creeping to the window.

Kevin opened the car door and rushed to hold her when she burst through the cabin door.

"Thank God you're here," she said, kissing him.

"Why?" His hand went under his jacket.

"I'm going crazy. Kevin, I can't take this. I can't stay here."

Kevin swept her into his arms and carried her inside the cabin, where he kissed her again and again. Despite all, Suzanne felt passion stirring. She wanted to make love, to hold him until the morning finally broke over the hillside. But most of all she wanted to be away from this place. She wanted her life back.

"I wish I could change this, but I can't. Until I know for sure who is after me, you must remain here where you'll be safe."

"How long? Give me a time!"

"I can't."

"You have to!"

"Don't you understand? This isn't a game we're playing. Nobody's going to say they quit and give themselves up. This isn't television! We all can't just go home at the end of the day and stop worrying about our job."

"What kind of job?"

"I can't tell you that. I'm sorry."

Suzanne detected a rising fear in Kevin's voice.

"Kevin, I can't take this. Can't you understand? My life is so helter-skelter right now that I'm going to explode."

He took Suzanne into his arms and warmed her until the shivers of fear raking her body subsided. He loved her so much. She became the one constant in his world that he had come to believe in.

"I love you, Suzanne. You're the only thing in my life I can count on. You're what keeps me going. I need to know I have you."

For a long moment Suzanne said nothing, fighting back the tears struggling to get out.

"I do love you. I love you so much that no matter what happens I will never turn my back on you."

They refrained from making love, somehow it seemed wrong at this moment, rather they sat nestled in each other's arms on threadbare burlap strap sofa long into the night. There was much Kevin wanted to say, so much Suzanne needed to understand, yet he knew it was still too dangerous to reveal secrets he kept buried deep beneath the surface.

"You still awake?" he whispered after a while.

She smiled, mumbled something, and tightened her arms around him.

"Every day I wake up asking myself what must I do this day to save someone's life. If I fail, Suzanne, innocent people die. I can't let that happen and live with myself. It's what I do."

"I love you, regardless of what you do," Suzanne whispered.

Three A.M A ringing telephone drew Squire from a dead-to-the-world slumber that began only two hours earlier. Sleep had become a devilishly elusive creature over the past few days, and for the first time in a week, Squire had successfully crawled into his bed in the hopes of emptying his mind. His body craved sleep, glorious hours of sleep. Yet his demon was toying with him, offering an appetizer to a starving man, then watching him beg for more. Still cloaked in darkness, Squire located something yellow on the night stand and forced his swallow as he staggered into a cold shower to cajole himself back into the world of the living. While he slept, an MI5 communiqué had been routed to Langley the moment the London station deciphered it. Any report regarding Leviathan got marked MOST URGENT and routed to a drop that went to Squire without delay.

The report indicated Leviathan might have been spotted less than two hours earlier in the south of London. Local time of the reported observation had been 2 A.M. However, the report had yet to be confirmed by MI5.

Squire was on the phone the moment he realized the meaning behind the words. The team was spread out. Only Remy seemed to be in a position to close in on their prey in a timely manner. With luck, he could get to London in time to fall in behind their target. No one on station could be trusted to set up the sophisticated surveillance a target like Leviathan required.

Squire's call to Housemother put wheels in motion. Housemother said he could be there in thirty minutes. Squire needed more. He had to arrange air travel to get the team to London before he could leave for his dungeon.

The exhilaration in Housemother's voice lingered in Squire's head after he hung up. What they had worked for—and one had died for—had suddenly appeared within reach.

Brax's cell phone awakened them after only a few hours of uncomfortable sleep on the sofa. Neither he nor Suzanne wanted to lose the moment by leaving the sofa for the relative comfort of the bed.

"Go, Squire," Brax said. With the first words, his eyes snapped full open and alert. Suzanne struggled to keep hers open enough to see Kevin's face.

"We got a sighting on the hard target," Squire said.

"Where?"

"Twenty kilometers south of London. Unconfirmed, but two agents from MI5 are en route to get some kind of confirmation."

"Who's closest?"

"Remy. He's boarding a Harrier right now. He'll touch down in England in less than two hours."

"Arrange transportation for the team."

"Already done. You'll be airborne in an hour."

"Get Housemother out of bed."

"Already done. He's here, grinning like the cat who swallowed the canary. Cody's in the air. But he can't get there for five hours."

"Cali, where's Cali?"

"On her way to an airbase. I've arranged a SAC bomber to transport her. With aerial refueling, she'll arrive around the same time as you.

"Instruct MI5 to keep him in sight at all costs."

"Brax, you think it's the Chunnel like Remy said?"

"Squire, I think we're going to get our chance. I need you to do something for me."

Brax waited. There was a uncomfortable pause before Squire answered.

"I need you to stay with Suzanne. I know how you feel, but it's important. You can set up temporary Ops here."

"Might as well. It's either there or the dungeon. No way you're letting me go to London."

After Squire agreed to the assignment, Brax hung up, offered Suzanne a quick description of what Sidney looked like and left in a flurry of dust in his Jeep.

```
Have made contact. Seems the
landlord was not at home.
                        Remy
```

An almost orgasmic exhilaration moved through Ranzami. He dressed in faded denim jeans with stains of gray and white, and a double-pocketed workshirt that had been scrubbed about sufficiently to infuse an aged appearance.

Sitting before a mirror lighted so brightly that most would squint, a wide-eyed Ranzami began the meticulous task of applying the precisely molded latex strips. He fitted each piece to his face and verified it against the snapshot beside him before gluing it in place. Afterward, he applied a thin makeup base to blend the appliance to his natural skin tone. After seventy minutes of cosmetic wizardry, he applied the bushy eyebrows and thin mustache to complete his transformation.

At the moment, the television in the background provided more a source of noise than useful information. When he gazed beyond his face in the mirror, he could see most of the twenty-five inch screen in the reflection. He cared little for anything the two talk show hosts had to say. What he anxiously anticipated was the weather report. The night sky outside the small apartment remained dull and dingy despite the passing of sunrise.

"What's on tap for the White House this Hallow-een," a feminine voice asked her male nameless co-anchor. Both seemed far too perky for this time of the morning.

"Well, the president and first lady will be hosting a Halloween party for a large group of underprivi-leged children in the White House garden later this afternoon. That is, if it doesn't rain."

Ranzami turned toward the screen hoping for more information.

"Rain could spoil trick or treating for a whole bunch of little ones this year. I understand when asked if the president would be in costume, he replied he was masquerading as a Republican."

The irony brought a wry chuckle from Ranzami.

Before rising from his chair, he inspected his handiwork once more with a critical eye, measuring it against the picture on the badge clipped to his right shirt pocket. Only the astute could discern the imper-fections. No one would suspect that beneath this face breathed the man the British Secret Service, American CIA and FBI desperately wanted dead.

Ranzami's heart pounded. He was indeed the master of strategy who directed his army of patriots to execute his cabals. He was the one man they must fear most. Now due to unfortunate circumstances, he himself would perform the one step most crucial to the success of his plan. He had never been this inti-mately close to any operation before. He had never allowed himself to be put to such risk. The adrenaline rush made him feel more than alive. His brilliant mind had conceived this plan and assembled every meticulous detail, now his very hands would carry it through to its final stages.

Standing three feet back from the mirror, Ran-zami critically assessed every nuance of his new appearance. His reflection appeared exactly as the guard would see him when he handed over his badge for verification. He was ready.

He filled his canvass bag with the necessary tools for his established cover, then he checked the badge one final time before tucking it away.

"Trick or treat," he said to the television set before switching it off.

The Washington traffic lived up to its reputation on Ranzami's drive to the Capitol building. But he had factored that into his plans and sat patiently amidst the clogs until he finally reached his destination. He parked in the construction crew parking area, after producing his badge for the guard at the gate. He had been waved through with no more than a glance at his authorization. The first checkpoint lay in his wake. He retrieved his bag from the trunk, using the opportunity to reconnoiter the entrance while his head hovered out of view beneath the trunk lid.

He waited patiently for his moment, feigning checking his tool bag. He would proceed only when the traffic entering the construction door became such that it minimized the risk of a guard inspecting too closely his identification. Long lines made people uncomfortable, causing them to rush to compensate for the delay. Rushing leads to inattention, so Ranzami waited for the line to build at the doors. All had been properly prepared and checked. Ranzami calculated that his chances for success remained very favorable. There, of course, were always variables beyond control. That's what makes living exciting. But Ranzami would address each errant variable if and when it arose to present a problem. Yet for all his preparation and careful planning, his heart still raced and his palms sweated as he waited in his car for a cluster to amass outside the door.

Sixteen minutes later, Ranzami left his car, set a battered Yankees baseball cap snugly upon his head, and with his bag in hand, headed for the construction entrance. A dozen or so laborers returning from lunch grumbled about the stringent security as they waited for reentry. The drizzle that had begun shortly after dawn remained, making the wait in the line extending out the door even more uncomfortable.

Ranzami had to exercise care to keep the water from loosening his appliances. He kept the cap bill low, deflecting most of the water away from his face.

For the first time since conception, Ranzami worried that his plan might be in jeopardy. Despite his efforts, a light mist accumulated on his face. He knew to wipe it away might expose his latex disguise. Luckily, he moved inside before sufficient moisture accumulated to disturb his makeup.

"We go through this a dozen fucking times a week for the last five months, you'd think those Bozos could move us through the line faster," a disgruntled carpenter three ahead of Ranzami commented. The two made eye contact. Ranzami smiled but remained silent.

Finally he reached the first guard station. He presented his badge in exactly the same manner as those before him, and he maintained a warm eye contact with the guard. The eyes would be the first to reveal suspicion. Ranzami mentally measured the distance from where he stood back to the door. But those behind him in line would impede any egress. This must work, because Ranzami had left himself with no escape.

"Were you passed through earlier?" the guard asked, clearly annoyed at the comments from those grumbling about, forced to stand in line so long.

"At eight-thirty," Ranzami lied.

The guard verified the picture on the badge and waved Ranzami through. This time the guard never even entered the name into the computer, though it wouldn't have mattered. Their cover had been established months earlier, just in case anything went awry.

Ranzami swallowed his relief while he moved on to the next line. There he endured a scant two minute wait for the guard to inspect his bag, even though most of the other workers carried nothing back in. A worker with a sack of electrical materials, it seemed, became a clog holding things up.

Ranzami cataloged the sharply dressed blue suit that strolled up to the guard station. He surmised that this might be a supervisor, since he took up a position of authority behind the guard checking clearances at the computer. How fortunate, Ranzami, thought, that he had made it through before the boss had showed up to check on his underlings. Would even he had been astute enough to detect Ranzami's ruse?

"Everything going okay?" Donley asked offering up no more than a casual glance at those waiting in line.

"Can't you guys do something to speed this up?" a swarthy-skinned Hispanic painter asked of Donley, concluding that because he wore a suit he must be the one in charge.

Donley smiled and shrugged as if to say it was all beyond his control, but he offered no words to appease the grumbling. He watched as the clearance for the badge in the guard's hand came up on the screen. Satisfied that all his security measures were being strictly adhered to, Donley slipped his hands into his pockets and strolled down the corridor, oblivious to the men moving in and out of the construction wing of the Capitol building.

Ranzami smiled as the suit drifted away.

"Trick or treat," he whispered to himself.

Complacent fools, he thought as the guard inspecting his bag removed an aerosol can and shook it.

"Test for leaks in pipes," Ranzami said.

"Don't you know these things screw up the ozone?"

"Until someone invents a non-aerosol replace-ment, I'm stuck with this," Ranzami offered. His eyes never left the guard's hand as it returned the can to the bag. A moment later, Ranzami strolled through the construction area whistling a tune that had been in his head since he climbed out of bed.

It took two passes by the utility room before Ran-zami felt at ease with his surroundings. This was the most perilous stage of his plan. This was the one time when discovery would indict him. This was the moment he had planned for with every breath he took. Three years of assembling every piece until he knew without doubt success would be his.

Three years of locating the right specialists capa-ble of constructing each segment of his complex device. Three years of arranging for the tremendous financing required to move his plan off the board. The Iraqis, coming through at the last moment, singly contributed to his presence here now. Success loomed on the horizon like the first glowing rays of an imminent sunrise.

Ranzami unlocked the door with fingers as calm as a brain surgeon's. He checked both directions down the hall to ensure no one observed him. With an easy fluid motion, he slipped into the utility room. He locked the door and stood there breathing deeply for a long moment. Using his shirt sleeve, he dabbed at the small beads of sweat that found their way to the surface from beneath the latex. Ten minutes of unin-terrupted solitude and it would be done.

He gazed up the ladder into the darkness of the crawlspace. With the renovation project so near com-pletion, he would have one shot at this. And it was unlikely anyone would disturb him, since the over-head work had been completed many weeks before.

Halfway through his ascent, Ranzami shifted the bag from one hand to the other. His heart hammered inside his chest, not from exertion but from exhilara-tion. When he reached the last rung, he gingerly set his bag on the transom and stared down into long tunnel of darkness.

Ranzami had reached the pinnacle of his world. A feeling of omnipotence that only he could truly fathom at this moment swelled inside. For only he knew. Only he understood what was about to become reality.

Moving mechanically on hands and knees down the transom, Ranzami located the Y-junction in the ductwork. The cover plate was exactly where the drawing indicated. In seconds, he removed three of the quick disconnect screws with a magnetic screwdriver. In his excitement, and despite his tool, he still dropped one. It disappeared amongst insulation and conduit. But he had brought spares.

Ranzami removed the fourth screw with one hand while holding the plate in place with the other until he could grab it securely with both hands. The plate he must not lose. It must go back exactly the way it came off. Removing the plate sent a rush of warm air across his face. The same amber wave upon which he would deliver justice to the filthy pigs.

The boisterous rhetoric of the self-centered Representatives below filtered into the duct. Ranzami chuckled as he listened to those bombastic imbeciles bickering over petty foolishness. While multitudes starve, and thousands slaughtered at the hands of the greedy, these decadent bastards quarrel about who shall have the most miles of highway or the largest slice of the worm-infested American pie.

Time meant nothing to him now. Only precise movements counted. No mistakes.

Ranzami unzipped his canvass bag and removed a small inspection mirror on a twelve-inch extension handle. He eased the mirror into the duct, angling it until the metal frame and triggering circuit came into view.

Retrieving the micro-antenna tape from his bag, Ranzami installed one end of the tape securely on the

metal strip of the triggering circuit board, then slowing unrolled the clear plastic until he could affix a 30
centimeter length to the outside of the ductwork. He
was certain he had unrolled longer than 30 centimeters, but longer was acceptable, shorter was not.
Using the inspection mirror, he checked the tape for
proper placement on the circuit. Afterward, he meticulously returned the plate to the duct using two
screws to hold it in place.

It was too soon to release a glint of a smile. Ranzami next removed a circuit breaker from his bag,
pried off the side panel with a small screwdriver and
palmed the remote device Kirkhammer had provided
him. Without fanfare, Ranzami pressed the button,
observed the green light illuminate moments later,
then he returned the device to the concealment the
circuit breaker afforded.

Foolish security guards, Ranzami thought, they
take everything at face value.

After unfastening the screws holding the plate in
place, Ranzami exposed the inside of the duct and
returned to his inspection mirror. The three small
lights cast an almost invisible glow. Their luminescence meant that his activation had awakened the
device and now all the circuits were properly functioning. The device had triggered just as Willie
assured him it would.

For a moment Ranzami paused to breath. The
remote activation proved itself as reliable as he had
paid for it to be. Willie Kirkhammer would have been
proud of his triumph for the cause...if he had lived to
witness it.

Ranzami slipped a hand into the duct to very
gently inspect everything with his finger tips. His
index finger stopped when it came upon the switch
necessary to disarm the trigger and return it to the
sleep mode. He pressed and held as he slowly
counted to ten. With the mirror in position, he con-

firmed the little lights had extinguished. The circuit had returned to sleep. He could proceed.

Ranzami endured sweat trickling down his back. He worried that the sweat on his face would in time loosen his latex. Something he had been unable to account for when Lonigan's compromise forced him to change his plan. The front of his shirt wore a deep blue sweat stain. The overflow began collecting in the waist band of his pants.

Having assured himself of the integrity of the triggering mechanism, Ranzami removed the first aerosol can and unscrewed the bottom. Packed securely in wadding, the first polished metal cylinder came out. It filled his palm and proved quite weighty for its small size. On the top of the cylinder, a special fixture about the size of a knuckle had been fitted. The canister resembled a large CO_2 cartridge. Alone, the gas inside this cylinder was considered dangerous, but not lethal. However, when combined with the gas in the second cylinder, the union became virulent. So virulent was Chevanovich's triumph that this small amount when combined from both cylinders would wipe out a stadium of people on a day when the wind was still. Ranzami only desired to kill six hundred.

Next, Ranzami removed a roll of double-sided tape from his bag. Biting off a piece, he placed it securely across his palm. The cylinder stuck to the tape with such cohesion that only a strong tug could pull it free. He could nil afford to drop either of the cylinders and have them roll away along the bottom of the duct.

But Ranzami paused. He was not ready to proceed. His heart pounded inside his head. His breathing turned to gasps. He must fit the cylinder into the two metal straps that would hold it securely in place, then tighten them down while keeping the discharge valve aligned with the trigger pin. No easy task. Ranzami had rehearsed the necessary movements a hundred times before coming here. Each time he wore a blindfold and each time he succeeded without incident. But those had merely been exercises; this was for real.

Ranzami slipped a hand into the duct. He had to maneuver blindly, relying on touch until the cylinder reached the approximate position with the release valve near the trigger pin on the circuit board. Then, using his index finger to locate the first metal strap, and steadying the cylinder in place, he manipulated the strap over the cylinder body and locked it down on the circuit board. Exactly as he had practiced in his room. With one in place, he removed his hand with a firm constant pressure. The tape yielded. His last steps for the first cylinder were to secure the second metal strap and visually verify that the valve and trigger pin were in alignment.

Using the inspection mirror, Ranzami rotated the cylinder slightly to slide the release valve beneath the trigger pin. The soft *click* told him half his job had been completed. One more operation and his deadly Landfill device would be complete.

Ranzami duplicated the procedure in exactly the same precise movements for the second cylinder, and once done, he visually verified both cylinders had been locked down on the circuit board and each mated with their respective trigger pins. Using his finger as a way to gage his accuracy, Ranzami rubbed the tip along the release valve and trigger pin of each cylinder. The alignment had been done without error.

For a long moment, Ranzami just knelt there, admiring his accomplishment. All logic warned him to seal the opening and withdraw immediately, but Ranzami, like any other artist, loved his creation, and therefore, hesitated before walking away from it even though it was complete. The culmination of years of planning, organizing and pitching sat asleep inside the duct. A lifetime of hatred had driven him to this place in history. No one would know that he was the one responsible. No one would ever clasp his hand to say 'good job.'

Ranzami's hands shook as he fumbled through his bag in search of a replacement screw for the cover plate. One by one he inserted the screws back into the cover. He made certain nothing looked even remotely out of place in the crawlspace.

Smoothing his fingers over the sheet metal beneath the plate, he felt for the tape antenna. Only the most scrutinizing eye could detect the presence of the micro-antenna outside the ductwork. And since all work in this area had been completed better than month ago, there would be no reason for anyone to come poking around the ducts.

It was done. Only one last task stood between him and success.

Ranzami withdrew to the ladder. Darkness engulfed where he had been. He gazed back down the transom one last time. In his mind, he ticked off, point by point, a checklist he had prepared for himself. During those moments, he mentally confirmed he had performed each item on the list. The last item brought a faint smile to his face: No evidence of his presence remained behind, no telltale sign that anything had been altered in this place.

Before beginning his descent, he examined the latex on his face with his fingers, making certain neither heat nor sweat would cast doubt upon his identity. As he stepped down the ladder, measuring each placement ever so carefully to prevent an accident, he listened intently for sounds beyond the utility room door.

All remained quiet.

He must escape unnoticed for his plan to remain uncompromised. No one can know that this place had been visited by a workman. No one can know that death now hovered over the heads of these gutless men.

As easily as he had slipped into this place, Ranzami exited the utility room, locked the door for the final time, then strolled down the corridor whistling the Battle Hymn of the Republic. He never once looked back at where he had been; he focused only on the future.

31

Gone visiting Aunt Sophie. Will call
with schedule to return home.
                              Squire

Sidney rocked and rolled, charged with a new-found energy, along a snaking dirt road through woody hills, all the time ignoring the picturesque landscape and focusing instead on an escape plan. A secondary road branched off to the north, flanking the cabin ahead, and if they could get to that branch, they could use it as an alternate route back to the highway. If *they* approached from the west, he could drive downhill to the south to return to the highway. He felt totally inept for what he had been tasked with, but knew he had to perform. The midnight blue Grand Cherokee coasted to a stop before the cabin matching Brax's description down to the last detail.

Sidney felt for the comfort of the Glock 22 poking his side, reminding him of the underlying gravity of the situation. Even before leaving the vehicle, he detected movement in the darkened interior. He made a mental note to brief Suzanne on how to behave inside the cabin.

"Suzanne," he called in advance of his approach. He paused at the single step leading to a four foot wide porch. Before entering, he surveyed the terrain to assess the degree of difficulty perpetrators would face in making an assault on the cabin. In any possible scenario, Squire would get at least a minute's

advance warning in daylight and thirty seconds in the
pitch. It wasn't much. Sidney revised his egress plan
to account for a shortened nocturnal evacuation window.

The curtain to the right of the door moved
slightly. Two frightened eyes appeared for a second
then disappeared. The door opened.

"Sidney?" Suzanne asked, abandoning all the cau-
tions Brax had instructed her to observe before
unlocking the door. She knew the moment she saw
Sidney's face that he was the man Kevin had
described. A sigh of relief slipped out. Her smile
spread all the way to her eyes.

"You've been briefed then?" Squire said, gesturing her back into the cabin while his eyes worked the
trees back to the road. He hid a sudden surge of terror wrenching his insides. They were so totally alone,
so completely isolated that they could expect no aid
in the event of an attack.

Squire locked the door. A small measure, useless
actually against the type of men he was charged to
protect Suzanne from. He peeled back the edge of the
window curtain to watch the road on which he had
just arrived.

"Kevin called this morning, said to expect you."

"Kevin? Oh yeah. I've got supplies in the back of
the Jeep. How we fixed for food?"

"Okay. I'll go bring them in."

Sidney reached out, snared her arm and gently
pulled her back.

"Not yet. I'll get them later."

"I'd love to sit down to a restaurant meal."

"I'm sure," Sidney commented almost absently.
He strolled the cabin, surveying the bedroom and the
bathroom with a keen eye. Two alternate exits, but little protection from a barrage of bullets. His best
strategy was to flee before they could get close
enough to fire.

Suzanne took notice of the small pager on Sidney's belt and a gun's bulge under his jacket. His thin frame and extremely tense demeanor did little to root confidence in her.

"Are you looking for something in particular?"

"No. How you fixed for food?"

"Hello. We just went through that. Shouldn't we move on to the harder questions."

Suzanne tried unsuccessfully to quiet the fear swelling inside her.

"Are you a spy, too?"

"I don't know what Brax has told you..."

"Brax?"

"Nash."

"Nash?" Suzanne was still puzzled.

"What did you say his name was?"

"Kevin. If we're talking about the same person."

"We are."

As darkness settled in over the valley, Suzanne and Sidney ate in silence at the small table, neither knew how much they could say to the other.

"Is the chicken okay," Suzanne asked more to break the silence than to discern whether he approved of her cooking.

"It's just fine."

"When will I see Kevin?"

"Can't say."

"How long are you staying with me?"

"Not sure," Sidney replied, realizing he sounded like a Bogart character in a typical B-movie.

"You're a real pleasure to talk to, Sidney."

"Sorry. I really don't get out much."

Suzanne's appetite faded halfway through the meal, so she quietly rose to remove her plate to the sink. She turned on the water, flinching from the sudden hammering coming from the pipes.

"You'd think after this long I'd be used to that."

"I'll do those," Sidney offered, "You cooked. The least I can do is clean up."

"Don't you have spy work to do?"

"I'm doing it." Sidney forced a smile. Suzanne was staring at the gun handle protruding from his jacket.

Sidney set his dish beside the sink and left Suzanne in the kitchen. While she cleaned, busying herself with the mundane to the extent that she made it obvious she needed the activity, Sidney took an inordinately long time unloading the car; in the end, lugging in only two bags of groceries and two suitcases. He set one case next to the sofa and the other on the table.

"You planning on being here awhile?"

Sidney said nothing. He opened a suitcase to reveal a laptop computer, fax machine, and telephone base station. He wasted no time getting on-line with his computer at Langley.

"Am I allowed to see any of this?" Suzanne asked over his shoulder.

"Just as long as you don't figure it out."

Seconds later streams of random numbers paraded across the screen.

"And you can understand that?"

Sidney chuckled. He tapped in a command with fingers that danced across his keyboard. The numbers tumbled into words racing across his screen like a ticker.

"You're an Evelyn Wood grad?"

"No. It's all being stored in memory. I'll recall it later and read it at my leisure. Right now I'm scanning for important stuff."

"I'm turning in. I'd appreciate if you and your friends would keep the racket to a minimum."

Her statement brought visible relief on Sidney's face. He wasn't sure how to handle her interest in what came in over his satellite link.

"Oh, don't lock the door," Sidney commanded before she reached the bedroom.

"I beg your pardon?"

"Sorry. Please leave your door unlocked. If a situation arises in the night, I have to be able to get you out in a hurry."

"What do you mean, a situation?"

"Brax says hello, he loves you like crazy, and he'll get here as soon as he can."

"I think we have a problem, Sidney."

Suzanne remained at the door, struggling with his request.

"I understand how you feel. You don't know me from Adam. But, Suzanne, you have to trust me. This is important."

Suzanne closed the bedroom door; she had to resist that driving need to rotate the lock on the knob. After a number of minutes in contemplation, she retired to the bed, where she crawled fully clothed beneath the blanket. Kevin had trusted Sidney enough to send him here. She had to afford Sidney the same trust.

She stared up at ceiling timbers for a long time. Images of the stars from her skylight back in California popped into her head. She tried to go back to that place, that time. But the present and its ominous implications tugged her back. Why did Kevin show up now? And why after being called away did he send one of his associates here to watch over her?

She hesitated formulating the answers to those questions. Before she could face the possible answers, exhaustion plummeted her into a dreamless sleep.

Long into the night, Sidney sat at his laptop conversing with Brax via the keyboard the way friends talk over the telephone.

The Pack had strategically dispersed throughout London waiting for confirmation on the Leviathan sighting. Eighteen hours had passed since their arrival and still no one on the streets could confirm if their hard target was in the country. As a measure of additional security, Remy contacted a close friend in

MI5 to warn them of a possible terrorist attack on the Chunnel. If the Pack deployed at the Chunnel and were wrong, they might miss Leviathan's next strike. If they were correct, or more appropriately, if Remy were correct, they could still descend on the Chunnel at the first hint of trouble and thereby corner their target.

Sidney informed Brax that he was tracking every intelligence report filed on the continent and that the FCA had been alerted. They were deploying their own team to the north of France to provide support should the need arise.

Sidney concluded his message informing Brax that an exhausted Housemother would be off line but still available to the Pack. The stress of the past few days had taken a toll on the seventy year old deputy director.

Throughout the following day, Suzanne and Sidney said little. Sidney seemed so totally immersed in his work that anything she might say would only distract him. When he wasn't tapping keys on his keyboard, he was tapping his feet or pacing the room. Suzanne spent her time scouring the few television stations for news. Boredom sent her to old books that had been tucked on a shelf in the cabin's only closet. A stack of mysteries and romance novels. Neither appealed to her right now. Romance was the last thing she wanted to think about, and mysteries only served to punctuate her own situation. Eye strain prompted her to walk the grounds.

"Always stay within sight of the cabin," Sidney cautioned without looking up from his computer.

"Yes sir," Suzanne replied, offering a left handed salute at the door.

"It's the other hand," Sidney corrected.

"You saw that?"

"It my job, ma'am."

Suzanne complied, always careful to remain within visual range of Sidney, who moments after her exit moved his laptop out of doors to maintain a near constant vigilance over her.

Earlier, she had overheard Sidney on the phone say to Kevin, at least he said it was Kevin, that the sighting had been termed a bust. No one could make a confirmation. Just the dejection in Sidney's voice told her they had yet to do whatever they were supposed to do. And that meant Suzanne would remain trapped in this refuge from reality.

She had been sequestered in the cabin for close to a month and now began to feel no harm could possibly come to her isolated from the rest of the world as she was. And if that were the case, why couldn't she have stayed with her mother in Sacramento, where at least she would be amongst other breathing, speaking individuals?

Suzanne found no fault in Sidney nor Kevin's sense of responsibility toward her. Like clockwork, Sidney surveyed the surrounding landscape through binoculars, and snapped alert at the slightest sound drifting in the air. At night he slept like a guard dog, when he did sleep, jolting alert at the creak of the old cabin timbers, and something told her he hid that same protective viciousness.

Sidney continued to spend his days studying computer files that he stayed up late into the night to download into his computer. He spoke more into the telephone than he spoke to her and rarely mentioned his work. When Suzanne queried him as to his role in the scheme of what threatened their lives, he ignored her question and changed the subject. He never talked about Kevin nor anything for that matter, that might help Suzanne make sense out of what had turned her life inside out.

On those occasions when he did communicate with Kevin, Sidney was curt and cryptic to a fault. But without fail, he turned the phone to her so she could hear Kevin's voice. However, he chose to stop that kindness after the third day, when tears collected in her eyes after a brief conversation with Kevin. Neither Brax nor Sidney knew how much more of this Suzanne could tolerate. Both knew, however, moving her prematurely could prove dangerous.

On the morning of her fourth day with Sidney, Suzanne awoke to the raucous chatter of blackbirds fluttering in the trees outside her window. She loathed facing another day of isolation. She had become the prisoner—the punished. She wanted to scream until her lungs were spent. Instead, she dragged her bones out of bed and looked for a fresh change of clothes. She still slept fully dressed, and even though she came to trust Sidney, she could not bring herself to remove that protective shell at night.

She emerged from the bedroom expecting to find Sidney asleep on the couch like previous days.

The sofa was empty.

"Sidney?"

No answer.

Suzanne whirled in a frightened three-sixty around the cabin. Panic spread through every fiber of her being. Sidney was gone.

She reached the front door and pulled it open before realizing that was the one thing he had briefed her never to do. Of course, he had doled out so many directives that first night that she no longer recalled half of them.

No Sidney. Her mind ceased to function. Her breathing came in gasps. She dashed to the leeward side of the cabin. The car remained. For a moment, Suzanne's heart slowed. She scanned the woody hills.

"Sidney?" she called, but not so loud that her voice would carry over the ridges.

Being suddenly alone terrified her. Was Sidney out there somewhere in the woods dead?

Instinct ordered her back inside to the tenuous safety of the structure. She ran and released a muf-fled scream when an arm snared her mid-stride the moment she breached the cabin. Sidney's hand clamped her mouth shut.

"Close the door," he commanded harshly.

Suzanne stood frozen in terror. Sidney's hands and face were sweated; his heart raced. Suzanne saw doom in those dark eyes.

"Stay away from the window."

Suzanne complied. With the door now locked, Sidney pulled her against him.

"I've got a bogie on the south ridge."

Suzanne's heart leapt into her throat. She couldn't breath. Flashes of the fireball and explosion from that nightmare in Aptos flooded into every corner of her mind, dousing her ability to think and function.

"Maybe it's Kevin..."

Sidney checked his pager. The device provided an electronic identification for recognizing friend or foe. It transmitted a uniquely coded signal for each member of the Pack. The receiver portion accepted only those frequencies.

No codes flashed on the device.

"Damn, no one we know," Sidney whispered. His eyes never left the ridge and the silhouette that slowly began moving in and out of the trees.

"How could they fucking find us?" he muttered.

Suzanne felt all her strength and courage desert her like water rushing down a drain. Her face went pallid and slack.

Sidney caught a glint of sunlight reflect off a vehicle door in motion.

"How can you be sure it's not Kevin?"

Sidney lifted the pager. I'd have confirmation of their ID by now."

"Who then..."

Suzanne stopped herself. She didn't want to know.

"What are we going to do?"

"You ever use a gun?"

"I teach fourth grade. I'm great with a glue gun."

"Okay. Let me think."

"Sidney, you're a spy, right. I mean, you're trained to handle this, right?"

Silence.

"Right?"

"Yeah, right. We let them come to us. Don't worry. I'll get us out of here. I'm a professional." Sidney wished he had sounded more convincing not only for Suzanne's sake, but also his own.

Suzanne began to quake. She grabbed Sidney's arm for support. Her breathing came in terrified gasps. Something about the way Sidney said 'professional' frightened her.

"Suzanne, I need you to hang on. I promise I'll get us out of this. But I need you strong."

Suzanne managed no more than a nod.

"I wish I knew how many."

Sidney readied his Glock 22 and afterward folded Suzanne's fingers tightly around the car keys.

"Whatever you do, don't drop these. Fuck."

Sidney left the window. All his stuff lay exposed on the table. The hard disk in his laptop held super sensitive information. The deciphering software alone would be a prize catch for those bastards on the ridge. Sidney punched off a quick message to Brax, then entered a series of keys that forced the laptop to smolder before it burst into a small flame followed by a billow of smoke. The secure phone went up next, bursting into a white hot flame that quickly died amidst a glob of molten plastic. Sidney then returned to the window.

Sidney's forethought to secure their Jeep in a secluded location now worked in their favor. When their aggressor approached, they would be unable to see the vehicle, which meant Sidney and Suzanne could get to the car undetected. The engine starting would be the first sign the perpetrators would get that they were bolting.

While Suzanne maintained a watch over the ridge, Sidney scanned the landscape behind the cabin through the bedroom window.

"Sidney, I just saw two bogies move off the ridge."

Sidney raced back to Suzanne's side.

"I got them. Oh shit. Here's the plan. When they cross the ravine, we go out through the bedroom window and get to the car. You get in behind the wheel and do exactly as I say."

Suzanne released a whimper.

"I don't want to die," she cried.

"We're not going to die. No questions. No talk. Just do everything I say. Exactly as I say."

Suzanne nodded. Sidney's eyes tracked past her to the rising woods. A pair of black silhouettes worked a slow descent toward the cabin. Suzanne and Sidney had run out of time.

A hundred and twenty years ago, the greatest of all our presidents delivered his second State of the Union message in this chamber. We cannot escape history," Abraham Lincoln warned. "We of this Congress and this administration will be remembered in spite of ourselves." The "trial through which we pass will light us down, in honor or dishonor, to the latest generation."

Well, that president and that Congress did not fail the American people. Together they weathered the storm and preserved the Union. Let it be said of us that we, too, did not fail; that we, too, worked together to bring America through difficult times. Let us so conduct ourselves that two centuries from now, another Congress and another president, meeting in this chamber as we are meeting, will speak of us with pride, saying that we met the test and preserved for them in their day the sacred flame of liberty--this last, best hope of man on Earth.

God Bless you and thank you.

Ronald Reagan, January 26, 1982.

32

Package in good hands
                    Squire

Sidney dove out the bedroom window first, somersaulting to come up on one knee, from which he leveled his Glock to return fire. No one had been positioned to fire at them. At best they had thirty to forty-five seconds before the two men flowing down the hillside reached the cabin. If they were bogies, they would approach the building with guns poised and take out anything that moved. They would determine later if they had achieved their target.

Sidney had great difficulty thinking of himself now as a target.

Suzanne was slow coming through the window, trying to pick her way cleanly. To help expedite the escape, Sidney steadied her right leg, allowing her to land on the ground without toppling.

"Keys?" Sidney whispered.

Suzanne uncurled a fist to expose an ignition key at the ready. Sidney smiled. A gesture that did little in the way of dampening the fear welling in Suzanne's throat. He motioned her to take the wheel.

"Stay low. As soon as the engine starts, ram it to the floor and go for the rutted road over there."

Sidney pointed to a barely visible path directly downwind from the cabin. They slid into the Jeep and eased the doors closed. While Sidney trained his weapon on the side of the cabin where the men would appear, Suzanne inserted the key, pressed the accelerator to the floor once, then waited for his signal. It came two seconds later.

The engine roared like a beast angered for being disturbed. Suzanne slapped the gear shift into drive and slammed the pedal to the floor. Whirling the steering wheel hand over hand, the Jeep circled out away from the cabin leaving a pair of rooster tail dust clouds in their wake.

"Go!" Sidney yelled. He leaned out the window, clinging with one hand while he lowered his Glock into firing position. As they cleared the structure, the two men broke into a run, tucking leveled Uzis under their arms. The rounds sprayed the Jeep like a sudden hail storm.

Suzanne tightened her grip on the wheel, scrunched down as low as she could get into the seat and still see, while she pounded the accelerator into the floorboard.

Another staccato burst of fire rang through the desolate woods. Sidney returned fire, emptying his clip without releasing his finger from the trigger.

They had a scant few seconds while the intruders slapped new clips into their machine guns.

"You hit?"

"No!" Suzanne screamed, "You?"

"I'm okay."

Suzanne swerved onto the rutted path at full pelt, fish-tailing off to the right before gaining stability and taking over the center of the infrequently accessed road.

"Take that, you fucking bastards!" Sidney chimed at the sight of the men abandoning their chase to return to the vehicle. Though they continued firing, their shots sprayed into the trees and well wide of their target.

"We are out of here," Sidney chimed. "Oh shit," he added when a black Ram pickup broke out of the trees and began picking its way toward the rutted road they now occupied. The driver had abandoned his two comrades in favor of taking up a fast pursuit.

"Sidney, what do we do?" Suzanne cried, almost losing it. She had to fight the steering wheel constantly to keep the Jeep centered in the ruts. Negotiating the road had become like fighting a bull by hanging on to the horns.

"Stay on this path. I'm going to try to take them out before they can reach that ridge there," Sidney said. He realized the pickup's strategy would be to cut them off on the road before the Jeep could crest the ridge. There appeared, in Sidney's quick appraisal, no alternate path to this road.

He slapped a fresh clip into his Glock and pulled himself out the window, sitting on the door and leaning all of his weight over the roof to fire at the pickup. When the road jostled them, Suzanne had the presence of mind to reach across with her right hand and snare Sidney's leg preventing him from toppling backward out of the car, while at the same time jockeying the obstinate steering wheel with her left.

Sidney went for the truck's tires, emptied an entire clip and never once hit rubber.

The driver angled his course, setting him in a trajectory to cut the Jeep off before the road rose over the ridge. It also provided him a line of sight to fire off some poorly aimed rounds from his handgun.

"So much for shooting out the tires," Sidney muttered while he slapped another clip into his Glock.

It took Sidney too much of the last minute they had to analyze the situation and come up with a possible solution.

"Sidney, he's almost on us."

"Suzanne, slow down. I want you to broad side him just as he hits the base of the ridge on our left. See that ravine. You hit him and he'll topple."

"Sidney, he's got a gun."

"I'll cover that. No matter what happens afterward, do not stop for anything. Even if I'm knocked out of the vehicle."

Suzanne eased her foot from the accelerator. Instinct urged her to slam it back down. As she held back, the truck roared toward its intercept on the path. A second later, Suzanne screamed, floored the pedal and angled the Jeep so her left corner would slam the truck just behind the passenger door.

Sidney took hold of his door, leaned out the window until he could place his extended arm over the roof and began firing in slow steady succession. The bullet spray kept the driver at bay until they made contact.

Suzanne's efforts landed the Jeep's left headlight into the rear quarter of the truck's door. And as expected, the truck lost its footing and began sliding into a four foot ravine. It toppled into the growth, rolling the driver into a heap of bloody flesh on its way down.

Neither Suzanne nor Sidney risked a celebration.

Suzanne found reverse, spun the tires to bring the Jeep back into the ruts and tromped the pedal. The Jeep lurched as it climbed the ridge and disappeared over the crest.

Then Sidney let out a wail of success. And Suzanne finally took in a breath.

33

New data coming in. Expect answers
soon.

                    Brax

As they had done twice before in the past three months, the team of six specialists assembled inside the now nearly renovated Statuary Hall. The time approached three A.M. As before, the dogs tugged at their leashes, anxious to perform their duty, but not so this time for the men. The handlers stroked their animals' ears as a way to keep their excitement peaked for what they were about to do.

While the others donned headsets and tuned equipment, the dogs began with great exuberance their sniffing routine along the walls.

"Three hours," Donley reiterated with three fingers raised as the team dispersed. So confident had he grown regarding the security measures he had instituted all along for this project, that there arose a strong temptation to make this last inspection more perfunctory than diligent. But one more night on the stinking shit detail mattered little. This would all be over by nine A.M. this morning, and after a day's rest, he would report for a new assignment. Or a new fucking if his supervisors felt he deserved still more punishment.

But Donley let the men meander off in their own directions, trusting they would perform to their expected exemplary standards. Donley took up a position near the doors to the House Chambers to wait. A week before Thanksgiving and this project was ready to be signed off. *Unbefuckelievable!* Who'd have thought any government project could ever get done on time. Of course, Donley concluded that in order to get the job done on time they had to incur tremendous cost overruns, which the good people of this country had to dole out. Excuse me, Mr. Taxpayer, could you bend over just a little more, so I can ram you deeper. Donley's mind ambled from subject to subject while he waited. All he could really focus on was the fact that this horseshit detail was finally over.

The team completed their first floor sweep in record time. The dogs detected no hint of explosive material nor did any of the sweepers locate the presence of hidden eavesdropping devices.

After an hour, the team had moved up the stairs leaving no inch of space unchecked. They began the more tedious process of sweeping each of the offices in the House Wing. This night Donley added a few extra security guards, primarily to unlock doors and shift furniture around to facilitate the team's task. The sooner this inspection was completed the better.

It all seemed so routine that after a while the guards coagulated in the hall to chat, without realizing their voices interfered with the sensitive devices meant to pick up minute resonating sounds off a clandestine microphone.

When a German shepherd became fascinated at a locked door, the handler commandeered the guard away from his little gathering to unlock it. Inside the small closet, a ladder lead to the crawlspace over the offices.

For a long moment the handler encouraged the animal to pursue its desires, while he contemplated the task of working the dog up the ladder. Though the urge to skip the overhead space nagged him, the handler decided he would be remiss if he failed to go up the ladder at least to follow the animal's instinct. The dog negotiated the ladder in the arms of its handler. It hesitated before stepping on to the suspended transom. The transom's clanking metal seemed to spook the animal, causing it to whimper rather than proceed.

The handler raked his light beam in both directions to quickly satisfy himself that the transom could support both man and animal. Wobbly as it was, when they began creeping down it, the animal seemed to acclimate well enough to overcome its apprehension. With each step the animal seemed to grow more intense in its sampling.

Working his way behind the dog on hands and knees, the handler lagged a few paces while the animal sampled the air. As they neared the House Chamber, the dog yipped, immediately dropping to its haunches.

Something had snared the animal's attention.

The handler angled his beam first overhead, then along the conduit spanning beneath the transom. At first he detected nothing out of the ordinary. Then a red-eyed mouse buried itself deep into the dirty cotton layer of insulation.

"Shit. All this for a friggin' rat," the handler moaned.

But before moving on, he swept his beam along the ductwork, settling momentarily on a sheet metal access plate held solidly in place with four screws. He brought the dog to the plate prodding it to sniff around for at least thirty seconds. The animal, however, seemed more interested in retreating to where it had come.

The bug sweeper waited at the base of the stairs for dog and handler to descend the rungs, with the handler carrying the animal down in one arm. The animal never once flinched during the climb down.

The handler embraced his partner with both physical and verbal praise, rubbing his coat vigorously in reward, despite the fact it turned out to be a fruitless endeavor.

With dog and handler gone, the bug sweeper refitted the headset over his ears before making the same climb. He crawled down the same transom, first in the direction leading to the center of the Capitol building, and finding nothing of any interest, reversed his direction toward the House Chamber. He listened with unwavering intensity, covering his left headphone with his hand while negotiating the crawl way with his knees and right hand. Every five seconds, his listening device sprayed bursts of radio energy outward. He thought at first he detected an echo, but when he failed to reproduce the occurrence, he attributed the false reading to the metal conduit and ductwork crammed one over the other in such a confined area.

After twenty minutes, he, too, retreated down the ladder, where he flipped the security guard a thumbs up, indicating the door could be locked.

Five thirty-seven. The team reassembled in the Statuary Hall to report their findings to an anxious Donley, who seemed more interested in getting the inspection completed, so he could return home and crawl into the warmth of his water bed. The final security inspection for the House renovation project awaited signatures. The FBI could consider the building sanitized, and therefore, turn the task of routine day-to-day security operations back over to the Capitol security force and Captain Dipwad.

A fucking job well done, Donley told himself.

As far as Donley and the team were concerned, they had detected no materials either electronic or otherwise, secreted into the walls during the project, nor had any surveillance devices been planted in any of the offices that made up the second floor of the wing. Though, Donley still had to worry that a device might be sleeping inside a wall or in the ceiling panels over one of the offices. For now, all the right paperwork could be signed off to show adequate security measures had been maintained throughout the duration of the renovation project. He still had to gain approval from the Head of the Secret Service, but rarely did the Secret Service question the methods of the Agency or the Bureau.

🔫

Squire returned to his dungeon with a new attitude toward his job. He had been in the field. He had faced the kind of peril that he imagined the rest of the team faced out their in the world of counterterrorism. He still wasn't sure which world he liked better. In this gloomy dungeon he was alone but safe. No one came after him with Uzi blazing.

And because of his efforts, Suzanne had returned safely to Brax. For the last five days Sidney raked his memory trying to figure out how anyone could have located the safe house. Neither he nor Brax could come up with a logical explanation of how they, whoever they were, had discovered the location of their refuge. Brax himself had removed that particular location from Company files six months before Wolf Pack came together in anticipation for its possible use. Only Remy, Brax, Squire and Jaffe knew of the cabin's existence. Even Cody and Cali remained ignorant of its location, since they joined the team later.

Squire sat at his computer entering the command for the system to update him on the overnights. While he waited for the data stream to begin, he ruminated over the past five days. The first anomaly to trigger in Squire's brain was that the intelligence stream had suddenly grown thin. He still received traffic from the stations, but for some reason, the volume of information had dwindled. As that thought churned, Sidney began to assemble bits and pieces in his mind. It wasn't what he was seeing that manipu-

lated his thoughts, rather it was what he wasn't seeing in the daily updates. The bulk of the reports
flowing through the system seemed overtly innocuous. Status reports from agents who were previously
uninvolved in early operations.

When Squire watched a redundant report flow up
his screen, he pulled himself closer to the terminal.

The implication working its way methodically to
the top of Sidney's mind was that someone had
begun turning off the spigot of information to the
dungeon. Subtle as the changes were, Squire had
detected them. Someone had altered the pattern.

This time, however, instead of receiving the
reams of data he expected, an encoded message
blinked across the bottom of his screen.

One of his sniffers had returned. One that had
been sitting in memory overnight waiting for his
login to be entered.

Squire's first instinct was to drop the sniffer data
into a file and get on with the day's business. Chances
were the sniffer had picked up Housemother's data
when he read one of Squire's reports to Brax. Then
something in the back of his mind kicked in. Something tugged at his mental shirt sleeve, craving attention like a spoiled little child. An intelligence report
that he had just read surged to the forefront of his
mind. It tugged at him. Then he realized he had read
that very same report less than two months earlier. A
second redundant report. Squire consumed precious
moments searching through his database. The report
had been generated in Italy. It had little significance
to the Pack. After searching through a dozen or so
records in the database, Squire located the report in
question. He called it up. It matched word for deciphered word. Someone was playing with him.

Squire decoded the sniffer. The sequence of numbers returned bore no resemblance to any series he
had received earlier and matched none he maintained
in his database. That presented a dilemma, since a

unique series now required him to worm his way
through the maze of internal data to locate the
source of the login. What stuck out as an anomaly
were the first three characters of the second
sequence of numbers on the screen. K6D.

He knew from previous explorations that servers
from the Congress side of the firewall carried an L as
the first character in the second series. That ruled out
any of the senators or their aides.

For hours Squire entered strings of commands
meant to hunt down the K6D identity on the network.
The lunch hour came and went. Candy wrappers,
Coke cans and any empty pill bottle accumulated on
his desk. Panic was forcing Squire to become careless.
His stomach tightened into a growing knot. He
became obsessed with uncovering the machine that
had within the last two days become interested in his
message traffic to the Pack in the field. His fingers
began to tremble; he mistyped nearly as many words
as he typed correctly.

Someone had tapped into his login. Someone had
learned where they were keeping Suzanne. Someone
from the inside had been investigating Jaffe before
his untimely demise.

The more zeroes Sidney came up with, the more
his concern flamed. More and more, he knew who the
eyes weren't.

In desperation, Sidney called the System Admin-
istrator for Housemother's machine, employing the
login codes he had extracted earlier. It was a risky
move to imitate the Deputy Director, but this thing
was growing darker by the moment. He complained
that he had been receiving chewed up secure messages from another server and needed to know whose
server the messages had originated on.

As Sidney had hoped, the Sys Admin, having the
highest security access as a super user on the network, tapped in the machine codes as Sidney read
them off. Offering Housemother's code first, the Sys

Admin verified it, then asked for the second set of numbers.

"Are you sure about this number, Director?" the Sys Admin said.

"That's what it decoded as," Sidney offered, feigning activity at his desk as if he were a pushy person who had little time for this nonsense.

"That's outside the Agency firewall. That's a Bureau... But you already... Is this Director Calfield?"

The Sys Admin stopped.

Sidney slapped down the phone.

"Fuck. Shit. Fuck"

Sidney was off his chair and circling. His heart was like a cannon, booming inside his chest.

"The FBI's got a trap-door on my traffic. And Housemother knew about it. Fuck. He rolled us over. He fucking rolled us over! That's how they knew about the cabin."

Sidney sat back down. He had to think clearly now. He stared at the screen for what must have seemed an eternity. Then he swung around on his chair. There was only one course to follow. He grabbed a secure phone connected to a scrambler, and handset trembling, punched in the speed dial code.

"Scrimshander. Scrimshander," he said trying to maintain an equilibrium in his voice. If the FBI had tapped into his traffic, they must have placed the team under surveillance. Something must have gone awry. And Sidney had no time to contemplate his decision. Do it and do it now. He couldn't wait around to find out why.

Before exiting the dungeon, Sidney sent the Scrimshander broadcast message out to the team via the network. The moment they logged on at their laptop computers, they would decode the urgent message. The operation had been compromised.

Sidney consumed a precious moment at the door gazing back at what had been his home for the past fourteen months. Did he need to take anything with him? No, he concluded. The Sys Admin could have already sounded the alert. The guards at the doors might detain him if he tried to remove anything on his person.

He raced back to his keyboard to punch in a string of fourteen nonsensical characters. He waited. Nothing happened. His destruction code had been disabled. Only a very select few could have breached into his secure profile to alter his destruct code. All his files became vulnerable to anyone who cracked his login password. He entered the command to erase his local hard disk. Nothing. The cursor blinked back at him uncomprehendingly.

"You sons-a-bitches, you turned on us," Sidney muttered.

Sidney had to abandon everything. He considered seeking refuge in Housemother's office. They wouldn't arrest him there. Or would they? Had Housemother insulated himself from the team? Was he now also working with the FBI?

Sidney realized he needed to get clear of this place first, then assess the extent of the compromise. Brax had a way to contact him. They could consider the implications of the situation and decide on a course of action then.

Sidney locked his dungeon door. He became acutely aware of the sweat accumulating on his forehead. No one in the corridor paid attention to his exit. He opted for the stairs rather than the elevator and sucked in a deep breath before opening the door to the main floor.

He thought about one thing and one thing only. Walk directly to the main doors and exit. Talk to no one. Listen to no one. Even if someone yelled for him to stop, he would bolt for the doors.

Sidney crossed the main lobby at a pace neither hurried nor slow. He never once looked over at the guards sitting in their rotunda station. His exit proved unremarkable. Sidney concluded that even if the Sys Admin had figured out who was behind the phone call, it would take many minutes to put anything into motion that could snag Sidney.

He was out, in his car, and blending in with traffic within fifteen minutes of learning that the FBI had been monitoring his traffic. Only the spy catchers would have any reason to be tapped into the pipeline inside the Agency.

Donley marched down the deserted corridor like a man on a mission. The excitement his step exuded would have turned heads. It was after ten in the evening; his day had started at two A.M. and yet he felt so invigorated that he couldn't sleep even if he wanted to.

Special Agent Gerald Lindsay waited outside the briefing room door to meet Donley when he walked up.

"You owe me big time for this one," Lindsay offered in hushed tones, holding his words until Donley was upon him.

"Thank you. If we have a moment, bend over so I can kiss your ass for this. That fucking renovation project was enough to make me want to blow my brains out."

"They've already started. So slip in quietly."

Donley eased open the briefing room to the light cast off a silver screen from a slide projector. Special Agent Roy Shelby stood outside the beam of light with his pointer poised at the screen. A dozen crisply attired agents filled the chairs arranged around an oblong table.

Donley and Lindsay worked their way to retral chairs furthest from the speaker. A few took notice of their entrance, most however, remained consumed by the picture on the screen.

"Target's name is Phillip Nash. He's a twelve year Company veteran with commendations as long as my arm. In the past, he specialized in counterterrorism and troubleshooting."

The slide projector clicked off to be replaced on the screen by a grainy video shot in questionable light. It revealed a darkened alleyway. Illuminated by headlights somewhere beyond the camera's eye, Nash stood over a crumpled body and fired a single shot into the mass.

"The man Nash just executed was Malackey Lonigan. An IRA lieutenant who showed up in New York a couple months ago. He approached one of our street weeds asking to make a deal with the FBI. He offered to turn himself in, in exchange for protection from the CIA. Claimed he had information about a renegade CIA field operative. Nash executed him before we could reach him."

"This street weed reliable?"

"Hard to know for certain. He's gone."

"Has the video been analyzed?"

"Absolutely. Our guys positively identified Nash. The morgue gave us a positive on Lonigan."

"How'd we pick up Lonigan?"

"An informant rolled the scum over after he entered the U.S. at the Texas border. We had him under our nose until New York."

"Then what happened?" the agent sitting near Donley asked.

"We got pulled. My opinion is executive order. Nobody else has the authority to wave off a terrorist surveillance."

"So you think somehow the CIA got to this weasel."

"We have reliable word from an informant that Nash has five notches on his belt. Don't let his mild-mannered appearance fool you. He knows more ways to kill you than any of our own Special Forces. I know because I spent a tour in Special Forces."

"He working this alone?"

"He's got someone with him. Notice in the video where Nash walks *away* from the direction of the car headlights. Someone had to drive the vehicle away from the scene. Nash disappeared on foot."

"What do we have on him?" another agent queried.

"You're looking at it. He went underground fourteen months ago. Company's refusing to give up anything on the guy. After we started digging, we turned up a bombing in Kano in March of this year. We believe Nash used the explosion to hide a contact he had made with a Jihad operative. This scum asshole went sour on us."

The slide projector returned, ejected the present scene and injected a new slide onto the silver. This one showed Nash with a bearded Mediterranean man in his early thirties. It was evident from the grainy texture that the shot had been accomplished using a telephoto lens from a significant distance away. Despite the texture and the distance, there was no mistaking that the man accepting a black case was Philip Nash.

We got his shot compliments of Interpol. Nash had been observed in the presence of one Al-Hadadd Shilil. He's HAMAS. The Brits believe Nash went rogue and has been feeding the terrorist underground with government information concerning potential U.S. targets."

Lindsay leaned to Donley.

"Now listen to me. Don't fuck with Shelby. He's a bastard if you fuck up, and I kissed his ass to get you on the team," Lindsay whispered.

"And that's why I want to repay the debt. I'll kiss your ass anytime you want."

"He the only one identified at the Agency involved?" someone near the front asked.

"No. We uncovered intelligence recently linking Nash to a Russian network in New York. And someone inside the Company has been feeding him information."

"We have an ID yet on the Company mole?"

"Not yet. But I've got two people assigned full time to get us a name and a face."

"Do you think Nash is still in the United States?"

"We don't know for sure. We had a tap on his communication network within the Agency, but it shut down before we could get a location on him."

"Who's paying him?"

"We can't tell that for sure. We know his inside man tipped him off. We don't know who or how they learned of our investigation. But the comm link died and the one who originated the transmission from the Agency has remained off the air."

A few murmurs moved through the gathering.

"We believe Nash may be involved in an assassination attempt. We don't know where, or how."

"Do we have any idea what operation this Nash was involved in with the Agency before he went rogue?" Donley asked from the back of the room.

A few eyes turned toward him.

"Nothing. All official channels to the CIA have been shut down. We don't know if there is inside involvement. We can't trust them. I've arranged to join forces with the Secret Service for the time being. Until we get an idea of where this Nash has holed up, we won't know how to approach the situation."

"Do we consider him dangerous?"

"Lethal. As far as we're concerned for operation Red Eagle, Philip Nash is a suspected terrorist. Consider him deadly and take him down without hesitation. If we can link him to any others, we'll pass the information down to you as it becomes available. For right now, we try to anticipate his target, and remember, he knows everything about us, the Secret Service and our security measures. Consider him capable of breaching our best security net and getting to a target, any target."

Lindsay tapped Donley's forearm.

"You take this Nash scum down, and you'll be back in the Director's good graces," Lindsay offered Donley as the lights came back up. Everyone in the room began to rise in anticipation. An eagerness infested the gathering.

Donley and Lindsay took information packets about their target, which included photos identical to the slides.

34

Looking forward to holiday vacation
in the sun.

                    Squire

December 23rd. A snow-covered road wound through a woody maze rolling over a hill to finally end at the drive for an A-frame chalet nestled out of view from the main highway. A Jeep Cherokee and a Suburban were joined by a grape Tracker beside the front entrance.

Squire entered, lugging a scrawny Christmas tree at the most three feet tall and still on the wooden cross stand. Though missing some vital branches, the tree still followed the general shape of what the Yuletide symbol should resemble.

"Ho, ho, ho, Merry Christmas!" he bellowed in a voice ill-fitted to take on the role. But his smile alone shone bright enough to warm even the coldest soul this night Pennsylvania winter's eve.

An almost funereal air hung over the room. Brax and Suzanne sat on a divan, staring blankly into the fire while Cody and Cali moved about in the kitchen. Remy stood at the window with arms locked across his chest, gazing at the falling snow.

Suzanne rose to lend Squire a hand with the tree. He set it on the floor beside the fireplace, as if to gloat over his triumph, and even before removing his gloves, he extracted an angel whose hair had been

365

formed with spun silk. Gingerly he set it atop the tree.

"Viola! Now that's Christmas," he said.

Cali and Cody entered the living room, with Cody serving steaming hot cups off a tray. As they moved about, Cali handed a mug to each. The gesture proved enough to draw Remy from his window, though he offered no more than a grunt of a thank you.

The Pack had been holed up in this place for almost two weeks. Instead of a time of celebration, it had dwindled to a somber time. A time when words of gratitude came with great difficulty.

"Cali and I can make something to string on the tree," Suzanne offered, appraising the leanness of Squire's offering.

Squire motioned for Brax. In such a small place seclusion became difficult. But over the last few days Suzanne learned to sense when she was unwanted, and she would drift off to allow them their time.

"They rolled us over, didn't they? They fucking offered us to the slaughter," Squire asked away from the rest.

"We can't know."

"Bullshit. Housemother rolled us over. He gave us to the FBI. It was the Lonigan incident."

Brax ruminated for a time, watching the steam rise and curl out of his mug. He had raked every inch of his memory looking for answers to what had went wrong.

"Somebody rolled us over. We can't know who right now," Brax offered.

Cody joined them, though his eyes lingered on Cali standing at the tree. She was attempting to place a star she had fashioned out of aluminum foil onto a branch.

"You getting anything off the street?" Cody asked of Squire.

"Word is we've been marked for extermination. I got onto the Company computer using an alternate login I had set up when we started. They haven't uncovered it yet, so I've still got limited access. Housemother's now out of the loop."

"All of us?"

"Brax and myself. Somebody's been keeping an eye on my apartment. I'm telling you, they rolled us over," Squire said, his voice rising an octave in anger.

Cody and Brax exchanged a look. Squire's words had drawn Remy to the group.

"What about me?"

"Can't determine that yet. There has been traffic from the DCI to MI5. But we may have buried you well enough that even our own won't be able to dig you up."

"How about Cali?"

"I think she's safe. The way I understood it, the only one outside our circle who knew her identity was Valentine."

"What do you think, Brax? Can we trust Valentine?" Cody probed.

"Do we have choice?"

"Is Valentine even powerful enough to get us out of this?" The question came from Sidney. From his furrowed brow and uncertain eyes, it became obvious he needed an answer to that question. They all did.

Brax had no answer.

"Valentine's isolated himself from us, along with the DCI. There's no one to come to our rescue. They'll let us go down," Cody said.

"Them fuckers."

"We knew that's the way it would be going in."

"You knew. Not me," Sidney shot back.

"Squire, can we get a risk assessment of this situation?" Brax asked. He needed to refocus the team's thoughts to a course of action.

"An FBI team's on the streets right now trying to hunt us down. I intercepted a message that intimates the Company also deployed a team to hunt us."

"How'd you find that out?" Remy asked.

"Still got a few tricks of my own. I ran a scam using Housemother's login to get into the DCI's message stream. I can only get what goes out into the network. But it's a enough to know the DCI gave the nod. Our information has turned up on the broadcast network to the station chiefs. They're feeding the field that Brax assassinated Jaffe in Kano. They're saying he's turned to the Russians."

"How'd everything get so fucked up?" Cody moaned.

His words snared Suzanne's attention in the kitchen. She turned then turned back away. Her action brought silence to the group for that few moments.

"I'm guessing that they've been monitoring my traffic for some time, and that's how they made us. Every time I sent a message to you in the field, there was somebody in the Bureau intercepting it and analyzing the information."

"Can we try to re-establish contact with Housemother?" Remy asked.

"I can't. I tried earlier to get to Housemother. He refused the call," Squire said.

"He may be trying to protect us," Brax offered

"Or fuck us," Squire added.

"Where do we go from here, boss?" Cody asked. He set his empty mug on the tray Cali carried with her when she joined them.

"Oh no. You're not going to ruin this for us. Cali and I are just getting into the spirit, and I am not going to let this screw it up," Suzanne injected.

Remy was the first to depart, returning to his window and the snowfall.

Cali removed the tray of empty cups to the kitchen. The smell of Suzanne's popcorn in the microwave began to permeate the chalet.

"She's our ace, you know," Squire added.

"Cali?"

"I know. Far as I can figure, they haven't been able to make Remy or Cali. But there is always a chance MI6 will roll Remy over."

"Won't be able to do that," Remy said from the window without turning around. "Didn't think I was listening, did you?"

Remy returned to the others, stilling holding his cup that remained nearly full and had become tepid by now.

"I set up elaborate dummy files to cover my tracks. It should take them months to weed through the paperwork before they figure out who Remy really is."

"Where do we go from here, boss?" Cody asked again. Sitting around in this place for so long had infected him with cabin fever. He longed to get back into the field. This waiting was getting them nowhere.

"We still have a mission. We've come this far. We can't give up on this yet. Leviathan hasn't struck. That means we still have a shot at him."

"Yeah, while our own people take shots at us," Squire put in.

"Someone may have set this ruse up to knock us out of the game. Until I know more about this, we're going after our hard target as before. Squire, can you still gather intelligence for us?"

"It's riskier now. But I can. We won't have access to the central data stream coming in from the stations, but I'll try to get taps into lower level traffic. I can piece the stuff together."

"Great. In the meantime, let's work with what we have. There's got to be an answer somewhere in all that information."

Later that evening, after the others had drifted off to their own corners throughout the chalet to sleep, Brax and Suzanne sat before the fire. For a long time neither spoke. The crackling flames spread an intoxicating air about the small expanse. Brax was the first to break the silence.

Before Brax could speak, Suzanne stopped him with a finger to his lips. Instead, she set a small package she had tucked away in her pocket into his hand.

Without saying anything, Brax unwrapped the present to reveal a small set of gilded angel's wings. These, however, were no ordinary wings; they were tarnished and ruffled as if they had been through difficult times.

"I don't know what you believe in, Kevin. But I want you to have these, so I'll know something far more powerful than either of us is watching over you."

"I hadn't wanted our Christmas to end up this way. I'm sorry it happened, and I'm sorry I put you at risk."

"Kevin, I love you enough to face anything."

After Suzanne pinned the wings beneath his collar, he took Suzanne's hands in his and looked deeply into her eyes. Eyes that sparkled before the firelight.

"Will you still marry me?"

"Are we going to live long enough to get married?"

"I will never let anything happen to you."

"But what about you. Can even a guardian angel help? Are *you* going to get through this?"

Brax had no answer.

"Kevin Chambers, Brax, Phillip Nash, whatever your real name is, my life would be meaningless without you. If you believe in what you're doing, then I believe in it, too. I can't imagine living my life without you after having experienced the joy of loving you. Just tell me we're all going to get through this."

Brax wanted with all his heart to reassure her. But above all else he needed to be honest. And that's what kept him from giving her an answer and the ring he kept secreted in his pocket.

35

We have a way to view the
essentials.

                    Squire.

Brax paced with a bottled-up ferocity, moving
from the bedroom to the living room window in the
cramped Washington apartment. They had relocated
their operation back into D.C. hoping they might gain
more intelligence off the streets. The risks were
greater here, but they had to bear them in the hopes
of learning more.

Brax had to gamble that they were close at hand
to their target. The money had moved, Leviathan had
positioned people. All that remained now was determining where his strike would take place. Brax half
expected Leviathan to strike over the holiday period,
when the impact would prove most dramatic. But for
some reason he waited. Maybe something had yet to
fall into place. Now January moved quickly toward its
close.

Squire monitored traffic from a laptop and a
login he had planted to safeguard himself in the
event something went awry. His presence of mind
had enabled him to intercept an intelligence report
which stated that the FBI had learned of a high ranking IRA terrorist's arrival in D.C. That made Brax
think Leviathan's next strike was now imminent.
Especially when the terrorist gave the Bureau the slip

and vanished underground. The FBI would believe they had just lost a stooge. Brax knew better.

Suzanne sat with her legs on the sofa, her head propped in her arm staring vacantly at the television screen. It was like she had become numb to her situation. Remy occupied a chair at the table, where he studied outdated intelligence reports through eyes that had grown blurred and puffy from a lack of sleep and near constant use. He tasked himself with uncovering something they had missed earlier. Something hidden within the jumbled maze of intelligence they had been collecting over the past eleven months.

Assured that a sighting of someone connected to Ranzami in the U.S. meant he was now poised to strike, Brax and Remy had to scramble to interconnect the pieces of a diabolic puzzle. Death loomed just over the horizon. How many? Where? and what would be his method of execution still remained at large. There had to be something in those reports they had missed, something that could indicate how to find the demon.

Suzanne increased the volume, surfing the channels for something, anything worthwhile in the sixty channel cable offering. She had grown desperate for any kind of diversion. Her mind throbbed from the grueling frenzy of activity surrounding her. She could feel the pressure crowding in on everyone in the apartment. Over the last few days, conversation dwindled to a minimum. Everyone had a specific task, and they raced a clock that ticked on relentlessly. Everyone but Suzanne. If they squeezed out even one answer, it might lead to others.

Suzanne chanced to pause on an in-progress commentary being delivered in a drone by a local news reporter. He spoke as he strolled languidly through a silent vaulting Capitol building. It wasn't the reporter's words that snared her attention. It was the background as the narrator moved into Statuary Hall.

Brax transplanted his inter-room pacing into intra-room pacing, moving back and forth in the living room. He paused to stare out the window as he had done habitually on previous laps. Then perchance he faced the television set. The stone figures of Statuary Hall captured his attention.

"The renovation cost in the thirty million range..."

Suzanne fired the remote.

"What! Go back? Hurry!"

"Why," Suzanne asked.

"Do it!" Brax snapped.

"Some guy babbling about the Capitol."

"What'd he say?"

Suzanne fired to recapture the channel on the screen. The reporter moved into a wide corridor.

"...and they completed the project ahead of schedule."

Remy rose.

"I don't know. I wasn't really paying attention," Suzanne said.

"What was he saying?" Remy asked, moving beside Brax in rapt fascination.

Suzanne felt a sudden burdensome weight flattening her shoulders. She had figured this to be some typical D.C. propaganda spot on the local news.

"He started out with something about the State of the Union address. Then he went on to describe some renovation that had recently been completed on the House Wing of the Capitol."

Suzanne fell silent while the narrator continued his tour.

"The last renovation performed on the Hall was in the late sixties. This latest endeavor took six months and was completed in mid-November. Visitors to the Capitol can view the new look in time for the State of the Union address tomorrow evening in the adjoining House Chamber. Renovations planned for the Chamber itself will begin two years from now at an additional cost of eighteen million. One can only wonder if taxpayers are truly getting their money's worth."

Brax, Remy and Suzanne stared at the screen while the camera panned the breadth of the hall from floor to ceiling.

"This turned out to be one of those rare occasions when a government project comes in both under budget and ahead of schedule. The original project was slated to be completed in early January, but work was actually finished shortly before Thanksgiving."

Brax snatched the secure telephone and dialed.

Remy swept the reports from the table with a wave of his arm and stuffed them helter-skelter into banker boxes beside his chair.

"What does any of this mean?" Suzanne asked. She listened.

"Squire, get over here right now," Brax commanded into the phone.

It took Squire fifteen minutes to navigate the D.C. traffic to arrive at the apartment. When he arrived they wasted little time.

"We need a look at the plans to the Capitol?" Brax asked.

"Sure. They're on the central computer."

"Can we access them without the Company finding out?"

"I don't know. Why?"

"Think back to the Spring," Brax asked of Squire.

Squire turned up his face as if to focus all his concentration. Thousands of intelligence reports had moved across his eyes since Spring. Literally hundreds of incidents had to be assimilated.

"You reported that local authorities found traces of Prussian Blue in Brussels, remember?"

"Yeah. I followed the story through the locals. They never caught the guys that escaped that Black September safe house. So?"

"They never recovered any Prussian Blue?"

"Okay. I couldn't determine that for sure. The police think they shut down a chemical processing operation before it got started. Why?"

Brax turned to Remy.

"How'd those junkies die in Geneva?"

"Shit. You're right. Why didn't we think of that earlier. Cyanide. Asphyxiation using cyanide gas. Those bastards were making Prussic acid from the Prussian Blue in Brussels."

"Exactly. We would have locked on to any movement in cyanide gas instantly. But we let the Prussian Blue, the major component needed to manufacture the gas, slip by. Leviathan was testing his plan. He locked them in a sealed room while he pumped cyanide in through the ducts. That explosion was meant to eradicate the evidence. The only reason we were allowed to witness it was because he figured we'd all die in the explosion."

"Fuck. Double fuck," Remy muttered.

Suzanne's stomach rolled. Another explosion. Kevin was almost killed there.

"Suppose our little scumbag has developed a way to dispense a lethal gas into a room."

"Or a chamber...the House Chamber," Squire added.

"Exactly. If you're Leviathan, when would you do it?"

"State of the Union. He's got every important government official in one place at one time," Remy said.

Suzanne shivered from her place on the couch. Goose flesh rose on her arms, causing her hairs to stand on end. How could anyone do something so diabolic?

"Can he really do it?" she asked.

"How?" Brax asked the group.

Cody began rummaging through the bones of intelligence reports. Cali, realizing her team member's intent, joined him in the search. They might very well have an the answer to that.

"Kirkhammer," Cody said, pulling out a single page report.

"We recovered ASIC electronic devices from the apartment where Kirkhammer died. Suppose Leviathan was the one who killed him. Why? Because he had performed a service for Ranzami and that made him a security risk. Ranzami kills him to protect the secrecy of whatever Kirkhammer did."

"But what did Kirkhammer bloody do?" Remy asked.

The room filled with silence that lasted a minute or more. The Pack had assembled around the table, Remy at its core.

"Using specialized ASIC devices, he designed the remote detonating device for the cyanide," Cali injected. Her eyes never left the intelligence report.

"Our lab boys checked out the devices we pulled from Kirkhammer's apartment. They were sophisticated frequency shift transmitting devices with extraordinary range."

"And that bloody means?" Remy asked.

"Means Kirkhammer designed remote detonators that could operate even if we attempted to jam them electronically."

"How?"

"By constantly shifting the transmission frequency."

"How can he do that?" Remy persisted.

"Do I look like a fucking engineer to you?"

"Cody. Find out," Brax instructed.

While Cody moved to the bedroom with his cell phone Brax and Remy leaned over the table to assemble intelligence reports.

"My guy says it's plausible. Not really very hard. By transmitting the signal over a wide band of frequencies," he paused to hear more, his head popped out from the bedroom, "it increases the possibility of one of the triggering signals getting through," Cody reported.

"We assume Ranzami has a device he can trigger remotely to release a high concentration of cyanide gas. Where does he plant it?"

"Inside the House Chamber," Remy offered.

"How? The house was in session for much of the renovation."

"Okay. Okay. They recessed twice during that time. That would give someone an opportunity to get inside and plant something."

"No good. Security's going to go through the place before the State of the Union. They'd uncover it."

"Not if they didn't know where to look."

Remy had spoken and the very words forced him to pause. Everyone in the room turned to him for more. His mind raced in a dozen different directions. The correct path had to relate to the renovation project.

"What if work crews had access to the ductwork?"

"And they can operate under the cover of a huge renovation project," Squire added.

"How does he get past security?" Cody asked.

"Procedure would call for every worker to pass through a security check and a metal detector. The Secret Service, FBI and the CIA would all be involved in security," Brax countered.

"But computers control the security. They had to have a database of those who legitimately had clearance to work inside the Capitol," Squire said.

"So Ranzami had to breach our security in order to get his people clearance into the building."

"How?" Remy posed.

For minutes no one could devise a plausible answer.

Then it buoyed to the surface. First as only a flicker of a thought inside Brax's head. There was only one answer. To even consider it made his stomach convulse.

"Jaffe," he said barely above a whisper.

The team stared at Brax in disbelief. How could he even consider such a notion?

"No, you're right. Jaffe hacked his way into the central computer at the Agency. He could have planted false identifications there," Squire offered.

"How could you know that, Squire?"

"Housemother maintained a soft file on Jaffe. I got into it after Jaffe died. He was moving money between a number of accounts, and he had reportedly broken into the system. At the time no one knew what that meant. Now we may have the answer."

"Leviathan needed an inside man to get his people past our security," Brax said. While he spoke he resumed his back and forth movement.

"You're saying Leviathan used Jaffe to get inside the CIA computer then took him out after Jaffe served his purpose?" Cody asked.

"Look, we worked off a standard password setup until the time the DCI cut us out of the loop. That's how I detected we were in deep trouble. When the DCI ordered the passwords changed, and they excluded me, I knew we had had it," Squire said.

"But then Jaffe's information would have been segregated out of the system along with us."

"Yeah, but it was far too late to matter. Jaffe could have planted all the false identities Leviathan needed. He could have even planted an identity for himself which would have authorized him to receive the new set of passwords."

For a moment no one had anything to say. The pieces of the puzzle began tumbling into place faster than the team could assimilate them.

"We assume for the moment Ranzami breached security and planted some kind of device inside the

Capitol," Remy started. Like Brax he also needed motion to clear his thinking.

"Once the project's complete, your people go through the place with dogs and equipment searching for devices."

"Searching for conventional devices," Cali clarified, "they wouldn't be looking for a cyanide device."

"But they would be able to detect the triggering electronics? Right?" Brax queried the group.

No one could answer.

"Right?"

"Not if it's a sleeper," Cody said.

They were groping. Sleepers could escape detection only to be awakened moments before a detonation code is transmitted.

"So what do we do?" Brax asked.

"Get to the president."

"How?"

Suzanne rose from the sofa to join the group. For the first time since arriving here, she felt she could make a contribution.

"Me," she said plainly and simply. So much so, that everyone in the room stopped to turn toward her.

"Does it sound that absurd?"

"You?" Brax said.

"Sure. You said the Secret Service, FBI, and CIA are all looking for you. None of you can show your face without risking arrest, right? They already think you've turned against the government. If you tell them about your theory, and that's all it is right now, and your wrong, they'll accuse you of acting as a diversion while this Leviathan strikes his real target."

"So?"

"So? If I go in with your theory, they will at least listen to me."

"Suzanne, we can't be sure you weren't made by the Agency when they tried to blow us up in California."

Brax turned back to the table.

"I think Leviathan couldn't risk us uncovering his plan before he could press the button. I think he's the one who turned the Company on us. Somehow he's got an inside man either in the Agency or in the Bureau. That's who put the hounds on us. He had to keep us away from our support systems just in case we put the pieces together. Housemother didn't roll us over. Someone in Leviathan's organization did."

Brax looked to Remy for some confirmation of his thinking.

"Plausible. He got to Jaffe. He could have set us up when we starting getting too close."

"Sidney, can we get a look at the HVAC layout for the Capitol?"

Squire had to think. The central computer had everything they needed, but they would never gain access to it without raising a security flag. They could try a satellite uplink to the computer but chances are the Agency would shut them down long before they could get at any important files.

"I may have an idea. I'm going see a friend of mine. Maybe he can help us get to the files."

Midnight came. The team huddled before a computer screen in the advanced computing lab at Georgetown University. Squire sat at the center of the circle while Brax, Cali, Remy and Cody crowded in behind the chair. All stared at the twenty-seven inch screen of an SGI Virtual Reality workstation, waiting for it to load the files Squire had accessed.

"I just need another few minutes for the software to render the building from the plan," Squire said. His eyes never left the screen. He punched in commands with the speed of seasoned typist.

A minute later the screen blanked. New lines began to populate the glass. As they accumulated, it became obvious what they were seeing.

"Okay, I've started us at the east entrance to the Statuary Hall."

"Where is the ductwork?" Remy badgered.

"I'm getting to it."

The screen progressed through the hall then ascended to the air vent on the ceiling.

"Watch this," Squire touted like a kid with a new toy he had just figured out how to operate.

The screen moved them out of the hall and into the air vent. The lines closed more tightly as they entered the narrow passage.

"Is this stuff cool or what? There are three main shafts feeding the House Chamber," Squire said.

Using his mouse, Squire directed them through the duct.

"Where are we now?" Brax asked.

"Second floor," Squire said.

"You turned the wrong way," Remy said, growing anxious. He had assimilated the exercise more quickly than the others and was already racing ahead in his mind to locate their target.

"No, I didn't," Squire said.

"Yes, you did. You're moving away from the House Chamber."

Squire stopped and reversed his mouse movement. He paused at an intersection of two main ducts.

"Now go the other way," Remy corrected.

"But this shaft is going up."

"I know. The ductwork has to incline to enter the Chamber ceiling."

"No. I think it enters the chamber on the side walls."

"Not according to the drawing."

Squire yielded to Remy's guidance. As the Brit has believed, the vent branched off into two different directions at a Y-intersection and then progressed another ten feet to a standard T-intersection.

"There it is!" Remy chimed with a vault of recognition.

"What?"

"The diagram from the card I swiped in Alabaster's room in Boston. The layout he was transporting was from the Capitol ductwork, not the Chunnel. See these lines here. They show up on the diagram. Alabaster was carrying the device's exact location back to Leviathan. How else would Leviathan know where to plant the device."

Remy's eyes worked the screen.

"He would most likely place the device in one of these two locations. However, we can't know for sure which one. All three branches eventually enter the House Chamber, and all three provide access from the outside. There are probably a dozen locations on these ducts where inside access could be obtained," Brax said.

"Well then, is any one location better than the others?" Cali asked.

"If I were Leviathan, I'd locate the device as close to the speaker's podium as possible," Cody said.

"I disagree," Remy injected.

Everyone turned to Remy. He offered them a look that intimated the answer should have been obvious, though to them it wasn't.

"What's going to happen when the gas floods the room?"

"Is this a pop quiz or something?" Cody said.

"People drop dead," Cali said.

"Exactly. And as soon as the second body drops, everyone panics. It's mass hysteria as everyone and I mean everyone scrambles at the same time to evacuate the chamber. Remember no one will have a clue as to what is happening around them. At the concentration I suspect Leviathan intends on using, the gas is odorless."

"So?" Cody said. Whatever bizarre British logic Remy clung to had failed to register inside Cody's brain.

"How long does it take for cyanide gas to kill?"

"Seconds," Squire said.

"Bloody damned immediate. So, he disperses the gas through the vents closest to the doors. That way when people attempt to escape, they inhale the gas and drop dead before they can get out. An accumulation of bodies forms a natural barrier to evacuation. Like a Landfill. Nobody in, nobody out. The president, vice president and members of Congress literally become trapped with the gas inside. No one can stop the flow. It becomes impossible for them to escape the cyanide. By the time anyone can figure out what's going on, it's too late."

Squire slid the mouse along the pad and moved through the ductwork toward the main doors of the House Chamber.

"This main shaft runs along the adjoining wall. It branches into two and feeds the vents near the front of the chamber."

"I think Leviathan would set his device up just before that junction," Remy said, pointing to a point on the screen. "That way the gas saturates the air as people try to evacuate and virtually ensures everyone will remain inside the room until they're all dead. You can't save the president because you can't get to him and he can't get out."

"Can we force outside air into the room?"

"Not without flooding the ducts and moving more of the gas into the Chamber."

"What about exhaust?"

"Nothing. All air movement comes through one central system. It's recirculated for efficiency through the heating system."

"So there's no way to prevent the gas from getting into the room?"

"None that I can see," Squire said. His eyes went to Remy's.

"Afraid not," Remy offered Brax.

"How do we stop it?"

"If it really is Leviathan's plan. What if we're wrong? What if his target is something else. What if while we're trying to find this device, he detonates a bomb in the chamber?"

No one had an answer.

```
Have received the date and time of
meeting. Hope you can join us there.
                              Brax
```

Back in the apartment, the table became the focal point the team assembled around to work through the night. A myriad of details had to be organized and scrutinized. They not only had to find a way to stop Leviathan, they had to do it while evading the FBI, CIA and Secret Service. Leviathan had indeed planned his next strike well, right down to setting the Wolf Pack up. Somehow Leviathan had turned the FBI on them.

All around them, people awakened, dressed, and were sitting down to breakfast before leaving for work. A robust January sun shone down over the Capital, though the air remained frigid due to an arctic blast sweeping in from the Midwest. Forecasters predicted the cold would remain throughout the week.

The talk on the hill this day would be the imminent State of the Union address to be delivered that night. The president customarily isolated himself the entire day, refining and honing his speech. Though a team of professionals created the words, the president reserved final say and attacked the delivery with the same ferocity as any actor preparing for his first starring role. No meetings, no interruptions. And no access from the outside.

Brax tugged at his brain for a way to reach the president without jeopardizing the team. The Secret Service and the FBI would swarm the moment he made a move. They would already have an offensive strategy in place should Brax or any of the others surface. All Brax could think about was how Leviathan could have manipulated Jaffe to orchestrate this elaborate ruse against them, and thereby prevent them from thwarting his plan.

At the table, the talk focused on how to neutralize the threat if it were in fact real. The team vacillated through the hours of darkness, looking at any and all possible ways Leviathan could reek havoc. Each time they came back to the evidence. The Prussian Blue detection, the mass slaughter in Geneva, the ability for Jaffe to circumvent security. It all made too much sense to dismiss.

The question as to whether Leviathan was in the U.S. plagued the team. If they could gain the slightest intelligence indicating Ranzami was in Washington, they would need no further evidence.

Squire stared out the window as cars began crowding the street below. He wondered if the traffic below contained Secret Service or Bureau agents cruising in hopes of spotting Brax, Remy or any other member of the team. Even Squire had to be careful in his movements now.

Suzanne returned shortly after nine with a bag stuffed with groceries. Preparing a breakfast of eggs, bacon and potatoes with Cali and Cody's assistance made her feel less like an outsider and more like a contributor. The team looked exhausted. She dared not speak for fear they would snarl at her. She never fully appreciated the meaning of what they did until now. She never fathomed the depth of their commitment to their government, despite knowing that the FBI, CIA and Secret Service would most likely shoot them down on the spot.

Yet all they could concern themselves with was carrying out the mission they had committed to a long time ago.

Few words were exchanged over breakfast.

"You need to sleep," Suzanne said at last, scanning the table at those present.

"It's up to us to stop it," Brax said after the long deafening silence.

"You can't keep going without rest."

"I should be the one to go in. They have the least chance of identifying me. I'll use my Reuters cover to get inside," Remy offered. He searched the team's eyes as he spoke.

Brax pushed his plate away using the moment to contemplate Remy's words. He had only a moment to weigh the risks.

"But I go alone."

"No. No one goes anywhere alone," Brax fired back with a sharpness that precluded an argument. "Cali goes in with you."

"How?" Squire asked.

"I have an old cover as an assistant to the Thai embassy here in Washington."

"You think it might still be good?"

"We can try?"

"Squire, can you tickle the files to see if we can use her cover?"

"Sure. I'll need the name and about an hour."

"She'll use that to get inside the Capitol building," Brax said with such a measure of control that Remy understood there would be no back and forth on this point.

"What if they made her?" Remy harped, he couldn't resist, even now.

"We take that chance," Brax replied with the same cutting edge to his words.

"Then I want her in well after me. I'm going in as early as possible."

Remy and Cali departed the table to begin working through the details of their task.

"What are we going to do, Brax?" Squire asked.

"Figure out where the device will be detonated
from."

"How?"

"Do I have to come up with all the goddamn
answers?"

Cody spent hours on the telephone, working on
something he told no one about. The frustration
mounted in his voice each time he failed to gain the
information he sought. But even after hours of fruitless effort, he continued his search.

He exalted a Texas holler when he hung up, tele-
graphing his ultimate success.

"Finally found someone who knew enough about
the electronic devices to help," he said. He left the
chair at the desk and cleared the papers from the
table to unfold a Washington D.C. and surrounding
area map, which now covered the surface.

"My man says the range of the device in that type
of a configuration is only two thousand feet. Therefore, the detonator must be located within that
range."

"Great," Brax said.

The three leaned over the map, drawing a circle
representing two thousand feet around the Capitol.
There would have to be a secure location within that
range of the Capitol building.

"Either he detonates from inside the building, or
within one to two blocks of the House Chamber,"
Cody said without lifting his eyes.

"You really think Ranzami would attempt detonation from inside the Capitol?" Squire asked.

"No. Too risky. He'll be the one to set it off, though. But he'll do it where he'll be safe," Brax said.

"And protected by goons," Squire said.

"Wait a minute. He could slip away easily in the chaos," Cody added to defend his theory.

"Yeah, but if the device were somehow detected, he'd be arrested on the spot. Ranzami's too smart. He always pulls the trigger from a safe location. A place where he knows he can escape and avoid being linked directly to the crime."

"Then I don't see how we can stop him from releasing the gas," Cody said with a sinking voice.

"Think about this. Suppose Kirkhammer figured out a way to extend the range of the transmitter. Suppose he could boost the power just enough to allow Ranzami a safer distance of say four thousand feet?" Squire asked.

Brax drew a second circle around the Capitol building at what he believed to be a distance of about four thousand feet.

"Look what we have here," Brax said as he ran a finger along the old warehouse district north of the Capitol building.

"He's going to be somewhere within that circle. All we have to do is find him," Cody said.

"How?"

"I think I know how we can get to him," Brax muttered more to himself than his team.

Remy fell in behind the throng of reporters waiting to gain entrance to the Capitol building through the west entrance. Two guards stationed just inside the doors scrutinized each press ID, and then singly, each person passed through the metal detectors. Security was always at its tightest during the State of the Union, so it was virtually impossible for Remy to determine if extraordinary measures were being taken this time.

Remy stood stone still while those before him went through the security gate. He could only hope his cover with Reuters had remained undiscovered. He would find out soon enough. The urge to survey over his shoulder at his escape route proved almost too overwhelming to control.

Everything right now rested on the premise that the team's secrecy had been guarded well enough that the two checking IDs had not already been alerted and awaited for him.

Remy had altered his appearance just enough to made a quick recognition difficult, and he intentionally wiped at his nose as he waited for the man in front of him to pass the checkpoint. His sneeze reinforced his facade, though he intentionally removed his handkerchief when he handed his pass to the guard. He had to give the man no reason to become suspicious.

This moment became critical. Remy sucked in a silent breath as the guard ran the name on the pass through his security computer. The delay seemed endless. Remy refused to breathe for fear the act itself might arouse suspicion. After another ten seconds, Remy began that first confident step forward, anxious to get beyond the guard station.

"Hang on, bloke," the guard said with a condescending edge, trying to gain a chuckle. Remy shot him a stern glare.

The guard gave another look to the ID picture and handed it back. The moment, like the press pass, hung between. Remy felt the first beads of cold sweat form under his hairline. Had someone uncovered his identity? The man behind Remy nudged him to get closer, frustrated by the delay.

"Come on through," the second guard ordered.

As Remy stepped forward, the first guard nodded approval. Remy held his smile until he had moved well beyond range of the guard station. The question still remained whether Cali's cover could hold up to such scrutiny.

Remy followed the trail of reporters moving through the Statuary Hall and then outside the House Chamber doors. This would be where the action was at the close of the speech. Every reporter in attendance would vie for a statement from the departing congressmen. Even now, some of the waiting vied for congressional statements as to what these important people expected from the State of the Union. Remy had only to blend with the others. He remained unobtrusively at the rear of the gathering, watching the activity. Within that first minute, he picked out three federal agents and what he believed to be a pair of Company men working the crowd. They made their presence known by exhibiting far too great an interest in the reporters and television people rather than the politicians working their way into the chamber. The direction of their eyes offered up telltale signs of security.

You could also always tell the junior senators and representatives. They were ones few reporters sought, and the ones most eager to talk.

Remy scanned the crowd once more, this time he saw no sign of Cali. He risked to check his watch with a quick glance. He would have to rely on his mental clock for now, since frequent time checks alerted security people to possible suspicion. They would be cutting it close if they failed to begin their search in the next few minutes.

While Remy and Cali worked their plan to gain access to the Capitol building, Brax, Cody and Squire took to the streets in the four thousand feet vicinity of the Capitol building. Even the best of the best made errors. They had to hope Leviathan had erred in some small way.

They were hunting, while at the same time being hunted. Everyone would be out on the streets watching for them. The Company knew them by sight and method, the FBI team received Company sponsored training to deal with espionage agents—their spy catchers would be deployed and ready—and the Secret Service were expert in aborting assassination attempts against the president. Yet none of them had an inkling that the real threat came from the one man more clever than the three agencies combined.

Neighborhood security around the Capitol mall became so tight you couldn't drop a dime without a half dozen going down to grab it for you. Brax spotted three government agents working the crowd that flowed back and forth in the vicinity of the Capitol. A huddled gathering outside the gates protested abortion while another group chanted for a tougher government stand on crime. Then there were the gawkers, who agitated about, just wanting to get a glimpse of the president when he arrived. All in all, the constant movement made it easier for the Wolf Pack to move about the area. There were so many faces flowing back and froth that no one could lock on to any one.

Squire drove. Brax and Cody watched out the side windows of a dingy blue van. They studied the faces of the onlookers with a practiced intensity. They knew who they were looking for. The thought that one of the protestors or gawkers could be Leviathan with his finger on a remote trigger sent chills up Brax's spine. But Leviathan would have to know exactly when to trigger his device for maximum effect. That meant he had to be in a position to monitor the address.

The white smoke puffing out the exhaust helped minimize suspicion on their vehicle.

"What are we looking for?" Squire asked after a fourth pass of the area turned up nothing that remotely appeared out of place. The van by its very recurring presence had begun to arouse the suspicion of police providing crowd control.

The sun's final glow along the western horizon had long ago completely disappeared. Time ticked away. Brax checked his watch. They had less than an hour before the House Chamber would come to order and the president announced. Brax hoped they were wrong. They had forced pieces together that might have otherwise not fit. They were racing to stop a phantom that might never materialize. Something inside told him that wasn't the truth. Ranzami would go for the heart of his enemy. Topple its leadership. That's the way Ranzami thought.

Brax surmised Ranzami would most likely wait until everyone became seated and the address well under way before triggering his deadly device. He also knew Ranzami right at this moment would be sitting comfortably before a television set selected to one of the news stations covering the event. What he didn't know was where and who else would be present to witness the carnage. They all knew Ranzami would be surrounded by his lieutenants. Men expendable at this late stage of his plan. They played a crucial function in his strategy: they would provide the firewall meant to keep anyone from reaching the monster before he pressed that final button.

"Slow down," Cody commanded with an edge of excitement in his voice that pulled both Squire and Brax to look to his side of the van.

"Never mind, shit," he said moments later as if a balloon had suddenly burst.

Squire sped up only to slow to round a corner. He scrutinized doorways and alleyways on his side of the street. Though he had only an inkling of an idea as to what he was looking for, and could only hope something would jump out at him.

"Here we go," Brax said.

Squire froze at the wheel. He neither sped up nor slowed, keeping the wheel straight, waiting for a further command.

Cody slid to Brax's side, where he observed a bundled form scurry like a rat along the side walk.

"Who?" Squire asked. He never turned his head.

"An IRA scum runner."

"Pull over," Brax barked. As soon as the van stopped, he slipped out the back and began moving back down the side from where they had come.

"Go to the end of the street. Pull into that alley and stop," Cody issued. His eyes never left the huddled mass flowing quickly through the foot traffic on the opposite side of the street as Brax.

Squire complied. The van came to a stop in the alley with the back end exposed enough to allow Cody constant surveillance on both the target and Brax. A minute later both disappeared around a corner.

"Get back into traffic, move it," Cody ordered.

Squire, however, hesitated.

"Fuck! Move it, will you."

Squire held the brake. A government vehicle loaded down with four agents passed just as he was about to make a move. Had he gone, he might have given the Feds an opportunity at an introduction.

"Move, Squire, now!" Cody snarled.

"Damnit, Cody, that's Bureau."

"Fuck, we're going to lose them," Cody muttered, watching the midnight blue Ford turn in the same direction as Brax.

"Jesus Christ, we've got to get Brax out of there," Cody snarled with the viciousness of a rabid Rottweiller.

37

Phone troubles prevent further
communications. Please advise on
arrival.

> Brax

Cali realized there was only one way to play her entry into the Capitol. She barged through the collection of men standing on the steps, and without a word, presented her credentials to the guard behind the computer console as if she expected to pass through without delay.

"Excuse me," the guard said, accepting her paper with a angry stare. "I don't know how you people do things in..." he paused to check her paper, "Thailand, but here you wait for everyone else."

"So sorry. We are honored guests of the president. I am late and the crown prince will have me beaten for not being in my assigned place. I will dishonor his highness."

Cali's face quickly fell under the shrouds of fear. The kind of fear great pain would elicit. Thus, the guard wasted no time in punching her name into the computer. Her terrified eyes never strayed from his. Even though she realized her ruse had rooted firmly in the man, she played it for all she could gain from it.

"Please, come through," the second guard said waving her on through the metal detectors even before her clearance appeared on the screen.

Seductive blue eyes have a way of melting most men.

Once cleared, Cali marched with an almost military cadence after grabbing her papers from the first guard's outstretched hand.

"Thank you," she said with the passion of one whose life had just been spared. She continued away without delay and fell in with the crowd.

A second later the computer screen flashed a message across the bottom of the screen approving her access to the Capitol building.

Cali located Remy standing near the exit to Statuary Hall scribbling notes into a notebook like so many other reporters were doing.

"What are you doing?" she asked.

"Acting like those morons over there. Any problems with security?"

"Those idiots think the crown prince of Thailand's here."

Remy laughed, though only slightly while he motioned her toward the stairs.

"We've got less than ten minutes to get to this thing."

The two moved virtually unnoticed, since the activity now centered around the doors to the House Chamber rather than the corridors further away.

Remy led Cali to the second floor corridor in search of the access door Squire told them to expect. However, they turned left down a side corridor when they should have went right, and as a result, ended up at the stairway leading back down to the west entrance.

"It's got to be back this way," Cali injected, taking over the lead and moving down the hall with urgent steps.

When they came upon the locked door, they assumed they had found the right access. As bad as assumptions were, they had no other choice. Remy removed his tools to work the lock. He stopped when

Cali set a hand on his shoulder. Sounds emanated from a side corridor.

"Faster," Cali urged.

They were caught in the midst. They could neither abandon nor explain exactly what they were doing.

"Damnit, not now," Remy muttered under his breath. He worked the pick deeper into the key hole and finally the mechanism tripped. The lock yielded. Remy pulled open the door enough for Cali to slide in first. Once he slipped inside he held the door closed. They had to pray no one tried the lock at this moment.

Neither breathed until the sounds faded. In the corridor, they were exposed and vulnerable. Inside the closet, they had at least achieved a tenuous security.

"Didn't MI6 teach you how to pick a lock?" Cali scowled.

Remy said nothing.

"Damned close if you ask me. American quality," Remy replied later after cleansing the sweat from his face. He endured a burning in his chest, attributing it to pressure mounting inside him.

They paused at the ladder. Both hearts raced out of control. Their assumption this far had paid off. Cali worked her dry lips as she gazed up into the pitch of the crawlspace. Remy made certain he locked the door behind them to avoid detection by a passing guard. They remained safe as long as nobody became suspicious and followed them up the ladder.

Cali started up. But Remy pulled her back down and clamped a hand over her mouth. Outside, feet strolled down the corridor in regular rhythm.

They waited, sweating, not breathing, expecting the door handle to rattle. It never came. The two must have left behind no telltale signs of entry, or the guard was satisfied that his responsibility for this event would remain routine.

This time Remy started up the ladder first.

"Didn't anyone ever tell you, you never precede a man up a ladder. He'll ogle your underwear."

"I figured you needed a cheap thrill to steady your nerves after that debacle with the lock."

"Fourteen seconds isn't that bad, you know."

Remy paused at the transom to gaze in both directions. The only light at this level bled upward from the office and hall lighting. And then that was widespread and sparse. They could make out the HVAC ducts and electrical conduits running in both directions for at least thirty to forty feet.

Remy signaled for Cali to begin checking to the right while he moved along the rickety transom to the left. They had agreed the most likely place for the device was would at a Y-junction in the ductwork, but neither had been able to spot the junction once they settled on the transom.

Remy inched methodically along, searching for anything that might even remotely indicate the duct-work had been altered. As he approached the House Chamber, flickers of light filtering through the cracks in the ducts mottled him.

The din of those assembling in the chamber below filtered into his ears and heightened his aware-ness of why he was there. Sweat rolled off doughy cheeks. Breathing became difficult in the overly warmed, stale air trapped in the crawlspace.

Then he saw it. Ten paces ahead on his left the ductwork split into a Y-formation, and the two ducts fed into the ceiling of the House Chamber. Remy stopped to signal Cali with a penlight beam.

He did nothing while he waited for her to rejoin him on the transom. Nothing beside steady his nerves and pray they had found the correct location. The increasing amplitude of human voices indicated the gathering had already moved inside the House Cham-ber. They were down to minutes.

"Here's the Y. If Squire's right, that blasted device is somewhere right around here."

Together, Cali and Remy began the tedious search beginning at the Y-junction and following the main duct back a few inches at a time, seeking an access panel.

Cali stopped. She brushed across screw heads flush with the surface in three corners of the access panel. A protruding screw head occupied the fourth hole. Without a sound, she gestured her findings to Remy.

They listened while the gavel came down twice and the Speaker of the House announced the President of the United States. A roaring applause filled the chamber.

"Fuck, goddamnit!"

Remy wiped the dripping sweat from his face. His shirt had become saturated. His breathing came now in gasps. They had to be right.

"This better be it," Cali said.

Remy shot her a sidelong glance as he worked the screws. When the first one came out his smile lit up the space.

"Quick disconnects," he murmured, moving on to the next screw.

Neither could have any idea how much time they had to find and deactivate the device. Remy carefully removed the remaining screws until he had one left on the access panel. As he put the small screwdriver to the last screw, Cali jerked his arm away.

"What if it's booby-trapped? What if removing the panel itself could trigger the device?"

Remy stopped and lowered to rest his quaking knees on the transom. Even in the weak beam off the penlight, Cali could see he was visibly shaken.

Squire exited the alley to follow the government vehicle at a safe distance. He released a sigh when he saw Brax slip unnoticed into a doorway behind the target. Whether he realized it or not, Brax had hid himself from the passing Feds, who continued on their way not only missing Brax, but also the terrorist stooge.

Squire slid to the curb and held until the FBI passed out of sight. He then moved forward until Brax came into sight again. But Brax suddenly stopped.

Cody emerged from the back of the van and approached Brax, who remained before a specialty store.

"He's in there," Brax said, motioning with his eyes to a two-story warehouse across the street on the corner.

"Definitely within range," Cody said, looking back over his shoulder and the illuminated Capitol dome.

A moment later, Squire came up the street only to pass the two as if they were strangers. He continued on for a dozen paces and turned into the entrance of a store. From inside he turned about to watch Brax and Cody through the window.

Cody entered the warehouse first, picking the lock on the same door the target had gone through a few minutes earlier. No one knew what to expect. But they prepared for anything.

Brax followed a minute behind. The two rendezvoused inside the foyer. Squire left the store, walked down the street away from the building and came up the other side disappearing into the building minutes after Brax and Cody.

"I figure the second floor in the corner closest to the Capitol building," Cody said. He had appraised the situation while he waited for the rest of the team.

Brax nodded.

Cody removed his Desert Eagle, checked the magazine and counted the number of spare magazines he carried in his coat pocket.

"You know we're going to need a hell of a lot more than this," he said.

Brax drew a Glock 22 that he handed to Squire. Then he removed a 9mm ASP for himself.

"Once we confirm the target, we go in hard with everything," Brax instructed more for Squire's benefit than Cody's. Cody already knew the drill and needed no coaching.

"What are you expecting?" Squire asked as they moved up the dimly lit staircase in single file. His face had gone slack and he expended tremendous force just to get the words out.

"You wanted fieldwork," Cody snickered while he affixed a silencer to his weapon.

"All fucking Hell is going to break loose," Brax said. His eyes never left the landing for the floor above. In the silence they paused.

"Squire, Can you do this?" Brax asked in a whisper.

The hesitation in Squire's face offered more of a response than words.

"Can you kill?"

Squire tightened his grip on his weapon.

"Let's go," Squire replied.

Cody shot him a smile and a thumbs up.

The sprawling open expanse appeared largely deserted, yet there remained sufficient crating and refuse to provide cover for anywhere from three to six men.

Cody breached the second floor first. He advanced slowly toward the east all the time tuned for signs of life. He heard nothing. For a moment, they paused solidly on the second floor to get their bearings.

Twenty yards away, at the right end of the expanse, a door opened. The three froze leveling guns at the target. The man Brax had tailed exited.

Cody's silenced shot hit the target in the temple. The man dropped into a splayed heap in the middle of the floor.

Squire eyes widened in amazement. He'd never seen someone kill with such calm, deadly accuracy.

"It's time to play!" Cody yelled and charged ahead with Brax and Squire right behind. They went through the open door to the flash of gunfire inside.

All three rolled or dove for cover behind boxes and dilapidated production tables. Brax fired until his magazine went empty to keep the assailants at bay.

Two, Cody signaled with his hand. He pointed them out at the end of the long room.

Brax slammed another magazine in and fired another volley, allowing Squire to advance and improve his cover.

"I've been expecting you, Brax," a calm, even voice said from across the dark chasm.

For a long moment neither Remy nor Cali spoke, neither moved.

"We've got to take that chance. We can't sit and wonder."

Remy removed the last screw and held his breath while he slid the access panel off the duct.

Nothing happened. At least nothing discernible. Both held their breath knowing the repercussions of breathing when the device went off.

Remy angled his head as close as he could to the nine-by-nine access hole and gazed in both directions along the inside of the duct.

"Bingo!" he said in triumph.

He withdrew, allowing Cali to get a look at what they were now up against.

"What do we do now?" she asked.

"I would think the answer becomes intuitively obvious. We disarm it."

"How we going to do that?"

"Minutia."

"Minutia? Everything to you is minutia. By the way, what does that mean?"

"Petty details. Don't sweat the small stuff."

"A goddamn cyanide bomb to you is small stuff?"

Remy inched much of his head into the duct and realized he would need an arm in there at the same time in order to work. However, the square opening left him without sufficient room to have both head and arm in at the same time. For a long moment, he memorized every aspect of the device. He would have to work blindly, feeling his way through the disarming process. A process he had little time to develop. Certainly this type of device would employ no ordinary triggers.

"I've got two tandem cylinders on a central mechanical trigger controlled by an electronic circuit. From what I could see at my angle. The remote electronic trigger releases two trip pins into cylindrical valves."

"So what can we do?"

"I'm not sure yet. Let me think."

Applause drifted up through the ducts from the House Chamber below.

Remy withdrew to clear his head and hopefully improve his thinking. Cali in turn poked her head in enough to appraise the device. Then she withdrew and stuck her arm in.

"Be very careful. It's mercury switch protected," Remy cautioned.

With her fingers she carefully brushed along the cylinders, feeling as much of the device as possible.

"Can we just pull it out," she said, grasping the device with her fingers around both the cylinders.

"No!" Remy yelled in a harsh whisper. He grabbed her arm with a painful vise lock.

"That mercury switch on the triggering device will detect any shift in equilibrium on the trigger. It will set off the device if it's moved."

"Fuck. So what do we do?"

Cali very gently released the cylinders and eased her hand from the duct. Her eyes had grown white in terror.

Remy said nothing.

"We can't do it, can we? We can't stop it."

"We've got no choice but to go for disarming it. I'll have to do it blindly, since I can't get both my hand and face in through the access panel at the same time."

"What if we can remove one of the cylinders?"

"Can't know for sure if they are both cyanide or a chemical agent meant to combine when the trigger's activated."

Remy slid his hand back into the duct to very gently ride his fingers over the upper cylinder. He then slid to the metal band holding the cylinder in place and felt for a locking clip or any other way to release the band holding it in place. Finding nothing, he worked his finger and thumb up to the valve and located the firing pin on the triggering electronics used to release the gas.

Very slowly, Remy began easing the cylinder back away from the trigger until the valve cleared, hoping to take it out of alignment with the firing pin. When he felt the device shift, he stopped. He looked in and determined that his trick had worked.

"One down," he said. He stopped to breath while Cali sopped up the sweat rolling off his face.

38

Hope to return to the coast for
another visit. Call with itinerary.

Brax

Brax knew immediately they had been correct.
Jaffe.

Brax slid in closer, using an overturned trestle
table to shield him from the shots flashing out of the
darkness. Cody honed in on the bursts of light and
leveled his gun with deadly accuracy. He fired thrice,
listened as the bullets pinged off the metal surroundings and knew none had found flesh or bone.

"How do you like the game I've set up for us? I
don't know how the fuck you survived back in California, Brax, but ever since that day I knew it would
come to this."

Still neither Brax, Cody nor Squire spoke.

Jaffe positioned himself between them and the
door that led to Ranzami. Jaffe had undertaken the
task of preventing them from getting through that
door.

All their assumptions had been correct. They had
deciphered Ranzami's plot and now could prevent
the carnage. If only he had uncovered Jaffe's intent
earlier. Had Housemother confided in Brax about
Jaffe's soft files this day could have been prevented.

Squire fired a volley into the darkness. Cody
advanced. But a moment later the return flash told
them their shots had missed.

"I guess right now you feel pretty much betrayed. Don't feel bad, they've been fucking me over for years. Of course, I've made certain they'll fuck you over just as bad. You only made one fuck up, Brax. Bad idea to knock off Lonigan in that alley. I made sure the Fools, Boneheads and Idiots got the video, along with a few well constructed intelligence reports indicating you've been turned. I figured you'd all be holed up in some prison by now."

They were running out of time. They had minutes before the president would enter the House Chambers. After handshakes and well-wishing, he would take the podium and begin his speech. Any time after that, Ranzami could release the gas. They had to get to Leviathan before the speech began and before the doors to those chambers closed.

"We're almost out of time, Brax," Cody fired just above a harsh whisper. This was not a time for patience and persistence.

Brax tried to focus on the target. Jaffe was astute enough to deduce what they would attempt. Brax figured they had to go with a novel approach, but before he could devise one, Cody rose and advanced through the darkness, firing John Wayne style at where he believed Jaffe to be.

"Jaffe, you motherfucking traitor, you're going to die for fucking us," Cody yelled above the staccato bursts of gunfire.

Like a wild west cowboy, Cody discarded his spent pistol only to pull a second to continue firing into the darkness, running until two shots nailed him squarely and sent him tumbling backward.

But Cody's valiant charge was not without some measure of success.

When the gunfire fell silent, Brax moved forward. No shots opposed his advance. He stopped near the door to find Jaffe splay-legged on the floor with blood gushing from his neck.

The Kevlar couldn't save him.

Even in the faint light from the street lamp out-side the tall windows, Brax could discern that Jaffe still breathed. Jaffe's eyes stared into Brax's. He saw something he interpreted as an apology. Then Jaffe breathed no more.

With Squire poised and ready behind him, Brax kicked in the door. They flooded the room with a spray of bullets. Squire rolled into the spacious loft room and leveled his pistol at a corner where a television set lit up the surrounding space.

A shot rang out, clipping Squire's shoulder, forc-ing him to lose his weapon and scramble for cover behind a row of crates.

When Brax breached the room, a foot shot out from around the door to kick the weapon from his hand.

Shigeo swung around the open door in a flying assault, and Brax countered it with a sharp punch to the inside of the knee.

Shigeo, however, landed on both feet, his arms in an aggressive posture, his eyes locked on Brax's.

"It is time to die," Shigeo said. He launched a rapid-fire assault with fists and feet.

Brax deflected each punch but had to withstand to two driving jabs from Shigeo's feet to his rib cage. Despite the pain, Brax held his ground, forcing Shigeo to retreat instead of advance.

Brax forced his way deeper into the room, where he chose his shots at Shigeo carefully. In the back-ground the voice from the television set grew louder. The Speaker of the House was announcing the presi-dent's arrival.

Shigeo struck, hitting Brax in the neck. But the blow missed the lethal spot, and as a result, Brax rolled backward and came right back up to his feet. Another shot rang out, but it pinged across the room from where the two men fought. The shot originated behind a wall, and as it was its intent, it kept Squire from emerging from his place of refuge in an attempt to retrieve his weapon.

When Shigeo launched another fierce attack, Brax countered, diverting the blow while at the same time landing a hard strike to Shigeo's face. When Shigeo shifted his weight to prepare a kick, Brax drove the butt of his palm into Shigeo's throat. The strike shattered Shigeo's larynx. Blood chortled from the Asian's mouth and nose.

For an unending moment, Shigeo stared beyond Brax's eyes. As if to surrender and pay homage, he lowered his hands, bowed slightly, then toppled face-first to the floor.

When Brax turned toward the source of the light, the president's face filled the television set. He waited patiently for the applause to dwindle into quiet. Then he delivered that all-important opening line of his speech. A warm and engaging smile crossing his face, the president cast his eyes over the crowd held silent by his presence. Whether the audience liked the man or not, whether they agreed with his principles or not, they afforded the office the respect it deserved.

Brax dove for his gun. Another shot rang out from behind the wall, forcing Brax to hold short his position.

"Bravo, Mr. Nash, or do I call you Brax. That *is* your codename in Wolf Pack, is it not?"

Ranzami materialized from around the wall, blotting out the light of the television screen. His face exuded more smug confidence than that witnessed earlier on the president's face. He palmed a Ruger P-85 in one hand and a small black remote device in the other.

"I have never lost faith in you, Mr. Nash. I knew if anyone were to stop me, it would have to be you. Why do you think I turned your man against you? From his absence, I conclude you have eliminated him as a threat to your government. Is that not what your mission is, Mr. Nash?"

The television's volume rose an octave.

"Please, invite your comrade to join us. I want so very much for the both of you to witness this most spectacular event. Seldom do people get the opportunity to behold my genius from my side."

Ranzami's voice held complete control. He had won. A moment that would change the history of the world—and he held it in his hand.

Squire crept out from behind the crates, at the same, eliciting a clumsy move toward his gun as he became visible in the light off the television screen.

Ranzami leveled his pistol at Squire's forehead.

"Foolish boy. Rest assured, I have sufficient shells left in my magazine to kill you and your leader before you can reach your weapons."

That little diversion, that moment when Ranzami had to focus his concentration in another place, proved just enough for Brax to withdraw the marble he carried with him always. He would get one shot. But he needed to be closer to his target. Much closer, though he knew in his heart the hour glass had run out. He had to take the best shot available and hope he succeeded.

"Come. Watch. I suspect you unraveled most of my plan if you were able to track me to this place. I am the deadliest of all my kind. As you will witness, Mr. Nash."

Brax scanned, hoping for anything in the room that might help him get to Ranzami before he pressed that button under his thumb. It seemed Ranzami had made certain nothing could be used against him, if all other measures to keep the team out had failed.

"Such an eloquent speaker, your president. How many people do you think are listening to his filthy propaganda? Fifty, eighty million? More?"

Ranzami released a slight laugh from his lips. So much power he wielded at this moment. So much control he clutched in his left hand. His eyes never strayed from Brax.

While Ranzami spoke, Squire edged closer to Brax, and Brax moved an inch at a time toward the man now half sitting on a table to the right side of the television as if he were a casual commentator to the momentous event.

"You know what is going to happen."

Just as Ranzami ended his last word, Brax fired the marble like a projectile, taking aim on Ranzami's eye. He had one chance to stop him...if he hit on target.

Ranzami fired off a reflexive shot, clipping Brax in the upper right chest quadrant, but he swung around too late to fire upon Squire.

The marble landed wide.

Squire's flying kick landed squarely on Ranzami's chest and dislodged the gun from of his hand.

"You motherfucker!" Squire yelled as he went for the device.

But Ranzami pressed the red button before the device left his hand and went sliding across the table.

"Always willing to sacrifice your life for your leaders," Ranzami said. Then he began to laugh as the little green light on the remote device illuminated.

"It is done," Ranzami said.

Brax and Squire stared at the small device as if time had become suspended.

"The green light means the device has triggered and cyanide gas right now seeps into the House Chamber. In less than five minutes, everyone will be dead. And fifty million of your American pigs will witness it."

With the same meticulous care that Remy used to misalign the first canister, he eased his hand down to the top of the second cylinder. He moved his fingers along the cold cylinder body to locate the valve at the neck. This one resisted his attempts to shift it out of alignment. When he looked in to check on his attempt, the release valve remained aligned with the firing pin. He slid his hand back in with a surgeon's gentle guidance and renewed his effort.

Suddenly, he felt the circuitry under his palm heating up. A flash of green bounced off the shiny metal of the inside of the duct.

The device had been triggered.

Remy could do only one thing. He shoved his fingers into the valve forcing the firing pin to drive into his skin. It felt like no more than a pin prick. His flesh kept the pin from puncturing the release valve and expelling the deadly gas.

"Damnit! Cali get out of here—NOW!"

"What happened?" Cali said. She shifted about on the transom but refused to retreat.

"It triggered. The firing pin's caught on the flesh between my finger and thumb."

"Then do something?"

"I can't goddamnit! I can't move my hand. If I do, the pin punctures the valve and releases the gas."

"Pull the device out and I'll help you."

"I can't. I can't gripe it. If I drop it now, we're both dead along with everybody in the House Chamber."

"Tell me what to do," Cali urged.

"Get out of here. Get the hell out of here."

🔫

Squire retrieved the gun from the floor and fired. The shot tore into Ranzami's chest and backed him into the television set.

Applause reverberated into the room, causing the president to pause for a third standing ovation. His words had struck a resonant chord with those charged with building upon the American dream. His smile charmed everyone in the chamber.

Ten seconds passed in agony. Ranzami stared at the screen, fighting for just enough breath to remain alive long enough to witness the pinnacle of all his hatred.

A minute passed. The applause continued.

Ranzami's rictus turned angry and vile.

The president resumed his speech. His smile exuded confidence.

Ranzami fell dead upon the floor to the resounding applause of the entire House Chamber.

Brax and Squire stared at the screen, waiting...

🔫

"I'm not leaving you, goddamnit. You let that fucking thing slip, and we both die. Now tell me what to do!"

Cali worked to keep panic from slipping into her words.

"All right. You need to work your hand inside with mine," Remy instructed. He locked his free fingers around the canister and held them as tightly closed as he could. Only his loose flab of skin separated them from certain death.

Cali eased her body gently against his and slowly slid her fingers into the opening.

"Finally I get your body next to mine," Remy said, though there was anything but levity in his voice.

Cali reached around with her other arm and molded her form against his. She ran her fingers along his hand until she came to the cold metal of the canister. With her index finger she could feel the firing pin pressed into Remy's skin. There had to be no more than a sliver of flesh separating the pin from the discharge valve on the canister.

"Now, together we have to move the device out..."

At that moment a flashlight beam washed over them, silencing Remy.

"Freeze!" a caustic voice erupted from a face on the transom at the ladder.

"Damnit, not now," Remy scowled.

For the first time in his life, Remy felt the grip of certain death around his soul. They were going to die. If not by a bullet, then from the deadly gas inches from his face.

"Don't make a move," Cali shouted, with more verve and authority than she realized she could muster in this situation. "We're federal agents, there's a bomb here."

Cali's words brought enough hesitation in the man holding the flashlight and the gun that he stood there uncertain of what to do.

The radio at his belt crackled.

"This is Donley, I've got a situation," he said into it in low tones that neither Remy nor Cali could barely make out.

"You FBI? I need to see identification," Donley asked.

"Does it look like we're in any position to flash our badges? Now get the goddamn hell back down that ladder before you blow us all into a thousand pieces."

"We've got to do it now," Remy said, just above a whisper.

In unison they dislodged the device from its underpinnings and inch-by-inch maneuvered it toward the opening.

"Stop!" Remy yelled when he felt his finger slip ever so slightly.

At the end of the transom the flashlight beam disappeared.

"I'm losing it," Remy stammered.

Cali tightened her grip on the canister and held it stationary.

"You got it now?" she prodded.

After a moment's pause they resumed. Two inches later, the device became visible in the duct's access. Remy could see his skin holding the firing pin at bay.

"Little more and we're out," he said.

Cali's precarious position against Remy prevented her seeing anything. All she could do was work her hand back toward the opening and trust that Remy remained in control.

The next inch brought the device out of the duct to where they could view it. Cali gripped the canister with both hands. She rotated it just enough to misalign the firing pin with the release valve. As she did, Remy's finger slipped. The pin struck the metal housing of the valve.

"It's done," Remy said, sucking in a breath he thought he might never get to take. Then he kissed Cali squarely on the lips.

39

This meeting is adjourned.

                         Brax

January 29th. Suzanne sat in a straight-backed victorian chair fashioned with a fine damask linen. She was no antique expert, but she knew enough to realize this chair had to be at least two centuries old. She wrapped her fingers together in her lap, refused to notice the men in suits parading back and forth down the corridor, and never once asked them why she had been brought here.

A gruff voice had telephoned her in the middle of the night three days following the State of the Union Address, said he was calling on behalf of Kevin Chambers, and requested she be prepared to be picked up at nine the following morning. She asked what she should wear. All he had said was black would be appropriate. She still thought of him as Kevin despite knowing now that his name most probably was Phillip. Maybe it wasn't. Maybe that also was a ruse.

Two men in black arrived in an indigo sedan to escort her at the time she had been told to expect them. They confirmed her name and asked that she make herself comfortable in the back seat. Her first thought was that Kevin had been killed, and she was attending his funeral. As she sat there in the ante-room to the oval office, she wondered what had hap-

pened. For days she had no knowledge of whether
Kevin was alive or dead. Even now she knew only that
she was to be here. She hoped in her heart she was be
reunited with Kevin, if he were still alive.

The door at last opened. Suzanne looked up into
the gentle eyes of a man with bushy brows. He
stepped clear of the office, closed the door behind
him, then turned to face her squarely before speaking.

"Miss Masters, my name is Theodore Calfield, I
am a good friend of your fiance. I believe we're ready
for you now," Calfield said, taking her hand and placing it under his arm. He made no effort to hide the
pleasure gleaming in his eyes at having her at his
side.

He flashed a smile obviously meant to allay her
butterflies, though from the trembling in her hand it
must have failed.

"A few things you must adhere to before we
enter. It is best if you speak only in response to a
question and refrain from offering anything unnecessary. This is a somewhat awkward situation. So
please bear with us, and we will try to do the best we
can.

Calfield opening the door brought the president
visible as he stood casually before his desk, his arms
across his chest, with a face impossible for Suzanne
to read. He warmed into a welcoming smile the
moment their eyes met.

Suzanne sucked in a breath. Why would she be in
the office of the president? Why had she been
brought here, what would be expected of her, and
what she possibly should say to the President of the
United States.

As Suzanne entered, she caught in her peripheral
vision Kevin, Sidney, Cali, and Remy. Remy's one
hand rested on the wheelchair where a bandaged
Cody sat. Cody struggled to get out his Texas smile. It

had lost much of its luster, but it still shone large enough to overshadow his bandages.

"Welcome to the office of the president, Miss Masters. I've been informed we owe you a debt of gratitude.

"Suzanne. It's Suzanne, Mr. President."

The president took her hand in both his, shook it mildly and refused to release it.

"I think our Mr. Nash is one very lucky man."

Before speaking, Suzanne glanced back at Calfield, her eyes projecting the confusion that cluttered her mind.

"Did he prompt you? Forget him. I'm no different than any of those men over there."

"Yes sir."

"Mr. Nash tells me you've endured quite the harrowing experience. Seldom do we call upon our citizens to perform under such pressure. I want you to know that your government is indebted to you for the strength and courage you've demonstrated under conditions of tremendous stress. And though we are not at liberty to divulge any of the particulars behind what went on, I can say with all confidence that every member of the Senate and House of Representatives feels you have performed a great service to your country."

"Thank you, Mr. President."

"You're here, Suzanne, today to share in the ceremony we are about to bestow upon these people. Realize Miss Masters, that everything that you have experienced, everything you have witnessed, including this ceremony, is classified Top Secret, for reasons of national security. Only those present in this room will ever know what went on out there and what you together have done for this country. We are here today, because of the courage and commitment each of you have demonstrated."

Suzanne took her place beside Nash. They shared a brief smile while she slipped her hand into his, feel-

J.M. Barlog

ing for the first time in months that they were completely free from danger.

"When I first conceived of Wolf Pack, I never dreamed Leviathan would be capable of penetrating so deeply into our core. You're Prime Minister, Remy, stood beside me, knowing Leviathan would never abate. We had to seize the initiative to end his terror. You collectively have saved countless lives and driven a new fear into the hearts and minds of terrorists worldwide. For that we owe you our deepest gratitude."

"Another jock strap medal," Remy muttered from the other side of Suzanne.

Calfield readied four black velvet cases he had retrieved from the president's desk. Standing at attention beside the president, which was something his withered old frame found unnatural, he waited while the president read the commendation printed on a fine gilt parchment. Words never to be heard outside the oval office. Afterward, he handed a Medal of Valor to his Commander in Chief, who placed it over the first recipient's head. As the president moved to the next in line, Calfield handed the next medal over, angled the open empty case out so the medal just awarded could be returned. One by one, each member of Wolf Pack received acknowledgment for his or her contribution.

The whole process appeared so contradictory and comical that Suzanne struggled to conceal her astonishment.

Each revelled in the bliss brought on by receiving medals from the president himself, however, fleeting it seemed, then they watched as Deputy Director Calfield returned their recognition to the president's desk.

That thrill-of-a-lifetime moment evaporated as quickly as it arose. The Wolf Pack awaited their next assignment.

Glossary of Terrorist Organizations

The following provides a brief description of terrorist organizations used in this book. These descriptions are in no way meant to be complete, nor is this listing intended to be exhaustive.

Black September

Also known as Abu Nidal Organization (ANO). Group claims a strength of several hundred and has carried out terrorist attacks in 20 countries. Targets include the United States, United Kingdom, France, Israel and various Arab nations.

Armed Islamic Group (GIA)

An Islamic extremist organization, the GIA's strength ranges from several hundred to several thousand. It utilizes hijacking, bombings, assassinations and kidnappings to carry out its terror. The GIA hijacked an Air France flight to Algiers in December 1994.

Aum Supreme Truth (AUM)

A cult that came into existence in 1987, the Aum's goal is to take over Japan and then the world. The group claims 9,000 members in Japan and over 40,000 worldwide. Their name became infamous across the globe after releasing deadly sarin gas on Tokyo subway trains.

Chukaku-Ha

The Chukaku-Ha is the largest domestic militant group in Japan. It contains a covert action wing known as the Kansai Revolutionary Army and has purportedly launched rockets against a U.S. military facility. Its strength in considered to be about 3,000.

Devrimci Sol (Dev Sol)

The Dev Sol is a splinter faction of the Turkish People's Liberation Party/Front. The group espouse's a Marxist ideology and is violently anti-U.S. With unknown strength, the Dev Sol carries out terrorist attacks mainly in Turkey.

HAMAS

Also known as the Islamic Resistance Movement. Claiming tens of thousands of supporters and sympathizers, HAMAS is fighting to root an Islamic Palestinian state in Israel. HAMAS clandestine units have used violence against Israel.

Hizballah (Party of God)

Also known as the Islamic Jihad, this radical Shia group seeks to create an Iranian-style Islamic state in Lebanon. Strongly anti-Israel and anti-U.S., the Hizballah is aligned with Iranian fundamental beliefs and is often directed by Iran. The Hizballah has established small groups in Europe, South America and the United States.

Irish Republican Army (IRA)

A radical terrorist group dedicated to removing the British forces from Northern Ireland. Uses bombings, assassinations, kidnappings and robberies. IRA operations have included bombings in mainland Britain. They are known to operate in Northern Ireland, Great Britain and Europe. The IRA has received funding and support from both Libya and the PLO.

Jamaat ul-Fuqra (FUQRA)

An Islamic sect seeking to purify Islam through the use of violence. Fuqra members have established isolated compounds in rural United States. Fuqra assassinations and firebomb attacks during the 1980s included targets across the United States. Most violent members of Fuqra in the United States have been convicted of terrorist attacks

Japanese Red Army

Also known as the Anti-Imperialist International Brigade. The JRA maintains long standing relations with Palestinian terrorist groups from which it receives support and funding. A JRA operative was arrested in April of 1988 carrying explosives on the New Jersey Turnpike. He had intended an attack to coincide with another attack being launched against a USO club in Naples.

Vanguards of Conquest

Also known as al-jihad and the International Justice Group. The Vanguards of Conquest specialize in armed attacks against high-level Egyptian government officials. Though it operates in Cairo, the Vanguards of Conquest appear to have members outside Egypt. Exact strength is unknown.

Kuristan Workers' Party (PKK)

The PKK operates in Turkey, Europe and the Middle East, claiming approximately 10,000 to 15,000 guerillas. Its primary targets are Turkish Government forces, but the PKK has also been active in Western Europe. They continue to receive safe haven from Syria, Iraq and Iran.

New People's Army (NPA)

The NPA serves as the guerilla arm of the Communist Party of the Philippines (CPP). Using city-based assassination squads known as sparrow units, the NPA carries out violent acts of terror against the Philippine government. A lack of funding keeps the NPA from gaining strength and organization.

The Palestine Islamic Jihad (PIJ)

A series of loosely connected factions, the PIJ seeks to create an Islamic Palestinian state and the destruction of Israel. It considers the United States a prime enemy because of its strong support of Israel. It carries out suicide bombing attacks against Israeli targets.

Revolutionary Organization (17 November)

A radical leftist group named for the November 1973 student uprising in Greece, the 17 November is anti-Greek and anti-U.S. Its goal is to force Greece to sever ties with NATO and remove all U.S. bases from its country. Uses bombings and assassinations to further its cause and is presumed small and financially unaided.